THE QUEEN

of the

VALLEY

LORENA HUGHES

KENSINGTON
PUBLISHING CORP.

www.kensingtonbooks.com

KENSINGTON BOOKS are published by
Kensington Publishing Corp.
119 West 40th Street
New York, NY 10018

Special book excerpts or customized printings can also be created to fit
specific needs. For details, write or phone the office of the Kensington
Sales Manager: Kensington Publishing Corp., 119 West 40th Street,
New York, NY 10018. Attn. Sales Department. Phone: 1-800-221-2647.

The K with book logo Reg US Pat. & TM Off.

ISBN: 978-1-4967-3629-1 (ebook)

ISBN: 978-1-4967-3628-4

First Kensington Trade Paperback Printing: September 2023

10 9 8 7 6 5 4 3 2 1

Printed in the United States of America

Praise for *The Spanish Daughter* by Lorena Hughes

"A lushly written story of bittersweet family secrets and betrayals that ultimately celebrates the healing power of hope, resilience, love—and chocolate!"
—Andrea Penrose, author of *Murder at the Royal Botanic Gardens*

"A lyrical and nuanced study of family and belonging. Readers will fall in love with *The Spanish Daughter*'s unique setting amidst the cacao plantations of Ecuador in 1920, its lush and vivid prose, and compelling and audacious heroine. I'm already looking forward to the sequel."
—Anna Lee Huber, *USA Today* bestselling author of *Murder Most Fair*

"A deftly written story entangling family, identity, chocolate, and murder, set in the lush golden days of Ecuador's cacao boom in the early twentieth century. Hughes gradually weaves the separate tales of her narrators into a single strong thread, drawing you into the world of three very different sisters united by deception and loss. An exciting debut from this fresh voice!"
—Shana Abé, *New York Times* bestselling author of
The Second Mrs. Astor

"An atmospheric and captivating mystery set against the backdrop of 1920s Ecuador, *The Spanish Daughter* is an engrossing, suspenseful family saga filled with unpredictable twists and turns."
—Chanel Cleeton, *New York Times* bestselling author of
Next Year in Havana

"Hughes portrays a small cast of characters while providing whodunit suspense and lots of background information on cacao plantations and insights into the way social classes are embodied in the production of chocolate. With an equal mix of historical fiction, dramatic family conflict, and mystery, this tale should please fans of Christina Baker Kline, Lisa Wingate, and Kate Quinn. Beginning with a map and ending with a reader's group guide, Hughes's tale of secrets, treachery, and chocolate will be appreciated by fiction readers looking for an extra level of engagement."
—*Booklist*

"An engrossing mystery/romance set in early twentieth-century Ecuador and Spain . . . Fans of historicals will appreciate the descriptions of dress, local foods and customs, social stratification, and the cacao industry, a source of an economic boom and bust in early twentieth-century Ecuador . . . As addictive as chocolate, this ends on a modern and satisfying note."
—*Publishers Weekly*

"Passionate and suspenseful, *The Spanish Daughter* is a satisfying historical mystery set in a lush tropical land."
—*Foreword Reviews*, STARRED REVIEW

Books by Lorena Hughes

The Spanish Daughter
The Queen of the Valley

In memory of Isa and Magdalena Abedrabbo,
who crossed seas and oceans for a better life

CHAPTER I

Lucas

Hacienda La Reina
Valle del Cauca, Colombia
March 7, 1925
The night of the gala

The night Martin Sabater disappeared had started with so much promise.

Tables draped with damask linen (embroidered by the sanctimonious Damas del Buen Vivir), centerpieces stuffed with purple orchids and carnations, china brought all the way from Cali, and enough *aguardiente* and rum to feed a battalion.

A band of musicians played *bambucos* in a patio filled with guests strategically positioned around a three-tier pond fountain. Barefoot brunettes in voluminous skirts moved their hips to the rhythm of the guitars while gaping gentlemen watched, their dolled-up wives elbowing them every few minutes. Despite the women's silk and georgette gowns, fancy hairdos, and the pearls hanging from their necks, it was the humble dancers who garnered every man's attention.

The "entertainment" had been Martin's idea. He was the one

who found our folkloric dances fascinating. We told him we should instead hire a string quartet or an opera singer, but he insisted that this kind of dance was an art form—whims of a foreigner, I suppose.

Months had gone into the planning and execution of a gala meant to save our old, beloved boarding school. From carefully selecting the list of *hacendados*, affluent *caleños*, and former students who might contribute with money and/or auction items for the cause, to the killing and roasting of five *lechones* and one calf to feed nearly a hundred hungry guests. No less important were the logistics of lodging and transportation and the recruitment of twelve waiters and four chefs to help Lula—the hacienda's official cook—with main and side dishes.

They even had a professional photographer—me.

My one and only contribution to the noble cause.

The two organizers and hosts of the evening, Dr. Farid "El Turco" Mansur and Martin Sabater—the hacienda owner—had dusted off the silk lapels of their black tuxedos, shined their patent leather shoes, and charmed every female in the region during the entire evening. Or most of it, anyway.

At least, that was how it appeared to be.

Appearances, after all, mattered. In this world—in a world like ours—perception was everything, even if it wasn't accurate or truthful. And the perception we wanted to convey was that we were lifelong friends doing our best to raise enough money to pay for scholarships and school repairs.

So, we found ourselves together after so many years: the doctor, the landowner, the photographer, and the nun. It had been long enough since we'd all been under the same roof. And maybe, just maybe, it might have been better never to cross paths again.

We did our best, of course, to feign normalcy. Though I could see the way Farid glared at Martin from time to time, his thick Middle Eastern eyebrows locked in a frown whenever Martin laughed with one of his guests.

Then there was Camila in her Siervas de Jesús ghostly habit.

The rigors of her life choices reflected on her face. She was paler than ever, as if she hadn't seen the light of day in months, and her face had thinned out. And yet, time had been kind to her. She was more beautiful now, at thirty-two, than she had been at seventeen. Her cheekbones were high, her gaze wiser. What a pity that someone so lovely, so smart, had confined herself to a life of prayer, fasts, and penances. It didn't escape my notice, either, the way she avoided Martin. She tried so hard to ignore him, she produced the opposite effect.

But I didn't have to pretend. I could hide myself behind my Kodak Folding Automatic Brownie and nobody questioned it. I was invisible. They only noticed me—for a few seconds—when the flashlamp in my hand went on.

I didn't care if they didn't see me or how they might perceive me—the least successful of the bunch. I had my own reasons for being here. And it had nothing to do with saving a school from bankruptcy. Neither was I here to socialize or reunite with old friends.

I wanted information.

And the person who could provide it was already here. I'd just taken his photograph.

His name was Iván Contreras and he had, up until a few years ago, owned this hacienda. He was also the only person in the world who knew where my mother was.

Martin held my arm, leaned over me, and spoke in a low voice.

"I found out something. I'll tell you in the morning."

I nodded, restraining the urge to inquire more. But he was right, this was no time to talk.

As it usually happens, the trigger to the looming tragedy of the evening had been a woman.

She was one of Martin's lady friends. One I had never seen before. And I prided myself of knowing everybody in the region.

This woman was worldly—that was one way to describe her. The other way was fragile, reminiscent of a porcelain statue with a long, smooth neck and her bare back fully exposed through a low-cut pearl gown. She was shrouded in feathers and the soft waves of her bob covered her head like a cap.

I never caught her name, though I heard Martin introducing her to another friend of his, an emerald mine owner named Gerardo, a ginger who was apparently visiting from Boyacá but had a house in Cali as well.

The emerald miner was older than us, closer to forty than thirty, and had a thick mustache of the same length and width as his eyebrows that perfectly matched his copper hair. Martin spent a long time speaking to him. And occasionally winked at me as if reminding me that he hadn't forgotten we had an important conversation pending.

That was one of Martin's greatest qualities, what drew people toward him. He always made you feel as if you mattered.

Someone bumped into my tripod, dropping my camera on the vermilion tile floor.

"Oh, I'm sorry, Lucas," the woman said, attempting to pick up the Brownie up with shaky hands. It was Farid's wife, Amira—the Arab princess, as I secretly called her.

Amira had been Farid's bride since childhood and had eventually married my friend. She was one of those women who knew exactly what to wear to enhance the modest curves of her body and how to bring up the best of her exotic features. Her fine upbringing in Bogotá showed as she was the only one in the crowded room who could compete in refinement and sophistication with Martin's mysterious friend.

But Amira was the opposite of Martin's friend in every way. Instead of the pale, nearly translucent skin and dainty nose of the woman in feathers, Amira had an unapologetic nose, olive skin, and obsidian eyes. She was wearing an aquamarine chiffon slip, beaded with embroidered leaves and silver sequin flowers.

"Is it broken?" she asked as I picked it up.

"It's fine," I said, hiding my annoyance to the best of my abilities. "But . . ."

Before I could finish my sentence, she tapped my shoulder and dashed away. Was she following someone?

I tested the shutter after her, and it seemed to be working.

Much later, I would piece together the events of the evening with those photos.

After the plates were empty, the auction had exceeded our expectations (thanks, no doubt, to the alcohol we generously served all night), and the foxtrot was in full swing, Martin's lady friend took the stage. She brazenly removed the microphone from the singer's hand and announced that Martin had recently purchased an Andalusian mare and he ought to show us his new acquisition.

Normally, the ramblings of an intoxicated woman would've had no effect on such a distinguished crowd, but being that the proposition came from such a beauty and everyone at the party was more or less swimming at her same level of inebriation—past the point of caring, that was—they all agreed with a cheer.

Martin reluctantly accepted and before he or anyone else at the gala could stop it, a group of six enthusiasts had climbed on Sabater's horses—he on top of his shining new mare—and went on a ride around the cacao plantation in the middle of the night, the moon as their only guide.

Martin never came back.

CHAPTER 2

Puri

Buenaventura, Colombia
June 7, 1925
Three months after the gala

Paco and I barely made it to the train in Buenaventura. In our hurry from the port to the train station, I'd hardly taken a peek at the town through the carriage window. All I had been able to determine was that the port of Buenaventura was no less malodorous or chaotic than the port of Guayaquil, where we'd come from.

A silvery plume of smoke gathered in the front of Ferrocarril del Pacífico, making some of us cough while we stood in a jumbled line. It was so crowded inside the train that we had to squeeze between passengers and piles of luggage to reach our car.

Our cabin was tiny, with umber leather seats across from each other and a nun sitting in one of them, hands on her lap. I greeted her, inhaling the smell of polished wood and stiff air inside. Almost effortlessly, my young assistant set my trunk in the back of the car. How did I live so many years without Paco? He'd been my salvation. With his long arms and slender frame, he could reach anywhere, quickly and efficiently. He was a calming presence in my life, more thoughtful than he'd first appeared. He always reserved his opinions about others, except when it came time to warn me about someone's bad will. It didn't cease to amaze me how someone so young, as evidenced by his smooth tan skin—the envy of any woman—could be so wise.

"*Gracias, mi alma,*" I told him.

"*A la orden, Doña Puri,*" he said.

The nun was dressed entirely in white, from her tunic to her scapular all the way to her long veil. Her only ornament was a round silver insignia over her scapular. She had that indefinable quality of some nuns who never seemed to age. Her skin was immaculate, her cheeks rosy, but she must have been in her mid-forties already, judging by the deep lines flanking her mouth and the wrinkles in the corners of her eyes. And yet, her complexion looked radiant. Maybe this was one of the benefits of a life of serenity: eternal youth.

I smiled back at her and sat next to Paco.

"You're Spanish?" she said, across from me.

I perceived the accent of a *madrileña.* It had been five years since I'd seen a compatriot of mine.

"Yes," I said. "*Andaluza.*"

"Oh, beautiful land. I visited it when I was a *cría.* Whereabouts?"

"Sevilla." My voice broke unintentionally. It was highly unlikely that I would ever go back to my homeland. "And you?"

"Madrid," she said. "I'm Sor Alba Luz."

"I'm Purificación—Puri," I said. "And this is Paco."

My assistant extended his hand, but changed his mind right away and tucked it under his thigh. How did one greet a nun?

"I went to Madrid twice," I said.

"On vacation?"

"No. To renew my grandmother's patent."

"A patent? How interesting."

"Yes, she was an inventor."

Paco turned to me. I'd never told him this story. In all truth, he and I didn't talk a lot; we had an unspoken understanding. He intuitively knew what I wanted and then, he did it.

A prolonged whistle signaled that the train was leaving the station.

"Inventor of what?" the nun asked.

I sat up straight, filled with family pride. "She invented a coffee and cacao bean roaster."

"That's extraordinary!" She clapped.

I clung to the armrest as the train started to move.

"The only problem was that her patent expired after five years because she didn't have all the required paperwork—her *cédula*—but she never got around to procuring it. I tried to do it after her passing but it was a futile effort."

"That's unfortunate," she said. "She sounds like an impressive lady."

"She was," I said.

"You know they have a chocolate factory in Medellín?"

"They do?" I was shocked. I was a pioneer in Vinces and had opened the first chocolate store in the area.

"Yes. I spent some time in Medellín last year," the nun said. "With the Siervas de Jesús, a fellow congregation."

Paco yawned. Of course he would. What twenty-one-year-old man would care about chocolate factories and nuns?

"Are you two family?" Sor Alba Luz asked.

"No." I tapped Paco's leg. "Paco is my guardian angel."

He shook his head. "More the other way around. She gave me a job when I most needed one."

"In Spain?" the nun asked.

"No," I said. "In Ecuador. That's where we live. I have a chocolate store there."

"Fascinating," she said.

Paco and I met when I first arrived to Ecuador in 1920 to collect my father's inheritance. Back then, he was still in his late teens. He'd had a raft to transport people from one river to another, mostly to the different plantations in the area. When the cacao industry collapsed, his work became so sparse that I hired him to help me with my brand-new chocolate store, which I set up in Vinces to great success—that is, until Martin Sabater stopped sending me cacao beans.

The smell of charcoal and oily metal was giving me a headache. As if reading my mind, Paco stood to shut the window.

"What brings you to this area?" I asked the nun.

"My congregation sent me to help with a new hospital. I'm with the Siervas de María in Panamá."

"Are you a nurse?"

"Not officially, but you could say that. Our charism consists of taking care of the ill so we have some nursing training."

Paco sighed and leaned back, extending his long legs against the nun's travel bag.

"Where exactly are you going?" I asked.

"It's northeast of Cali, by a village called El Paraíso. They are opening a hospital in the area. I volunteered since I've worked at hospitals before."

"Oh, that's where we're going, somewhere near El Paraíso, right?" I turned to Paco, who nodded distractedly, his eyes focused on the pastures outside the window. "We were trying to figure out how to get there from the train station."

"You just have to rent a carriage in Cali. That's what I'm going to do."

It was getting harder to hear the nun's melodious voice through the track noises. Outside, trees, hills, and livestock passed by in a blur. I squeezed the strap of my reticule.

"You all could come with me, if you'd like," the nun said.

"You just read my mind! I was thinking about asking, but I didn't want to inconvenience you."

The nun waved a hand. "Oh, no, not at all. One doesn't meet a compatriot in these lands every day." She rested her hand on her stiff veil.

I wondered if it got hot underneath those mountains of fabric.

"So, Puri, what brings you to these lands?"

Paco lowered the rim of his straw hat and shut his eyes.

"I'm looking for a friend from Ecuador," I said. "Perhaps you know him? His name is Martin Sabater. He has a cacao plantation near El Paraíso."

"Oh, no, *cariño*. I'm afraid I don't know anyone in the region. The Reverend Mother is from Valle del Cauca and she's the one who told me exactly how to get here, but this is my first time down south."

She fanned herself with her plump hand.

"But I don't think you'll have any trouble finding your friend," she said. "El Paraíso is a small village, from what I hear, and everyone knows each other. At least, that's what the Reverend Mother said."

"I hope so," I said, feeling Martin's letter through the satin of my pouch bag.

CHAPTER 3

Camila

Hacienda La Reina
June 7, 1925

Farid had a talent to infuriate me like no one else. Who *exactly* did he think he was? The Almighty? What he was doing was inconceivable, tyrannical. But when had he cared about anyone's desires but his own? He was used to getting his way *all the time*.

Underneath my scapular, I dug my fingernails in the palms of my hands until they hurt. Sometimes I would leave deep indentions and if the provocation was too high, I might even draw some blood. But it was the only way to unleash the anger boiling inside my veins. I was expected to "curb my passions" at every provocation, to be a model of perfection. And it wouldn't sit well for a nun to yell at her brother, the charitable Dr. Mansur, who was now inaugurating a much-needed hospital.

Who cared if the property belonged to Martin Sabater?

What did it matter if Farid's methods to transfer the estate to his name were more than questionable? I'd yet to know all the details, but I couldn't be too inquisitive or show too much interest. I just had to fill my role as head nurse and shut up.

Sporting a cream-colored suit, Farid stood out among the small crowd gathered in front of the hacienda's front porch. My brother was much taller than the average Colombian, but it wasn't just his size or his wide *toquilla* straw hat. He was imposing, with his wide shoulders and a gaze that could see right through your soul. His voice was deep and thunderous and he often used big words he'd learned in his college years in Bogotá.

Not a lot of people in the valley understood him, and so they simply nodded and acquiesced.

Just like Padre Carlos Benigno was doing at the moment. It didn't matter that it was Sunday, his busiest day of the week. He had found the time to come here from the boarding school to give his blessing to Farid's brand-new hospital. Padre José María would've never agreed.

"O heavenly Father, Almighty God, we humbly beseech Thee to bless and sanctify this hospital and the hands of those called to heal." The priest then turned to my brother. "You are the presence of Christ to his people."

Farid stood a bit taller. The priests at his former school had always adored him.

Such arrogance my brother has.

I pinched my palms deeper.

Why did I always think the worst of him? Medicine was his calling. It had been since we were children, since that infamous night when everything changed for us.

The priest continued to bless the sick, the nurses, and another doctor I'd just met. Then, Father Carlos Benigno thanked God and the community for making this all possible. The plan was to proceed with the inauguration ceremony outside and then go into the hacienda and bless every single room with his hyssop and bottle of holy water.

Mayor Guerrero stood by my brother as he cut the red ribbon to symbolize the inauguration of the hospital.

Behind me, the flash of Lucas's camera went on.

Annoyed, I turned my eyes from my brother and faced the hacienda's façade. It was six thirty and the sun was about to set. Rows of Baroque wood columns flanked the portico. Luscious ivies and bougainvillea branches clambered along the walls, giving the two-story structure the appearance of an enchanted castle.

I could see why Martin had fallen in love with this property.

It was now my brother's turn to give his inaugural speech and thank the dignitaries in attendance. I couldn't stomach it one more minute.

As my brother garnered all the attention, as usual, I discreetly distanced myself from the group and circled the hacienda toward the back. In the distance I could see the chicken coop, the servant's quarters, and, a little farther down, the stables. A drop of water hit the tip of my nose. I looked up. Rain? In June? Fat clouds had gathered in the sky and the air felt thicker—an anomaly at this time of the year. The seasons in this region were clearly defined. It was either rainy or sunny, no in-betweens. And this was definitely not the season for rains.

I kept walking, but something stopped me.

The crackling of leaves behind me.

Someone was following me.

I turned around.

"What are you doing here?" I said. "Aren't you supposed to be taking photographs?"

Lucas offered a shy smile, his camera hanging from his neck, his folded tripod in his hand.

"I have plenty of photos of Farid speaking. I don't need to hear him, too." He stood beside me. "I'd rather take photos of the place." His gaze scanned the area. "Where were you going?"

I hesitated, then pointed at the *cacaotales*. "Just for a walk. I suffocate around too many people."

One thing I'd learned with the Siervas was to appreciate solitude. I never thought I might, but so many years of silence and prayer had made crowds repellent to me.

"How are you going to deal with the hospital when it opens?" he said. "I know everybody in the region has been eager for the opening."

I shrugged. "I can deal with patients."

I just hated social engagements. Everyone always stared as if thinking, *What a waste, too bad she couldn't find a husband and* had *to become a nun.*

If they only knew the entire story.

Lucas seemed distracted with something else. "Do you see that?" He pointed at the hacienda's pitch roof.

I followed his finger toward the aquamarine plumage of a peacock perched between the terra-cotta tiles.

"Isn't it beautiful?" he said, unfolding his tripod.

The bird climbed toward the top of the roof, his cobalt neck elongated, his ornate turquoise feathers expanding widely.

Lucas looked around bright-eyed and spotted a wooden ladder resting by the chicken coop.

"You've never seen a peacock before?" I said.

"Not that high."

He grabbed the ladder and, without taking his eyes off the bird, dragged it toward the servants' quarters. The building was a smaller version of the hacienda with the same adobe walls and brick floors, but it was only one story and had a flat roof that extended over the porch. Before I could say anything, Lucas leaned the ladder against the wall.

"He seems agitated, wouldn't you say?"

He didn't wait for an answer and I didn't bother offering one.

"So strange," he said as a cool wind hit me. When he was halfway up the ladder, he turned to me.

"Hand me the tripod, will you?"

I did as was told. Nearby, the hens clucked as if a wolf had broken into the coop.

"You're going to get your camera wet," I said as the raindrops multiplied, but he didn't listen. He was rapidly setting up the tripod on the edge of the roof and pointing to the building ahead. He leaned behind the camera.

"*Divino*," he said, taking shot after shot.

"We should go inside," I said, shielding the rain from my eyes with my hand.

"Just one more," he said.

I rested my hand on the ladder. It seemed to be moving. I looked at it.

It *was* moving.

But how?

Under my feet, the ground trembled. A roar, like a sustained double bass note, echoed throughout the patio. The building was swaying like a hammock. An unmistakable shudder followed and all the windows vibrated in protest, as though someone had grabbed the globe and had shaken it like a maraca.

I took a step back, but the slab under my feet was moving as well.

"Lucas?"

His answer came in the form of a groan followed by an audible ruckus and a loud "*¡Jueputa!*"

Down came the tripod, and then Lucas himself.

He landed on his right side, but miraculously the camera was intact in his left hand.

I darted toward him over the unsteady ground. It didn't escape my notice that the hacienda and chicken coop were also shaking.

There was much screaming nearby. The women were the loudest, but I could also hear my brother and the priest calling for the crowd to stay calm, while someone thought it necessary to yell "*¡Terremoto!*" as if we hadn't noticed that we were in the midst of an earthquake.

Horses neighed from the stables and the roosters, not wanting to be left behind, did their part by crowing in unison. The relentless rain only added to the overall chaos.

"Are you all right?" I shouted, offering Lucas a hand. Through the pouring rain and the impending dusk, I could see that he was attempting to sit up but seemed unable to lift himself.

He tried to grab my hand. First with his right, but failed and switched to his left hand. Using my arm as leverage, he sat up and then stood.

"*Carajo*, my ankle!"

Another ruckus above us startled me.

Lucas shoved me away from the building a second before the cornice over our heads fell down. I watched the building in terror. Was the whole structure going to collapse?

"Mila! Mila!" Farid called out, using the pet name he'd used for me since we were little and he couldn't pronounce my full name.

"Over here!" I said.

"We have to go to the open field where it's safe," Farid said. Then he turned to Lucas, who was flinching in pain. "Are you all right?"

"Yes," Lucas said. "Let's go."

The ominous grumbling from the depths of the earth continued.

"But there may be people inside the buildings!" I said.

"There's no one here," Farid said. "Come on!"

My brother grabbed my arm and led me toward the group. Carriage drivers were doing their best to calm their horses and mules, which were rearing and neighing, while the more impatient guests and future hospital staffers attempted to climb on wagons and landaus. Others, less courageous, threw themselves on the ground— cross-shaped—asking God to forgive their sins and promising never to falter again if only they could survive the cataclysm.

As if I were still a little girl, Farid lifted me toward the step of his landau and pushed me in. Apparently, his horse knew better than to disobey my brother and was the only animal in sight that showed restraint. Lucas followed me inside the carriage with a pained expression.

I glanced back at the hacienda, a pit stuck in my throat.

Later, my brother would say that the harrowing ordeal had taken less than a minute.

CHAPTER 4

Puri

Cali, Colombia
June 7, 1925

There was something about Martin's letter I couldn't quite grasp.

I assessed my two travel companions, one in front of me and the other one beside me. Both snored in the crammed car, their heads bouncing up and down and occasionally tapping against the windowpane. It had been nearly six hours since we left Buenaventura and they'd been sleeping for the last two.

I removed the letter from my purse.

> *January 16, 1925*
>
> *Dearest Puri,*
>
> *I saw this stuffed bear on a recent trip to Medellín and thought of your son, Cristóbal. They have a fantastic store there with a variety of imported toys and books. You would love it. I hope he likes the bear and guards it, as it is one of a kind.*
>
> *Things here are not as good as I expected. I think I mentioned in my last letter the droughts we've been*

*having. That's not the only problem. To be honest, I
don't know if I'm going to make it here in Colombia, but
I have a plan that will hopefully work. It may be my last
chance.*

    I miss you dearly and think of you often.

    *Please give my love to little Cristóbal and to your
sister Catalina.*

    Sincerely,

    Martin

What exactly did he mean when he said he may not "make it" in Colombia? Was he talking about his business as a cacao exporter, or did he mean something more sinister? I hadn't received my regular shipment of cacao since the beginning of March. I'd sent him letters and telegrams, but there had been no answer. His last letter was the one in my hands, sent in January.

It was out-of-character for him to disappear like this. If he'd sold the property or if the bank had repossessed it, he would've told me. Martin had always been quick to respond. If he cared about one thing, it was his business and his reputation among the exporters. Why had he fallen silent for the last three months?

"Oh, we're here." Sor Alba Luz sat up and pointed at the colonial houses outside the window. "I wish we had time to do some sightseeing in Cali, but the Reverend Mother's sister is waiting for me in El Paraíso." She paused. "For us."

"Don't worry about us," I said. "We'll find accommodations elsewhere."

"Absolutely not. Doña Rita is an altruist. She's one of the most magnanimous benefactors of our convent and has an ample house. I'm sure she won't have a problem hosting the two of you."

"I would hate to impose."

"Nonsense. The Reverend Mother would be appalled if you stayed somewhere else. Vallecaucanos are well known for their hospitality. *Y no se hable más*," she said, putting an end to the discussion.

At the train station—a bright two-story structure filled with arched windows—we had no problem finding a horse-drawn carriage to take us to El Paraíso. We only had to look outside the station where a handful of carriages and a Model T were parked. The landau driver, a middle-aged man with a belly so large the buttons of his linen shirt were about to give, was standing between a food cart and a gigantic palm tree. He devoured some corn cakes Sor Alba Luz called *arepas*. They were flat and circular, the size of the palm of my hand. Paco and I hadn't eaten in hours as we had been in such a hurry to reach the train station.

I purchased a dozen *arepas* and shared them with Paco and Sor Alba Luz. She warned me that, according to her Mother Superior, "*arepas* without coffee are not *arepas*." Hence, I went back to the food cart and bought three cups of black coffee. The *arepas* were delicious, and among a mild corn flavor, I tasted cheese.

The driver pointed at the carriage rental office so I could sign the agreement. The plan was to stay the night at El Paraíso and in the morning, Sor Alba Luz would go to the hospital and I would go to Martin's hacienda.

The thought of seeing Martin in just a few hours gave me a small thrill.

It was a fact that Martin was my only supplier of cacao and I needed his beans if my chocolate store in Vinces was going to subsist. But the truth was my trip to Colombia was not only a business decision. Martin was important to me. I still had feelings for him even though I hadn't seen him in four years. He was, after all, the father of my son, though nobody knew it—not even Martin.

As I pulled the door open, a blend of cedar and body odor hit me like a wave of steam. It was a tiny office with only one ticket booth. A barefoot man sat on the stone floor, holding a tin cup for charity. Another man, a gangly one with a wiry nose, leaned by the booth, arms across his chest, face and hands soiled. He stared at me from head to toe. Among all this poverty, I suddenly felt self-conscious in my brand-new, two-piece beige suit, my maroon silk crepe blouse, and matching cloche hat—a perfect attire for traveling, I'd thought, but an imprudent choice as every pore in my body was boiling in this heat and my fancy shirt was clinging to my back. No wonder they called this area *tierra caliente*. I deposited a couple of coins in the beggar's cup to clear my conscience.

As I stepped out of the office, I removed my jacket and grabbed my son's stuffed bear from my trunk. It was the one Martin had sent him in January. Little Cristóbal had fallen in love with the bear's soft plush ears and his big round eyes. He'd lent it to me with the condition that I would bring it back, but it would protect me during my travels, he'd said.

After Paco and the driver strapped my trunk to the back of the landau, the driver turned to the nun.

"And you, Sister? Is that all you're bringing?"

Sor Alba Luz tightened her grip on a leather travel bag hanging over her shoulder.

"*Sí, hijo*, a simple woman like myself doesn't require much. Everything I need is in this handbag." She fanned her cheeks with a straw fan she'd just purchased from a peddler. "Please leave the hood down, unless you want us to cook inside."

Nodding, the driver helped her into the carriage.

"*Doñita*," Paco said, offering me his hand.

The landau's leather seats were somewhat worn-out, but I was glad to have found transportation. With an "*¡Arre!*" and a cluck of his tongue, the driver guided the horses onto the road that would take us to El Paraíso.

"So Doña Puri, are you married?" the nun asked.

Paco grabbed another *arepa*—his fifth—from the paper bag, which had oil stains throughout.

"I'm a widow," I said. "My husband passed away five years ago."

Sor Alba Luz made the sign of the cross. "May he rest in peace and rise in glory."

I was supposed to say "amen" but in the last few years, I'd become somewhat disconnected with the Church. I attended mass on Sundays with my sister Catalina, mostly for her sake and for my son's, but I'd never held a strong conviction about Catholic doctrine and rituals—a fact that I'd only shared with my husband and, in his absence, kept to myself.

"Any children?"

"Yes. One son."

"Can I have the last *arepa*?" Paco asked.

"Where do you put all that food, *hombre*?" the nun said, laughing.

He tapped his flat belly with pride.

"Of course, *cariño*," I said.

I removed a gold locket from my neck and opened it.

"This is my little boy," I said, handing the nun the open locket. I'd had my son's photo taken during a trip to Guayaquil. He hadn't smiled once during the photo shoot.

"*¡Qué majo es!*" she said in praise of my son's good looks.

I agreed with her that he was beautiful, but as his mother, I was partial to his looks and how adorable he looked with his bow tie.

"And I suppose that plush bear belongs to him?" she said.

I lovingly squeezed the stuffed animal in my lap.

"Yes." My chest ached. I hadn't seen my little Cristóbal in so many days. We'd never been apart before but I was lucky that my sister Catalina had offered to take care of him. Fortunately, Cristóbal loved Catalina—he'd known her since he was born, so she was like a second mother to him.

"I've never seen one of those toys before. Look at his tiny button nose."

"My son loves it. He lent it to me so I would remember him. As if I needed something to remind me of him."

"Sweet boy."

The sun was already setting and a warm rain started to fall. Around us was nothing but copious vegetation.

"Driver!" Sor Alba Luz said. "It's starting to rain. Please put up the hood."

The man kept driving without turning around.

"*¿Señor?*" She leaned forward. "*¿Señor?*"

A deafening gunshot interrupted her.

In the front of the carriage, the hefty driver fell to his side, wounded.

It was so sudden and unexpected I didn't have a chance to react. Paco leaned over to protect me with his body. The nun screamed.

A man on a palomino caught up with us and jumped onto the driver's seat. I recognized his crooked nose—it was the man I'd seen at the rental office.

"*¡Madre de Dios!*" the nun said.

The man took over the reins while elbowing the driver out of the carriage. He fell out of the seat and rolled on the muddy soil. Flanking us were two other horseback riders. One of them was the beggar I had given some coins to. The third man had a black bandanna over his nose and mouth.

Paco threw himself against the bandit in the front. The two locked in a desperate struggle interrupted by another gunshot.

Paco shuddered and a second later, there was a hole in the side of his shirt.

"No!" I screamed.

The gunshot had come from my right side. It had been the man with the black bandanna, still riding his horse.

Paco, my dear boy, turned to me in despair.

I squeezed his clammy hand. "Be strong, Paco. You're going to make it."

I tried not to stare at the red circle growing on his shirt.

The carriage came to a halt. Paco spit blood by our feet. The men at either side of us stopped their horses. The one with the bandanna climbed onto our seat.

"*A ver, señoras,* you're going to cooperate with me if you don't want the same fate as those two men," he said.

I dared not move a muscle, but I could see through my peripheral vision that Sor Alba Luz clasped her hands in prayer. I shouldn't have been flaunting my riches at the train station.

Why had I asked Paco to come with me on this trip?

"Here, you can have all my things"—I removed my bracelet, my rings, my pearl earrings, the locket with my son's portrait— "but please, let me take my friend to a doctor."

Tears and raindrops mingled on my cheeks.

"*¡Cállese!*" one of them said.

Paco took a sharp breath. I wanted to reach out to him, but the man with the bandanna stood between us.

"Please, please," I said.

Sor Alba Luz had started praying the Pater Noster.

The beggar took my jewelry. "Where's your money?"

I handed him my purse.

"This one's really pretty," said the man with the bandanna.

"No time for that," the one with the wiry nose said. "Not in front of the nun, anyway."

"Says who?" The man removed his bandanna, revealing a missing front tooth and a mole that covered a big chunk of his cheekbone.

He grabbed my arm and dragged me out of the carriage.

"*Venga, mamacita.*"

"No!" I said, but the man had such a tight grasp of my forearm I couldn't escape. As I was pulled toward the bushes on the side of the road, soil and wet leaves clung to the rims of my shoes like leeches.

A *thump* made me turn my head toward the carriage. Paco's body fell to the ground. I flung my body toward him, but the man wrapped his arm around my midsection and forced me into the woods. The other two followed us while Alba Luz watched me with horror.

They'd spared her because she was a nun.

It seemed that criminals had their own set of principles. Killing was fine, but raping a nun wasn't.

Behind an oak, the man with the mole tore my shirt, exposing my camisole to all. By now, the rain was implacable and my bell hat and hair were soaked.

I tried to run but one of them held my arms. I was sure they could see my nipples as all of their eyes were focused on my chest. If only I could free my hands to cover myself.

"Let me go!"

The one with the mole slapped me so hard it burned my cheek. As his face came back into focus, my eyes fixated on the craters in his skin. The beggar closed the distance between us and forced me to the ground, but my legs were shaking so much I could hardly comply. The one with the mole pounced on top of me and attempted to kiss me. I shook my head in both directions.

"Stop!"

His mouth landed on my throat. A horse neighed. But there was something else: a low, rumbling sound. Under me, the ground moved. The leaves above my head were shaking. The rain hitting my face made it hard for me to see clearly, but I could definitely perceive movement.

The men froze.

"What's happening?" one of them said.

"¡*Terremoto!*" said another.

"The horses!" yelled the third.

Their weight lifted. Two of them scurried away.

"I repent, I repent!" the former beggar said, weeping.

But nobody answered his pleas. The ground was moving up and down, as if breathing. The earth attempting to expel us. But the most intimidating part was the gloomy reverberation that seemed to be emerging from the center of the earth.

A foul smell had taken over. Flashes of light blasted sporadically.

In the distance, the nun screamed.

I tried to hold on to a branch to stand up straight, but it was also shaking. One of the horses ran past me and the beggar darted after him.

As if walking on slippery eggshells, I made it to the road. The carriage was no longer there, the men had taken off, and the nun was lying on the ground, rubbing the back of her head.

"Are you all right?" I said, helping her sit.

"One of the horses bumped into me and I fell. I think I hit my head." There was a bulky rock behind her. The wind was blowing so hard I could barely hear her.

"Do you think you can stand?" I said.

She stared at my ripped shirt and wet camisole. It was so embarrassing.

"Give me a moment," she said.

The branches stopped shaking.

"I think it's over," I said, looking around as the earth stilled again. "Did you see where the men went?"

She pointed in the direction where we had been headed.

"We should go back to Cali before night falls," I said. "We're still close." It had only been a few minutes since we left the city when the men had attacked us. Besides, it was our only option to save Paco.

I offered a hand to the nun and the two of us went to check on the boy. His eyes were still open, his body stiff. The blood on his shirt had turned darker. I gently shook him by the shoulders, calling his name.

"Paco, please." My tears were making everything blurry.

Sor Alba Luz wrapped her arm around me. "He's gone."

It couldn't be. He'd been so full of life.

I had one of my coughing spells—I always did when I was distressed. Sor Alba Luz suggested that we move his body out of the road. Somehow, we managed to lay him under the branches of a ceibo filled with scarlet and crimson flowers.

"I'm sorry," I said, kneeling beside him and holding his hand.

Sor Alba Luz sat on a rock next to me, rubbing the back of her head.

"He was too young," I said, staring at his lifeless gaze through the little bit of light still left in the sky. His expression would forever be locked in a grimace. "This is my fault. I never should've asked him to come with me."

I looked around this trembling, foreign land. Why was I here?

Was Martin worth this much trouble? Our only saving grace was that it had stopped raining.

"You couldn't have known this would happen. Only the purest souls die young. It means they're ready to be in the company of Our Lord."

I found no consolation in her words.

Had it not been for me, he would've been in París Chiquito, having a *puro* with his friends or fishing by the shore of Río Vinces.

"We should pray for his soul," Sor Alba Luz said.

Paco would've probably liked that. He had been a superstitious person and he would probably be afraid of what were to become of his soul without his last rites.

Maybe that would help ease my mind, too. I wanted so badly to be out of my head right now.

She opened her leather bag. Inside was Cristóbal's bear.

"You saved it," I said, picking it up, negotiating with a big lump in my throat to let me speak without breaking down.

"At least that," she said.

Underneath the bear was a folded white garment.

"Why don't you wear this until we get to town?" she said. "You'll feel much more comfortable and you won't have to be covering yourself the whole time."

I'd been holding the torn fabric of my shirt together for so long that my fingers were getting stiff.

She removed a habit identical to the one she was wearing and handed it to me. It was entirely white, but the scapular was beige.

"*Gracias.*"

I removed my blouse, which was so torn it was probably beyond fixing, and slipped Sor Alba Luz's habit on. It was warm and dry.

"It fits you perfectly," she said. "Maybe it's meant to be yours."

I thanked her. I didn't really care how I looked, but I was grateful for the comfort of being properly covered once again.

"Let's pray," she said, lighting a candle and handing it to me.

There was something soothing about Sor Alba Luz's voice. I never cried in front of anyone, not even my mother, but this nun's kindness made me feel at ease. Pressing the cross of her rosary, white-marbled beads entwined between her fingers, she repeated the Ave María while I sobbed quietly. I was in a trance, as if this act somehow cleansed my soul.

When my tears subsided, I gave Paco a kiss on the forehead and promised I would never forget him. The twilight only gave us about twenty minutes before the sky turned pitch-black.

"We should go before it gets dark," I said.

The nun nodded, but something had changed in her. If she'd been in a trance, like myself, she wasn't out of it yet.

"Can you walk?" I asked.

"Yes, but I have the worst headache of my life."

We slowly walked away. A dull feeling had taken over me and I was grateful for it—it prevented me from thinking too much, from the agony of remembering. I was focused on getting to Cali, finding a place to stay and then, finding a way to bury Paco.

Sor Alba Luz grabbed my arm. She was so pale.

"I can't walk anymore. I'm too dizzy. You go on. I'll sit next to these heliconias."

She pointed at a bush of carmine blossoms along the road that appeared to grow in a pattern, and whose shapes closely resembled leaves. I'd never seen flowers like those before.

"We're almost there," I said, pointing at the houses straight ahead. "You can't stay here by yourself. What if there's another earthquake? Or the men come back?"

"I hadn't seen those flowers in years," she said. "They're my favorite."

Her lips were so dry. I wished I had some water to give her.

Letting go of my arm, she folded over to sit on the roots of a tree.

"This is not good," she said. "My vision is getting blurry."

"What do I do?"

"Go into town. Ask for a doctor, a healer, or an apothecary and bring them to me. I'll wait here."

I nodded.

"Take your son's bear," she said.

She was handing me her bag. I looked at her in confusion. Her eyes were brimming.

"Please, make an effort," I said, stupidly.

"Take it," she said. "There's some money inside. You may need it."

This was wrong. I couldn't just leave her here, but she looked exhausted.

"All right," I said, grabbing her bag and rushing down the trail toward a cobblestone street.

It was hard to discern what was in front of me as the city was covered in white dust, but I kept going. There was chaos all around me. People were crying and praying in the middle of the street. A house was missing a wall and the people inside had been caught sitting around the kitchen table, drinking coffee. Now their neighbors watched as if the diners were going to star in a *tonadilla*.

A man was urging the rest to go to some church nearby. "What could be safer than the house of God?"

There was a bakery at the end of the street.

An overweight clerk was sliding down a metal door. I asked him if there was a doctor nearby.

"There's a *droguería* two blocks down the street and the apothecary pays home visits in the evenings, but good luck finding him in this madness."

I didn't wait for him to finish speaking. I rushed in the direction he had pointed.

By the time the apothecary and I arrived to the tree, I knew something was wrong. Thanks to the gas lantern he was carrying, we spotted a white bulk that I recognized as Sor Alba Luz's body lying down. I ran the last stretch to reach her. Her eyes were closed, her arms on her sides, her legs stiff, but she had a serene expression on her face. The apothecary, a middle-aged man with a thick white mane, checked her vitals, then turned to me with a somber expression.

"She's gone."

Then he added an explanation. As if that changed things. "It was probably a subarachnoid hematoma, with that head trauma you described."

I had no idea what he was saying. I looked at him, confused.

"The space between the brain and the skull probably hemorrhaged."

"But she was fine after the blow. She was walking, talking, making perfect sense."

"Sometimes it takes some time, but then, I'm afraid, there's nothing to do."

I couldn't believe it. Another person who'd died trying to help me. I was like a bird of ill omen. I covered my eyes with my hands. Maybe I should go back to Ecuador, to my son, but the *boticario* was already grabbing me by the shoulders in a parental gesture, telling me not to worry, he will take care of this "*alma de Dios*."

I couldn't process what he was saying, only that he mentioned a boardinghouse where I could spend the night. "Now sit there," he said. "I left a message for my son to bring the wagon. He will be here shortly. *En un momentico*," he said in his Colombian singsong.

I nodded—it was all I could do.

Under my feet, the ground was still rumbling.

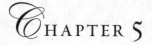

Chapter 5

Camila

One week after the earthquake

Out of all the things I had to do as a nurse, childbirth was the one I couldn't stand. But I was afraid there was no escaping it this time. My brother had gone to Cali and Dr. Costa was tending to a new wave of patients who had showed up in the morning.

At least another Sierva had arrived, but she seemed like the nervous kind. Certainly not ready for the demands of this hospital, but she'd have to do for now.

I was *that* desperate for help.

So it was up to Nurse Celia and me to tend to this delivery. Why hadn't this woman given birth at home? So many did. Her cervix was dilated and I could see the baby's head, but after twenty minutes of pushing, we hadn't made much progress.

If only Farid were here.

In spite of how much he annoyed me, I could always rely on him to take charge of a situation or handle a difficult case.

Maybe he wasn't so bad. He could be extremely selfish and narcissistic, but underneath that shell of pride and enormous ego, he had a soft heart reserved for the weak and the innocent. This hospital was the culmination of his dream, of his innate need to help others.

We had been two twigs, Farid and I. Nothing but long arms and legs and not an ounce of fat on our bodies. Mama used to say our most distinctive traits were our eyes, and everyone always talked about them. She said I was born so small that all you could really see were my eyes and long eyelashes. Back then, I thought Farid could do it all, from climbing the tallest trees to memorizing poems in Arabic and writing letters and numbers with beautiful penmanship. And he was only eight. Who knew what he could do when he reached *secundaria*?

"Mila," he said, two days after I'd turned six years old. "Come here and be quiet. If you say a word, I'm kicking you out."

I'd fallen asleep on top of the covers with my clothes still on. It was already dark and they'd never called me to dinner. But I was grateful that Farid invited me on one of his adventures and not our little brother, Omar, who was no longer a baby.

Rubbing my eyes, I nodded. Then brought a finger to my lips in solemn promise.

Baba was pacing in the hallway. When he turned away from us, Farid signaled me to follow him. The door to my parents' room was ajar, and from what I could hear, there was a woman inside with Mama. The woman was leaning over the bed, pressing her wide hips and soiled apron against the mattress. It was dim, but I could make out their shapes and my mother's voice.

Farid crawled toward the drawn curtains and hid behind them, pointing at a spot beside him for me. "Be quiet," he whispered.

"What's happening?"

"Shhhh . . ."

I could barely make out Mama's body on the bed. She was lying on her back, her legs wide spread. But why was she crying?

"The baby's coming," Farid said.

They'd been telling me for months that there was a baby inside her tummy but I couldn't quite picture a tiny human inside another one. How did the baby get in there? And *why?* From this angle, I could see her belly rising like a mountain over a pile of blankets and Baba's relentless pacing in the hallway.

Mama moaned softly while the older lady kept appeasing her, giving her precise instructions on how to breathe and where to put her legs. It was all very boring.

A long time passed—minutes or maybe even hours—before we heard the woman's voice again.

"*Puje, señora, puje,*" the woman said.

Mama screamed at the same time as the big woman pulled something out from between my mother's legs. And that something let out a cry almost immediately.

"The baby!" Farid said with a grand smile.

I tried to stand to see it, but Farid pulled me down.

"If they see us, they'll kick us out," he hissed into my ear.

Baba stepped into the room, praising Allah out loud, giving Mama kisses on the forehead. The big woman bundled the baby with blankets and placed it over Mama's belly. I let out a deep yawn. Hunger and exhaustion competed inside my body.

"Can we go now?" I whispered.

Farid shook his head. "You go."

I didn't have to be told twice. I crawled outside the room. On my way out, I turned to see Mama one more time and I noticed a dark liquid dripping onto the hardwood floor. I meant to say something, but then I remembered Farid's admonition. He was giving me one of his murderous looks, so I crawled all the way to Omar's room.

My baby brother was already sleeping inside his crib. Oddly, Baba had put him to bed—which almost never happened—and not Charito since it was her day off. I pulled out my one and only doll and hugged her. Then I rested by Omar's crib, where he barely fit anymore. I didn't know why, but I didn't want to be alone.

A pinch woke me up. Who knew how long I'd been sleeping on the rug by my little brother's crib. Farid was right next to me, his face wet, but it took me a while to understand that he'd been crying.

I removed my thumb from my mouth as Charito or Mama always scolded me when I "acted like a baby."

"What happened?" I said.

"She's gone."

"Who?"

"Mama."

"Where did she go?"

"To heaven."

"What do you mean?"

He started crying again. There were also boogers coming out of his nose and the two liquids—tears and boogers—were mixing all over his face.

"The midwife said Mama had a hemorrhage that couldn't be stopped."

I couldn't understand the words he was saying: *midwife, hemowhat?* I stuck my thumb back in my mouth.

"She bled to death," he said. "They let her die." There was a bitterness in his tone I'd never heard before.

I couldn't understand what he was saying. Mama couldn't die. That only happened to old people like our grandmother, who'd passed away last year, but not Mama. Who was supposed to run the kitchen and take care of us now? Charito never put us to bed or sang to us, like Mama did.

"A doctor should've been here," Farid said. "But Baba couldn't find one in time."

"Who was that big lady?" I asked.

"Not a doctor!" he said, resentful. "She was just a *partera*!"

There it was, that word again: midwife. But I was too sleepy to ask for further explanations. In the distance, a baby cried. I gasped.

"Yeah, she made it," he said, not too enthusiastically.

She?

"Who?"

"We have a sister, I guess," he said.

A sister? I'd always wanted one. I'd been so disappointed when Omar was born and he turned out to be a boy.

"Don't smile so much," Farid said. "That girl killed our mother."

Farid was never the same after our mother died. It was almost as if he aged overnight. Gone was the rambunctious kid who was always hiding to scare me or playing *Pepo*, a game that annoyed me but boys loved—probably because it had to do with explosives. But this new Farid was more concerned with adult affairs and books that he would borrow from his teachers.

He was also callous and indifferent toward our new sister, whom Baba had named Nazira after Mama.

People said I also grew up quickly, but I had to. Charito was not a maternal woman. Her one and only concern was feeding us exorbitant amounts of food every day. For Baba, meals were of utmost importance. He often said Arabs "lived to eat, not ate to live," and one of the reasons he chose to immigrate to Cali was because he found good meats and a variety of fruit in the region.

As Charito was too busy making the Arab delicacies Mama had taught her, I had to look after Nazira. Like the indigenous women I'd seen at the marketplace—the Nasas—I would wrap my sister to my back with a thin blanket and tie it across my chest.

"*¡Ahí va la turca con su hermana!*" they would say as I walked up and down the streets of Cali.

Everybody called us Turcos even though Baba had immigrated from Palestine. He explained to me, filled with irritation, that since Palestinians had been under Ottoman rule, they traveled with Turkish passports, which was why everyone in Latin America called us by that inaccurate term. The other assumption they made about us was that we were Moors, but in reality, we were more Catholic than the Pope.

As Baba explained, most of the Palestinians who fled the region were Christian, and that included my devout mother, who'd been engaged to my father since she was a little girl. In addition to being her husband, Baba had been her second cousin.

One of the consequences of losing my mother so young was that I also lost the little Arabic I spoke. Being that Baba had no one else in the house to speak Arabic with, he reverted to his heavily accented Spanish, and that was all us kids learned. He would occasionally meet with his cousin and other *paisanos* at the store or his favorite café, but they spoke so fast I couldn't understand a word they were saying. The only words that had stuck were food names, terms of endearment, and curses, but Farid or Baba always slapped me if I voiced them aloud.

I still did. Like Baba often said, "This one has a temper."

I knew I did, but that was the only way to survive in a house full of alpha males. Even Omar had strong opinions and frequent moodiness. It was increasingly difficult to discipline him, which had been my job since the morning after Mama passed away— Baba and Farid were too distressed to care. But Nazira was as sweet as a spoonful of *arequipe*. She was always smiling and doing everything in her power to please everyone in the house. I sometimes wondered how she handled the men in our family after I went to the convent. It was probably the reason why she married so young and moved to Buenaventura, where her husband's family lived.

"There's the head!" Nurse Celia yelled behind my ear, as if I couldn't see a crown filled with fine black hair myself.

As I pulled the baby from the birth canal, a big lump formed inside my throat.

I couldn't help it. It happened every time I saw a birth. I handed the baby boy to Nurse Celia.

"Bathe him," I said. "Make sure you use boiled water."

I walked out before anyone could see the tears in my eyes.

CHAPTER 6

Lucas

I didn't know which was worse: the persistent pain in my ankle and wrist, being stuck in this room all day, or the series of aftershocks we'd been experiencing for the last week.

"There has been a surge of cholera," Camila said. "The hospital is already filling up."

Well, this topped it all.

"You can give my room to someone who needs it more."

It felt wrong to be in Martin's hacienda without his consent, enjoying this comfortable bed and the spectacular view of his cacao plantation with its groves of trees forming a green ocean. Too bad the pods had been left to dry, awaiting a collection that never came.

"Are you crazy?" Camila said. "Farid would kill me if I sent his best friend downstairs with the cholera patients."

I attempted to get out of bed, but a sharp pain extending from my ankle to my back stopped me.

"What do you think you're doing?" she said.

I must have upset her because Camila rarely raised her voice.

"El Turco said it was just a strained ankle," I said. "I don't have to sit still like an invalid. I can help."

"Great, then go downstairs so you can catch cholera, too. You'll help us *a lot*." She adjusted a couple of pillows under my injured foot. "Look, we're managing fine with the hands we have. We certainly don't need your *broken* one."

We both stared at the cast on my wrist.

I leaned my head back against the headboard.

"What's wrong?" she said.

"I just got dizzy, that's all."

She seized my chin and lifted it. "Your lips are too dry. When was the last time you drank water?" She glanced at the metal tray by my bed. The pitcher was full. She served me a glass.

I took a small sip. How could anyone drink without being thirsty?

She growled. "Your ankle is still very swollen, Lucas. The more you rest, the sooner you'll heal. Do me a favor: just stay here and sit still. You help me more by not getting in my way."

I saluted her with my good hand as if she were a military officer. *"Como diga, mi coronela."*

Less than an hour later, she came back, followed by another nun.

At first, I didn't pay her any attention. What was there to see underneath that rigid veil and shapeless tunic purposely hiding women's natural curves?

But then I noticed her Mediterranean eyes.

"This is Mr. Ferreira," Camila told her, "a personal friend of Dr. Mansur, the head physician. You'll take care of him and report to me about his condition once a day."

The young nun widened her eyes.

"Mr. Ferreira had a bad fall during the earthquake," Camila said.

It was awkward hearing her talk about me in the third person, as if I weren't present.

"He sprained his ankle and broke his wrist. We just have to check how the ankle is healing and make sure the bandage is not too tight." She glanced at the water pitcher, still intact. "He's also a little dehydrated." She rolled the IV pole sitting in the corner of the room toward me. "We're going to give him an IV, just to be safe." Her tone changed as she faced me. "I told you this was going to happen if you didn't drink enough water, Lucas. You never listen."

I hated when she spoke to me as if I were a child.

When she turned around toward the equipment, I stuck my tongue out to her.

The new nun fought a smile.

"And you hardly eat." Camila didn't skip a beat. "Look at all the weight you've lost. Your leg is going to be so weak you won't be able to stand, much less walk."

"Well, the food here is . . . how should I put it kindly?" I twisted my mouth. "Substandard?"

With the same attention one might give an ant, Camila hung a bag of fluid from the top of the pole.

"Make sure you flush all the air from the tubing," she told the new nun, squeezing the liquid out of a tube connected to the bag. "It's the most common mistake around here." She was moving fast, snapping things here and there with the efficiency of someone who's had years of experience. "Hand me the antiseptic, will you?"

The new nun turned to a steel side table filled with jars, then glanced at me. I pointed at a brown-tinted glass bottle with my eyebrows. When she touched the cork of the tallest bottle, I nodded.

"Sister?" Camila said as she tightened a torniquet around my arm with a yellow rubber strip.

The nun handed her the brown bottle.

Camila felt one of my veins with the tip of her finger. I despised having her this close.

"Gauze?" Camila said.

The other nun removed one from a tin box and handed it to

Camila, who wiped the area with iodine and then felt my vein again.

"Here you are," Camila told my vein and poked it with a needle until a little bit of blood entered the catheter. "Stay still, Lucas."

I stared at the new nun. She seemed nervous and more than a little lost. Odd for a Sierva, but maybe she just had the jitters from the earthquake. Most of us did. Our whole world seemed to have changed in a matter of minutes.

She must have been around our same age, but there was something about her that seemed different. She wasn't from here, that was obvious. She was taller than the women in the region and had a sort of dignified stance.

"¿Hermana?" Camila said.

She flinched. "Yes?"

"The trash can." Camila pointed at a metal bin by the door. "I've asked you three times."

The poor nun looked mortified, but it was hard not to tune out someone who was constantly barking orders.

"Sorry," she said, circling my bed and grabbing the bin.

After Camila threw all the trash and made sure my IV was working fine, she gave more instructions. I pitied anyone who had to work under Camila.

"You must empty and rinse the chamber pot regularly. With the state of affairs, hygiene is essential. Always remember that. Cholera is a disease passed down by dirty water. This means clothes, linens, utensils, food—absolutely everything we touch must be in immaculate condition. We don't have the manpower or the time for any complications."

"Thanks for the complication bit," I said.

The new nun displayed a shy, pearly smile.

"You must check Mr. Ferreira's vitals once a day and write the information here." Camila pointed at a clipboard sitting by the jars.

"Aren't you going to show me how?"

"You've never taken vitals, *hermana?*"

"Yes, yes, of course I have."

"All right, then follow me."

I spoke before they left the room. "Wait! What's your name?"

"María Purificación," she said, and then added with a lovely accent, "Sor Puri, for short."

CHAPTER 7

Puri

I rushed behind Sor Camila down the stairs, lifting my habit to avoid stepping on the hemline. Never in my wildest dreams had I envisioned wearing a nun's habit. I'd never been a devout woman, much less with a religious calling, but this disguise was a necessity if I didn't want any more calamities to come my way.

I'd already decided I would keep the habit until I had a chance to speak to the person in charge of this hospital—Dr. Mansur?— and ask him about Martin, since nobody else seemed to know him. I'd already probed a couple of nurses but they had no idea who he was. I'd yet to ask Sor Camila, but she seemed so busy and short-tempered I hadn't dared. I must earn her trust first. If I rubbed her the wrong way, she might shoo me away without answers.

Apparently, Dr. Mansur had left for Cali in the morning and they didn't know when he was coming back. I hoped it wasn't too long. This last week felt like a year without my son.

After seven days of turmoil in Cali, I'd finally been able to find a man willing to give me a ride in his mule-drawn wagon. At the boarding house where I'd stayed, I heard from a couple of day workers from El Paraíso that Martin's hacienda had been turned into a hospital. At first, I didn't make the connection, but once they mentioned that the hacienda's owner had disappeared three months ago and nobody knew his whereabouts, I'd realized it was the same place where Sor Alba Luz was headed to—especially because there were no other rural hospitals in the area.

Down the timber staircase, Sor Camila's feet were light, quick, as if she were used to climbing up and down all day long. We walked past a courtyard with an enormous stone fountain in the center. Ferns and flowerpots—filled with those heliconias Sor Alba Luz loved—were scattered sporadically throughout the patio. This hacienda was a gigantic step up from Martin's old house in Vinces.

The nun was giving me yet another set of instructions.

She'd been doing plenty of that from the minute I arrived and the nurse who opened the door—Perla?—had introduced us.

Sor Camila hadn't been able to hide her disappointment upon meeting me. I told her Sor Alba Luz had perished in the earthquake and I was the only one left.

"What a pity," she said. "She was such a kind woman. I met her last year when she visited us."

"Yes, she was."

"I was hoping for more help," she'd said. "We've lost two sisters already."

"In the earthquake?"

She shook her head. She wouldn't elaborate, but being that the hospital was still in one piece and they had talked about nothing but cholera since I'd arrived, I assumed that was what had killed them.

It had been a relief to know that Sor Camila was from a different congregation than Sor Alba Luz. Instead of a scapular like mine, her tunic was covered with an apron. More importantly, the insignia on her chest was different from mine.

Apparently, we were the only nuns here and the rest were secular nurses. Sor Camila said she'd requested help from the Siervas de María because the ones from her congregation had their own sick to tend to in Medellín and the Carmelitas in Cali were cloister nuns. However, some nuns from her congregation were due to come soon.

Of course I wouldn't be here for that.

"Can't you move any faster?" Sor Camila said, creasing her brow.

When I'd first met her, I'd been stunned by her looks. You couldn't look away from her hazel eyes. Her nose was a little long but it stood in perfect harmony with the rest of her features. A small nose would've looked out of place on that exotic face of hers. I'd never met a nun like her. Sor Alba Luz had been graceful, but more in a kind, pleasant way. Sister Camila was one of those women men turned to look at when they walked by. She must have had more than a few admirers in her youth.

I rushed behind her past a shut door that she said was the cholera room.

"As you can see, we're severely understaffed," she said. "And now with the cholera outbreak, we don't exactly have a line of people wanting to work here. You'll start on the day shift but I eventually want you to cover nights."

¡Por los clavos de Cristo! All I wanted was to find out where Martin was, I didn't want to work here! I knew nothing about cholera or broken bones or who-knew-what-other-diseases, nor did I want to.

But how else could I stay? Unless I was a patient, I had no business here. Plus, after those men attacked me, the nun's habit made me feel safer. Not to mention they needed the help—desperately, it seemed. The problem was I couldn't ask too many questions. I was supposed to be a Sierva de María and according to Sor Alba Luz, they received nursing training. My only saving grace was that I had some experience caring for the ill as I'd been my mother's caregiver for the last four months of her life.

"Padre José María is the parish priest of El Paraíso," Sor Camila said. "He will be coming once or twice a week, depending on his availability, for mass, confession, and, of course, to deliver the last rites for those who need it. You'll also have the opportunity to observe the Grand Silence at the end of your shift every day. We have designated one of the rooms as an oratory for this purpose."

I was not familiar with this Grand Silence concept, but I nodded, nonetheless. I wasn't surprised they'd had to assign a room as an oratory; Martin hadn't been a religious man.

She took me to a well by the *cacaotales*, where I could get water, but she warned me that I had to boil it before using it, even to wash clothes and linens. I immediately recognized the mild scent of papaya and banana leaves.

The sight of Martin's plantation made my heart ache.

Hundreds of cacao pods had been left to die.

The Martin I knew would've never let this happen.

The banana trees, planted next to the cacao plants to give them shade, were already in bloom. Hands of green bananas hung upside down and a large purple flower in the shape of a drop sagged below the fruit. I always thought of bells when I saw those gorgeous flowers. Among the banana trees were rows and rows of ripe cacao trees. All of them in need of pruning. How could they have let all this product go to waste?

"*¿Hermana?*"

I turned to Sor Camila, who was watching me with a frown.

"We don't have time for all this daydreaming, Sister. Follow me."

She took me to the kitchen, where the nurses were having lunch. But she left without eating.

CHAPTER 8

Puri

Perla's sweet, syrupy voice reminded me of honey and *buñuelos*. She was the first person I'd met at the hacienda. A young nurse with a patched apron, white bonnet, and skin as smooth as tempered chocolate.

"I'm sorry you can't have your own room and you'll have to sleep with us," she was saying as we waited for our lunch to be served. "We have to take turns with the night nurses, but don't worry, I don't snore."

I'd already seen the nurses' room—I'd been instructed to leave Sor Alba Luz's bag in there.

"Oh, I don't mind," I said.

Perla's Colombian accent was so different from the ones I'd heard in Ecuador—not to mention mine. Among other things, she used the "j" instead of the "s," so instead of saying "*nosotras*" she'd said "*nojotras*," and there was a nice cadence to all her sentences.

We were in a spacious kitchen with two other nurses who were paying us no mind. Thick vigas crossed the ceiling above a dining table that sat eight. The counters were supported by terra-cotta brick, a pattern repeated throughout the kitchen. A brick oven, located in the back of the kitchen, was topped with bronze *pailas* and pots, and more hung overhead. Five or six metal buckets of water were stored on the floor within easy reach. This kitchen was not for show—it had a utilitarian feel—yet in its own way, it exhibited a simple rustic elegance.

"So how did you end up here?" I said.

"I worked for Dr. Mansur in his private practice, but this is my first time in a hospital." She cautiously glanced at the other two nurses. "Dr. Mansur always dreamt of opening a hospital to help the people from this area since he'd gone to school near El Paraíso. So, when the opportunity arose, he took it. And he brought me with him."

Opportunity?

"But this used to be a cacao plantation, as far as I know. How did it get converted into a hospital?"

"That I don't know, *hermana*. I know nothing about businesses! I just packed my luggage and moved here when Dr. Mansur told me to do so. I was so worried that I was going to lose my job that I didn't even ask any questions."

"So, you never met the previous owner?"

"Is it this the man you asked me about earlier?"

I bit my lower lip. I had asked all the nurses, discreetly, I thought. "Yes. I heard about him from some day laborers who worked here. They said his disappearance had been *extremely* mysterious."

She raised an eyebrow. "Mysterious, huh?"

I nodded as the elderly cook approached us with a bowl of soup, her sandals shuffling across the floor.

Perla whispered into my ear. "If I were you, I would ask Don Lucas Ferreira. He knows *everything* about everybody in this region."

The cook placed the soup in front of me.

"*Sancocho*," the old woman said. She had hardly any teeth left but had no qualms in smiling frequently and showing off her red gums.

The soup looked so appetizing. I swirled the spoon, counting the different ingredients: a chicken thigh, potatoes, yuca, corn, plantain, carrots, and lots of herbs—including cilantro, my favorite.

"*El sancocho valluno*," the cook was saying, "is different from *sancochos* in other parts of the country." She spoke slowly, her spectacles resting on the tip of her nose. Her fingers were wiry, her spine crooked. "We use long carrots cut in *rayitas* and our broth is thick."

I eagerly tried a spoonful. But I was shocked beyond words.

It was as sweet as meringue.

Perla watched me with a smile of solidarity. As the cook went to grab another bowl, the nurse whispered that Doña Tulia or Tuli—as she lovingly called her—often confused salt for sugar but everybody ate nonetheless because the cook was so adorable and it was nearly impossible to find people to work at a place bursting with cholera.

"So we're grateful to have anybody in the kitchen," Perla said, flinching a little as she took a sip of her own soup. "In this region, if someone prepares a *sancocho* for you, it means they're welcoming you to their home."

In other words, I had to be gracious and finish the soup whether I liked it or not. And I *was* hungry—I'd eaten so little in the last few days. Perhaps the chicken wasn't so sweet?

I'd tasted this kind of soup in Ecuador but they'd prepared it with beef instead of chicken, and of course the cook hadn't mistaken sugar for salt.

"Don Martin loved it," the cook said behind the counter.

My hand froze, leaving the spoon midair.

I looked around the table. Perla was now talking to the other nurses. Nobody seemed to be paying attention to the old lady. This was the first time someone had mentioned Martin! I wanted to ask her about him, but I had to be cautious. The cook might not speak so openly in front of the others, though she didn't seem to have a lot of self-awareness.

When the nurses finished their *manjar blanco*, which I first feared would have salt instead of sugar, they left. Perla explained that this dessert had been prepared by the other cook, which was why it had the right amount of sugar and no salt whatsoever.

"Should we go?" she said.

I glanced at the old cook.

"I think I'm going to have another serving of *manjar blanco*. You go ahead," I told Perla. "I'll be there shortly."

I wasn't even sure where we were supposed to go—our room?—but I didn't want to lose the opportunity to speak to Doña Tulia about Martin. After Perla and the nurses left, I carried my empty bowl to the kitchen.

"This is delicious, Doña Tuli. Did Don Martin like this dessert, too?"

"Oh, yes, but he's more of a savory kind of man."

She spoke about him in the present tense. Good.

"I haven't seen him around. Do you know where he is?"

"He went for a ride."

"A ride?"

"Oh, yes, he loves those horses."

He was *here*? And he'd gone for a ride? Maybe he was leasing the hacienda to that doctor they mentioned. But if that was the case, why hadn't he answered my letters and telegrams? Also, wouldn't Perla and the other nurses have known who he was?

"Could you take me to him, Doña Tuli?"

She smiled her toothless smile.

"Do you know where he is?"

"Who?"

"Don Martin."

"Oh, he's so sweet. *And* handsome." Her eyes opened wide. Then she laughed. "He always tells me that if he ever marries, he'll marry me because he hasn't met a woman who can cook as good as me."

"Doña Tuli, could you take me to his bedroom or his office?"

"I told you he went for a ride."

"All right, then can we go to the stables? Could you show me his horse?"

"*Sí, señora,*" she said, nonchalantly.

A woman with a hazelnut skin tone and an ocean of coils around her head entered the kitchen. She hummed as she tied a white embroidered apron around her waist.

"Good evening, *madre,*" she said in my general direction.

It took me a moment to figure out she was talking to me. Of course, some nuns were called "*madre.*" But the older ones, as far as I knew. Had I aged so fast? I was only thirty-three years old.

"*Hermana,*" I corrected. "And you are?"

"Lula, *madre.*"

While our introductions took place, Tulia kept her gaze on the *sancocho* she was swiveling with a long wooden spoon as she attempted to hum, too. Reaching over the elder cook, the newcomer immersed a spoon in the pot and brought it to her mouth.

"*¡Ave María!*" she screamed, startling me. "You're going to be the death of me, Tuli! You mixed up the sugar with the salt again!"

Tulia kept humming, or so she thought. Her hums basically consisted of blowing out air through her gums. I wondered if her lack of teeth made the task more difficult.

"*¡Mira ve, esto está dulcísimo!*" Lula said.

She dug a spoon inside a small basket of salt and poured some of it inside the soup.

"Don't you touch my soup!" Tulia said, shaking the spoon. "I was making this soup before you were even born!"

"Oh, come on, Tuli, be good!"

"Don't you get near my soup with that basket of yours again!" She kept threatening with the spoon.

"It's just salt," Lula said.

"Doña Tulia looks tired," I said. "Maybe she needs some air? I'll take her outside for a moment."

"Thank you, *madre.*"

I rested my arm around Tulia's shoulder and guided her toward the door. "Now about those stables . . ."

"Yes, the stables."

We stepped outside the kitchen to a garden full of herbs and vegetables.

"Which direction do we go?" I said.

"The stables," she repeated. Then pointed away from the building. "That way."

We followed a trail flanked by dense grass and wild orchids, past a chicken coop about eighty meters from the main building. There was a man—swarthy and hefty—fixing the fence around it. He tipped his straw hat at me as we walked by. I made a note to talk with him later.

The stables were not far from there and Tulia headed toward the wooden structure with determination.

Inside the building were about a dozen stalls, most of them empty. I unwillingly inhaled the stench of manure and hay.

"*Aquí está*," she said, pointing at a beautiful Andalusian horse, white from head to toe, like my not-so-pristine habit. It was just like Martin to get the best horses. I'd seen this kind of animal near my hometown in Spain, though I didn't know how to ride a horse back then. Not that I was skilled now, but at least I could get on the horse without falling. Martin had been the one to teach me.

"Giralda," she said, petting her muzzle.

I gasped. Martin had named his mare after a famous cathedral tower in my hometown—I recalled telling him about it years ago and how I longed to hear its bells toll again. I didn't think it was a coincidence he'd gotten a Spanish mare and named it after my beloved Giralda. I had a desperate urge to see him again. I instinctively looked around the stable, but the stalls were empty except for five more horses.

"Why don't we go get Martin so he can ride his mare?" I said.

"He never came back," she said.

"When? What do you mean?" I was trying not to push her too much, but I was growing impatient with her half answers.

"That night," she said. "The night of the party."

"What party, Tuli?"

"The fundraiser."

"What fundraiser?"

"For the school." Tulia trailed away.

"Wait," I said, lifting my heavy tunic before I would drag mud and manure everywhere with it. "You said Martin never came back, but the mare did?"

"Oh, yes, she did. She's a good girl."

"But what happened to Martin?"

She shrugged. "He went for a ride."

I sighed. This was harder than giving a manicure to a hen. "So, he never came back?"

"So handsome," she said, shaking her head, almost to herself.

"Do you know where his room is, Tuli?"

She kept walking.

"Hermana! Hermana Puri!" Perla said from a distance, waving her hand. "There you are. Come, I want to introduce you to someone."

I recognized him immediately. His dark hair had grayed in the last five years and he could use a haircut, but he still carried that preoccupied expression, lips like cherries and pasty skin contrasting with his dark eyebrows, just like I remembered. He looked like he hadn't shaved in a couple of days, or slept well, but it was apparent that he enjoyed a good meal.

"Sor Puri, this is Dr. Costa, a compatriot of yours," Perla said.

The man, wearing a white smock, stared at me, squinting a little. I nodded, hiding my hands under my scapular. If he were to look at me long enough, he might remember where we'd met.

"You're from Spain?" he said.

"Yes. Andalucía."

"I'm from Barcelona," he said, his arm seemed to be struggling between remaining folded or stretching toward me. What was the proper etiquette to greet a nun? I'd encountered this same uncertainty in the last couple of days, this look of ambiguity. Since I'd put on a habit, people looked at me with reverence, as if I were an angelic creature too sacred to be touched or to be looked at directly, like the sun.

I felt so much safer with it.

I already knew Dr. Jaume Costa was a Catalán. I also remembered his wife, Montserrat. She'd helped me during the most trying time of my life—the day after my husband got murdered aboard the *Andes*. The doctor had given me a sedative to calm my nerves that night. What a coincidence to find him here. He'd come to Colombia back then to fight the Spanish influenza. I supposed he never left.

"You look so familiar," he said. "Have we met before?"

If he remembered me, he would know I wasn't a nun. I'd been married to Cristóbal de Balboa when we met. I avoided his gaze. I needed more time.

"People often say I have an ordinary face."

"Hermana Puri is with the Siervas de María," Perla interjected.

Good thing the sun had already set and our faces were partially dim.

"Well, thank you, *hermana*, for coming to help," Dr. Costa said. "Now go get some rest. We have a long day ahead of us tomorrow."

I stiffly walked away, feeling his gaze on my back. I could always say I'd entered the convent after becoming a widow. But would he believe it? Only five years had passed since we'd met. Would I still be a novice at the convent or would I have taken my vows already?

I really hoped it didn't come to that.

But maybe I was worrying too much. Dr. Costa must have met hundreds of people in the last five years. He was an important doctor, and apparently he'd been moving around. Surely, he wouldn't remember a compatriot he'd met so long ago during a particularly ominous night.

CHAPTER 9

Lucas

I woke up to the placid smile of the new nun.

"What are you doing here, *hermana*? There are other patients who need you more than I do."

"Good to see you, too," she said, shutting the door behind her. "Don't you remember that Sor Camila said I should exclusively tend to you, Señor Ferreira?"

"Oh, yes. La Coronela Camila."

"May I?" she said, pointing at my sheet.

"Yes. And call me Lucas. Señor Ferreira was my father, *que en paz descanse.*"

She looked at me, uncertain. Then, she recited: "May he rest in peace." A long pause. "And rise in glory."

There was something awkward about the way she said those words but I couldn't pinpoint why.

"Everything looks fine," she said, examining my ankle and my wrist.

I still hadn't been able to place her accent.

"Aren't you going to take my blood pressure?" I said.

She hesitated. "Not now. I forgot my . . ."

I snapped my fingers. "Stethoscope?"

"Yes. That."

She opened the curtains and stared at the view for a long time.

"Where are you from, Sor Puri?"

She turned around, avoiding my gaze. "Spain."

"You're a long way from home."

"Well, that's what happens when you dedicate your life to the service of God. You travel all over." She approached me. "Your color is so much better today. Are you ready for breakfast?"

I shook my head.

"But Sor Camila said you needed to eat and drink more."

I sighed. "I will, just not at six in the morning. I'll throw up if you feed me this early."

She adjusted the pillow behind my head. I perceived a light rose scent. "Are you comfortable?"

"Yes, but I'm so bored I'm about to start eating the curtains."

"I thought you weren't hungry."

I liked her wit.

"I can try to find you a book?" she said, resting her hands on her waist. I could see that she was thin underneath her tunic. "Though I have no idea where."

"I have a couple in my valise. Would you hand it to me?" I pointed at my hard leather suitcase, which was sitting by the armoire.

She picked it up and turned back, too fast.

"Just be careful with—"

But the clasps gave out and the suitcase fell open.

"—the clasps."

"Sorry," she said a little too late, her cheeks flushed.

My trousers, vests, shirts, books, and, worst of all, the photographs from the gala littered the floor.

I had meant to fix the clasps, but alas, here we were.

"Don't worry," I said. "I'll take care of it."

"What? With that cast on? No, thank you, I don't want you to fall and break something else."

She started putting stuff away.

"All these photographs," she said. "I've never seen so many. How come—"

"I have a photography studio in Cali. These are photos from a gala we had here a few months ago. I was going to deliver them to the party guests when I had that stupid fall, so they'll have to wait a little longer."

"A gala?"

I nodded. She looked down again and something caught her attention. She'd found the one photograph I didn't want anyone to see.

She studied it for a long time. I'd seen it so often, I'd already memorized every detail.

It had been taken in this very hacienda. The woman was standing on the front porch, slightly leaning against one of the wooden columns. She was wearing a light dress with leg o' mutton sleeves and her hair fixed in a puffy updo. In her arms was a baby girl. The photo was over thirty years old.

Sor Puri lifted her head to meet my gaze and parted her lips. After a moment, she finally spoke.

"I'm sorry. I'm being meddlesome." She hastily picked up the rest of the photos and organized them in a pile. It didn't escape my notice that she paused an extra-long time on one of the photos. Her fingers might even have shaken a little, but I couldn't be sure.

I looked down.

She was staring at a photograph of me, Farid, and Martin Sabater.

Chapter 10

Lucas

When I remember the first time I met Martin, I always think of wood. Those first days at our school, he always carried a chess set under his arm with carefully carved wooden pieces, a pine scent following him everywhere he went. He would sit on a bench on his own and play against himself. A few kids would surround him and watch. Martin was a skilled player, but he was also impatient and would easily lose his temper and throw the pieces all over the ground. What was it about that game that he seemed to both love and hate? It would take years for me to understand.

In the fall of 1907, Martin was a tall, thin, fifteen-year-old kid, slightly pale—or maybe it was the jitters of being the new boy at school. Not that he had been a nervous kind of person, but anybody moving to a new country and meant to live with strangers would be slightly uncomfortable and apprehensive about his new life.

On his first day at Colegio Internado Oro Verde, Padre Carlos Benigno interrupted our work to present him to the class. Martin—or Juan Sabater, as he first introduced him—was already wearing our school uniform: white buttoned-up shirt, black tie, and a navy-blue jacket with the school insignia. He was somber, which wrongfully led me to believe he wasn't friendly. Back then, I had no way of knowing he had just gone through the most traumatic experience of his life and his aloofness had nothing to do with us and everything to do with growing up with a lunatic father—which, by the way, were his own words, not mine.

I assumed his father was the man waiting for him in the hall, a man I heard speaking to the school principal with a marked French accent. He was a distinguished fellow, obviously European—his stance, his mustache, his tall hat. He was fair-skinned and too stylish and overdressed to be from this area—the men here almost always wore white because it could get really hot, really quickly. But this man, with his ostentatious arrogance and brown striped suit, seemed oblivious to mundane details such as the weather or the poor villages surrounding our boarding school. He stared inside the classroom from time to time while Martin avoided his gaze, keeping his head straight, focused on a fixed spot in the back of the classroom.

Later, I would learn that the man with the French accent was Martin's neighbor—someone who'd inadvertently become his guardian and who would play an important role throughout his entire life.

Padre Carlos Benigno continued telling us about the new kid. Juan Martin was from Ecuador, he said, and had just arrived in Colombia so we were to be kind and welcoming and teach him the School Principles. He assigned me to be his guide and introduce him to the school grounds once theology class was over.

I smiled at the new boy but he didn't smile back. He remained solemn and apathetic—he didn't even wave goodbye at the elegant man who'd brought him here.

Padre Carlos Benigno determined that we would call him by his middle name, Martin, as there were already three *Juanes* in class and he wanted to avoid any confusion.

I could tell that Farid, my best friend—and dare I say, worst enemy—was taken aback by the new kid's presence. In spite of Farid being our prefect, which basically gave him all the advantages over this new student, El Turco had the look in his eye of an alpha male about to compete with another for his rightful spot in the pack. For the last two years, Farid had been the tallest, the toughest, and most brilliant student in our class. Nobody had challenged him. In fact, everyone bowed to him and blindly followed his every whim. But Martin might have been slightly taller than Farid and he looked like someone who was not afraid to fight. At least that's how I took the defiant look he gave all of us while Padre Carlos Benigno introduced him to the entire class.

Martin sat behind me. I resisted the urge to turn around and say hello. He'd already shunned me by not smiling back. Farid always said I smiled too much and that men didn't need to smile to each other. Being overly friendly only made others take advantage of you. Honestly, the only one who took advantage of me was Farid. But there were perks to being his best friend, too, like sitting at the head table in the dining hall and being assigned to only light chores, such as cleaning the sacristy instead of taking care of the farm animals or cleaning the stables and weeds—a task for the younger kids or the new ones.

When class was over, every last one of us stood up. My classmates dispersed into small groups. I was about to turn to greet Martin when Farid stopped me with a stern frown and a nod toward the hall. Being his closest friend meant I was in a constant state of both annoyance and pride. Sometimes I wanted to tell him to go to hell, but then, I liked the status and respect I got from the other kids from being El Turco's buddy. I followed him to the hall.

"What?" I said.

In the last year, Farid had filled up and looked way older than his fifteen years of age. His eyebrows had also thickened, giving him a sort of menacing look. "Don't tell me you're going to hold *el nuevo's* hand and take him sightseeing."

"But Padre Carlos Benigno said—"

"Whatever. *Que diga misa.* You and I have more important things to do."

I glanced inside the classroom, where Martin was sitting alone. I didn't want to disobey the priest, but I didn't want to lose favor with my friend, the prefect, either.

I stuck my head inside.

"Hey, *nuevo!* What are you waiting for?" I told Martin. "Come on!"

Farid smirked. I think it gave him a small measure of satisfaction to see that I was finally making up my own mind and that I'd been rude at addressing the new kid. Martin gave me a look of annoyance, but stood up nonetheless.

El Turco walked away.

"Hey, where are you going?" I said.

He ignored me—so typical of him. Martin reached me, a camel leather satchel across his chest.

"Follow me," I said, leading him outside the building. I intended to give him a short tour of the school grounds until I had to go to my next class.

First stop: the barn, where we kept hens and goats for eggs and milk. The smell of poultry manure and ammonia always repulsed me.

"You'll probably have to feed the chickens and clean up," I said. "That's what the new kids have to do."

Martin remained impassive, but everything changed when we reached the stables. His eyes brightened at the sight of the *percherones*.

"They're so big and muscular," he said. "I'd never seen horses like these."

Before he could get any ideas, I said, "Only the priests can ride them. And occasionally the prefect, my friend Farid. The rest of us can ride them on excursions."

"When are those?"

"I don't know. On holidays, mostly."

"Can't I come here and take care of the horses instead?"

"Doubt it."

I dodged a pile of manure and pointed at a white building in the distance. "That's the residence hall, and the small building next to it is the dining hall." I walked past the director's carriage. "They'll probably assign you a roommate. Pray it's not a sixth grader."

He didn't answer; he seemed more enthralled by the mountains overlooking the school.

El Internado Oro Verde was located in the middle of a valley, not far from the Cauca River, amidst a rich vegetation of pines, eucalyptus, and *robles*. You nearly tripped with rose bushes and orchids everywhere you went.

"I've never lived near a mountain before," Martin said.

"We go there on hikes sometimes. And to the river."

"For fishing?" His expression softened.

"Sometimes, but not too often. Let's go, we have shop now."

"Shop?"

"Carpentry."

Martin gave me a half smile. "I think I'm going to like it here."

Martin was probably regretting his words as Pacho Ruiz and Jairo Perez beat him senseless behind the dormitory. His transgression? Being the new kid at school and daring to sit with me and Farid at the head table. We didn't have to do anything—other kids at school with a lot less seniority than Martin knew he had to earn his place. As soon as he sat with us, Farid stood up and left. I hesitated—I liked the kid, but as the prefect's best friend I had to follow through. At least that was the way I behaved back then, before I knew any better. So, we left Martin alone and after he was done eating, the other kids—the *enforcers*—waited for him outside the dining hall and told him we wanted to speak to him behind the building.

I couldn't imagine what was going through Martin's mind as Pacho Ruiz—a stocky, not too bright kid a year younger than us—was kicking his stomach and sides (Pacho said that those areas left fewer bruises than the legs or face). Martin somehow managed to get hold of a fallen tree branch on the ground and in a surprising recovery smacked Pacho's legs with it. Pacho's knees folded and he fell down. When Jairo came after Martin, he was already on his feet and ready to punch him on the nose, which he did.

Jairo brought his hand to his face. It quickly filled with blood.

Martin retrieved the thick branch from the ground and before Pacho could stand up, he threatened him with it. "Try to hit me one more time, *hijueputa*, and I'll break every bone in your body." Then he turned toward Jairo. "The same goes for you."

Jairo extended his hand. "Calm down, *hermano*, we're just playing around. Can't you take a joke?"

Martin prodded him with the stick. "*Estás advertido*. Don't ever get near me again."

Three stories up, behind our bedroom window, Farid and I watched as Pacho Ruiz and Jairo Perez scrammed. Martin stood behind, heaving. El Turco didn't say a word, but he had a satisfied smirk on his face.

For the next few days, Martin didn't speak to me—to any of us, really. He alternated between playing chess on his own and sitting unassumingly in the back of the dining room with his new roommate, a Brazilian kid two years younger than us who'd arrived a month prior. Apparently, his father was a merchant in Buenaventura and had sent his kid to our boarding school. The kid was studious but barely spoke any Spanish so the two of them would often sit in silence, though a couple of times when I'd walk past them, I heard Martin attempting to learn Portuguese. They seemed to have hit it off because I would often see them walking together down the halls and working side by side during shop.

Martin never said anything to the priests about the beating.

One day, out of nowhere, El Turco told me to bring Martin to the stables. As the school prefect, Farid had certain privileges. Ordering his peers around was one of them. Riding horses with the priests on weekends was another. It was no surprise he was a much better horseman than the rest of us.

Martin didn't answer when I told him to come with me, but he followed nonetheless.

Farid was standing outside a stall, his hands resting on the banister. The school's latest acquisition, a jet-black Spanish mare, was rearing out of control. Apparently, El Turco had tried to ride it again, but I could only guess how that attempt had gone. Behind me, Martin suddenly seemed more interested.

"I heard you're good with horses," Farid told him. It was the first time he'd spoken to Martin since he'd arrived two weeks ago.

"I know a bit." Martin approached; his eyes fixed on the animal's gallant mane. "Is it a female?"

"Yes."

"It doesn't surprise me."

Farid hid a smile.

Ever so carefully, Martin opened the stall door and took a step inside. The mare reared some more, then started pacing frantically back and forth. Martin just stood there, hands at his sides, watching her. Once in a while, he would say something soothing like, "Easy," or "It's going to be fine."

The mare continued pacing for a while.

And then it stopped.

Martin did nothing. He just stood between the stall door and the mare.

She had no way of getting out other than to trust the man standing in front of her. Did she realize that? Slowly, Martin stretched out his arm and grabbed her leather halter. The mare acquiesced, somehow, and eventually lowered her head.

Martin petted her side and then her back, while softly whispering to her.

Farid eyed him with newfound respect. After that day, nobody beat Martin again.

CHAPTER 11

Puri

"How come someone as pretty as you chose to lock herself in a convent?" Lucas said, his head leaning against the headboard. A mischievous expression—the sum of a smirk and a beaming gaze—seemed to follow him at all times. Underneath his shabby appearance, I suspected, dwelled an attractive face.

"I'm not locked in, am I?" I said.

"You know what I mean."

I had just brought in a lunch tray for my sole patient and was setting it on his lap when he bombarded me with questions. I had to admit I was surprised that he would speak to a nun with such freshness. Either he was irreverent by nature, or he didn't truly buy the idea that I was a nun.

"Eat while it's still warm," I said, sounding like my mother.

There was a broth of some sort in a ceramic bowl, tamales *val- lunos*, and a banana for dessert. It was disturbing to think that Tulia and Lula didn't have to cook for too many people because most patients had cholera and didn't eat anything other than broth or *avena*, if they were doing better. Otherwise, they were on IVs.

"Well, let's see," I said, setting a napkin on his lap. "I wanted to help others."

"You can help others without consecrating your life to the Church."

I agreed with him, but I had to play the role. "I suppose."

I fiddled with his silverware as I tried to arrange it for him. Oh, wait, I was going to have to cut the *tamal* for him as his right wrist was in a cast.

"Tell me the truth," he said.

Had my actions somehow given me away?

"What do you mean?"

"Did you not have enough of a dowry to marry well? Did you have a forbidden love? Which one is it?"

"None of the above."

He shook his head.

"What?" I said.

"It doesn't make any sense."

"What doesn't make sense?"

"You don't seem like the kind."

"I didn't know there was a kind."

"Well, there is a kind."

"Is Sister Camila the kind?"

He grabbed the spoon with his left hand and dipped it inside the broth. Then he blew on the liquid before sipping it quietly.

"Well, is she?" I said.

He shrugged.

The door burst open. It was Perla.

"We need you, *hermana*."

I followed her outside, barely catching up with her quick steps. From the moment Perla woke up she was running around the hospital—she and the other nurses. What a slacker I was, assigned to only one patient.

"What happened?" I asked.

"Dr. Mansur brought his father. We need you in the cholera room since Sor Camila is going to be tending to their father exclusively."

Dr. Mansur was back!

"Wait. Did you say *their* father?"

"Didn't I tell you?" She scratched her forehead. "Sor Camila is Dr. Mansur's sister."

I paused before taking my next step. "What?"

There was some commotion in the courtyard. We peeked over the second-story banister. A man in his early thirties—hair already thinning—led an old man, much shorter and rounder than him, across the patio. The older man seemed to be complaining—half in Arabic, half in Spanish.

"That's them," she said.

A languid adolescent followed the men and, behind him, a woman whose heels clacked against the cobblestones just as loudly as the men bickered.

The woman was dressed in the latest style—a pink silk blouse and a long pencil skirt hugging her legs. A wool cloche hat and a bob completed her chic look. She looked like she was ready for a luncheon at the tennis club or a tea rather than a rural hospital visit. Sister Camila was also with them, but remained aloof and indifferent to the bickering.

"What's wrong with their father?" I said.

"I think he hit his head or something, but apparently, they lost their house in the earthquake, so the whole family came," Perla said, nearly skipping.

I followed Perla downstairs and she handed me a cloth mask. With the news and the scandal in the patio, I hadn't quite grasped that I was going to enter the infamous cholera room.

They had warned me about it, but I wasn't expecting this.

The fetid odor, the buckets of bluish liquid underneath the cots, the pale patients slowly turning into breathing cadavers—it was not a pleasant sight.

There were over a dozen patients here. Perla instructed me to make sure their IVs were open and they had a constant saline drip. I was to clean and change their chamber pots and essentially offer them comfort in their last hours of life, if it came to that.

I swallowed.

"No one has survived this, so far," Perla said, "so make sure you clean everything well so you don't get it, too." She was frowning, shaking her head, as I tried to catch up with her. "We've told the people in the region how important it is to boil their water before they drink it or wash their vegetables, but they won't listen. *They just don't listen.*"

A man grabbed my hand as I walk past him. "*Hermana, ayúdeme.*"

His cheekbones protruded, his face so thin I could see the shape of his skull. His skin looked leathery, stretched out, and his lips were dry. Instinctively, I searched for a glass of water, but then I saw he was hooked up to an IV. And still his body wasn't holding any liquid.

How could I help him? I knew nothing about cholera or spiritual matters. But Perla had just said that some people only needed comfort during those last hours in this world, someone who would listen to them, to keep them company. It didn't cease to amaze me how many people reached out to me because of this religious habit. It was almost as if it gave me supernatural powers. I nodded and sat by him, listening to a labored confession of his sins.

This was wrong. He needed a priest, not a nun, much less someone pretending to be a nun. But there didn't seem to be anybody else and Sor Alba Luz had told me that the Siervas' charism, their calling, was to tend to the ill, to the hopeless, and offer them comfort. Well, I could do that, just like she'd done to me after Paco died.

We started praying.

I couldn't help but think of the last day I saw my mother alive. She'd been suffering for about four months with a liver that had been fighting her body as if it was its own worst enemy. Her eyes had been dimmed on her last day, but she'd had a slight smile on her lips when she looked at me. She told me she'd done everything she wanted to do in life, though she had some regrets—which I suspected had to do with my father—but she never said what those were. I remember holding her hand, but I hadn't been there when she passed. I'd gone to sleep in my childhood bed-room for a few hours. I always regretted not being there when she took her last breath. Had she been afraid—terrified—of what was coming? Perhaps I could've offered some comfort and much needed company.

I held the man's hand and he squeezed mine. We remained like that for a few minutes. I looked into his eyes until he slowly released my hand, his muscles relaxed, and his head fell to the side. I gasped.

Someone squeezed my shoulder. I turned to look at Perla, a somber but exhausted expression on her face.

"You nuns are so good at this," she said.

"At what?"

"At transmitting peace to our patients."

Her words only made me feel worse about my imposture, but what else could I do, at this point? My only clear option was to speak to Dr. Mansur. And I intended to do so, just as soon as Perla let me go.

Fighting back tears, I ran my hand over the man's eyelids, at-tempting to close them, but they didn't.

Yes, I was a phony, but I'd offered this man the comfort he needed in his last moments—that had to count for something, right?

"Sor Camila has the same gift, despite her bad temper."

That had been obvious. In Spain we said irritable people had *mala leche* and she had plenty of it.

"We need to notify Dr. Costa about this death," she said, lead-ing the way outside the room.

I was taken aback by her nonchalant tone. Perhaps that was what it took for someone to work in this field.

They said cholera could kill someone in a matter of hours. They said it was highly contagious. I, myself, had just witnessed the death of a man. I might find out what happened to Martin, but at what cost? And what would become of my son if something were to happen to me?

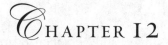

CHAPTER 12

Camila

Keeping a secret for most of my life was like having a rubber ball permanently stuck in my throat. Every time there was the slightest possibility of the secret being revealed, the ball would press against the walls of my throat, threatening to come out.

I'd had a desire to retch all morning—and it had nothing to do with the epidemic around me. It had everything to do with my brother's decision to bring our family here. Why here of all places? My brother knew the effect seeing them would have on me. But he couldn't care less. He did it anyway, he simply shrugged it off and said, "I couldn't leave Baba in the street. Could I? Besides, he hit his head."

I'd seen his head. He barely had a scratch on his forehead. He could've stayed with Tío Ibrahim or our brother Omar. There was plenty of room in their homes for my father and for Farid's family. But clearly, my older brother wanted to see me suffer. He still hadn't forgiven me.

At this point in our lives, his actions shouldn't come as a surprise. Farid had always been that way. The only thing that mattered was what *he* wanted, what *he* needed. It was bad enough to have Lucas here.

Baba smiled at me coyly, his forehead showing nothing more than a pink scrape. I turned away, not granting him another look, and faced the carriage.

"Good morning, Tía Camila," Basim, Farid's eldest, said stepping out.

I was breathless—as though I'd received a punch in the gut. Basim had grown so much since I'd last seen him. He was almost a head taller than me and so thin, just like his father had been.

"Hello," I said.

He kissed my hand, as if I were a priest, and quickly followed Baba. I nodded at Amira, my sister-in-law, who emerged after Basim. As usual, she was wearing the latest fashion, from her glossy mahogany heels (so out of place in the country) all the way to the feathers poking out of her bell-shaped cloche hat.

I hadn't purchased or sewn new clothes in years, whereas Amira never wore the same outfit twice. But it wasn't her fault that I'd made a vow of poverty fourteen years ago and that it had been instilled in me that vanity and pride were faults to be expelled from the root.

My brother knew all about his wife's vanity when he married her, but he hadn't had much of a choice. Amira was destined to be his bride since she was a baby.

"Where are my nieces?" I asked my sister-in-law.

Aside from Basim, Farid and Amira had two girls who, according to my calculations, must be eleven and twelve years old now.

"They stayed in Cali with Omar and his family," she said.

My brother Omar was now in charge of my father's fabric store and there was no human power that could remove him from work—not even an earthquake.

At a cautious distance, I followed Baba and Farid's family into the hacienda. I couldn't let Farid see how much his imposition had affected me. I took in a deep breath as we crossed the courtyard, and caught up with my brother before he reached the stairs.

"Where will Baba stay?" I asked.

"Upstairs. In the back room," he said.

"Your bedroom?"

"Of course."

So he was giving Baba his room, the largest one in the hacienda, and a space that had once belonged to Martin Sabater.

It was surreal to be in Valle del Cauca after so many years of living away and having barely had any contact with my family. The Siervas had become my family, as much as some of them often irritated me. But now, I would be confronted on a daily basis with people who'd inhabited my memories—and nothing else—for years. I wasn't sure I was ready to have them as part of my life again. Especially under these circumstances. With all the chaos at the hospital, I barely had any time to think, much less to face the emotional drain from the past.

It was at times like these that I missed my mother the most; times when I needed a confidante, someone to guide me through the hardships of life. How many times in the last fourteen years had I wished I could turn to one of my sisters at the convent and share my burdens? But I couldn't. Just as soon as we arrived, we learned that we were supposed to forget our past lives and never speak about them again.

But I couldn't forget, hard as I tried.

People said you could never replace a mother. I believed it. I didn't have many memories of her since I had been barely six years old when she died, but I clearly remember a time when I fell down and cut my knee. She'd immediately come to my aid and told me, as she cleaned my wound with iodine, that I was supposed to let the scab fall off on its own—when it had dried and healed—or it would start bleeding again.

"You can't take it out yourself. You can't rush the healing process with your will."

Well, she was right. I'd tried to remove the scab from my past many times and it always bled.

But I would get through this—somehow. I just had to focus on my duties, like I always did.

No time to think.

After Farid set up Baba in his room and checked his head one more time, he determined that I was to devote every waking hour to our father's care.

"Make sure he doesn't start saying weird things. We can never tell what will happen with a brain injury."

He called *that* a brain injury? My brother's devotion was getting in the way of his good sense. I followed him to the hall.

He squeezed my shoulders with those big hands of his, destined to heal. "Don't worry, they won't be here long."

"But *akhuy*, don't you think we're putting Baba and everybody else at risk here? You know how contagious cholera is."

"We'll take all the measures. As long as we keep everything clean, Baba will be fine. But I want him here, near us. He practically lost his home, *ukhti*, and I don't trust Omar to take good care of him. If it doesn't have to do with work, he's oblivious." He looked me square in the eye. "I only trust *you*, Mila."

Farid always melted my heart when he called me "Mila." He knew exactly how to appease me.

Who would've thought that at this stage of my life, I would have to look after my father again? After everything that had happened between us.

I looked after Farid as he walked down the dim hall of the hacienda, in a rush as usual, leaving me with the responsibility of our father's care.

I went back to Martin Sabater's—Farid's—room. Baba was looking at me from the bed.

"This is ridiculous, *habibti*. I don't need to be here, like an invalid. Farid exaggerates."

I didn't answer. I never did. Baba had hurt me too much throughout the years and I was not ready to talk. If Farid wanted me to take care of our father I would do it, just like I would care for any other patient, but that didn't mean I had to speak to him.

"Camila, Camilita . . ."

I didn't even look at him. I simply arranged the covers.

"I should've told you this a long time ago, but for whatever it's worth, I'm sorry."

I looked up.

"What we did to you . . . it was wrong. And . . ." He sat up. "I've always regretted it."

"And you think that saying 'I'm sorry' is enough?"

I headed for the door. How did I get sucked into this? Things were going well for me. And now, thanks to my brother, thanks to my father, a pair of men who'd always controlled the course of my life, I'd been swept away by a tornado of events and emotions. All because of one little letter sent to the convent three months ago.

CHAPTER 13

Puri

A man in a white smock was coming in my direction. As we got close to each other, I couldn't help but notice his eyes. They were what my mother would've called "deep," with thick, imposing eyebrows and long eyelashes. They seemed to have a brown tint to them, initially, but as the light shifted, they turned hazel.

He stopped in front of me.

"You're new," he said.

"Yes, I arrived two days ago. My name is Purificación." I refused to add "Sor" to my introduction.

"I'm glad you're here, *hermana*," he said, extending his hand. "We need all the help we can get."

I shook his hand. I remembered from the days that I impersonated my husband how important a handshake was for men, so I'd gotten used to responding with a strong grip and by looking directly into the person's eyes.

"I'm Dr. Farid Mansur," he said.

I figured as much: the chief doctor, Sor Camila's brother. No wonder the resemblance. His name was definitely not Latin, but Arab, if I wasn't mistaken. But he didn't sound like a foreigner.

He let go of my hand.

I had to ask him about Martin, but how would I bring up the subject? *By any chance, do you happen to know where Martin Sabater is, and why have you taken over his property and converted it into a hospital?*

"And I hear you're Spanish?" he said.

"Yes," I said, studying his demeanor.

His stance was relaxed, his shoulders wide and straight. He had an ease about him, a confidence that was captivating. A medal of some saint hung from his neck.

"And you're from this area?" I asked.

"Yes."

"But your name?"

"My father's a Palestinian immigrant, but I was born here."

"No wonder. You look like the *moros* in Sevilla. In fact, you could easily blend with my people."

"Of course, Arabs were in the Iberian Peninsula for eight hundred years. But my family is Christian."

This was my opportunity. I'd been waiting for his return and now I had him in front of me, conversing in such a friendly manner, I could ask him about Martin. But here? In the middle of the hall?

"Have you been in our country long?"

"Just a few days."

"You arrived at an interesting time," he said.

"Yes. Unfortunately." I cleared my throat. I was just going to ask him about Martin. Blurt out the name. How would I even bring it up? *Talking about interesting times . . .*

"Doctor, I wanted to ask you something," I said.

He folded his arms across his chest. "What?"

His stern reaction made me waver.

"Dr. Mansur!" A nurse named Celia emerged from one of the rooms in the hall. "Could you come over, please?" Her voice was urgent, her face covered in sweat.

The doctor tried to walk past me, but I blocked him.

"Doctor, I . . ."

I must've looked like an absolute idiot just standing there, unable to finish my sentence.

Say something. This is your chance.

"Excuse me, Sister," he said, impatiently. "We'll continue our conversation some other time."

"Yes, yes, of course."

I moved to the side so he could follow the nurse into the room. Something had stopped me, something other than Nurse Celia.

Farid Mansur was the third man in Lucas's photograph.

He was still youthful now, but a little fuller. He'd also lost some hair. His face, however, hadn't changed at all. And when he'd crossed his arms, he'd looked exactly like the adolescent in the photo. Martin had once told me he'd spent some of his best years at the boarding school in Colombia. It was apparent, too, that he'd run into these old friends when he returned to the area a few years ago.

So, what happened?

Why had they taken over his property? People didn't just go missing for no reason, and nobody had seen Martin in months or had an answer as to whether he'd sold the hacienda or simply abandoned it.

How did Sister Camila, Dr. Mansur, and Lucas, even, connect to Martin?

Did they?

During my conversations with Martin, back in París Chiquito, he'd been reserved about his life in Colombia. He'd only told me about a few pranks he and his classmates had played on their teachers during high school. One had involved explosives and a shattered roof, and the other one some frogs that Martin and his friends had fed the priests during a special meal, claiming they were pieces of chicken. But he'd never mentioned any names.

If there was, in fact, a connection between all of them, would this illustrious doctor give an explanation to a stranger? Particularly if this property's takeover had been less than honorable. It had been one thing to ask Perla. She was just one of the many nurses who worked here. Or Tulia, the cook. But it was something else to give the director a reason to suspect my true motivation for being here or start questioning who I really was. If he didn't like what I had to say and saw me as a nuisance, he could send me away—at best.

There had been something dark, something intimidating about Dr. Mansur that I hadn't expected.

After everything I'd seen in the last few days, I was apprehensive about this land. I could barely walk without fearing that the earth was going to crack open and swallow me. I'd been having a hard time sleeping since Paco and Sor Alba Luz passed away, and the slightest noise made me flinch. My middle-of-the-night thoughts kept warning me I might be next.

I needed a plan that would get me as much information as possible without exposing myself. And I needed to find the right time. If I started digging openly about Martin, and someone didn't want his story uncovered, I could be in danger. I had to be cautious, patient, not my usual reckless self.

I headed to the cholera room, where I'd consoled the dying patient yesterday, and put on my mask before entering the room. The stench of bodily fluids greeted me nonetheless. I walked past a couple of patients, making sure their IVs were open, when a familiar voice startled me.

"Hermana Puri! What a pleasure to see you."

It was somewhat jarring to see Lucas here.

"What are *you* doing here?" I said.

He was standing by one of the patients, a crutch under each armpit to hold himself up, sporting a walnut robe halfway open and a crooked cloth mask.

"You abandoned me, Sister."

I fixed his mask. "I'm sorry, Lucas, but Perla told me to come here this morning. She said she'd look after you. Are you feeling fine?"

"Yes. A little bored, to be honest."

And he came here for what? Excitement?

"Should you be here? The last thing we need is for you to get cholera."

He shrugged, as much as someone can shrug with a pair of crutches under his arms.

"You should go back to your room."

"I can't be lying in bed all day with this epidemic going on. I can help."

"You? But you can barely walk on your own!"

"Oh, I'm fine," he said, squinting a bit.

"Then why do you look like you're in excruciating pain? Besides, you look pale." I pressed his back. "You're coming with me."

He offered no resistance as I led him outside the room. Hard as he tried to act normal, he flinched with every leaden step he took.

"I can't believe you descended those stairs all by yourself," I said. "You could've fallen again, Lucas. Have you had any breakfast yet?"

"If I promise I won't leave my room without your permission again, would you stop scolding me?"

I sighed. "What about breakfast?"

"I could definitely eat, but can't I have my meal at a table? I hate eating in my room by myself. I've been doing that for days."

I could see by the sweat on his forehead and his pained expression that he was trying to conceal the toll this little stroll had taken on his foot.

"All right," I said, heading for the kitchen.

The shuffling sound of Lucas's slippers against the pavement was making it hard for me to stay annoyed at him for his escapade. There was something endearing about him.

The kitchen was such a contrast from the cholera room with that pleasant aroma of fresh baked *pan de yuca*, some kind of meat cooking, and *agua de panela*. Tulia, her back to us, was squeezing oranges. She filled a pitcher with juice and grabbed a small bowl with a white powder.

"Wait!" I said, rushing behind the tile counter that separated the kitchen from the dining room table. I inserted my pinky inside the bowl and tasted the powder that got stuck to my finger. As I feared, it was salt.

"I don't think this juice needs any more sweetening," I said. "If you don't mind?" I took the pitcher from her hands and poured a glass for Lucas.

Tulia tapped her lips with her finger, as if trying to recall what she was about to do. When she remembered, she reached out for a pan hanging above the oven.

"*Huevitos?*" she asked Lucas.

"*Sí, mi señora divina.*"

Bracing myself, I handed Tulia a basket filled with eggs, but clung to the bowl of salt as if my life depended on it. All these ingredients and cooking utensils made me miss my kitchen so much. Hardly anything brought me as much comfort and ease as preparing chocolate.

"Have you tasted chocolate, Lucas?"

"You mean the drink?"

"No, solid chocolate."

"I'm afraid not," he said.

"When you're feeling a little better and the doctor clears you from your diet, I'll prepare you some. That is, if I can find any decent cacao beans around here. From what I've seen, most have dried out, but I should be able to procure some since this used to be a cacao plantation, right?"

Ignoring my comment, Lucas finished tucking a napkin inside his pajama top.

"Right?" I repeated.

His gaze fluctuated between Tulia's back and me.

"How do you know that?" he finally said.

"People have made comments, you know?" I added a pinch of salt to the eggs in the pan. "Besides, I'm not blind. I've seen the cacao trees."

"Yes, this was a plantation," Tulia said, "owned by Don Martin Sabater." She sighed. "Such a charming young man."

I glanced at Lucas.

"You knew him?" I said.

With as much proficiency as anyone with a cast could, he picked up a knife and fork and held them upright, on either side of his empty plate.

"Did you?" I repeated, hoping he wouldn't lie to me. After the photo of them together, he couldn't deny it.

"Yes," he said.

I leaned over the counter, forgetting all about Tulia's cooking.

"What happened to him?"

"Tuli, you're the best," he said as the elder woman came around the counter with a plate of scrambled eggs and *pan de yuca*. "I'm so hungry I could eat a horse."

"No, not a horse," Tulia said. "They're too pretty."

He dug into his food.

"Well?" I said, folding my arms.

He barely looked up.

"Aren't you going to tell me what happened to the owner of the plantation?"

"Not here," he mumbled, glancing in Tulia's direction.

The cook seemed lost in the kitchen again. Lula shouldn't leave the old woman here alone anymore. When things were slow between meals, Lula was nowhere to be found.

I sat in front of Lucas while he ate, filling his coffee cup once in a while. It seemed like Colombians like their coffee a lot. He was on his third cup already when Doña Tuli stepped outside.

I cleared my throat. "Now will you tell me what happened to Martin Sabater?"

"You are persistent for a nun."

"You're filled with ideas about what a nun should or shouldn't be. We're all different people, not one big mass of praying creatures, you know?"

He sighed. "Why is this so important to you?"

"I promise to tell you why if you tell me what you know first."

He brought a piece of bread to his mouth and studied me while he chewed. I was ready to tell him the entire truth if he would just give me some answers.

After he was done chewing, he wiped his mouth with the napkin, and looked at me with the most serious expression I'd ever seen on this man's face.

"Martin is dead."

CHAPTER 14

Puri

I didn't believe Lucas. I *couldn't* believe him.

"Are you sure?" I said.

"Reasonably."

"What do you mean?"

He stared at his blue ceramic plate. "Farid told me he died."

"The night Martin went riding his horse?"

He looked up, lifted an eyebrow. "A few days later."

No, this couldn't be true. Martin couldn't be dead. He was too young, too eager to live, to do extraordinary things. My heart shattered. *He never met our Cristóbal.*

"Please . . . tell me what happened."

He collected bread crumbs into a neat cluster. The creases on his forehead reminded me of a confluence of rivers. And his eyes were the same color.

"No. I already answered your question." He was still gazing at his plate, his head tilted sideways. "Now you have to tell me why you care about Martin Sabater."

I couldn't share the *entire* truth with Lucas. I'd just met him and didn't know if I could trust him. Now that I was learning that Martin might be dead, I couldn't make myself vulnerable. Something about the ominous way Lucas was delivering the news seemed to me like Martin didn't exactly die of natural causes, *if* in fact he was dead.

"I met him a few years ago in Ecuador," I said. "We were good friends."

"Martin friends with a nun?"

What was it about this man and nuns?

"So, you came here looking for him?" he said.

I awkwardly ran my fingers along the stiff veil covering my head. "I already answered your question. Now you have to answer mine."

"Which one? I've answered so many already."

"How did Martin die?"

Lucas took a sip of juice. He fiddled with his eggs for a bit, then started talking.

"Martin, Farid, and I went to the same boarding school. In the last few years, it started losing students, probably because it's so expensive. It's also in the middle of nowhere and they've opened new schools in the area, including some really good ones in Cali. Well, the board decided to close the school because it kept losing money every year and they weren't even able to pay the teachers' salaries anymore. Both Farid and Martin were devastated by the news as both of them considered their high school years the best of their lives."

"Martin did mention that to me," I said.

"Anyway, the two of them organized a massive fundraising gala with the most powerful landowners of the region for the purpose of giving out scholarships to those students who couldn't afford tuition. Martin offered his hacienda as a venue. There would be dinner, dancing, and an auction. It was a big success. Way into the night, after everybody had had too much to drink, someone asked to see Martin's new Andalusian mare—a lady friend of his from Ecuador, I think."

A lady friend?

"Do you remember her name?" I interrupted.

He thought for a moment. "No. I'm sorry."

"Continue, please."

"I thought it was stupid that Martin had spent so much money on that horse since, as he'd confided in me, he was struggling to keep his hacienda afloat, but he was sort of a dreamer, you know? All his life he'd dreamt of owning a plantation, so he moved heaven and earth to get it. Well, his next whim was to get a Spanish horse, and so he got it. It must have cost him an eye, but he did it anyway. His lady friend asked to ride it. Apparently, she was a skilled horseman. Other people wanted to ride, too, including Martin, and off they went with the rest of the horses. I was too drunk to remain standing, much less ride a horse.

"About two hours later, the group came back, but there was no sign of Martin. Farid said they had encountered a jaguar that spooked the horses and everybody got separated. Farid said he shot the jaguar but didn't know if he hit it or not as it ran off.

"We waited for Martin for a while, but seeing that he wasn't coming up, a caravan went looking for him until dawn, but couldn't find him. He was missing for three days until Farid found him agonizing. Apparently, he'd fallen off the horse and had broken his neck. Farid couldn't save him."

"Did you see Martin's body?"

He kept his gaze on his plate. "No. I left the day after the party. I got a telegram from one of my neighbors in Cali telling me my mother was in the hospital. She has diabetes and her insulin had gotten really low."

"How is she?"

"Stable. She's close to our neighbors, so they always look after her."

"Do you know who else saw Martin's body besides Farid?"

Lucas shrugged. "I think Camila did, too."

"Sor Camila was here? At a party?"

"The Mother Superior sent her and a couple of other nuns to

support the school effort. Apparently, they had some experience with this kind of charity."

"But there's something I don't understand. How is it that Martin's hacienda turned into this hospital?"

"Farid said that was Martin's dying wish. When Farid found him, Martin told him that since he didn't have any descendants or family left, he wanted to help the people in the region with a hospital."

That sounded very charitable, but not exactly like the Martin I knew.

I studied Lucas's face attentively. He was avoiding my eyes. Something about his demeanor, his discomfort perhaps, told me he was either hiding something or lying about it. It wasn't that Martin wasn't a person capable of a good deed, such as this one, especially during his final moments, but it seemed too convenient for Dr. Mansur that he would be the sole recipient of such a generous donation.

Since he didn't have any descendants or family left . . .

Lucas's words drilled into my mind. Martin had died not knowing he had a son—*our* son. Guilt crept through my veins. I should've told Martin a long time ago that he had a son. Perhaps he would've come to Vinces to meet him. Maybe he would've let go of this place and whatever problems he was having. Had he gone back to Ecuador, he might still be alive.

Why didn't I say anything?

It wasn't that I wanted this place for myself—or for Cristóbal. It just wasn't fair for my son to grow up without a father—like I had—or to be stripped of his inheritance.

How could I have allowed my son to grow up without a father when I had gone through the same thing and it had been so hard? As a child, there was nothing I wanted more than seeing my father. I'd longed my entire life to be with him. And yet, I'd carved the same destiny for my Cristóbal. All because of my own shame since I didn't want people to know that I'd been intimate with a man so soon after my husband passed away. The man my sister Angélica loved, at that. I'd been so selfish. I'd let *el qué dirán* dominate my actions, *knowing* they were wrong. But how easily and quickly had I judged others who let society's rules dictate their own behaviors.

"Are you done?" I said, pointing at his plate.

He nodded quietly. He was studying me as well. It must also seem like a big coincidence to him that I came to this hospital ·after having met Martin in Ecuador years ago.

"Just one more question, Lucas. Were you and Martin still friends when he came back from Ecuador?"

His eyes widened.

"Yes, of course."

He sounded certain, but there was something about his manner—the way he was shifting in his seat, avoiding my face, adjusting his pajama top. Something wasn't quite right.

I helped him back to his room, questioning if his answer had been truthful or if he was trying to hide something. But if so, what?

CHAPTER 15

Lucas

May 1909

I knew something was wrong the minute Padre Joselo whispered into Padre Carlos Benigno's ear and they both looked at me. We were in the middle of Theology when Padre Joselo had busted into the classroom with a sense of urgency and a pallid face.

My body tensed up when Padre Carlos Benigno walked in my direction. From the desk next to mine, Martin gave me a compassionate look—as if he already knew what had happened, as if he'd seen this same look directed toward him in the past.

"Mr. Ferreira, would you come with me outside?"

I followed him to the door, my knees locking from time to time. He held the door for me and then turned toward the rest of the class.

"Mr. Mansur, please continue with the reading."

I stopped listening to the rest of the instructions imparted to my classmates, my attention limited to the movement of the priest's lips without comprehending a word he was saying. The building was cold, probably due to the fact that the walls were made out of adobe. He took me to a small inner patio flanked by

large windows. There was a single jacaranda tree filled with laven-
der flowers. My gaze rested there, the only safe place I could find.

"There's been an incident with your father," Padre Carlos Benigno said.

I knew it had to do with him. Not sure why.

"His heart failed him."

I peeled my gaze off the bushy tree and turned to the priest.
"Did he die?"

Padre Carlos Benigno rested his hand on my shoulder. "You
have to be strong, Lucas."

"Did he?"

"Unfortunately, yes."

I shook his hand off my shoulder. I hated the pity I saw in his
eyes.

"Are you sure?" I said.

"Yes."

There was something breaking inside me, but I couldn't let it
take over or I would collapse right there and never, ever, be the
same again. I stood up.

"Can I go back to class now?"

"But Lucas, we have to arrange for your trip back home, the
service—"

"Later," I said, a little brusquely. "Later, Padre, we'll talk about
that later. I need to finish my work."

To think that I would never utter that word—*padre*—toward
my father again, just men in cassocks. But I wouldn't let myself
go on that route. The "never agains." Any second now, someone
would come and tell me this was nothing but a big mistake.

I was numb. Numb to everyone around me, to the voices whispering nonsensical words, to the cooling temperature, to the smells
of coffee and cigarettes and bodies sitting too close to one another—some behind me, others next to me—numb to the people,
both old friends and strangers, coming to hug me, but especially
numb to the casket holding my father's body in front of me. I still

hadn't gathered the courage to go see him and make sure it was truly him. My mother had told me to go, she had urged me with words and with a poke in the arm to say goodbye to my father, but I hadn't moved from my chair.

I didn't want to see him. I'd never seen a dead person before and I wasn't going to start with him. But then, if I didn't get close to him, if I didn't corroborate that, in fact, it was his body in there, how would I know he had truly died? I still had my doubts. The casket seemed too small to hold someone like my father, someone who'd always been larger than life, whom I'd always thought of as immortal—too intense to be resting quietly in that tiny box. He should be walking around the room, greeting everyone, making jokes. The irony of it was that in spite of the coffin appearing to be too small to hold him, when I'd first arrived from the boarding school, I couldn't believe that they'd managed to fit a casket in our living room. My mother and the neighbors had removed all the furniture from the parlor and replaced it with the ghastly coffin, long-standing candles, and chairs. Black curtains had also been hung in the house's entrance, which had given me the chills when I'd arrived with Padre Carlos Benigno.

A jolt passed through my legs, as though they were urging me to get up and go see him before they closed the coffin. It would be the last time I would lay eyes on my father. I told myself it might be the only way I could wake up from this sleepwalker state I'd been immersed in for the last two days, but other parts of my body opposed the idea and prevented me from getting up.

"Mire, mijito, sus amigos."

My mother's voice sounded distant even though she was right next to me, propelling her coffee breath into my ear, squeezing my arm. She was saying something about my friends. Were they here? I thought she'd said that, but I couldn't be sure. I turned around, facing dozens of strangers. When did this place fill up? It had only been me and my mother and Padre Carlos Benigno for a long time. But it seemed like the entire town of Cali was here. It made sense, though. My father had been one of the few photographers in town and everybody knew him. He had a way with people—a gift, if you will—and it showed in his images, the trust, the complacency between the person and the camera. Most portraits from other photographers were stiff, mechanical, but my father found a way to bring out the person's humanity so you could almost smell their flesh, touch their cheeks, see through their eyes and into their hearts. That ability of his was what made people so fond of him.

He'd had that gift with everyone but me.

And now, those faces, those countless images were coming to life and taking turns to hug me, pat my back, shower me with condolences and words of praise about my father. Behind all the heads I recognized the inscrutable gaze of El Turco, my best friend, and right next to him the lanky frame of Martin Sabater, who was one of our *panas* now, as he would put it in one of his Ecuadorian idioms. The sight of those two guys stirred something inside me, a millimeter of emotion that I was afraid would tear through something unstoppable. I swallowed hard, dismissing the feeling, the pain in my chest, and put on my best smile—at least I tried to, though I wasn't sure what kind of expression came out in my attempt to show them that everything was all right.

Farid hugged me first, and it was the first warm hug I'd received all day. Martin was more distant. He patted my arm and said in a low, grave voice:

"I know what you're going through, *hermano.*"

Martin had mentioned soon after he came to El Valle that his father had passed away recently, which was the reason why his guardian had sent him to a boarding school in another country. "People will tell you things get better, but honestly, they don't. It's always shit."

I believed it. It was the most honest statement I'd heard all morning. People had been telling me I should rejoice because my father was now in the presence of Our Lord, but I couldn't find an inkling of consolation in those words. Mostly because I didn't believe them. How would they know? Had anyone here died and gone to Heaven before? But some people seemed to think that if you repeated that chant long enough it might become true.

I recalled something else Martin had told me soon after I met him—had it been two years already?—something like, "I have nobody and nothing left." And I'd felt sorry for him, the same way people were probably feeling about me now.

I couldn't stand it.

"My father wanted to see you," Farid said, opening his chest, stretching his arm to bring his father to my side—being my best friend gave him that right, I supposed.

Yusuf Mansur was a short, bald man with a generous belly that sat over his belt. His eyes were highlighted by heavy purple circles, which had caught my attention the first time I'd met him. ("Did someone punch your dad in the eyes?" I'd asked Farid.) But with time I'd realized it was an Arab trait. The more I got to know and visit Farid and his family, the more I was exposed to this group of immigrants who'd done so well in my country. Don Yusuf had a large group of friends in Cali, all of them business owners, merchants by blood, and fond of good food, good coffee, and women.

After a heartfelt and somewhat painful hug, Don Yusuf grabbed my face with his pudgy hands and kissed my cheek, his eyes watery. This was another cultural norm I had learned. Arab men often kissed other men. They were intense, devoted friends. Farid had inherited this trait *al pie de la letra*. I nodded as Don Yusuf gave me some kind of blessing with his heavily accented Spanish and threw some Arabic words in there, too, for good measure. I should be consoling him instead, such was the pain I saw in his eyes. But I had to remember that he had lost his wife only a few years ago and was raising four kids by himself in a foreign land, away from the family he'd left behind in Palestine.

After Don Yusuf moved on to greet my mom, Farid's siblings approached me. It had been a couple of years since I'd last seen Camila Mansur, back when she was thirteen. But she was fully grown now. I'd always thought she was pretty and had befriended her since she was one of the few girls I knew. That was what you did when you went to a boarding school full of men: you took any opportunity to meet girls. But now, the word "pretty" didn't even begin to describe her—she was nothing less than breathtaking.

Camila Mansur was one of those women who demanded attention whenever she entered a room, from a perfect poise highlighting her delicate frame—narrow shoulders, long neck, slender waist—to her stunning eyes, accentuated with black eyeliner, like a modern Cleopatra. Those were wise eyes that examined the world with confidence and acumen. Her black lace dress softly delineated her figure and presented me with a pair of breasts that hadn't been there before. Her body, her beauty, made it impossible for me to look anywhere else. She had what could only be defined as a regal presence.

She stood patiently as Farid reintroduced me to her, as if I needed to be reminded of who she was.

"You remember my sister Camila?"

I nodded. Camila extended her hand toward mine. Her long, straight mane seemed to blind me with its shine. "I was very sorry to hear about your father, Lucas."

Her voice had changed, too. She sounded older now, slightly hoarse. There was no trace of the child I'd met before.

I cleared my throat before answering—I'd been quiet for so long I didn't know if my voice would come out. "Thanks," was all I said, but what else do you say under these circumstances? I was lucky to have been able to get any word out.

Her younger siblings, Omar and Nazira, came next. He was barely hitting puberty, with a shadow of hair over his lip, and Nazira was not ten yet. Both of them had Farid's eyes—their father's—and Nazira had her curly hair up in a ponytail tied with a ribbon. She clung to her older sister's arm as soon as she gave me her quiet condolences. Frankly, the young girl looked more upset than I was.

As the Mansur family walked away, I noticed a middle-aged woman in the back of the room, watching me. There were several people standing between us, but we exchanged a glance for an instant. I didn't recognize her at first with that black veil around her head, as if she were going to church. I'd seen her at school events before. She was one of the benefactors, her and her husband, but she'd been so sophisticated then. It wasn't that she wasn't properly attired for a wake—it was that she looked like she'd aged a decade since I'd last seen her, only a few months ago. I nodded at her, expecting her to approach me, but she turned and walked away. As Padre Francisco, the priest from my mother's parish, crossed the room and stood by my father's coffin to start mass, I wondered why that woman had been staring at me. It was as though she'd been searching for me, as if she wanted to say something but couldn't gather the courage, sort of like me walking to see my father for the last time.

I didn't see her at the funeral.

I never saw my father's dead body, either.

That night, I got drunk for the first time. Somehow Farid and Martin landed a couple of bottles of *aguardiente* and the three of us drank in my bedroom until dawn. Before we were ready to go to bed, Farid and Martin decided to explore my parents' house.

"What's this door?" Martin said after we descended the staircase, holding onto the railing, barely able to keep our legs from collapsing.

"*Ron't wooopen it,*" I said. My words came out slurred, distorted, barely understandable.

Martin opened it anyway. "Why? What's the big mystery?"

"*My father'sssss . . . pho . . . photo studio.*" I spoke slowly to give a semblance of sobriety. *But don't go in there.* The last part didn't come out and Farid and Martin entered the studio anyway.

I stood by the doorframe. I couldn't stand to see that place tonight.

I despised it.

"Nice," Martin said, pointing at my dad's Brownie box camera.

"Careful," I warned, as he nearly tripped over the tripod on his way to touch the camera.

The two of them were standing in the middle of my dad's studio. It hurt to see his things, which he so meticulously cared for. He'd been a tyrant about this place, about his camera, about his expensive lights. I was not allowed in here because as a little boy I had opened the darkroom when he was working and let in all the light, ruining a pile of his very expensive paper, which he'd traveled long and wide to find.

And now my friends were desecrating his shrine as if it were a cheap whore open to exploration.

I took a step into the room. Martin stood behind the camera, peeking to the front through the viewfinder. Hanging lights flanked a simple wooden stool, where hundreds of people had sat throughout the years. A white sheet hung loosely behind the stool, creating a neutral background for portraits. Papá had my mother wash that sheet once a week.

"I told my sister your father left you his studio," Farid said. He'd drank just as much as Martin and I had, but he sounded perfectly sober. "She wanted me to ask if you would take a photograph of her."

"Me? I barely know how to use the camera."

"You'd better learn quickly as this is your business now," Farid said.

I sat on the wooden desk in the corner of the studio, where my dad kept his paperwork, where it was safe to be. "Ugh, don't remind me."

Martin was still pacing around, examining the place from floor to ceiling. He grabbed one of the black curtains leading to the darkroom. "Hey, *pana*, don't complain. I wish my father would've left me a business, *any* business."

"Even something as . . . use . . . useless as this?" I opened one of the drawers and dug through dozens of portraits. Grabbing a pile with both hands, I tossed them upward. A rain of photos covered the gray linoleum. "This is what he loved most in the world—these flat, soulless pictures of damn strangers."

Martin picked up one of the photos from the floor. "I think it's incredible that a single moment can be recorded forever on a piece of paper." He flipped the photo over. "Simply fascinating."

Why did everyone else sound so much better than me when we'd all been drinking? More importantly, why didn't anybody really *listen* to me?

"I think you should do it," Martin said.

"Do what?"

"Take his sister's photograph. It would be good practice for when you start working. You can't just let this place and all this equipment go to waste. Besides, she has an angelic face."

Farid punched Martin's arm. "Hey, you're talking about my sister. Wash your mouth before you ever mention her."

Martin shoved Farid's arm and the two of them started wrestling about, good-naturedly. They often did. I stared at them and that numbness took over me again. Normally I would've tried to stop them, I would've forced them outside of this sacred place, but somehow, I didn't care. Touching the photographs in the drawer, seeing those prints scattered across the floor, as if they were unimportant objects—which they were—had somehow lifted a burden. I stepped on one of the photos and watched calmly as my friends jostled about the studio, trampling over chairs and pulling on curtains. My father's fancy camera—his most prized possession—sat vulnerably on its tripod. My mother would never forgive me if something were to happen to it.

And yet, I remained by my father's desk, looking at the Brownie, waiting for my friends to kick the tripod's legs, to knock the camera down, waiting for it to collapse, to break into tiny little pieces any minute.

I waited and waited and waited.

Maybe it wasn't such a bad idea to take Camila's photograph, to be alone with her—assuming that Farid would take his eyes off her for a few minutes, which might never happen as he was annoyingly possessive of her. But despite my limitations as a photographer, it might be amusing to be with her again. I had enjoyed her company when we were younger. She'd been fun to be around, playing ball and running around, just like us boys. It didn't hurt that she was so beautiful, either.

After Martin and Farid were done twisting each other's arms, rolling on the ground, and Martin was the clear winner sitting proudly on top of Farid's chest (dangerously close to the tripod), I turned to Farid.

"Sure, tell Camila I'll take her photograph."

CHAPTER 16

Puri

I was somewhat relieved when Sor Camila informed me that I had to work the night shift. It was the only way I could go into the head doctor's office without being seen and gather information about Martin. I had finally figured out where Dr. Mansur's office was and I'd been itching to get in there for the last two days. I *had* to find out if what Lucas told me was true. I still couldn't believe that Martin might be dead. I *needed* confirmation. I briefly considered asking Dr. Mansur himself, but what was the point if I didn't trust him? He made me uneasy.

As I neared his office, I heard two voices echoing down the hall: a man's and a woman's. It seemed that they were arguing. I stood by the door, listening.

"How much longer am I supposed to stay here?" the woman said.

"As long as needed." This might be Dr. Mansur.

"Farid, this makes no sense. I don't understand why I need to be here. Your father is fine. Basim and I are bored out of our minds and, on top of it all, we're at risk of contracting this damn cholera at any given time."

"Do I need to spell it out for you?"

There was a moment of silence. Then, a *thump*—the stamp of a shoe?

"You're being unreasonable, Farid."

"You cannot be trusted."

"What did you do to him?" she shouted.

I stiffened. *Him?*

There was a long pause.

"I don't know what you're talking about," Dr. Mansur said. "Now leave me alone. I have to finish writing this report."

As the clatter of heels approached the door, I rushed away from the office and stood behind a wall. As I suspected, it was Mansur's wife—Amira? She dashed out of the office and slammed the door shut. She strode past me—without seeing me—in the direction of the staircase and then rushed downstairs.

What did you do to him?

Was it Martin they were talking about?

I'd been wondering myself why the doctor had brought his family here. Why put them at risk unless it was absolutely necessary?

The only thing I'd gotten from Perla was that Basim, Farid's son, was close to his grandfather and had asked to come, but what about Amira? Why didn't her husband trust her?

Dr. Mansur stepped out of the office and headed toward his bedroom. The second story was built in a U-shape overlooking the central patio. The Mansurs were all staying on the other side of the floor.

I waited about five minutes in the shadows to make sure neither one of them was coming back. I couldn't take too long as the nurses downstairs might complain to Sor Camila about me, but I couldn't waste this opportunity, either. When all was quiet, I removed a candle and a match from my side pocket and lit it. Making sure no one was around, I headed for Mansur's office.

I carefully closed the door behind me and pointed the candle toward an oak desk. There were two piles of folders meticulously stacked by each other and an overflowing bookshelf behind the chair, right next to a large armoire. The room smelled of old books and wood.

This must have been Martin's office.

I could feel his presence here. I brought a hand to my chest to ease the pressure. In spite of being married for eight years to a good, honest man, my feelings for Cristóbal had been tame in comparison to the passion that Martin had ignited. He had touched something inside me that was infinitely more chemical and visceral than anything I could control or reason. It was hard to explain why since I hadn't known Martin for long. I often thought it was something that worked on a subconscious level. Just like some magnets attracted certain metals and repelled others, Martin and I had been drawn to each other since we first met. We were similar. We understood each other.

I set the candle on the desk and rummaged through the drawers. I didn't know what I was looking for, but I was certain I would know once I found it. I searched for a while, looking inside binders and folders—a certain violation of patient's privacy—but I only considered this for a second. It wasn't as if I was *reading* their records.

Right when I was ready to give up, I came across the paper I was looking for.

Martin's last will.

Or what appeared to be his testament.

I sat down. I didn't have much time so I scanned through the document as fast as I could. *"In full use of my faculties . . . No descendants . . . Donation . . . I name Dr. Farid Mansur the executor of my Will and properties."*

In a nutshell, the contents of the will coincided with what Lucas had told me about donating the property to Mansur. Everything seemed to be in order. Stamps. Signatures.

I got closer to the paper.

There were a couple of things that didn't make sense to me. First, wasn't it too convenient that Martin had this document ready at the time of his death, considering it had been an accident, and he was an otherwise healthy thirty-three-year-old man?

And the second, more disturbing matter, was that upon closer inspection I realized there was something wrong with this document. As Martin had been my father's plantation administrator and right-hand man for seven years, I had seen his signature plenty of times on purchase orders, payrolls, and various other documents I'd come across as I cleaned up my father's office when my siblings and I sold the property. Martin's signature was distinctive. For one, the first letters of his name and last name were notoriously large. The rest of the letters were somewhat round and straight. This signature was slightly tilted to the right and all the letters had proportional sizes, unlike Martin's ostentatious calligraphy. There was no doubt in my mind that this wasn't Martin's signature.

This document must be forged.

A noise in the hall startled me.

Mansur was back! Where could I hide? Under the desk? I couldn't possibly fit in there!

I stood up and dropped the document in the bottom drawer, where I'd found it. Then I rushed to the door and extinguished the candle. I stood still by the door for a moment. The steps were approaching. I had two options: being caught inside the head doctor's office, or leaving the room and hoping the darkness would shield me.

I chose the second option.

I snuck out of the room as quietly as I could. I couldn't see anything but a stream of light coming toward me. I inserted the candle in my pocket, squeezing it. Then, I created as much distance as I could from the door.

"Sor Purificación, what are you doing here?"

Sor Camila was the only one who called me by my full name.

"You're still awake?" I said, recalling my mother's admonition of never answering one question with another.

She seemed taken aback by my inquiry, and for the first time, I saw the young woman underneath the veil: a girl who was roughly my age and under different circumstances could have been a friend.

"I don't sleep much," she said. "There's a lot to do here, *as you should know by now.*"

"I just wanted to take a walk."

"A walk? Aren't you supposed to be with the patients downstairs?"

The kerosene lamp in her hand partially illuminated her face. The shadows under her eyes and the white cloth wrapping her face made her look spectral—and somewhat daunting.

"Yes. I'm sorry. I needed to take a break. I wanted to pray."

My last statement seemed to soften her a bit. But it made me feel ashamed. How could I lie about something so sacred?

"I understand. It can be . . . emotionally exhausting." Her voice was tempered now and had a sweetness to it I'd never heard before. "I haven't told you this, *hermana*, but we're all grateful for the work you're doing here, in spite of everything."

In spite of everything.

Well, I didn't blame her for saying that. I had to admit that I wasn't the smoothest of nurses as I'd made several mistakes along the way: tripping over buckets of urine, shutting my eyes at the sight of various bodily fluids, having to poke patients' arms several times until I found the right spot for the IVs. But I was pleased to have her approval, even if it came with a disclaimer.

"How is Lucas doing?" she asked.

"He seems almost fully recovered," I said.

"Good. He should be leaving soon, I suppose."

The thought of him leaving disheartened me. I liked his wit, his easygoing nature.

"You've known him a long time, right?" I said.

In the dark, people were more prone to make confessions and I'd never seen the nun so unguarded, maybe due to her exhaustion.

"Didn't they teach you, *hermana*, that you're not supposed to talk about the past?"

I stiffened. "I apologize."

She sighed.

"I suppose there's no harm in telling you. Yes, I've known him for many, many years."

I was silent for a moment, debating with myself whether or not I should mention Martin. It might get me dismissed from here, but it might also give me an answer. "You know something, *hermana*," I started, "the other day Mr. Ferreira was telling me about a friend we have in common."

She lifted an eyebrow. "A friend?"

"It's such a coincidence," I said. "Years ago, in Ecuador, I met a young man in the cacao export business. His name was Martin Sabater. It turns out he used to own this hacienda, according to Mr. Ferreira. I couldn't believe it when he told me."

Whatever color Sor Camila had on her face drained completely.

"Yes, well, I should go back to bed. And you . . ."

What was happening to her voice? It was cracking.

"You should go back to work. They're probably wondering where you went."

"*Sí, hermana*," I said, but kept my gaze on hers for a while.

She broke eye contact and turned around, heading toward the nurses' bedroom. Under dire and stressful circumstances, I hadn't seen her display an inkling of weakness, but the sole mention of Martin's name had been enough to demolish the monument of strength and confidence that made up Sor Camila.

CHAPTER 17

Camila

Hacienda La Magna
July 1910

Martin was practically part of our family now. Since he was an orphan and had nobody in Colombia, Farid brought him to Cali during every school break, summers included. This time, though, Lucas had invited all of us to his godparents' ranch southwest of Cali. Lucas's godmother, Doña Juana Torres, happened to be his mother's best friend in addition to her *comadre*. Baba had declined the invitation because who would run the store if he left? But he'd begrudgingly agreed to let me, Omar, and Nazira come with Farid, Martin, and Lucas—*los tres mosqueteros*, as they called themselves.

This summer was going to be the last one Farid spent with his friends since they had all graduated from high school and were going in different directions: Farid was moving to Bogotá to study medicine, Martin was headed for Popayán to get a degree in agronomy, and Lucas was staying in Cali to run his father's photography studio. The plan was to spend a week in this area since there was a river and waterfalls near the ranch. I could barely hold my excitement as I hardly ever left my house and, like my Tía

Lidia said, I deserved a vacation after tending to my siblings and father the entire year. Tía Lidia and Charito, to some extent, were the only mother figures I'd had after Mama passed away. Thanks to them, I'd learned my father's favorite Palestinian dishes: *shish barak, wara' dawale, malfuf.*

But that was all I'd gotten from them. Charito had no patience for me and my aunt had too many kids and too many chores at home to teach me what I really wanted to learn: sewing. In the afternoons, when I was done with all my household chores and Omar and Nazira were busy with their schoolwork or playing outside with the neighborhood kids, I would stop by my father's fabric store and help with sales. My dream, which I'd never told anyone, was to turn the business into a dress shop one day. It was entirely possible since my older brother had no interest in the store and had decided to study medicine, and Omar was still a young boy who had no claims to the business, which meant I had to act quickly— before he came of age. In other words, I had to learn how to sew. This holiday was the perfect opportunity since Lucas's mother, Doña Matilde, was going, too, and as far as I knew, she was an accomplished seamstress. Once I honed the basic skills, and with my extensive knowledge and access to fabrics of all kinds, I could start working. Just as soon as I learned, I would propose the idea to my father. I'd already been drafting some designs. I just needed to make them. How hard could it be?

I'd met Doña Matilde a few times. One of them was the summer after Lucas's dad passed away. Mother and son lived in a two-story home in one of the oldest neighborhoods of Cali, Barrio San Antonio. That was, when Lucas wasn't boarding at Internado Oro Verde. The photo studio that had been Don Gregorio "Goyo" Ferreira's pride and joy occupied most of the house's first story. I'd been pestering Farid for months to take me so Lucas would shoot my photo, but it was only until the boys were off school last summer when it finally happened.

Such a sweet boy Lucas was. I'd never met anyone like him. So shy he would barely look me in the eye when he talked to me. I was certain he'd been grateful to hide his face under a black cloth when he took my photo. It was odd since we'd been so close when we were younger.

After several attempts, a sweaty forehead, and sleeves rolled all the way to his elbows, Lucas finally succeeded—he made it clear he was just learning and might never be as good as his father. He said it would be ready in a week and apologized profusely for the wait. My uncle Ibrahim, who had businesses in the area with other merchants, took me in his carriage to pick up my portrait a few days later.

In my excitement, I felt like skipping to Lucas's house, but my Tía Lidia had warned me that rushing like that was something young girls did, not respectful ladies, so I simply clasped my umbrella shaft in anticipation as Tío Ibrahim and I waited for the door to open.

At the other end of the doorframe was Lucas's mom and closely behind her, Lucas.

Doña Matilde didn't look like her son at all. Whereas Lucas was fair with light eyes and auburn hair, his mom was significantly darker and her features were coarser. She had an infectious smile that immediately softened her demeanor and put you at ease.

When Lucas handed me the photo, I accidentally dropped the umbrella on my uncle's foot and he immediately voiced his discontent. I looked so sophisticated in the photo, so much older. It was unbelievable that you could capture someone's likeness on a piece of paper. I clasped the photo close to my heart and then gave Lucas a hug in gratitude, to which my uncle responded with a forced cough.

My uncle Ibrahim was the reason why I'd been born in Cali. Most Arab immigrants went to Barranquilla, or other cities in the Atlantic coast, and Baba did the same when he first left Palestine, but his cousin Ibrahim somehow ended up in Cali a few years prior. *Divide and conquer* was their family motto. They had opted to spread throughout Colombia and be pioneers in the textile industry in different cities. When Tío Ibrahim offered Baba a position at his store, he'd agreed to come. First, to visit, but then he fell in love with the region and stayed. After working with his cousin for some years, Baba managed to save enough money to open his own store across town. And now his heart and soul were devoted to it. He'd once confessed to me that it had taken extraordinary courage and lots of *Arak* for him to travel across seas and oceans to make it to the American continent. So he wouldn't have lasted in Barranquilla anyway, he'd said. He didn't want to be anywhere near the water.

Lucas stiffened in my arms as I hugged him. I let go. His cheeks had turned sanguine.

"Well, we'd better go," Tío Ibrahim said. "*Shoukran*, young man."

Lucas stuttered a bit as he voiced his goodbye—he often did when he was around me. Farid always teased him about it while Martin laughed and laughed.

How I wished Martin would give me as much attention as Lucas, but my brother said Martin had a girl back in Ecuador, a girl he was going to marry one day.

And yet, there was something there. Martin had, after all, given me a quick kiss outside the gymnasium a few minutes before his graduation ceremony had started. *On the lips.* I hadn't been able to think of anything other than that kiss for days. And now, we would be in the same place for a whole week.

Not that it would do me any good. Martin was leaving soon and our paths would likely never cross again. I'd better focus on my plans. And my plans involved Lucas and his mother, the seamstress.

Hacienda La Magna was stamped in the middle of a green paradise of tangled vegetation, hills, streams, and indigo skies. How tall and exuberant the fruit and palm trees were, so large they resembled giants towering over me.

A sweet scent permeated the moist air all the way to the big house.

I pretended not to see Martin when he got off a horse. It had been a couple of weeks since The Kiss, but he barely greeted me—as if it *nothing* had happened between us.

I picked up my skirt and walked past him toward the portico.

Lucas's mom was already at the hacienda. I offered to help her and her Comadre Juana in the kitchen since they said the maid was in bed with an ear infection. If you counted the three of us, my siblings, Martin, Lucas, Doña Juana's husband, and the sick maid, there were several mouths to feed. I didn't want to impose, especially because this wasn't even Lucas's house and Doña Juana had said she was "simply" preparing *empanadas vallunas*.

Beef and potato *empanadas* for ten people, including *five men*? *This* was a simple dish?

She clearly hadn't seen how much my brothers ate.

I believe I won Doña Matilde over that night. I helped the two women prepare the dough, peel and cut potatoes, shred beef for the stuffing, in addition to frying the *guiso* and the *empanadas* themselves. I even got a burn on my hand as a result. The food was a big success among the men and kids. The three of us ate later, after everyone else was full. Such was the servitude of Latin and Arab women. Both cultures blended well in that respect.

While we ate, I mentioned my interest in learning how to sew because if I were to wait for Lucas to ask his mother, my hair would've turned white. Doña Matilde was excited at the idea of teaching me and asked Doña Juana if we could borrow her sewing machine in the morning. She'd always wanted a daughter, she said, and Doña Juana agreed that sewing and knitting were desirable skills for any lady who respected herself. And so it was set that I would start my lessons first thing in the morning.

Nazira sat with us for about ten minutes before she declared it was the most tedious activity she'd attempted in her entire lifetime and she would rather go to the river to fish with the boys. At least she would get to see nature and explore. She had so little opportunity to do that.

I made a lot of progress with my sewing that day, though I wasn't sure Baba would agree to buy me a sewing machine. I had some savings from my allowance but I doubted I would be able to afford it without his help. I had to find a way to convince him. Perhaps I would sew him a shirt.

"Let's start with a handkerchief," Matilde said. "A shirt might be too ambitious for your first day."

After two days of learning and a completed handkerchief and two pillowcases, I was ready to leave the house. While my siblings and Farid's friends had gone fishing and exploring the area, I'd been stuck at Doña Juana's house—and all for what? A handkerchief and two pillowcases?

"Don't be discouraged," Matilde said. "Next time I'll teach you how to sew a curtain."

We were supposed to go to one of the nearby waterfalls. Matilde warned me that it would take about an hour to hike there, but I didn't mind. I was excited to get out and see the sights and sounds my siblings had been talking about. The flora flanking the river was so coarse that if it weren't for a faint trail guiding us, I would've been certain that no human had ever set foot in this wild land. What neither Matilde nor the boys had told me was that we would have to cross Río Meléndez *by foot*. At first, I didn't think anything of it. Normally, I'm not a nervous person, but as we stepped on the slippery stones and the rapids hit our calves, I screeched, nearly losing my balance. I could already picture my head cracking against one of those massive rocks and my lifeless body flowing down the river.

I shouldn't have come.

Sewing handkerchiefs seemed like paradise in comparison. Behind me, Martin grasped my arm and stabilized me.

"*Tranquila*," he whispered into my ear. "I won't let anything happen to you."

His soft voice did something to my stomach. I hadn't noticed how bright his eyes were when he looked at me.

Leading the way, my brother was giving a long explanation of the area that I *really* didn't want to hear. He attempted to stand in front of us, soaked shirt stuck to his chest, as he hollered.

"We're about to arrive to Cascada del Alemán. It was named after a group of Germans who came here some time ago and built a large house nearby. Supposedly, these Germans took all the gold in the region. Legend has it that the spirit of an indigenous woman dressed in gold from head to toe appears in these waters. If you see her at night, her custom glows in the dark—right, Lucas?"

Behind Martin, Lucas nodded, pressing a handkerchief against his mouth. What was it about this family and handkerchiefs? He seemed just as distressed about crossing the river as I was.

As usual my brother was imparting information to show how smart he was. He could be so annoying sometimes. No wonder his friends were in awe of him, but I knew better. I knew all his flaws.

My tulle hat flew off my head, but Martin caught it midair before it got lost in the current. He handed it to me with a smirk and a bow, nearly slipping with his gallant attempt.

"Gracias," I said, my nerves in constant conflict between the things he made me feel and the fear of falling into the water. Not to mention the fact that my dress was getting soaked as we crossed.

By the work and grace of the Holy Spirit, we made it alive and arrived to dry land. But we had little time to celebrate our small victory as Farid was already heading uphill. I plowed through for the next ten minutes, but just as I was ready to complain of exhaustion, a stunning view appeared beyond the foliage.

A magnificent waterfall of about twenty meters—according to Farid—stood in front of us, imposing and proud.

"¡Miren!" Farid pointed at it as if we were too blind to see it.

Meanwhile Martin held my hand to prevent me from tripping over a sharp rock.

As we approached the bank, I squeezed his fingers and dug my shoes into the mushy soil. With my free hand I lifted my rosewood muslin skirt. I should've worn something less voluminous, but this fabric was fresh—and nearly transparent now that it had gotten wet. I should've worn the bathing gown my neighbor had lent me—a short dress that even though it exposed my calves was made out of an impermeable fabric called Mackintosh and was the fad in Mar del Plata, according to my friend.

My siblings rushed toward the waterfall and so did Farid. Now what? Was I supposed to get in the water, too? It wasn't deep and I'd been to a *balneario* as a little girl, but the waterfall and the rocks were more intimidating than a swimming pool. Particularly after Lucas had told me that he once had an encounter with a caiman in a river.

As far as I could see, Lucas didn't intend to get into the water, either. He'd found a spot to sit on a nearby rock to smoke a cigarette. *In front of his mother?* That would've certainly earned me a smack from one of the family elders—even one from my brother Farid. But we women lived under a different set of rules and expectations.

"Aren't you getting in the water?" Martin asked me as I settled on a rock of my own, right next to Doña Matilde.

"Not today," I said. I was embarrassed to admit that I had nothing appropriate to wear. How life changed. As a child, I could have swum naked, but now I was supposed to cover every centimeter of my body at all times.

My sister, however, didn't seem to mind that her dress was getting soaked as she positioned herself directly under the waterfall, giggling with shut eyes as the water drizzled her face and soddened her long, curly mane into strands that attached indiscriminately to her mouth and cheeks. Standing next to her was Omar, the spitting image of Farid at twelve with his long eyelashes and his square jaw, but he was more mellow than our older brother had ever been.

It was truly a beautiful place.

Too bad I had to sit here while everyone else was having fun.

In the morning, I woke up to a sharp *thump* against my window. Nazira and I were sharing a room on the second story, but my sister was so exhausted after yesterday's expedition that she didn't even flinch at the noise. I opened the window, feeling the warm breeze hit my face, and spotted Martin standing by a horse. The sun was barely rising.

Had he thrown a stone against the window? I didn't even want to imagine what would've happened if he'd broken it. Lucas's *padrino* seemed like a stern man.

"Get dressed and meet me downstairs," Martin said. "I have something to show you." Before I rushed inside to collect my clothes, filled with excitement, he added, "And bring something you can swim in."

He met me downstairs and handed me a piece of sugar cane for "breakfast." I loved anything sweet.

"Where did you get this horse?"

"I have my tricks."

"Do you know how to ride it?"

"A little." He smiled and offered me a hand to step on the stirrup.

"Wait. I'm not getting on top of this horse if you don't know how to ride."

He looked me in the eye. "Do you trust me?"

I squinted.

He helped me up and then climbed behind me. With ease, he guided the horse toward a trail, always in control. He'd grown up in a hacienda such as this one, he said against my ear, but they grew cacao beans and he was going to own it one day.

"Where are we going?" I said.

"You'll see."

I'd never ridden a horse before. The feel of the creature's back muscles bulging under my hamstrings was so unnatural I feared I might fall at any given time, but Martin's composure reassured me. I only hoped my brother wouldn't see us.

I placed my hand on top of his as he held the horn.

"I was wondering how long it was going to take you to do that."

His Ecuadorian accent was so different from ours. I liked it. It made me think of the sound a broom made when sweeping the floor.

As the trail became narrower and curvier, the horse slowed its gait and stepped slowly into a path of stones. The smells of the forest—moist soil, rotting wood, moss—grew stronger as the vegetation enveloped us.

"Are we almost there?"

"Yes," he said, pulling on the reins to bring the horse to a halt.

I was so focused on climbing down without hurting myself that I didn't immediately realize that beneath the overgrown vegetation was a stream of crystalline waters, and beneath it a thin waterfall.

"It's called Cascada La Reina," he said as we both admired the timid waters barely competing with the magnificence of Cascada del Alemán, but displaying a sort of intimate beauty. "Since you couldn't get into the water yesterday, I thought I'd bring you here today."

He offered his hand to help me along the stone path toward the stream, saying he wanted me to experience the water "without fear or shame."

I shyly removed my dress, exposing my neighbor's swimming gown inspired by those magazine pages of the elegant swimmers at Mar del Plata. It was a knee-length sailor suit and I was self-conscious that Martin would see my legs, but with the current so low and the water so crystalline, I couldn't resist. I took off my shoes and sunk my toes in the olive waters, feeling the slippery rocks on the sole of my feet. Martin remained close and vigilant.

Before long, the water was caressing my ankles and I briefly thought of Lucas's caiman, a story he repeated *all the time*. I suspected that incident had more to do with his decision not to get in the water yesterday instead of the molar pain he'd claimed to have.

Martin removed his shirt and trousers, but kept his muslin undergarment on, much to my relief. However, he wasn't wearing his union suit—like he and my brothers did the previous day—so his chest was bare. It was the first time I'd seen a grown man without a shirt. As he stood under the cascade, the water soaked his head and shoulders, his muscles more defined than they appeared underneath his clothes. Blushing, I focused on the water wetting my calves.

"Camila!" he called out with a bright smile and happy eyes. I'd always thought true bliss could only be expressed through the eyes, just like every other emotion.

He waved at me.

"Come on!"

"It's too cold!" I said, frozen to my spot. No human power would make me stand under those frigid waters.

He waded toward me. Oh no.

"It's more fun under the waterfall," he pleaded.

I shook my head.

He splashed me. The drops chilled every fraction of my skin. I screeched.

"You're getting wet anyway."

I tried to run to the bank, but one, the stones were too slippery to advance fast enough, and two, Martin got hold of my waist. How dare he? I wanted to slap him, but the whole thing was so ridiculous I chuckled instead.

My knees gave in. It was too hard to fight him while laughing so I let him hold my hand and lead me to the waterfall. To my surprise, my expectations turned out to be worse than reality because once I was standing under the water, it wasn't as cold as I'd imagined. One might even say it was invigorating. I stood there, his hands on my waist, my eyes shut until my hair got soaked and the weight of my mane pressed against my back. When I opened my eyes, Martin was staring at me.

"You're so beautiful," he said. "Like a heavenly apparition."

I laughed. But he wasn't joking.

He held my hand and drew me toward the deeper end of the pool, never letting go, his eyes on mine, as though there was nothing else in this world he'd rather look at. Now that I was drenched, the water felt warm and comforting. I submerged my head. With

Martin so close, I felt confident and forgot all about Lucas's caiman.

When I emerged, I couldn't help but remember the hasty kiss Martin had given me outside the gymnasium.

I wondered if he was thinking about the same thing as he kept staring at my mouth. I licked my bottom lip, unconsciously, and he stopped smiling. He moved closer to me, his strong legs touching mine, his hands on my lower back. This was it, the long-awaited kiss.

Something stopped him. Dry leaves rustling behind us. The neigh of a horse.

I turned around but there was nothing other than overgrown bushes and Martin's horse tied to the trunk of a tree, chewing on grass.

I splashed water on Martin's face.

"Really?" he said. "You're going to pay for that."

He chased me, splashing water all around me. I couldn't stop laughing and that made it difficult to get away. When he caught up with me, I knew I was lost, but instead of soaking me, or worse yet, sinking my head inside the water, like I'd feared, he held me close. Drops trickled from his hair and along his cheeks. His eyes were beaming. I ran my fingers over his drenched eyebrows in an attempt to comb them. He kissed my wrist softly as I did, his hands tight around my waist.

"I can't fight this anymore," he whispered, against my mouth. "Whatever *this* is."

I'd had no idea he'd been fighting anything, but I didn't want to ruin the moment with questions. So I just let him kiss me. And there was nothing rushed or incomplete about that kiss.

We didn't stay there too long as we didn't want to awaken any suspicion. When we were close enough to see the house, I got off the horse and walked the rest of the way, hoping my hair would finish drying by the time I arrived. Martin went around and would claim he'd just gone for a horse ride.

At the hacienda, everybody was up. They'd already served breakfast and there were no more pastries left, which I'd been looking forward to.

Farid, being Farid, told me that was what I got for taking such long walks.

"You should've eaten first."

Martin entered the dining room just in time to hear my brother's nasty remarks. He frowned, but quickly composed himself and greeted me and everybody else as if this were the first time he'd seen me today. He left shortly after and was gone most of the morning. When he came back, he'd brought me a box full of sweets from town: *suspiros*, *alfajores con arequipe*, *cucas*, *polvorosas*, and lemon cookies.

"Since you couldn't have dessert earlier, I thought I'd bring all of them to you."

CHAPTER 18

Puri

I was having problems sleeping during the day. Even though the nurses drew the curtains and tried to make the room as dark as possible, the light still found a way to filter in through the cracks. Having to share the room with strangers didn't make things any easier. The two other nurses who worked the night shift weren't half as friendly as Perla, who'd remained on the day shift. Plus, I'd had the misfortune of having Bertha—the Snoring Nurse—as a roommate.

Instead of tossing and turning, I could be doing something productive.

When I'd gone to the stables with Tulia a few days ago, I'd seen a room with the door shut. I'd assumed it to be the sleeping quarters for the cooks or the man who cared for the chickens and collected eggs—I'd been meaning to speak to him as Perla said that the current employees had also worked with Martin. There were not that many employees left because pickers were temporary workers who only came during the harvesting season. I'd met some of them in Cali.

I could explore the area and see if I could find this man now that I didn't have Sor Camila on my back. Plus, I needed to wash one of my habits anyway as I only had two and Perla had reminded me of the importance of keeping everything clean.

It could be the perfect excuse if someone saw me.

I got up, as quietly as possible, and donned one of Sor Alba Luz's habits. The truth was this costume was much more comfortable than my days of dressing up as a man. Back then, I'd had a whole set of details to worry about: a corset around my breasts, a fake beard and a mustache, voice, gait, attitude.

I supposed attitude was something I'd been struggling with since I got here. I wasn't used to people telling me what to do. I'd always been my own boss and my husband followed my lead without objection, unlike my mother, who used to butt heads with me. Perhaps that was the main reason I'd married Cristóbal so quickly—to leave my mother's house and her prying eyes and do whatever I saw fit.

But as a nun, I was expected to be obedient above everything else. Everyone's needs came before my own. And I had so many people to account to: Sor Camila, the doctors, even Perla, who was much younger than me but despite her age, knew plenty about nursing. Lucky for me, she'd taught me the basics, including how to take patients' vitals and how to administer an IV. She never questioned why I didn't know these simple tasks. I could only speculate she had no idea that the Siervas de María were supposed to know all these skills.

Habit in hand, I left the room. The hall was empty, but that was not unusual as the action was always downstairs. I crept toward the stairs. Perla was stepping out of the cholera room with Nurse Celia; both were talking and looking at a report. I hid behind a column wrapped with vines until they wended away. If Perla saw me there, she would give me a hard time about not sleeping. She often said a good nurse needed to rest well if she was going to be of service to anyone.

I scurried to the back patio and set my habit inside a rectangular wooden washtub my mother called *artesa*. Fortunately, someone had left a big pot of boiled water next to it, which meant I didn't have to go to the well to fetch water and boil it.

Next to the tub was a yellow bar of soap—which looked like a rock and stunk bad—and a bulky brush. I soaked the habit in the tub and stood up straight. There, my alibi was perfect.

I meandered by the chicken coop to see if I could find the worker, but he didn't seem to be around. I then headed to the mysterious room. Hopefully, it wouldn't be locked.

It was.

I looked around, checking for windows, but there were none. It must be a storage room since not far from here, near the stables, was a small building filled with rooms, which I assumed to be the servants' quarters. This room, however, was isolated from the rest.

Now, who would have the key? The most likely candidate seemed to be Dr. Mansur, since he was the one in charge of the hospital and everything in it. Would he keep it in his office? I hadn't seen any keys when I searched through his drawers. His bedroom? It was possible, but it seemed difficult to enter when Amira and his son apparently spent a lot of time there. Perla had told me the boy slept on the sofa there and sometimes with his grandfather as he was so devoted to him.

It would be impossible to find it. Maybe I could force the lock open with a tool or a knife? Even if I broke it, it wouldn't matter that much as so many people lived here. They wouldn't necessarily know I had been the one to break it.

As I pondered and tested the doorknob again—to no avail— I heard a sound inside.

I leapt away from the door.

Someone was in there!

I fled the room and knelt down by the *artesa*. I grabbed the soap and dug my hands in the cool water. From that angle, I still had a good view of the infamous room.

The door opened and I couldn't believe what I was seeing.

Lucas?

What was he doing *there*?

He looked around and spotted me. I lowered my head, focusing on scrubbing the fabric with the soap. I pretended not to see him as he came along on his crutches.

"Sor Puri?" he said, nonchalantly.

"Hello," I said. "What are you doing here?"

"Shouldn't you be in bed right now?"

"I can't sleep during the day. Besides, who's going to take care of my habit if not me?" I didn't see him locking the door. "What's in that room?"

"Oh, it's just a storage room. I was bored and wanted to see if I could find anything interesting in there."

He seemed to do a lot of strange things out of boredom.

"And did you?"

"Not really." He scanned the area when he said this. "Just old trash."

Martin's old trash?

"Well, you won't be so bored anymore," I said. "Sor Camila thinks Dr. Mansur will discharge you soon."

"Is that so?" he asked, his gaze lost somewhere in the cacao fields behind us.

"Will you go back to Cali?"

"I don't know. I may." His finger tapped his upper lip. "But they need help around here. Farid told me they're getting a new wave of patients today or tomorrow. I would feel bad leaving when there's so much work to be done."

"Last I heard, you were a photographer, not a nurse."

"How difficult can it be to wash sheets and pots?"

We both looked down at my lousy attempt to wash my habit. The water was spilling all over the ground and I had entirely too much soap and bubbles. I'd always had maids doing this kind of work for me, both in Sevilla and in Vinces.

"I'm not trying to be dismissive," he said. "I just want to help."

"But your bones are barely healing, even if you feel better. Surely you shouldn't be exposed to the disease."

"Let me do that," he said, kneeling. "You're driving me crazy."
He rolled up his sleeves and squatted next to me.

"You had maids at the convent or what?"

I could feel my cheeks warming up. A nun was supposed to be self-sufficient, humble. She wouldn't have maids.

"Must be my exhaustion," I said. "I've barely slept since they switched my shift."

He grabbed the brush with his healthy hand and scrubbed my habit against the washboard. Even with one hand—his left, at that—he was doing a better job than I did.

"You're going to get your cast wet," I said.

"But at least your habit will be spotless."

I smiled.

"If Sor Camila saw you doing that, she would scold you for exerting yourself."

"Who cares what she thinks?" There was so much derision in his tone it couldn't just be that he was annoyed with the bossy nun barking orders to everyone at the hospital. There was more there—a history.

A soap bubble comically landed on the tip of his nose.

"I'm surprised you want to stay," I said. "I would've thought you were eager to go back to your family. You must have a wife and kids?"

"No, neither one."

"How come?"

"I haven't met the right person."

My mind started racing.

"I know a woman who would be perfect for you!"

He lifted his gaze from the wet fabric. "Really? Who?"

"One of my sisters," I said. "I mean *real* sisters, not Jesus' brides."

"What a relief."

"The only problem is she lives in Ecuador. But honestly, that's not too far. It only takes a few days to get there, especially when it comes to something as important as finding the right mate. She would be perfect for you, Lucas. She's gentle and an exceptional seamstress. She's well read and on top of it all, she plays the violin. Did I mention how pretty and young she is?"

"How young?"

I swallowed. "Only twenty-seven."

He gave me a dismissive look. Twenty-seven was way past the marriage age.

"*Only?*" he said.

"Well, you haven't married, either. How old are you anyway?"

"Thirty-three."

"See? That's a perfect match. Younger women can be so difficult."

"And what is the name of this wonderful dame I won't be able to resist?"

"Catalina."

I'd been trying relentlessly to find a partner for Catalina ever since we moved in together and I opened my chocolate store in Vinces, but as much as it pained me to admit it, she was way older than any man in the region would've desired. Most eligible men were already married. But I kept thinking I might be able to find her a nice widower.

Lucas was even more perfect as he was still fairly young and, above all, kind.

"Well, there is an obvious problem here." He was rinsing the habit now.

"What do you mean?"

"How am I ever going to meet her if we live so far? You're obviously engaged here and with your congregation. It's not as if you can travel south if you please."

I waved a hand. "Oh, don't worry about that. I'll find a way."

He gave me an odd look. I leaned down.

"Allow me," I said, taking the habit from his hands and wringing it to drain the water.

He stood up. "All right. I think my work here is done."

"Thank you, Lucas."

"Go get some sleep, *hermana*."

The way he said *hermana* was almost burlesque, especially followed by his wink. When was I going to learn to be more discreet? In my *celestina* attempts, I may have given myself away.

"I will," I said, but really, I was just waiting for him to leave so I could go do some of my own digging in the storage room.

He tipped his beret, which he'd started using every day since he'd become mobile, and grabbed his crutches, whistling all the way to the kitchen door.

Once Lucas was out of sight, I hung my habit on the clothesline and headed directly for the storage room. As I suspected, he'd left it unlocked. I'd been thinking that if he'd locked it again, I would have to confess the truth and ask him for the key (or search through his things while he slept? *Por Dios*, what was I turning into?). This was so much better.

The room was filled with trunks and cardboard boxes. It would take hours to sift through all the contents. There was a loosely open box by the door. Lucas must have been looking through it. I lifted the flap and peeked inside: there were letters from vendors, from the bank, purchase orders, payrolls—nothing out of the ordinary. I picked one that looked more personal.

Cali, January 2, 1925

Estimado Martin,

It was such a pleasure to have you among my guests at the New Year's celebration. As I offered during our conversation, here is the breakdown of the mine's earnings and expenses last year. Of course, the offer to come to Boyacá and visit the mine in person still stands. I would love to have you as an investor.

Sincerely,

Gerardo

Following the missive was a detailed income and expense report of an emerald mine.

Emeralds? Since when was Martin interested in emeralds? His passion had always been cacao beans. But of course, he had mentioned climate problems and competition in the area. He'd also said that other landowners in the region were turning to coffee bean and sugar cane production instead of cacao—both products that were booming in Colombia. It wouldn't have been foolish or senseless of him to be looking for other alternatives, even if it required him to move somewhere else, like this place—I peeked at the letter again—Boyacá?

I needed to find out about this town—my knowledge of Colombia was so limited. I would ask Perla or Lucas. No, not Lucas; he already suspected me.

What if, in reality, Martin had gone to Boyacá? I dared to hope for an instant. Maybe he wasn't dead after all. Maybe he'd just left.

If that was the case, though, why would Lucas say Martin had died? And why had I found a last will and testament that didn't mention emerald mines whatsoever?

Another interesting detail was that this letter had been penned only a couple of weeks before Martin last wrote me and sent me the stuffed bear for little Cristóbal. This meant the emerald mine investment could have been the plan he'd mentioned when he said this was his "last chance" to make things work.

I searched through other boxes. There were books, office supplies, paintings, items of clothing, shoes, and boots. Finding all these personal items deflated me. If Martin was truly alive and had gone to another town to start a new business, he would've taken his clothes.

In another box I found a large pile of letters wrapped with a string. The handwriting on the envelopes looked familiar and the stamps came from France.

My stomach turned into a knot.

I knew who'd sent these letters. I opened one of them just to confirm my suspicions.

My beloved Martin, it started.

These were different kinds of letters—love letters—all written by my sister Angélica, who'd had an off-and-on relationship with Martin since she was an adolescent. But my sister was still married to Laurent, as far as I knew, and had gone to Europe shortly after we'd sold the hacienda. She was supposed to have ended things with Martin for good.

At least that was what he'd said.

But in spite of everything, Angélica was still madly in love with him.

Not only in love, according to the dozens of letters in this box, but fixated on him. From what I could see by skimming through a couple of them, she'd never stopped thinking about him and she dreamt that one day in the near future they would visit those European landmarks together. Apparently, she'd been writing to Martin for the last five years—since I was expecting little Cristóbal.

Of course, she'd never known the details of my relationship with Martin, only that we'd become close friends.

My fingers trembled as my mind started exploring the painful possibilities.

If Martin had left with Angélica, he certainly wouldn't have told me. Even though he and I had remained friends and never agreed to continue our romantic relationship, he must have known I had feelings for him. He must have known how devastating it would be to know he'd chosen my sister over me.

But there was the situation with the clothes again. Wouldn't he have taken them with him?

Not if he went overseas. He was a practical man and probably wouldn't want to carry along trunks of clothing. Besides, if he'd left with Angélica to Europe or even Boyacá, he simply would've sold the property to Farid Mansur and I would've found a bill of sale, not a will.

I dropped the letters back in the box. I should read them all—there might be more answers—but I didn't have the fortitude to continue reading about how much they loved each other.

Not when I'd had a son with him.

Another thought came to mind. What exactly had Lucas said the other day? Something about Martin's lady friend from Ecuador?

His lady friend asked to ride his new Andalusian mare.

Of course, Angélica was a fine horseman. She could have been at the gala. But why the secrecy? Nobody here knew that she was married. Lucas couldn't even remember her name. In addition, why would they have left if he had a gorgeous plantation here? She could've simply stayed and become the mistress of the hacienda.

No, the more I thought about it, the less sense a possible escapade made.

Of course, it was hard to think with this desire to retch, with my body shaking and my mind clouded, when the rage, the shame, the shock was taking over.

I kicked the box to the side. I had to get out of here. I needed to calm down, think things through and then come back with a fresh mind, with my emotions in check.

Yes, I would do that. I needed to get some rest as my shift started in the evening and I hadn't slept at all. I was telling myself this knowing, of course, that I wouldn't be able to sleep after learning that Angélica was still somehow present in Martin's life.

I spun to leave, but the glimpse of something bulky, something metallic, stopped me.

I turned around again. Behind the box I'd just kicked was a metal safe.

CHAPTER 19

Puri

"Am I dying, Sister?" Lucas mumbled, juggling the thermometer from one corner of his mouth to the other, as if it were hard candy.

I lifted my head from the sheet I was tucking under his mattress.

"Why do you ask?"

"Well, you've been taking my temperature for almost ten minutes."

"Oh, sorry." I rushed to his side and pulled the thermometer out.

He massaged his jaw with his good hand. I'd been so distressed by everything I found out in the storage room that I was forgetting important steps, such as removing the thermometer from the patient's mouth after three minutes.

"You're so distracted today," he said. "And you haven't stopped yawning."

Madre mía, I'd never met a more vigilant man. Then again, he made a living out of observing people.

I set the thermometer on the metal tray by his bed. I'd known I wouldn't be able to sleep after finding Angélica's letters.

"Lucas?"

"Yes?"

"You mentioned that your friend Martin had a lady guest from Ecuador at the fundraiser. Was she a blonde?"

"You mean *our* friend Martin?"

"Sure." I avoided looking him in the eye.

"I'll only answer if you're honest with me."

"What do you want to know?" I said.

"This interest in Martin. Was there more than friendship between the two of you?"

I wished the veil would shield my face, not just my hair. "Yes," I said, cautiously. "Now tell me about that woman."

He studied me, unapologetically.

"Yes, she was a blonde."

Then it *could* be her. Angélica had inherited our French father's coloring and there were not a lot of blondes in this area of the world.

"Was her name Angélica?"

"It's entirely possible."

"And what happened with her? I mean, after Martin disappeared?"

He sat up and stared at me. He could've been less obvious about his examination of my every reaction, but he didn't seem to believe in discretion. Did he still believe I was a nun? Somehow what he thought of me mattered.

"She went into hysterics; I do remember that."

I stopped fiddling with the bottles of medicine. "What do you mean by *hysterics*?"

"Screaming, you know? Out of her mind?"

Angélica did have *strong* feelings for Martin. I could see how she would've been upset, but this meant they hadn't left together. It was a flawed theory anyway—it didn't make any sense that they would leave in secrecy.

"And then?"

"I don't know. I had to leave the next day, remember?"

"Do you know where she is now?"

He cleared his throat. Stretched his arms behind his back.

"Rumor has it that she's at an institution in Cali."

"An institution? Do you mean a *mental* institution?"

He nodded.

I had to sit down to take the news. And I did, right next to Lucas's leg. He flinched, bringing his hand to his ankle to protect it.

A mental institution?

The words didn't make any sense.

The Angélica I'd known had been an assertive woman who ran her household without delay or hesitation, a gracious hostess who knew exactly how to engage her guests and make them feel at home, a lady mostly in control of her emotions—except for a jealous outburst against Martin I once witnessed.

She was *not* a mental patient.

"Do you know her?" he said.

I couldn't picture her in a place like that. It was *wrong*. "If it's the person I'm thinking of, then yes." I gave him a quick glance. I *really* didn't want to explain my complicated relationship with my estranged sister.

I had to do something about this, though. I *must* see her.

But how?

I couldn't believe we'd been in the same town for a week and didn't know it. That meant she'd been there during the earthquake!

Lucas leaned forward. He was about to ask more, I could tell. It was probably safer to change the subject.

"What were you looking for in the storage room this morning?" I said.

He parted his lips. Then seemed to think better of it and grabbed a glass of water.

"Like I said, I was bored."

I placed my hand on his arm. "You can trust me."

He glanced at my fingers. I removed them as quickly as if I'd touched a hot pan. It had been a natural, involuntary act, but probably not appropriate for a nun.

"Trust you with what?" he said.

"I think you're trying to figure something out."

"What would I be trying to figure out? I told you Martin died."

"In that case, where was he buried?" I had the sudden urge to see his grave.

"At the cemetery in El Paraíso, I suppose. Farid took care of all the details. As I mentioned, I had to leave the day after the party, but Farid sent me a telegram after Martin was found."

"Did you attend the funeral?"

"No, Farid wrote me after Martin was buried."

"*After* the funeral? Why would they bury him so quickly?"

"It's customary."

"But you were one of Martin's best friends. Couldn't they wait for you?"

Lucas shrugged. "Farid knew I was at the hospital in Cali with my mother. She nearly fell into a coma. I supposed he didn't want to disturb me at that time."

"And why did you come back to the hacienda?"

"What is this, a police interrogation? Or in your case, the Spanish Inquisition?"

I hid a smile. His gaze fell on my mouth for a split second.

"It's just that some things don't make sense, Lucas," I said. "Martin's disappearance, his supposed death, the funeral, the donation. It all seems so rushed. So convenient."

He watched me in silence.

"And what is it to you?" he finally said.

I gazed at my nails. "I guess curiosity has always been one of my biggest character flaws."

He gave me a smug smile.

"But if we're going to spend so much time together," I added, "we might as well know each other."

"I suppose there's no harm in answering your *many* questions,

Sister." He sighed. "I came back because Farid wanted me to take photos of the hospital inauguration. Plus, I had to deliver photos of the gala to the guests from the area."

I wasn't sure I believed his presence here was just a coincidence. I had a feeling Lucas had come for a reason other than taking photos. It would also explain why he insisted that he wanted to stay and help.

"There's a safe in the storage room," I said, testing him.

"I know." He rearranged the buttons of his pajama shirt as they were mismatched. Our eyes met for a second. "I saw it."

"It must have belonged to Martin."

"Would you hand me my briefcase *without* throwing all the contents to the floor?"

"I can try."

With both hands I grasped the sepia valise sitting by the armoire and set it on his lap. Lucas opened it and went through the contents. His facial hair was shabby and gave him, at times, a haggard expression, but there was something appealing about him.

He retrieved a rectangular cardboard box and removed the lid. The pile of photos I'd dumped on the floor the other day was neatly organized inside. He took one out and showed it to me.

It was the image I'd seen before, the one of the woman standing in front of the hacienda's entrance with a baby girl.

"Who are they?" I said, holding the picture between my fingers.

"She's the wife of the former owner of this hacienda, and that's her daughter. The mother went missing a few years ago and I've been curious to know what happened to her. That's all."

She'd gone missing, too?

"But did you know them? I mean, it's a little unusual that you would take it upon yourself to investigate this missing person."

"Yes, they were benefactors at our school. In fact"—he searched through the gala photos—"this man here was her husband and he came to the gala."

He pointed at a man standing behind a trio of women in beaded and fringe dresses. He was alone, looking away from the camera, holding a champagne glass in his hand and sporting a tuxedo with a white bow tie.

"His name was Iván Contreras, and the wife's name was María Belén."

"So is this a local mystery, I assume?"

"Sort of," he said, organizing the rest of the photos. "I know Martin was also intrigued by what happened and mentioned it to me. In fact, the night of the party he said he'd figured something out and wanted to talk to me about it the next day, but I never saw him again."

"Interesting."

Could this woman's disappearance have something to do with what happened to Martin?

I studied Lucas's eyes. My mother used to say you could know if someone was trustworthy by the sincerity of their gaze, or if they maintained eye contact. Lucas did. I decided to take a leap of faith.

"I can help you find out about the lady in your photograph if you help me find out the truth about Martin."

"I told you—"

"I don't believe he's dead, Lucas."

He frowned. "Why not?"

"The signature in his will is forged. I knew his signature well and that wasn't it."

"You saw his will?"

I nodded.

"I don't think Farid would've . . ."

He was suddenly quiet. He stared out the window at the sad remains of Martin's grandiose plantation. Would he go against people he loved if it meant doing the right thing?

"All right, Sor Puri. I'll help you."

"Great," I said, standing. "But we can't start until I shave that wild beard off of you."

* * *

"Don't move," I told Lucas.

"It's called breathing," he said.

"Do you realize one false move could turn me into a murderer?"

I was holding a sharp razor blade up against his throat and attempted to shave him with slow, upward movements, but I was dangerously close to his jugular vein. The blade created a path through the soap covering his skin, like the freshly plowed roads I'd seen in Granada during a snowstorm many years ago.

I leaned over him a little, my bosom pressing against his shoulder. This time, he held his breath.

"*¡Respira, hombre!*" I instructed, but his chest remained still. "Come on. Let all that air out."

As soon as I turned toward the end table to rinse the blade in a bowl of water, he exhaled.

"Ready?" I said, standing in front of him. He sat on the edge of the bed, his cast carefully placed on the floor.

"I'd better be," he said. "I wouldn't want to anger a woman with a blade."

For once, he didn't refer to me as a nun. I returned the blade to his face.

"You have a beautiful smile, *hermana*."

"Lower your chin, please," I told him.

I hadn't even realized I was smiling.

"My apologies if I offended you."

When I failed to respond, he narrowed his eyes.

"Despite what you may think," he said, "nuns are worthy of compliments, too."

My cheeks warmed as his eyes met mine.

"Then again, I wouldn't want to condemn you to a day of penance by encouraging vanity."

I sighed. "How am I supposed to shave you if you won't stop talking?"

"Sorry." He smiled. "I'll be good from now on. I promise."

I took a step closer to him to reach the other side of his face. His Adam's apple moved as he swallowed.

I hadn't been so close to a man since, well, since my little Cristóbal had been conceived. The simple, mundane act of shaving Lucas—which I had done on occasion for my husband—felt more intimate than helping him walk or feeding him. It may have had something to do with the trust instilled in me not to hurt him.

The moment I was done, I stepped back and he smiled. It was then that I discovered various dimples on his face: one on his chin and two on his cheeks.

They were adorable.

I almost mentioned them but managed to hold my tongue before I condemned *myself* to a day of penance.

CHAPTER 20

Lucas

Hacienda La Magna
July 1910

I had mixed feelings about this holiday. I'd always enjoyed visiting my *padrino*'s ranch as there was much to do. And if there wasn't, he would find something—pleasant or unpleasant—to occupy me and any friend I might bring along, such as milking the cows at four in the morning or cleaning the horses' stables. But aside from those inconvenient chores, I had greatly enjoyed my summers in the country: fishing in the river, hiking, riding horses, climbing trees. A person could get lost in the serpentine paths of leaf litter scattered throughout the forest. I could never get enough of the scent of moist trunks and leaves the morning after a downpour, of the cacophony of swallows, woodpeckers, and parrotlets, or the creek's gurgle in the distance. I never felt more at peace than here—as long as I didn't have to get in the water.

My godparents had three girls, all married, all gone. My mother said my *padrino* saw me as the son he always wanted, which is why he and his wife insisted that I visit every summer and was free to bring friends over. With a perpetual cigar in his mouth and an oversized hat, my *padrino* often spoke in monosyllables. He was the opposite of my father, who was always quick to tell a story, but the irony was that this man of few words always showed a lot more interest in what I was doing—my school, my friends, my plans—than my own father.

The problem was that Camila was coming. I hadn't been able to stop thinking about her since I photographed her over a year ago. Her beauty was sublime, but there was something else about her, a confidence, a determination that I'd seldom seen before in a man or a woman. I should've been ecstatic to be able to see her again, to have her around for a week, but there was a small inconvenience. Something happened to me when she was near.

I was normally an easygoing person. I liked to be around others, to dance, sing, play my guitar, but I became a ball of nerves, an idiot, in front of her. My mind would often go blank, I sweated profusely, and I didn't speak, I mumbled.

How was I supposed to compete with someone like Martin, who was obviously comfortable around women? I'd seen him interact with other girls in Cali in the summers. He had no qualms about talking to any of them, in dancing. Why couldn't I be at ease like him?

On top of it all, we were going to the river or a waterfall, or some other atrocious place.

Swimming was the one activity I didn't partake of on my godfather's property. I didn't swim. I didn't get in the water. I had made that mistake before; as a ten-year-old I had more courage than now at eighteen. I'd been too close to death. A caiman had gotten hold of my leg—I still had the scar—but my *padrino* had thrown himself in the river, knife in hand, and stabbed the reptile, freeing me from his grasp. That had been enough for me to never, ever, get into any body of water again.

I saw my friends—Farid and Martin—enjoying the water, splashing Farid's younger siblings, my mother submerging her legs all the way to her knees. But Camila was just sitting there, staring at them. I could've seized the opportunity to talk to her. It was my chance since everyone else was distracted, but I couldn't. I didn't know what to say—normally I was full of ideas. But again, the mental paralysis had taken over except for smoking one cigarette after another.

I said I had molar pain, which had worked since I was a kid and didn't want to do something, and had actually been true at one point, to which my father had reacted by leaving me at home with a bottle of *aguardiente* in hand to take sips as the pain increased. But now, it was my one and only excuse, which I'm sure my mother already knew to be exactly that—an excuse—but didn't say a word about it. She would simply give me a sideways glance.

The truth was I was furious at myself, at my cowardice. Camila was just a girl, just like any other, and I'd had a girlfriend before at fifteen, but that girl was *nothing* compared to Camila.

"Get in, *hermano*!" Martin was saying. I would beat that *hijueputa* after this was over. I lit another cigarette, and glanced at Camila.

She was looking straight ahead—at Martin—as he swam back and forth. Her dress had gotten wet and the fabric had become somewhat transparent. Farid would kill me if he knew the impure thoughts I was having as I noted how the pink fabric snugged her breasts and hips.

She caught me watching her.

I smiled.

She did the same.

Go talk to her. This is your chance.

But the window of opportunity shut down as Martin got out of the water and approached her.

I saw them leaving together the next morning. Martin had taken one of my *padrino*'s horses, Sancho, named in honor of Don Quijote's sidekick. I'd learned to ride on that horse, which only added to my frustration when I saw Martin grasping Camila's waist and helping her onto Sancho's back. That damn idiot. He already had a girlfriend in Vinces, a girl he talked about all the time and had assured us he would marry one day. It was especially maddening when he was drunk. Then Farid and I would hear of nothing else but that girl's blond hair. *Have you ever met a blonde?* he would say. *That hair is like no other, it's soft like cotton and it shines so much you're drawn to it like a magnet.* And Farid and I would just roll our eyes and tell him to shut up already, we'd heard enough of that blond nymph.

So where was she now?

Camila was the exact opposite, her hair dark as the night.

If I knew Martin, which I did—I'd seen him every day for the last three years—he would take her to the waterfall by the *finca*, Cascada La Reina. I'd shown it to him just a couple of days ago and he'd loved it. He said the creek reminded him of the place where he used to fish growing up.

I borrowed one of the mares named Juanita, after my *madrina*, and headed over there. Juanita was mellow. She was old, shorter than the other horses, and had an abundant white mane. I had a soft spot for her, maybe because after Sancho had thrown me once, I'd started riding Juanita and she'd been obedient and sweet.

Sure enough, they were there.

Under the waterfall. *Holding hands.*

It hadn't taken long for Camila to remove her dress. She wore a navy-blue sailor dress underneath, but she'd removed her tights, which infuriated me as Martin was the beneficiary of such exposure. If Farid saw them.

I could tell him.

In Martin's defense, I'd never told him about my feelings for Camila. But I thought it was obvious. Why else would I sit there like a mumbling idiot staring at her all the time?

Besides, he had a girl already.

They were laughing, delighted. Martin's claws were grasping her waist, as if she were *his*. He led her into the pool. When her head emerged from the water, she was giggling, her long hair floating around them. She reminded me of a goddess rising from the waters, of Botticelli's *Venus*. He held her close, no longer laughing. And then the idiot did the unthinkable, he crossed a line that should've never been crossed, and kissed her.

He *kissed* her.

And she *let* him.

She set her hands on his shoulders and responded to the kiss with the fervor of a diligent student.

An ember lit somewhere inside me. I wanted to punch him until his skull collapsed, until that stupid smile disappeared from his face. I wanted to destroy him—have him beg for forgiveness.

My hands balled into tight fists and I found myself clenching my teeth.

I could do no such thing. I wasn't that kind of person and I had no claims on her. She had barely spoken two words to me in the last four days.

It was all Martin's fault.

Padre Carlos Benigno once told us that everyone had their limits, that anyone could do unthinkable acts, mortal sins that might change the course of their lives. They only had to have the right— or the wrong—stimulus. Was this it for me? At that moment, I knew I would never see Martin under the same light again. To me, he was dead and one day I would get back at him.

Somehow.

I just had to wait for the right moment.

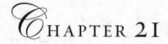

CHAPTER 21

Puri

I was tired of death and illness. But instead of scaring me off, it was making me more determined. By God, I wouldn't let this woman die.

"Come on, have a little more," I said, bringing a spoonful of broth to the mouth of the skeletal woman I was tending to. She was half sitting, half lying on her bed, but making an extraordinary effort to put some food in her stomach.

There were two large cholera rooms now—the former dining room and the former living room, according to Lula's explanation. The ones in the dining room were the sickest—they couldn't eat or drink anything so we had them on IVs. The patients in this room, however, still had hope and I was putting all of mine in this woman who was barely a few years older than me. Her cheeks were hollow and her ears stood out after I'd fixed her long hair in a braid. They all seemed to lose their facial fat almost immediately. And stink.

"What is this broth?" she asked.

"Chicken."

She shook her head. "But it's sweet."

Holy Mother, Tuli had done it again.

"But otherwise it's good, right?" I said.

She gave me a look, as if I were some kind of idiot. Only my habit prevented her from insulting me, I supposed.

"*Vamos, maja*, one more spoonful," I urged.

The woman grimaced.

"You need it," I said.

She conceded, not too happily. There was a certain gratification in tending to others—I'd done some in the past with my chocolate, but never so intimately. Earlier today I'd shaved Lucas and I had to admit I'd enjoyed it. Although the satisfaction of taking care of him had more to do with a certain attraction that was undeniable. This was an entirely different feeling. Serving others without getting anything in return other than the pleasure of helping, of seeing improvement in the other person, gave me a different kind of satisfaction.

The strings of a guitar filtered into the room, followed by some rhythmic applause.

I set the bowl on the nightstand and followed the sounds of the music to the patio, where Farid's son sat on the edge of the fountain, playing the guitar.

He had so much skill. His fingers traveled up and down the instrument's neck with amazing speed into complicated arpeggios. The sounds he emitted were simply beautiful, intricate chords that had a Moorish feel to them, similar to the music of my Andalucía, but somewhat more ornate.

I hadn't spoken to Mansur's son yet. I'd only run into the doctor and his son once in the kitchen, just as they were leaving. Mansur had elbowed Basim so he would greet me and the boy had shyly said hello without looking up, but that was about it. I was always mesmerized at how young men grew, how their bodies stretched out like rubber in all directions, producing broom arms and endless legs that didn't fill up until they reached their mid-twenties.

Paco hadn't filled up yet.

I would never know Paco as a full-grown adult.

The realization shook me to my core. I brought a hand to my

compressed chest—I couldn't even complain that my corset was too tight as I didn't wear one anymore. If Paco had been here, he might have become friends with Farid's son—they were the youngest people here. But that would *never* happen.

Perla waved at me from across the patio.

I waved back and, through teary eyes, tried to focus on Basim as he plucked the strings and suppress Paco's image from my mind.

There was something deeply familiar about Farid's boy, but I couldn't pinpoint exactly what. The more he played, the more people gathered on the patio, drawn by his natural magnetism. Nurses had emerged from the rooms, even the ones who were supposed to be sleeping, and some patients who were recovering from other illnesses or had broken limbs were out, too.

"*Dale*, Basim, *dale*," Perla said, enthusiastically.

Other nurses cheered the kid on and applauded. I did the same—mechanically—as I was still thinking about Paco and Sor Alba Luz with a mixture of sorrow and guilt.

Basim played two more songs and the upbeat melodies started soothing my soul.

Music was powerful. It could fill you with longing or pain, but it could also uplift your spirit, transport you. And the melody Basim was playing did just that.

We needed this. We needed a moment of joy in the midst of so much grief.

Across the fountain, sitting on a bench outside the kitchen was Mansur's wife, Amira. Her legs were crossed and her mauve dress slightly lifted, showing off a shapely calf. With an opera-length cigarette holder between her fingers, she watched her son's performance with an expression that didn't match the mood on the patio. She was an attractive woman, but in spite of her fine gowns and the emeralds hanging from her ears, she looked forlorn. I couldn't blame her—this was a sad place. Death practically surrounded us and was waiting for the next person to take.

I approached her. She continued smoking without saying a word or even looking at me.

It had come to my attention that the nun's habit caused distinct reactions. Some people treated me with deference and respect, others (like Lucas) seemed intrigued by it, but there was also a minority who seemed to resent it or be repelled by it, as if I had the power to read their sins. Amira was one of those people.

I sat next to her.

"I didn't know your son could play so well," I said as soon as he finished the piece.

She slightly kicked her leg up and down. There was an elegance to her face with those high cheekbones and charcoal eyes.

"That's all he does," she said. "He sleeps with that guitar."

"Well, it's good that he has a passion for something. We all need that."

She stared at me blankly.

"You have a peculiar name," I said.

She turned her gaze back to the fountain. "It means *princess* in Arabic."

She was certainly as pampered as one, with those nice gowns and jewelry. But there was something off between her and her husband. From what I heard the other night, he'd brought her here against her will and she'd made some accusations in his office that I still couldn't make out.

"Your name is not so common either," she said. "Purificación."

This was the first time we'd spoken and yet both of us knew each other's names. Well, what could be expected in such a small community?

"Someone once told me of a Puri who makes chocolate," she said.

Her comment was so unexpected I would've been less shocked if someone had thrown a bucket of water in my face.

"Who?"

She faced me for the first time. "You wouldn't know him."

"Try me."

She shrugged. "A friend of my husband's, a man called Martin Sabater."

I had to tread carefully.

"I've heard of him. He was the former owner of this hacienda."

She sighed, took another drag of smoke. "Yes."

"So, you met him here, then," I said.

She looked me in the eye, but didn't answer.

"What did he say about Puri?"

"He said she made the best chocolate he'd ever tasted. Actually, he said she *introduced* him to chocolate, just like I introduced him to some Arab desserts."

I tried to read something in her expression, but it was empty. Frankly, she seemed more annoyed than anything. There was no longing in her voice when talking about Martin, no distress. But she must know he was dead.

"What a pity that he died so young," I said. "Don Martin."

"Yes. It is. But we all have to die one day."

"True, but I like to think we'll die when the time is right."

"Will there ever be a right time?"

"I don't know." I sat with her words for a moment. "Probably not."

I was going to ask her about the night of the fundraiser gala when I spotted Dr. Costa staring at me.

Oh, no, had he recognized me?

He was coming toward me. I still hadn't thought of what I was going to say if he asked if I was the same Puri from the ship. I certainly didn't want to offer explanations in front of Amira.

"I'd better go back to work." I stood up, hands under my scapular.

Amira followed my gaze toward Dr. Costa. Well, it wouldn't be so strange that I got nervous when the doctor saw me taking a break without permission, would it?

I turned in the opposite direction and escaped.

CHAPTER 22

Puri

It was undeniable that Farid Mansur was a handsome man. But perhaps his greatest asset was his confidence. When he spoke, everyone listened. Around the dining table in the kitchen—for lack of a better space—we all watched him, enthralled by his knowledge, by the way he kept his cool under duress. He had something else, an innate leadership quality only a few people possessed and which seemed to originate in the womb.

In the last two days we'd had an invasion of patients. So much so that we even had people lying on the hall benches. I'd been so busy helping with the patients that I hadn't had any time to continue my investigations. Neither did Lucas, who'd given up his room to other patients in dire circumstances, and was now boarding with Don Yusuf Mansur.

I admired Lucas's decision to stay. He could've easily returned to his safe life in Cali, but he said he felt an obligation to help now that he'd seen firsthand the gravity of the situation.

"It's essential that we educate the people of El Paraíso about cholera," Dr. Mansur said, to which both Sor Camila and Dr. Costa nodded. Most of the nurses were in our impromptu meeting as well. "We must address the issue of the contaminated water with the mayor. We must test all the bodies of water in the region and close down the ones that test positive for cholera. Otherwise, we'll have the entire town here."

"That seems ambitious," Sor Camila said.

There was a subtle hostility between the siblings that showed up at times. I couldn't tell if it was the effect of two strong personalities butting heads or a history I didn't know about, but Sor Camila frequently found ways to contradict her brother or outsmart him.

She was the only one.

Even Dr. Costa, who'd had plenty of experience with epidemics and was nearly an eminence in my country—having been brought here by the Catholic Church a few years back—was deferential to the head doctor.

"But not impossible, Camila," Dr. Mansur said.

He was the only one here who didn't call her *Sor* or *Hermana*.

Annoyed, she faced me. "Tell them about your patient, *hermana*."

All eyes turned in my direction.

"Well . . ." I cleared my throat, conscious of Dr. Costa's attention on me. "The strangest thing happened to one of my patients. This woman in the cholera wing was very sick, she could barely eat. But I gave her Doña Tulia's broth, and it was . . . how should I put it?" I glanced at the cook, who was oblivious to our conversation. "It was seasoned with sugar instead of salt. Well, the next day, the woman was feeling a lot better. She'd gained some of her strength and said she was hungry."

Everyone turned to Tuli, who whistled and continued with her cooking chores.

"Well, it makes sense," Dr. Costa said. It was so strange to hear a familiar accent in this area. "There are different electrolytes in sugar, which may have improved her condition."

"*¡Bravo, Tuli!*" Perla said, applauding. The old lady simply turned toward us, perplexed.

The inviting aroma of *pandebono* served as an odd backdrop to this solemn conversation, but it was a morning meeting, after all. I'd become infatuated with this cheese bread, which Perla told me was typical in every *caleño* home. I glanced longingly at the bread, not able to decide if I was hungry or sleepy.

I could barely keep my eyes open after staying up all night tending to the patients. Not even when my son was a baby had I missed so much sleep. These nuns were admirable.

"Should we try sugared water with other patients, then?" Sor Camila asked.

"It couldn't hurt," Dr. Costa said. "Right, Farid?"

Dr. Mansur rubbed his chin. He looked exhausted. The doctors had been working double shifts and it showed in their rugged appearance. Gone were the trimmed haircuts and perfectly shaved faces—I'd just spotted a patch of hair on Dr. Costa's jaw. Meanwhile, the bags under Dr. Mansur's eyes had grown considerably. He resembled his father more and more every day.

"Sure," he said. "Anything else?"

Nurse Celia reported some of the patients were also making a recovery and the two doctors discussed if they should move them to another room. My eyelids felt heavy, their voices—more distant with each passing second—were lulling me into a daze until the creak of the door startled me; startled all of us.

We all turned to see Lucas coming in.

"Sorry to interrupt." He struggled to get in, but he was getting better at walking on crutches. He looked much younger without the beard. His features, his eyes, stood out.

Lucas stared at me, his chest heaving from the effort of maneuvering his injured leg.

"You need something, Lucas?" Dr. Mansur said.

His gaze paused on Sor Camila's face for a second longer than the rest of us. "I need to speak with Sor Puri, but it can wait."

The urgency of his voice contradicted his words.

"She's free to go," the head doctor said. "I think we're mostly done here."

I stood. "If you'll excuse me."

Nurse Celia took the floor again. She was one of those people who liked to hear themselves speak and rambled incessantly.

I followed Lucas to the patio. As he tripped with a step, I grasped his arm to break the fall.

"*¡Carajo!*" he said, eyeing my hand.

We were standing too close.

I let go of his arm and resumed my walk.

"What happened?"

"Let's go to the back," he mumbled.

When we reached the chicken coop, he removed a couple of papers from his *guayabera*'s front pocket and handed them to me.

There were two letters, addressed to Martin.

"Where did you get these?"

"In a tin box inside the storage room. Read them."

> *Don Martin,*
>
> *You're in possession of a valuable emerald necklace that must be returned to its rightful owner. It would be a pity if your hacienda were to suffer from a fire or some other mishap or that, God forbid, something disastrous were to happen to you. To prevent any of these unpleasant incidents, please return the jewel before dawn tomorrow morning at the abandoned chapel on the way to El Paraíso. You will deposit it inside a paper bag and under the frontal pew and leave immediately.*
>
> *Trust me, you won't like the consequences if you don't follow these instructions to the letter.*

The letter had no signature or date and it was typed, not handwritten. I looked up at Lucas, who was watching my every expression.

"Read the next one," he said.

The next letter only had one sentence:

> *We warned you.*

Whatever somnolence I had earlier dissipated.

A rooster crowed. I turned toward a shuffling noise behind the bushes.

"This has to be it," I said. "The reason why Martin disappeared."

Lucas nodded. "It would certainly explain some things."

"Do you have any idea of what this was about? Did he ever mention emeralds to you?"

Lucas shook his head. "Wait. At the fundraiser gala. There was this man, an owner of an emerald mine in Boyacá. Martin introduced me to him."

"Gerardo," I said.

"How did you know?"

"I found a letter where a man called Gerardo invited Martin to visit his mine. Apparently, he wanted him as an investor."

The hen's caretaker emerged from the bushes. There was something eerie about the way he ogled me.

"Maybe he knows something?" I told Lucas in a low voice.

Lucas gave me an odd look. "That won't work."

"Why?" I said, somewhat indignant. I despised when people told me I couldn't do something. It immediately made me want to do it more.

He took a step toward me and leaned his head. I marveled at his perky nose with its upward slope—a work of art—and took in the scent of bergamot and amber from his toilet water. Ever since I'd shaved him, I felt uneasy about standing too close to him.

"Because Nestor is mute," he whispered.

No wonder he'd never greeted me.

I was a horrible person for thinking he was eerie.

The poor man.

From the servants' quarters, Lula came in our direction. Apparently, this was not the private place Lucas had been hoping for.

"Look, I haven't had any sleep," I said. "Let me rest for a couple of hours and then we'll figure out what to do next."

Lucas nodded.

"One more thing," I said, trying to think of the perfect words to frame my next question. "Is there a specific reason why you and Sor Camila don't get along?"

The color left his cheeks.

"Why do you say that?"

"I don't know. There seems to be some hostility between the two of you."

He shrugged and started back toward the hacienda. "No, not at all. You're just seeing things."

CHAPTER 23

Camila

Cali, Colombia
October 1910

Baba was unrecognizable. I'd never seen him this upset. It had been two weeks since everything exploded, but his body still showed debilitating signs of the aftermath. His eyes were bloodshot, his tie undone, and his thinning hair was wildly disheveled. Baba, who always prided himself in being well dressed, had his shirt untucked and a maroon stain by the collar, which I assumed to be the red wine his cousin had brought him for his birthday.

As he entered my room, bringing in the scent of alcohol in every one of his pores, I braced myself, expecting him to yell at me again, or worse yet, to beat me.

"Your brother is here," he said. He hadn't spoken to me in days. "All the way from Bogotá, leaving his important studies and his fiancée just to fix the mess you've made."

"He didn't have to come."

He brought a finger dangerously close to my face. *"Ikhrasi!"*

I shut up, as told. Baba had never spoken to me this way before—not like he did to the boys. He'd always spoiled me. In fact, it had been easy for me to gently persuade him to do what I wanted, but this time was different. Things might never be the same between us.

Farid entered my bedroom with a leather valise in his hand. This was the first time I'd seen him since he went to medical school. He'd grown a beard and had lost a few pounds. He would probably gain them back when he married Amira, his eternal bride. She had the reputation of being an excellent cook.

"Leave us alone, Baba," Farid said, dropping the valise on the floor. "*Min fadlak.*"

Baba was about to protest but he was so depleted and Farid had such a stern look on his face that he must have concluded it was best not to argue with his firstborn.

As soon as Baba left the room, Farid approached me.

I raised my chin.

"Tell me who did this to you," he said.

I held on to the post of my canopy bed.

"Talk!" he said. "I'm going to kill that *malparido.*"

I'd inadvertently touched my belly and now his gaze fell on my midsection, which seemed to infuriate him more.

He slapped me and hissed a "*ramera*" under his breath.

How had I fallen from grace this low? Because I'd fallen in love? Christ, the worst part was that I didn't regret a single moment. I'd been reliving the week at Doña Juana's hacienda over and over again. I brought a hand to my cheek—it was burning. How dare Farid call me a whore! How dare he slap me! He hadn't hit me since we were little kids.

"Is it one of my friends?" he said.

"No!"

"I'm going to beat that name out of you."

"Do it. You can kill me if you want. I'm never telling you his name."

What was the point of telling them? Farid and my father would only give Martin a good beating—though I wasn't sure he would let them. Farid had said Martin was feisty. But violence would only make things worse and if they were mean to Martin, he would never want to hear from me again. No, I had to be smart. I had to do things my way. I would find him myself. I would talk to him and then we would get married and raise this child together. We didn't need Farid's or Baba's interference.

"Fine. Don't tell me," Farid said. "But you're going to do what we say. Pack your things right now. We're leaving in an hour." He picked up the valise and threw it on my bed.

I panicked. "Where?"

"You'll find out soon enough. Just pack whatever fits in that valise."

"Who do you think you are? I'm staying right here."

A tremor had taken over my extremities. I sat on the edge of the bed and crossed my arms.

Farid grabbed me by the arm and pulled me off the bed. "Do as I say! You've lost all your rights in this house. Baba doesn't want you here anymore, and I don't blame him. He's not going to raise the bastard child of a stupid seventeen-year-old." He threw me against the armoire. "Pack all your shit and meet us downstairs."

As he was walking out, I removed my shoe and threw it at him. The heel hit his calf, but he didn't even turn around.

Damn Farid.

What was I going to do? I didn't even know where they were taking me or for how long. Baba didn't want me here anymore? That couldn't be true. I'd always been his favorite because he said I reminded him of my mother. How could that end so quickly, out of *one* mistake? I'd always done everything right. I'd raised *his* children. I'd taken care of *his* house. I'd even worked at his store. All of that didn't count for something?

Fine!

I'd leave. He wouldn't last without me for more than a week. I knew Baba. He depended on me for everything. How would he find the simplest things: his shoes, his wallet, his pocket watch? He never knew where anything was.

I opened my armoire. Farid's valise wouldn't be enough for my voluminous dresses. What was I supposed to pack? And for what kind of weather? I wouldn't be able to fit in these gowns for much longer anyway—my waist and stomach were already growing. Maybe they were planning to send me to this mysterious location until I had the baby and then Baba would send for me. He had to.

I should've never trusted Tía Lidia with my secret. I thought she would help me find Martin. We hadn't heard from him since he'd moved to Popayán and I'd been hoping my aunt could send someone from the store out there and locate him. If only my aunt would've helped me, Martin would've come back—I knew it; he would've asked for my hand in marriage and Baba would've never known I was expecting a child until after the wedding. But Tia Lidia had betrayed me. She'd gone off and told Baba everything.

I would never forgive her.

I picked three looser-fitting afternoon dresses, undergarments, a hairbrush, two pairs of shoes, and the jewels my mother had left me. I would go, but that didn't mean I was going to stay there, wherever *there* might be. As soon as I had a chance, I would sell my jewels and find my way to Popayán.

We arrived at the outskirts of Palmira at night. Farid had barely spoken to me during the entire carriage ride, which took about four hours. I refused to respond as I was outraged that Baba and Farid hadn't even let me say goodbye to my little siblings, who had been sent to Tía Lidia's house without my knowledge. According to Farid, I was a bad example for Nazira and it would be best if she never knew about this calamity and would not be given the opportunity to ask where I was going to or why.

Apparently, my uncle and aunt had known of a home for girls in trouble, like myself, where we would spend our pregnancy in seclusion and utmost secrecy until we had our babies. What they wouldn't tell me was what would happen to my baby afterward. Would I be forced to give my child up for adoption? Many times during the ride, I was compelled to tell Farid about Martin. He might tell the driver to turn around and take me to Popayán instead, but there was also the possibility that my brother and my father would kill Martin, as furious as they were. And what if Martin had returned to Ecuador instead of continuing his studies in Colombia? In July, he'd been uncertain that his guardian—a Frenchman who'd been his father's neighbor—would follow through with his offer to pay for his university education.

No, the risk was too great. I had to find a way to solve this on my own. Perhaps I should wait to have the baby before I went searching for Martin.

But how would I support my child?

Would Baba welcome me back home or would I be persona non grata for the rest of my existence? Neither Baba nor my brother had explained any details to me.

We stopped by what appeared to be a two-story house surrounded by a grassy field. All I could really see were whitewashed walls illuminated by one tall light post that reminded me of a wide-shouldered man with long arms holding a lamp in each hand.

A woman carrying a gas lamp stepped out of the house, her hair held up in a high bun, her long dark skirt nearly touching the floor. Although the woman's hair was black, there was a thick strand of white hair that extended from her forehead to her bun.

"*Buenas noches*," she said.

As she approached us with a severe expression on her face, I realized I would not only receive scorn from my family for being a single mother—and therefore, a sinner with the same status as a criminal—but from society in general.

"This is where you stay," Farid told me.

"Wait, you're not coming in with me?"

"No."

"You're not going to Bogotá this late, are you?"

"I'm spending the night at a *hostal* and leaving first thing in the morning."

I couldn't ignore my shaking hands anymore. I'd never been away from my family. And with the rain and the woman's surly demeanor, this place felt so uninviting.

"*Entra un momentico, ¿sí?*" I told Farid, my pride out the window as I begged him to come in at least for a moment. I picked up his hand. "It's me, Mila."

He dropped my hand and didn't answer. I took it as a no.

"Will you come see me once in a while?" I said.

"I'd better go before it gets too late."

And just like that, my older brother, the man whom I'd loved and admired more than anybody else, left me alone in an unknown world.

CHAPTER 24

Puri

I didn't know what time it was—or whether it was day or night—when Sor Camila woke me up. I sat up and looked about the room. A sliver of light was filtering through the gap in the curtains. Beside me were the two other nurses who worked the night shift.

Sor Camila stood by my bed, her hands crossed over her midsection.

"Padre José María is here," she said.

I'd yet to meet the parish priest. Apparently, he'd been sick himself and hadn't been able to come see us until he got better. So far, the religious aspect of my disguise had not been too complicated being that we'd been so busy and Sor Camila and I had different schedules, but I knew she expected me to pray and communicate with God at least once a day during the Grand Silence, as she called it, which I mostly used to sit in the small improvised chapel she called "oratory," and analyze all the clues to the puzzle surrounding Martin's disappearance. Good thing I'd been raised Catholic so some of these concepts were not completely foreign to me. Still, I was nervous to meet the priest. Did nuns confess the same way as other mortals did? Or was there some kind of code I needed to learn? I'd been taught some Latin during elementary school, but I'd barely paid any attention and my mother had practically dragged me to mass on Sundays as I'd rather stay home practicing my grandmother's chocolate recipes.

Religion had always been too ethereal for me. For as long as I could remember, I wanted to experience life, not listen to a priest talk about it and then give me a set of rules to live by.

But now I was confronted with the realities of my farce.

I was pretending to be a nun, but I was expected to act like one.

"What time is it?" I said.

"Ten in the morning."

I'd only slept three hours today, but I couldn't complain. This mess was my own doing. I nodded and stood up.

"Sister . . ." Camila said. "I'd like to have a word with you first. I'll wait outside for you to get ready."

I didn't like her tone. Perhaps she suspected I wasn't a nun. Who knew how many mistakes I'd made along the way? There seemed to be so many codes of conduct and expectations. It wasn't just about donning the habit.

Sor Camila was waiting for me in the hall, her expression unreadable.

"Sor Puri, it has come to my attention that you and Mr. Ferreira have been spending time together outside your regular nursing duties." The light shone bright on her face, displaying a perfect complexion. What could have prompted such a beautiful woman to turn to God instead of a man? Perhaps her family had forced her. She might not have had enough of a dowry for a good marriage. "He said you shaved his beard. That is absolutely not in the scope of duties of a Sierva de María. Neither should you engage in idle chat with him. You must continue to observe your Inner Silence, even outside the convent. I'm sure you learned this, *hermana*."

"But his right hand is in a cast. How could he shave himself?"

"You could've asked Perla or any of the other nurses."

I nodded even though her reaction seemed exaggerated to me.

"Mr. Ferreira is a man, a bachelor," she said. "You don't want to feed rumors, do you? A bride of Christ must have exemplary conduct, not to mention what this behavior might be doing to your soul."

I hadn't considered how my innocent exchanges with Lucas might be viewed by a nun, how something as simple as an outfit, or someone's appearance, could change people's expectations of them.

When I disguised myself as a man a few years ago, there had been an entirely different set of expectations. In fact, visiting a brothel and drinking copious amounts of alcohol had been applauded. But to Sor Camila, this was more than an outfit, it was a commitment, it was her life.

"I'm sorry," I said. "I allowed these unusual circumstances to make me more lenient with the rules of conduct."

"I understand, *hermana*. It's not every day that we experience death. But that's when you turn to God and prayer. If this questionable behavior continues, I'm afraid I will have to report you to your Reverend Mother."

"No, please." If she reported me, they would surely discover me—now that I was so close to finding out the truth. I just had to be more cautious with my investigations. I couldn't believe Lucas had told her about me shaving him. What had he been thinking? "You won't have any more complaints about me, Sister."

Cervantes's description of Don Quijote came to mind when I saw Padre José María: an ancient man with an eagle nose, a shrunken face, and a brown cassock that required a rope wrapped twice around his lean waist. His gaunt appearance left no doubt that he'd been ill and that the thirty-minute mule ride from El Paraíso had taken a toll on him.

His poor sandaled feet.

In spite of his exhaustion, he seemed like a kind man. I considered for a moment being truthful in my confession. It might certainly relieve some of the guilt of my deceit, but then I'd be a slave to his reaction. Sure, he was obligated by canonical law to keep my secret but what if my offense was so magnificent than in his outrage, he accused me in front of Sor Camila? My mother always said that once you told a secret to someone, you were at the mercy of the recipient.

Between the priest's sneezes and frequent nose-blowing, I told him about my sins—deceit, lying, jealousy—but didn't give him any details about my wrongdoings. My penance consisted of six Pater Nosters and two Ave Marías, which I planned to follow through, but my good intentions got shattered as I ran into Lucas on my way to the oratory. He was still on crutches, but he'd gotten out of his pajamas and was wearing a casual suit with a tie covered with blue diagonal stripes. When I glanced at him, he flashed his arm at me and smiled. The cast around his wrist had been removed.

The sight of his beardless face made me furious. I hadn't taken him for a tattletale, but that was exactly what he was. He would get a piece of my mind just as soon as we reached the stable.

He struggled to catch up with me, but I didn't offer any assistance. Not that he needed much help anymore. With his free hand, he could maneuver his crutches much better now and was moving faster than ever.

At the stable, I waited for him, arms folded across my chest.

"Why did you tell Sister Camila that I shaved you?"

He caught his breath. "Well, hello to you, too."

I swatted a fly circling my nose.

"I didn't tell her," he said. "She guessed it. And I didn't deny it."

"I got in a lot of trouble because of that. It's the last time I do something nice for you."

"Don't say that." His voice was soft. He reached out for my arm. "You can't help yourself, Puri. You're the kindest person I know."

Puri? Where had he left the *Sor*?

Did he *know*?

Even more worrisome was the colony of ants that seemed to be crawling inside my stomach as I felt his touch. I freed my arm and cleared my throat.

"I'm sure you've met kinder people."

Was I fishing for a compliment?

"Sor Camila or Nurse Perla, for example. They're both sweet."

He laughed. "Sor Camila sweet? Maybe as sweet as a lemon. And I don't know about Perla. I've hardly spoken to her. She's always running around like a busy bee. Neither one of them has ever taken the time to talk to me, much less tend to me. Not that I'm complaining. I understand how erratic it's been around here and I already feel bad for keeping you away from the patients who really need you."

How could I still be angry at him after that? He was such a nice man. In some unexplained way, he reminded me of my late husband.

"I see they took off your cast," I said.

"Farid did. This morning, while you were sleeping."

"I'm glad," I lied. I doubted he would stay after he had fully healed.

"So where are you going anyway?" he said.

I stammered, "P-Padre José María gave me a penance."

"And you have to do it now? It's so rare to see you awake at this hour. I was hoping you would come somewhere with me."

I looked him in the eye. "I am a nun, you know."

I hated lying, but after Sor Camila's admonishment I knew I had to be more careful. My disguise was the only way I could stay here and find Martin. Dead or alive.

"I know exactly where Martin's lady friend is," he said.

Angélica?

My pulse raced. I'd been thinking about her a lot. I still couldn't grasp what Lucas had told me.

"Where? How?"

"I asked Farid. He confirmed that she lost her mind after Martin's disappearance and he took her to an asylum in Cali. He didn't know what else to do with her as she wouldn't tell him where she lived or where she wanted to go."

"But a mental institution? It seems highly insensitive."

"What else could he do? They didn't want to leave her here alone. She was a danger to herself and everybody had to go back to their lives. Since Martin couldn't be found, Farid had to take her somewhere." He looked over his shoulder, lowered his voice. "He said they found Martin after they'd already taken her away. But I thought we could go see her today."

"Today?"

"Well, since you're up and don't start your shift until the evening. We'll take Farid's carriage and be in Cali in an hour."

"And he agreed to lend you his carriage?"

"Of course. I told him I wanted to visit my mother and would be back today."

"And you can drive with your bad leg?"

He feigned seriousness. "Absolutely."

"But what about Sor Camila?"

"She's too busy to worry about your whereabouts every single moment of the day, isn't she?"

Leaving with Lucas might mean Sor Camila would report me to Alba Luz's Reverend Mother, but in order to do that, she would have to go to town and find a telegraph office or a telephone, if they had any in El Paraíso. Would she go through all that trouble when, to her own admission, they were severely understaffed and desperate for a pair of helping hands?

I might not have another opportunity to help Angélica out of her predicament—if, in fact, Martin's blond friend was her—or at the very least come up with a plan. I needed to talk to her. My entire purpose for being here was to find out what happened to Martin, not to be doing penances or nursing patients back to health.

Now that Sor Camila probably thought me asleep, there was no reason for her to go looking for me. She'd already interrupted my sleep once.

"All right. Can you wait here ten minutes?"

He gave me a puzzled look. "Sure. I'll get the horse ready."

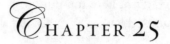

CHAPTER 25

Lucas

Cali, 1924
One year before the gala

The last time I'd seen Martin Sabater, we'd been two scrawny high schoolers with our whole lives ahead of us and a world of opportunities. At least we'd hoped so.

After fourteen years, I still recognized the two cowlicks on the back of his head and the distinctive gait that had been so indisputably his and that so many had tried to imitate in our boarding school days. He'd always had a confident walk—arrogant, if you will—and apparently it hadn't changed. If anything, he now seemed more sure of himself with those wide shoulders pushed back and his head held real high. I called him as he crossed the street toward Banco Hipotecario del Pacífico.

"Sabater!"

From a preoccupied, almost stern expression, his demeanor transformed to one of surprise and obvious satisfaction when he saw me. He flashed a smile, one I remembered well.

"*¡Hermano!*" he said, meeting me in the middle of the cobbled street.

We hugged and he patted my back loudly.

"What are you doing here?" I said. "I thought you moved back to Ecuador."

"I did," he said. "But it's a long story. It'll take a full bottle of *aguardiente* to tell it."

"How about a coffee—for now?" I said, pointing at the hotel cafeteria next to the bank.

He glanced at the bank's entrance before speaking.

"Fine, if there's no other choice."

As we waited for our *tinticos*, Martin was full of questions about everyone we'd ever known at Internado Oro Verde: teachers, classmates, friends, even janitors. Apparently, he'd been back in Colombia for nearly four years, but I was the first person from school he'd run into.

"I don't come to Cali often," he said. "Only for business. All the pleasure is in El Paraíso." He laughed. "Do you still have your photography studio?"

"Unfortunately, yes."

"Why unfortunately?"

I stretched my back. "You know I always wanted to travel the world."

"And? What stopped you?"

"It's called adult responsibilities. Not sure you're familiar with the term." I winked at him to soften my comment. He'd already told me he'd never married and had purchased a cacao *finca* near our old school, but had full freedom to do whatever he pleased. "My mother has diabetes so she needs me nearby," I said. "Plus, her medicine is expensive."

A waiter with a crooked bow tie brought us two miniscule porcelain cups with our espressos.

"What about Farid?" Martin irreverently sprinkled cinnamon in his coffee. "Have you heard from him?"

"I saw him a couple of years ago. As far as I know, he's still in Bogotá, but he mentioned he wanted to come back and open a clinic here, or something like that." I took a sip, burning each and every one of my taste buds. "He could be here already for all I know."

"What about . . . what about his sister Camila? Did she ever marry?"

He didn't know? I'd always suspected he was the guilty party—after what I'd seen at my godfather's hacienda—but I'd never been sure.

"No, she never married," I said, cautiously. "At least not to a human."

He frowned, smirking at the same time. "What the hell are you saying?"

"She married Jesus Christ."

He let out a guffaw. I'd always had a good sense of humor, but Camila's doom wasn't anything to laugh at. Although I was starting to think that Martin didn't believe me. In fact, when he finally shut up, he seemed confused by my reaction.

"What? You're serious?"

"Yes."

"A nun? But she was so beautiful."

"Beauty has nothing to do with it." Although, arguably she might have gotten in trouble because of her good looks. "Frankly, I'm a little surprised you hadn't heard. You seemed *very* close to her during that vacation at my *padrino*'s hacienda."

He fingered his napkin, avoiding my gaze.

"I wrote her some letters from Popayán, but she never answered," he said. "I thought she'd found someone else."

It had taken me years to get over my anger toward Martin. *Years.* And I'd thought I was over it when I saw him crossing the street a few minutes ago, but the nonchalant manner in which he spoke about Camila made me want to beat him again. He *had* to know that the things they'd done at that damn hacienda could've had consequences. Unless she'd had another boyfriend I wasn't aware of, this *someone else* Martin suspected.

"Well, I might as well tell you what I know in case you run into Farid one of these days."

He leaned forward.

"What happened?"

"This is something Farid told me in confidence, in a drunken stupor, years ago, so you can't tell anyone."

"All right." He unbuttoned his white jacket. He had filled up in these last fourteen years. I wondered if I had, too.

"Camila got pregnant the year we graduated from high school."

His lips parted; his color drained. Whatever suspicion I had that Martin had known the truth all along dissipated. He seemed genuinely surprised.

"What? A baby?"

"After she had the child, she didn't want to come back to Cali but insisted that she wanted to enter a convent. They took her all the way to Medellín, where nobody knew about her baby."

"Where's that baby now?"

I shrugged. "Farid said they gave it up for adoption."

Martin sat still for a long time, his face a kaleidoscope of emotions. He removed an El Sol cigarette from his front pocket and lit it, his hands trembling slightly.

"I can't believe you told me something like this over coffee. We should've gone to a *cantina* like I suggested."

I wasn't listening. I wanted to ask him what I've been wondering all these years.

"Martin, is there *any* possibility that this child could be yours?"

Holding the cigarette with his lips, he removed a handkerchief from his inside pocket and brought it to his forehead. He was sweating. Sure, it was a warm day, but this had nothing to do with the climate.

"Yes," was all he said.

"You know Farid is going to kill you when he finds out it was you." And I wasn't throwing the word "kill" lightly.

"Yes." He took a long drag of smoke. "I know."

CHAPTER 26

Lucas

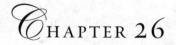

A woman in peach chiffon cautiously approached me.

I could barely recognize Sor Puri without the habit. She wore a tea-length, short-sleeve dress with a tier skirt. A matching white bell hat with a coral bow covered her bob. The color suited her. She looked younger, vibrant.

She kept glancing behind her shoulder as she approached me and the cabriolet.

I was about to give her a compliment but I didn't want her to think I was flirting. I continued petting Farid's horse.

"Nice carriage," she said, pointing at its shiny red wheels.

"Farid got it recently," I said, unable to come up with anything brilliant to add, but at least I had said something, unlike those painful years when I couldn't speak to a pretty girl. It turned out Sor Puri had some curves underneath her dull habit.

I offered my hand to help her climb into the back seat but she requested to go in the front with me.

"I'm not some kind of queen to go in the back, you know?" she said.

I took her gloved hand and helped her up. We sat side by side and I did my best not to stare.

"We should hurry before someone sees me," she said.

"Is that why you're wearing . . . that?"

"Yes. I don't want anyone to tell Sor Camila they saw a nun leaving. Now, will you hurry, please?"

I took hold of the harnesses' lines and steered the horse down the road.

Once the hacienda was out of sight, she turned back to the front, setting her hands on her lap. She let out a long breath.

"Calm down. She's not going to find out. She doesn't have time to care about what you do all day."

She nodded.

"You see that trail?" I said, pointing at a dirt road to our left. "It leads to our old boarding school."

"Is it still open?"

"Yes. In spite of Martin's disappearance, Farid managed to collect quite a bit of money that night."

"It must have been an excellent school for all of you to go through so much trouble."

"It was. We excelled in academics over our peers, but the priests also taught us several useful skills like horseback riding, carpentry, welding. I wish they'd taught us photography because I had a hard time learning my father's profession after he passed away."

"I would love to see the process in the darkroom. The idea of taking an image from life and sealing it on a piece of paper is magical. In an odd way, it reminds me of the process of turning hard cacao beans into a smooth delicacy. The capacity of certain things to transform into something completely different never ceases to amaze me."

"You seem to know a lot about chocolate."

She licked her lower lip. "Yes, my grandmother. Well, she was a chocolate connoisseur. So, how did you learn your father's trade?"

"To be honest, I don't know how I learned. I guess I remembered more than I thought from watching my father throughout the years. My mother also helped. She had some recollection of what chemicals were needed in the darkroom and in what order to use them. But I can tell you that I ruined a lot of film and paper in the process of developing photos. And, of course, I made a lot of people angry when they had to come again for a reshoot. My interaction with clients was not the smoothest, especially at the beginning."

"How so?"

We turned into a winding trail. The abundant vegetation covering the hill at the side of the road always made me think of a gigantic furry animal lying down—a green bear removed from a fantastic fable. Had it only been two weeks since I came to the hospital's opening ceremony?

It seemed like it had been longer than that.

"When my father died and left me the business, I was bitter as all I ever wanted was to play my guitar and see the world. On a subconscious level, I suppose, I wanted to turn off all clients so I would have an excuse to close the business. I remember this one lady who complained that she didn't look good in a portrait and I told her '*Señora*, the camera doesn't lie.'"

I loved the sound of Sor Puri's laugh.

"I was such an idiot," I said. "But fortunately, my mother was there with her endless kindness, patience, and *don de gentes*. So, people kept coming back. At first, it was only her clients. She's a seamstress so she would offer them the opportunity to have their photos taken with their new outfits. It was a novel idea that people loved."

"She sounds like a wonderful person."

I released the pressure on the leather rein and the horse turned into another curve.

"She's a born salesman," I said. "She taught me how to treat customers and I eventually learned to enjoy my work. The daily interactions with people, the challenge of getting the perfect shot, even the smell of chemicals became so familiar it felt right after a while."

"Do you ever take photos of places or landscapes?"

"Not really."

"That could be an opportunity for you to travel while doing your work, since that's what you've always wanted. I suppose there might be someone who would pay for those kinds of photographs."

Her head was tilted sideways and a soft shadow caressed her jawline and neck. A strand of chestnut hair rested on her cheek. I felt compelled to take her photograph.

"I've never thought of that before," I said.

Not a lot more was said during the next hour. I could tell she was nervous, like the day I'd met her. What connection did she have with Martin's friend? What connection did she have with *him*? I knew there was a lot she was not telling me.

I was nervous myself at what I would encounter in my hometown. I'd been fretting about it for days. This Angélica wasn't the only reason I wanted to come home.

As we reached the city, two- and three-story brick buildings materialized on either side of us, some more cracked than others. But still, they had preserved their colonial beauty. Most of the balconies still stood as well as the terracotta rooftops. Men in hats walked along the cobblestone streets and a few Model Ts passed us by as we headed toward Puente Ortiz, the bridge that overlooked the Río Cali. Sor Puri mentioned something about a river in her hometown, the Guadalquivir and the Puente de Triana, which she said was the oldest bridge in Sevilla.

I gasped when I saw the destruction before my eyes.

"*Ave María.*"

In front of us stood a mountain of rubble that had been, not long ago, the oldest church in Cali. All that was left now was debris, particularly piles of *bahareque* sticks—the material that had once conformed the walls of what we called La Ermita de Nuestra Señora de la Soledad y del Señor del Río.

"I can't believe it's gone," I said. "I came here so many times with my mother. I guess not even San Emigdio could save this one."

"San Emigdio?"

I turned to her, perplexed.

"The Italian saint of earthquakes. I thought you of all people would know that, *hermana*."

"Well, Lucas, the truth is . . ."

She swallowed, avoided my eyes.

"I-I wasn't the best of novices," she stuttered. "I always got the saints mixed up."

She faced the ruins of the church.

I resumed our ride until we reached a cluster of looming palm trees. Behind them, was the bell tower of La Catedral de San Pedro Apóstol.

At least the cathedral was still standing.

We circled the plaza, its brilliant metal fence restraining robust trees bursting with mangoes and pomegranates. In one of those *carbonero* trees I'd once carved Camila's initials.

I stopped the cabriolet by our monumental cathedral, which had also suffered significant damage—but not quite as bad as La Ermita. The side tower was somewhat skewed and the clock tower marked 6:37.

"The time when the tragedy began," I said, pointing at the main building. "There were four spires on top of the façade."

Only one remained.

The curb leading to the church's entrance held a bed of rubble—pieces of the spires.

A deep sadness took over me. Once again, I was confronted with the futility and absurdity of life.

CHAPTER 27

Puri

The smooth fabric of Perla's borrowed dress clung to my moist back. Borrowed without her consent, that is. I'd been trying my best to keep my composure as we approached the bleached wall surrounding the property where Angélica had been living for the last few months. It wasn't tall, so we could see the extensive property below, abundant with trees. Beyond the shrubbery, there were three or four visible buildings with red roofs. Apparently, there was no significant earthquake damage other than a diagonal crack across the main entrance.

As Lucas rang the doorbell, I started hyperventilating. I didn't know what to expect, in what state I was going to find Angélica.

Could it *really* be her?

The porter was a short woman holding a ring full of keys. She was so short I first thought she was a child. She seemed hesitant to let us in when we asked to see Angélica de Lafont. She said we needed authorization to go inside. After Lucas told her I was a nun, a Sierva de María, her demeanor changed and she kissed my hand. She said she would always be grateful to the nuns because one of them had taken care of her father during his last days.

"*Pase, hermana,*" she told me, oblivious to Lucas.

We crossed a long flagstone path flanked by grass and ruby begonias all the way to a garden behind one of the buildings.

Angélica—it was truly her—sat on a bench, her gaze lost in a gray sparrowhawk resting in the bushes in front of her. A few other patients walked the trails or seemed to be fascinated with the butterflies flying about.

I got a sense that they didn't receive enough attention.

Angélica's blond hair had grown and sat in waves over her shoulders. Her porcelain face was washed-out. Where she'd always applied rouge and lipstick, there was now a pale transparency that reminded me of the European friends I had left behind years ago. She wore a simple, loose-fitting beige gown that was probably made of cotton or percale, not the fancy silks and satins she owned in Vinces.

"It might be better if you let me talk to her first," I told Lucas. "She may get nervous if she sees you."

He nodded and kept his distance while I approached her. She didn't seem to notice, much less recognize me.

"*Hola*, Angélica," I said, sitting next to her.

My sister and I had never been close. For one, we'd met as adults, but the two of us were too similar. Those similarities made us repel each other at times. We were both stubborn, ambitious, driven, somewhat dominant.

And we had both loved Martin.

"Remember me?"

Her mouth was moving but no sounds came out. It seemed like she might be singing. Or repeating the same words over and over again.

"It's me, Puri."

I looked over my shoulder, wondering if Lucas could hear me. But he seemed distracted enough with an old man pacing in circles around him, repeating some sort of mantra.

"Angélica?"

Was she speaking French?

She'd been married to a Frenchman for years. And our father

had been French, so it wouldn't be too strange. The last I'd heard from her and her husband they'd been traveling in Europe with the money from the sale of our father's hacienda.

"Where's Laurent?" I said, referring to her husband.

She whispered the name ever so quietly.

I needed to contact him and tell him Angélica was here. He might be worried. But how could I find him? I had no idea where he lived. If not him, then I needed to take Angélica back to Ecuador, to our siblings, Catalina and Alberto.

I couldn't just leave her here.

It was painful to watch her like this.

"And Ramona?" I said, mentioning her beloved cockatoo. "Did you leave her with Laurent?" My sister loved her pet so much she couldn't part with her and had taken her to Europe years ago.

She touched her own shoulder, where Ramona used to perch, but didn't answer.

I held her hands between mine. I didn't know how to reach her. All I could do was follow my instinct and do my best. People at the hospital had been comfortable confiding in me. I leaned forward.

"Angélica, *hermanita*, I want to help you."

This was the first time I'd called her "sister." Just uttering the word aloud did something to my insides. It brought a tenderness I'd only experienced toward my son.

She looked at me for the first time. Her eyes narrowed.

"Do you know where you are?" I said.

She stopped her mumbling.

"Martin," she said.

"Yes, you came to see him. You're in Colombia."

"Martin," Angélica repeated.

"Do you know what happened to him?"

Her eyes filled up with tears. I braced myself for the possibility of an outburst like the one Lucas had mentioned, but Angélica looked more confused than anything.

"They took him," she said.

"*They?* Who are *they?*"

She shook her head.

I squeezed her hands. "It's all right, *hermana*. We'll find him. Just tell me who took him."

She started shaking her head.

"It's all right, Angélica, it's all right. We'll find him."

"Puri?"

"Yes. It's me."

For the first time I saw an inkling of lucidity. "The wagon. Where is it?"

"What wagon?" I said.

"They took him in it. There was a gunshot. He fell down. Behind the trees. I looked and looked but couldn't find him. Then another gunshot." She placed both hands over her ears and shook her head. "Where is he? It was so dark. I looked everywhere."

She was crying now. I hugged her.

"You have to help him," she said between sobs. "Don't let them hurt him."

"It's all right, Angélica. I'm going to find him and I'm taking you back home."

In my arms, she seemed to calm down. But she didn't say anything else. A male nurse snuck behind us.

"Who let you in?" He was a giant. "You can't be here."

"I'm her sister." I stood up. "I'm taking her with me."

The man extended a hand in front of me and hoisted Angélica up by the arm. "I can't let you do that. Not without the director's permission and he's not here."

"But there's nothing wrong with her!" I said. "She's just distraught."

Lucas approached us.

"I'm sorry, *señora*," the man said, "but you can't take a patient just because you want to. She was brought by Dr. Mansur himself."

"When can we speak to the director?" Lucas said in a rational tone.

I could see Angélica was getting upset. "Let go of me!" She was trying to hit the nurse with her free hand. He grabbed both of her wrists.

"Hey, you're hurting her," Lucas said.

I quickly assessed if Lucas and I could take the nurse down. Lucas with his crutches and me with Perla's airy dress and pump shoes—it didn't seem likely.

Angélica bit the nurse's arm. He groaned and dragged her toward the building.

"You both have to leave! Now!" he said, struggling with Angélica and the door.

I tried to follow him inside, but Lucas held my arm.

"It's not going to work," he said.

He was right, but I was still furious. "I'll be back for you, Angélica!" I said as she gave me one last glance before the nurse shut the door.

Back on the carriage, I couldn't fight the feeling that I'd done something wrong. I'd disturbed Angélica's nerves at a time when she was too fragile.

"I want to come back for her," I said. "She doesn't belong here, Lucas. I can't believe it's so easy to commit someone. She would be much better at home, with her family."

"I agree. They commit people for the stupidest reasons."

"Like?"

"Melancholia, hysteria, any kind of"—he glanced at me for a split second—"problem of a sexual nature."

I flattened the creases on Perla's skirt.

"Sorry," he said. "I didn't mean to offend you."

He was a shy man, this Lucas, despite his little flirtations. He didn't seem entirely comfortable around women. Not like Martin had been.

"I'm not as easily offended as you think," I said.

A faint dimple on his cheek told me he was holding back a smile.

I glanced back at the place where Angélica was staying—hopefully not for long—as it got smaller in the distance. Would they commit a woman for pretending to be someone else?

I turned to Lucas. "Did you hear what Angélica said about Martin? She thinks someone shot him and took his body away."

"Yes, I heard."

Had he heard the *entire* conversation? "We need to find Martin's grave."

That was the only way we could see if Martin was truly dead.

"Farid said he's at the cemetery in El Paraíso."

"We have to go."

"Not today. We don't have time."

I could insist, but I didn't want to annoy him or have him distrust me more. I'd been making one mistake after another, starting with the mysterious Italian saint *he* had to teach me about.

"Lucas, why are you helping me?"

"Martin was my friend, too. I also want to know what happened to him. I'd always thought the way he disappeared, his death if you will, had been strange, and after you mentioned the forged signature on his will, well, I had to know."

"Do you think Farid is . . . capable of hurting Martin?"

He was, after all, the one who benefitted the most with Martin's disappearance. That would also explain why he'd brought Angélica, his only witness, to this awful place. But I didn't voice all my concerns. Farid was a good friend of Lucas's, much closer to him than me and his loyalty may lay with him.

Lucas shrugged. "Farid and I have been apart for years. The Farid I knew—the young man from my high school years—had a dark side, but I don't know if he would go as far as killing someone."

The sound of drums came from a nearby house. A trumpet followed. We turned toward the music as we drove by. Through an open window, we saw a couple dancing.

"That's what I like about my people," Lucas said. "In spite of the tragedy, they still have a reason to celebrate."

"To celebrate what?"

"That they're still alive."

Why did he sound so melancholic, then? I sat with his words for a moment. The dancers were right. While there was life, there was hope. For Angélica. For all of us.

"Now, I have to ask you something," he said.

"What?"

"Are you and Angélica sisters?"

I took a deep breath. "Yes."

"But I thought you said your sister was in Ecuador and her name was Catalina."

"She's my other sister."

He brought a hand to his chest. "Good. For a minute there, I thought you wanted me to marry this lady."

"If you could've seen Angélica before, you wouldn't speak like this. She's the shadow of what she once was. Whatever she saw that night traumatized her." After finding all the letters she'd written to Martin, I had no doubt that he was an obsession for her— more so than for me. "Catalina is our youngest sister. I only met my sisters a few years ago, but that's a different story. Like I said, I want to help Angélica. I want to come back for her and take her to Vinces. It feels wrong to leave her here alone."

"Well, there's not a lot you can do for her now. Unless you think that taking her to a growing epidemic is a good idea."

"It's not. But before I go back to . . . the convent, I'll come for her."

"I don't understand," he said.

"What?"

"What does Martin do to women? You also hinted that you'd had some kind of relationship with him."

"I'd rather not talk about it," I said. "If you don't mind."

He didn't push the subject any further, but his words kept ringing in my ears.

What *did* Martin do to women? How to explain the effect he'd had on me all those years ago?

He was a man whose entire attention was devoted to the woman he had in front of him. He listened, *really* listened, more than any other man I'd ever known. He would look at you as though you were the most interesting, the most beautiful creature he'd ever encountered, and he couldn't believe his luck at having found you. There was no one as important, as intelligent as you. You were special for the first time in your life. So, you chased that feeling again and again because you wanted to feel good about yourself and only he could do that. It wasn't that he himself was a fascinating person, or that he did marvelous things no one else did, though he had a confidence about himself, a certainty of what he wanted in life that was appealing. But mostly, it was that you loved who you became when you were with him.

With Martin I'd felt truly accepted. He'd been a kindred spirit.

But my visit to Angélica made one thing absolutely clear. If Martin was alive, whatever notions I had had to raise our son together—even if I didn't want to admit it to myself or to anyone else—a relationship between us was absolutely impossible. I could never go back to the man who had shattered my sister's sanity.

An acute pain extended throughout my chest as I realized my true motivation, my *real* reasons for this reckless search. I had been stupidly hoping that, one day, Martin would meet my son and that there might be a future for us. Deep down, I'd always known I could find another cacao bean vendor, but I wasn't sure I could ever find another partner.

"There's somewhere I need to go," Lucas said, interrupting my turbulent thoughts. "It'll be quick, but it's important."

CHAPTER 28

Puri

Lucas stopped the carriage by a mint corner house. The balconies on the second level were bursting with pots of purple orchids and sporadic palm trees adorned the quaint street. He didn't descend right away or offer any explanations.

After a moment, he finally turned to me.

"This is my mother's house. I wanted to see if it was still in one piece."

After seeing some of the earthquake damage around the city, I couldn't blame him.

"Of course," I said. "I can wait for you here while you visit her."

"No," he said, shaking his head. But there was something else he wasn't saying. "I don't have to go inside. I just wanted to make sure it was fine."

"But of course you have to go inside. You probably haven't seen her in days. Don't worry about me. If I'm late for my shift, so be it."

"It's not that," he said. "I don't know if it's a good idea. We're not on the best of terms."

I wanted to ask him why, but he'd already complained that I asked too many questions. For once I bit my tongue. After a couple of minutes, he turned to me.

"Do you want to meet her?"

"I'd love to."

It surprised me that he rang the doorbell. Wouldn't he have a key to his own house? But that was not the only surprise. Lucas's mother, whom he introduced as Doña Matilde, looked absolutely nothing like him.

Her curly hair, which at some point must have been black, now resembled a cotton ball covering her skull. Her skin was dark, which created an interesting contrast with her hair, and she was tiny.

Her eyes filled with tears as soon as she saw Lucas.

"*Mijo*." She opened the door wide and gasped at the sight of his crutches. "What happened to you?"

"I'm fine," he said. Gone was the kindness and playful attitude he always displayed toward women. "I fell. That's all."

"During the earthquake?"

"Yes."

"I've been so worried about you."

That was it. Nothing else was said for an awkward moment. She attempted to hug him, but he remained stiff, his knuckles white from squeezing the grip on both crutches. Detangling himself from her arms, he introduced me as Sor Puri.

Upon learning I was a nun, she wiped her hands with her apron and kissed my hand. To say I was uncomfortable didn't even begin to describe my feelings. Why did people always want to kiss the hands of the religious?

"We can't stay long," Lucas said, as if the moment wasn't tense enough. "I just wanted to make sure you were all right."

"At least have a *champús* or a *jugo de naranja*."

"The juice sounds great," I said before Lucas could decline. Not only was I thirsty and hot, but I felt sorry for the woman. There was no question that something unpleasant had happened between them. Perhaps that was why Lucas had brought me along, to avoid being alone with her.

Inside was a set of stairs and a closed door to our right. Lucas said that was the photo studio and the living quarters were upstairs. If we weren't so pressed for time, I would've asked to see the darkroom.

He refused my help to climb the staircase and, with obvious effort, followed us to the second story.

The parlor was cozy and bright. Flower arrangements and vibrant rugs and tapestries abounded. Even the sofa's upholstery and the wallpaper were filled with vines and roses.

"Beautiful home," I said.

Doña Matilde disappeared through a swinging door, while Lucas and I settled on one of the couches. He dried the palms of his hands on his trousers and looked about the room as if seeing it for the first time.

Lucas's mom came back with three glasses of orange juice and something to eat.

"I'd just fried some *yuquitas*," she said, placing the bowl of what appeared to be fried potatoes in front of us. "They're Lucas's favorite."

I picked one. "What did you say this was?"

"*Yuca*," she repeated. "It's a tuber. Try it. I didn't have time to make the sauce, though."

I gave it a bite. It was exquisite—a new delicacy in the infinite collection of flavors and smells I was discovering during my travels. It tasted a lot like a potato with a rougher texture. To break the silence, I inquired about the sauce she mentioned.

"It's called *hogao*."

"*Hogao?*" I repeated, watching Lucas in an effort to engage him in conversation.

But Lucas found his nails more interesting.

"Yes, like *ahogado*," she said bringing her hands to her throat as if choking herself. "It's made out of tomato, onion, garlic, cumin."

"Sounds delicious."

"I can make it in just a few minutes." She stood up.

"No," Lucas said. "We have to leave soon."

Doña Matilde sat down cautiously and placed her hands on her lap, her blue tubular skirt hugging her wide thighs.

"Have one, *mijito*," she said.

"I'm not hungry."

I barely had time to finish my own *yuca* when Lucas awkwardly announced that it was time for us to head back to the hacienda as my nursing shift would start soon.

Along the wall down the stairs to the front door were dozens of black-and-white portraits, but I hardly had an opportunity to glance at them as Lucas hopped down in haste, swinging his leg on his way down.

Outside, Doña Matilde managed to get another sentence out.

"When are you coming back?"

Lucas responded by donning his hat and helping me onto the carriage.

"Have a nice evening, Doña Matilde," he said, climbing on the seat next to me and holding on to the horse's reins.

"Thank you for the juice and the *yucas*!" I said as the carriage started to move. "It was nice meeting you!"

I received no response as the woman simply brought a handkerchief to her eyes. As we turned into the road that would take us back to the hacienda, I couldn't hold my tongue any longer.

"Would you care to explain what that was all about?"

He kept his gaze on the road as the houses became scarce and the vegetation more pronounced. "I figured you would ask. Although I was hoping you'd learned discretion in the convent."

"Well, I didn't," I said. "Why are you so mean to your mother?"

He sighed. "I guess I have no choice in this matter?"

"No, you don't." I crossed my arms over my chest. "You have one hour to explain."

He groaned.

CHAPTER 29

Lucas

February 1925
One week before the gala

Even though this was my first time at Martin's hacienda, I had an eerie feeling that I'd been here before. The *comino crespo* columns at the entrance were striking, not just because of their intricate design, but they were the first detail in this place to give me a sense of déjà vu. I knew I had seen that porch before, but I'd never been here—*had* I?

As we sat in the courtyard, surrounded by the chirping of canaries camouflaged in nearby trees and the burble of the water fountain, we relished the pieces of cheese Doña Tuli had brought us—along with more than enough rolls of *pandebono*. These appetizers, of course, couldn't be enjoyed without a bottle of *aguardiente* in front of us.

Martin was talking about how he came to find out that this property was for sale. He mentioned running into the previous owner in El Paraíso.

"Who?" I said. I'd barely been listening. I'd been racking my brain for an answer as to why this place was so familiar.

"Iván Contreras. Remember him? His wife, Doña María Belén, was always at our school."

Suddenly everything fit into place.

The woman in the photo; the one standing by the entrance with the baby girl—it was her. But why had I found her photograph tucked inside my father's bible shortly after he passed away? I'd never shown it to my mother—I didn't think it would be a grand plan to torment her with the thought that her husband may have had a mistress or a long-lost love.

I hadn't really recognized Mrs. Contreras in the photo because she'd been so young, but when I pictured the woman watching me at all times—even at my father's funeral—I'd realized it was the same person. The same round eyes looking a little bit scared, a little melancholic, the pointy chin, the placid, reluctant smile.

Of course it was her.

"Yes, I remember them," I said. "She was always at school for the Christmas musical. Even for the rehearsals."

Our school organized an annual charity fundraiser every Christmas. I sang *villancicos* in the choir, but I'd been trying to convince Father Rafael, the music instructor, to let us organize a dance with the girls from the region and allow me to play my guitar.

Invariably, he said no. It would be highly inappropriate for a religious school to sponsor such a risqué activity.

"I never saw the wife during our negotiations," Martin said, "even though I came a few times to look at the property." He refilled my glass. "You know, something odd happened shortly after I moved here."

I leaned forward, ignoring the drink.

"A woman about our age came to see me. Her name was Olivia, I think. She said she'd grown up here with her mother and stepfather, but she'd married young and moved to Pasto with her husband." Martin paused, staring at the bottle with appreciation.

If María Belén was the woman in the photo, then Olivia must be the baby she was holding.

"She said that one time she came to visit, but her mother was gone. Her stepfather, who'd always been stern and cold toward her, told her that María Belén had left him for another man. Olivia didn't believe him. She said it was completely out of character for her mother to do that, but when she expressed her doubts to her stepfather, he kicked her out and never let her in again. When she'd heard the old man had sold the place, she decided to come."

"What for?"

"She wanted to look around, to see if there was anything that might give her an answer about her mother's whereabouts since Olivia never heard from her again. Don Iván hadn't finished moving out yet and there were still some boxes and bookcases here, which he'd promised to pick up soon." He squinted at the recollection in typical Martin fashion. "Olivia asked to see his things and I couldn't say no."

"And?"

"She found a locket. She said it had belonged to her mother and she would've never left without it. Apparently, she never removed it from her neck, even at nighttime."

"Did you see what was in the locket?"

"Two baby photos of a boy and a girl."

"Who was the boy?" I asked, a little too eagerly.

"Olivia didn't know, but she was certain she was the girl in the photo. She said her mother had never let her open it."

I swallowed. "Is it here?"

"No, Olivia took it. It was the only keepsake she had of her mother."

"What else was in the box?"

"I don't know—papers, books, I didn't look."

"Is the box still here?"

"Contreras sent an employee once to take some of the boxes, but I don't know if he took everything. I suppose he did. I didn't really look." Martin stretched out his arms behind his head. "Maybe I'll invite Don Iván to the gala next week."

"I think that's a great idea," I said, nestling my drink. "I'll bring my camera."

* * *

When I got back to Cali, I went directly to my studio and re-moved María Belén's photo from the desk drawer, where I'd kept it for years. I found my mother in her sewing room.

"Lucas, *mi amor*, how was your visit with Martin?"

"Fine," I said, not in the mood to elaborate.

Her brow furrowed. "Are you hungry? I made *ajiaco*."

"No, thank you," I said, placing the photo on the sewing machine, right next to her hand. "Who is this woman?"

She donned her spectacles and examined the image. Something changed in her expression. I believe she turned a shade lighter. She removed the glasses and set the photo down.

"I don't know."

"It was inside Papá's bible."

She got up. "How would I know? He had photos of everyone in this town." She dried her hands on her skirt, scrunched up her hair. "You want some *ajiaco*? I'm hungry."

"I already said no. Please tell me who she is."

She headed for the door. I followed her all the way to the kitchen.

"Mamá, you can't ignore me all day."

She went directly to the pot of chicken soup and swirled it with a wooden spoon. Her hand shook almost imperceptibly.

During my ride back to Cali, I'd remembered something else. I'd seen my father once talking to María Belén in one of the school gardens. What struck me as odd was that it looked like they were arguing. In the shortsightedness and innocence of my seventeen years of age, I'd assumed they were discussing my petition for a school dance. My father had agreed with me and saw no harm in the idea, but the rumor was that some members of the school board opposed it, not to mention the majority of the Salesian brothers. Now I thought their discussion was of a more personal nature.

"Who is she?" I said aloud.

My mother turned, eyes filled with tears. "I'm sorry, Lucas. I

should've told you a long time ago, but"—her lower lip trembled—
"I couldn't."

"Well, tell me now. Is she my *real* mother?"

She didn't deny it. When Martin told me about the baby boy
in the locket, I'd immediately wondered if it was me. That would
explain so many things, including why Doña Matilde and I looked
nothing like each other. I didn't look anything like my father, either.

"Am I adopted?"

"Not exactly," she said, avoiding my eyes. She was stirring the
ajiaco so much the chicken was coming apart.

"Goyo is your father, but María Belén is your mother."

I sat on a nearby stool.

"And I have a sister."

"Yes. Your twin."

The realization that I was not an only child and that I had a sib-
ling was just as shocking to me as finding out that Doña Matilde
de Ferreira, the town seamstress, beloved by all who knew her,
was not really my biological mother. Growing up, I'd wanted a sib-
ling so badly. My parents had always been too busy with work to
give me any attention. I always believed that was why they sent
me to a boarding school. I'd never been convinced that their only
purpose was to give me the "best education possible."

"It's my fault," she said. "I'm somewhat relieved you figured it
out already. It's been weighing on my conscience for thirty-three
years."

"Would you care to explain?" I said.

She made the sign of the cross, asking the Holy Spirit for courage to speak.

"My mother sewed clothes for María Belén's family. Since they
were always at my house with new fabrics, María Belén and I became friends. Her mom was compulsive about fashion and my
mother had the talent and skill to do whatever this lady pleased."

She avoided facing me as she peeled and sliced an avocado for
the *ajiaco*.

"She met your father for her *fiesta de quince años*. He was five years older than María Belén and had saved enough money for a camera and was starting his own business. He took her photo and, apparently, they felt an immediate attraction." Matilde nearly cut her finger off.

"Watch out!" I said.

She froze her hand in midair.

"Give me that." I removed the knife from her hand.

"*Carajo*, I ruined the *aguacate*," she said. She'd chopped it in tiny little pieces, too small to swim in the broth without sinking to the bottom of the bowl.

"Just let it be." I helped her to the kitchen table.

Who cared about avocadoes at a time like this?

"María Belén and Goyo saw each other in secret for nearly two years. I was her confidante, but I secretly liked your father. I always had." She covered her eyes.

My head suddenly felt too heavy.

"I . . . I admit I was angry when she told me about Goyo because I'd known him for years and he'd never paid me any attention. The truth is I was jealous and the feeling only intensified with time as I'd never had an admirer of my own. When she confided in me that she was expecting, I couldn't hold it in when her mother questioned me about María Belén. She'd noticed her daughter was acting strange and wanted to know why. I told her about Goyo with the condition that she wouldn't tell María Belén I'd disclosed her secret. María Belén's mom agreed and acted as though she'd figured it out on her own."

I was getting that numb feeling I always got when confronted with bad news. The last time had been when my father died.

"I was elated when María Belén told me her parents had found her a rich man to marry: Don Iván Contreras. He was a widower and had been looking for a wife for quite some time. He was enthralled with María Belén's beauty, so much that he didn't mind that she was expecting another man's child. Your mother wanted to marry Goyo and he did, too, but her family didn't want her to marry a poor photographer without a future."

She was already calling her "my mother," not realizing that I still had to process the sharp words she was saying.

"Goyo was devastated when María Belén got married. And I was there all along, offering him a shoulder to cry on." She was speaking faster now. "When María Belén delivered two babies, instead of one, Mr. Contreras was furious. He said he'd only agreed to one and this was too much. So María Belén sent for Goyo and asked him to take the boy as Mr. Contreras was adamant about not raising another man's son; a girl, he could tolerate."

"And you kindly offered to help him raise me."

"Well, yes. By then, we'd gotten close and Goyo, he needed a woman to help him with the baby as his parents had too many children and not the resources or desire to feed one more mouth."

"I suppose I should thank you."

She was sobbing openly now. "I'm sorry, Lucas. I have loved you like a son."

I stared in silence. I couldn't believe she'd lied for so long. Had she orchestrated this? It sounded like she did by telling María Belén's mother about the pregnancy. What would've happened if she hadn't told her? Would things still turn the way they had?

"But you shouldn't think ill of María Belén." She dried her nose with the back of her hand. "She was always interested in you. Goyo sent her photographs of you every year, and then she offered to pay for your boarding school. She was adamant about it. She wanted you to have the best education."

"I suppose that mitigated her guilt."

Matilde's eyes were swollen, her nose red. "Do you hate me?"

"Of course not," I said, curtly.

How could I? She'd raised me. But I had to admit I was furious. Electricity seemed to be running up and down my legs at full speed. I couldn't sit still anymore. I didn't want to be in Matilde's presence anymore.

"I need to be alone," I said, standing. "For a while."

I didn't know what bothered me more: the deceit, the rejection, not growing up with my biological mother, or how easily she'd given me away and picked this shadowy sister. Did she think that by donating money to the school I attended, she would find atonement for her wrongdoings?

"Wait, Lucas. Don't leave like that. At least have something to eat."

I was out of the door before she finished her sentence.

CHAPTER 30

Puri

I walked in a specter-like state all night. I hadn't been able to stop thinking about Lucas's story and how he'd opened himself to me, how he'd shared those intimate and painful details that had been tormenting him for months. The only thing I'd been able to do was squeeze his hand. He'd interlaced his fingers with mine and confessed that a weight had been lifted off his shoulders after sharing his thoughts out loud. We'd stayed like that for a moment and then he'd let go of my hand and grabbed the reins to continue with our trip.

What was happening to me? Lucas was making me feel things I hadn't in years. Long forgotten sensations—tingling in my stomach, racing heartbeat, sudden euphoria—were all emerging. Lucas had a vulnerability, a tenderness that Martin never had. Neither had Cristóbal. But Lucas thought he was confessing to a nun. What would he think of me if he knew the truth? I didn't even want to think about it.

I could barely keep my eyes open, but I couldn't let anyone notice my exhaustion after the trip to Cali. Fortunately, tonight was a quiet night. The only perceptible noises were the grumblings of the house—windows rattling, floors creaking—as if the materials holding the structure together were stretching and restoring itself now that its inhabitants were resting.

After making sure that all the patients' bags had enough saline solution and the tubes in their IVs were free of any obstruction, I settled in the corner of the room. The soft breeze pleasantly filtered through one of the open windows and I started dozing off.

A noise in the courtyard interrupted my borrowed sleep. I wasn't sure what awoke me. Was it a woman singing or had it been a scream?

I rushed outside, bypassing beds and emaciated patients.

Sitting by the fountain was Farid's wife in a pajama negligée made out of the finest crépe de Chine in a jade-and-purple pattern. Amira wasn't singing or screaming, she was sobbing.

She flinched when she saw me, but remained still.

"Do you need anything?"

"A friend."

I sat by her side. "What about your family?"

"Farid is not my family. The people I trust are in Bogotá." The aroma of magnolia wafted through the air. "The nights are the worst. At least during the day, I can take walks and pretend I'm somewhere else."

"Why doesn't your husband let you go?"

She let out a scoff.

"Because he wants to control me."

I didn't know what to say. One thing I had learned about the nun's habit was that it excused you from having to fill in uncomfortable silences. In fact, silence and contemplation were expected and praised. Sometimes people opened up more when I just listened.

When Amira's tears dried up, I spoke again.

"Did you have an opportunity to speak to Padre José María today? He might have been able to offer some advice for your predicament."

She shook her head. "I don't like talking to priests. In my experience, they don't really care about what you have to say. They're just ready to give you your penance and move on to the next person. Besides, I don't want to shock them with my sins."

"I don't think they're easily shocked. They've probably heard it all."

"But how does praying help me? I need someone to convince my husband to set me free."

In the dim light coming from one of the gas lamps hanging from the walls, I could see her moist eyelashes, so thick and long, and her reddened nose. I wondered what it would be like to be your husband's prisoner. I'd never experienced anything like that. My husband Cristóbal had been kind and accommodating. I'd been lucky to have him.

"If anything, I'd rather talk to you," she said. "At least you're a woman. You can understand."

There was so much I wanted to ask, but I just sat there, watching her. If I hadn't been so sleep-deprived, I might have been more strategic and talkative, but I could barely hold my head up.

"You asked why my husband keeps me here against my will and the truth is he doesn't trust me." She sniffed. "And I don't blame him."

The water gurgling behind us offered a soothing effect, at least to me. An owl sat on the rooftop covering the upstairs bedrooms.

"The night of the fundraiser gala Farid found out that I'd been unfaithful."

Her confession was enough to bring me back from my daze. *Madre mía*, was Amira another one of Martin's conquests?

"I'd lived in Bogotá all my life, but over a year ago, we moved to Cali. Farid wanted to be close to his father and younger brother. He wanted to open his own clinic. Actually, he wanted a hospital. He's so damn ambitious. But all he could afford was a small office and he hired Perla as his assistant. In the mornings, he worked at Clínica Garcés and in the afternoons, he had his private practice."

She held something between her fingers. A bracelet, maybe? She didn't look like the kind of person who'd be holding a rosary. Not after her apparent disillusion with Catholic doctrine.

"It's not easy to be married to a doctor, *hermana*. You spend all your life by yourself. Raising kids alone, eating meals alone, sitting on your expensive furniture and in your beautiful parlor alone. At least in Bogotá I had my family. But in Cali I had no one. Not even Farid's sisters since one lives in Buenaventura and the other one is a nun." She looked up. "I'm sure you know about Sor Camila?"

"Yes."

"Sure, he has cousins and an ancient aunt, but they never accepted me. They had preconceived ideas about the people from the capital and they considered me vain and a thoughtless spender. They never really gave me a chance."

My body started shaking in anticipation. Soon she was going to tell me how Martin had paid her all the attention she needed. He was an expert in that department. But I wasn't sure I was ready to hear about yet another woman in his life.

"The weather was awful, too. So humid, so hot. I was used to the cold climate of Bogotá and the people there, who are much more cultured and refined." She sighed. "And don't even get me started on the trip to Cali. It was so rough and dreadfully long." She placed her hands on her head, as if she had a headache. "But Farid didn't care. He didn't make any effort to introduce me to his colleagues or their wives and my girls were too big to like me anymore. I'd had an active social life in Bogotá but here, there was nothing other than going to the plaza on Sundays to listen to a band of musicians after mass. Not my idea of entertainment."

I was growing tired of her rant.

"One of those Sundays at the plaza, I met two ladies from Bogotá. We recognized each other's fashion sense and immediately knew we were from the capital. They befriended me and started inviting me to parties and other social events. I finally fit in." Her raven hair brushed against the edge of her collarbone. "It was in one of those get-togethers that I met him."

"Who?" My voice came out hoarse, as if I hadn't spoken in a month.

"He was not the most handsome man I've met. In fact, I consider my husband to be better looking, but there was something irresistible about him. I think it was the way he looked at me, as if he could read my mind and was in on my darkest secrets, as if he approved of all my imperfections. He had this self-assured smirk that drove me crazy."

Had she not heard me? I'd clearly asked the name of this man.

"We ran into each other a few times. He had his own Model T, so he offered to take me on a ride so I could get to know the city. I knew it was wrong, but Farid had stopped paying me attention altogether. He was barely home and when he was around, he would often be immersed in his books and his studies and never, ever, talked to me.

"I ended up accepting this man's invitation and it was the most fun I'd had in months. We met a few times a week, usually in the mornings while the girls were with their tutor and Basim was at school. This man said he'd never met anyone like me and admitted on my thirtieth birthday that he loved me. He also gave me an exquisite gift." She smiled in childlike wonder as she mentioned this precious gift. "You want to know what Farid gave me?"

"What?"

"Nothing! He didn't even remember my birthday."

"Do you think he suspected something?"

"Not at all. He would've had to pay me attention to notice. In reality, he was delighted that I'd made new friends. That way, he didn't have to hear my complaints. He accompanied me to some of the gatherings and he befriended many people there, but he didn't have the time to go to every single event. The last straw was that he wouldn't come with me to a New Year's Eve party we were invited to. He was on call that night. I was so upset that my husband wouldn't even consider coming with me that I went on my own anyway."

The New Year's Eve party. Martin had attended that party. Of course it was him. It had to be. This was a new low in Martin's character. Having an illicit relationship with his friend's wife?

"Tell me about the party," I said, my mouth parched.

She gave me a surprised look. I was done being discreet and nun-like. I had an urgency to know if this man, Amira's lover, had been in fact Martin. If it had been, I would leave at the crack of dawn; I would go back to my child. I simply wouldn't care anymore if Farid or anyone else had killed Martin.

"What do you want to know, *hermana*?" she said.

I was taken aback by her bewildered look. Did I really want to know? That all-too-familiar tremor—the one I'd felt upon finding Angélica's letters—took over my legs.

"That man you speak of," I said in a low voice, as cautious as a hunter treading behind a deer. "What's his name?"

The lines in her forehead deepened and she didn't even blink as she said:

"Gerardo."

I'd never been happier, or more relieved, than when I heard from Amira that her lover wasn't Martin. I could now go to sleep with that knowledge and peace of mind.

It was dawn already and the room was getting too bright to sleep. I didn't know how the Siervas and the nurses could do this all their lives. I had nothing but admiration for these groups of women who devoted their lives to caring for others at the expense of their bodies' deterioration.

The nurses lying next to me promptly shut their eyes and dozed off. They were so used to sleeping at odd times that they said their bodies were trained to fall asleep as soon as their heads hit the pillow.

Such was not my case. The events of the evening played out in my mind. I couldn't make a single coherent thought but my mind simply flashed images of Angélica, Martin, Amira, and this mysterious man, Gerardo—or whatever my mind assumed this man would look like. With my eyes closed and their figures slowly dissipating, I entered the delicious stage between sleep and wakefulness. I lost my body in the softness of the mattress and the thin blanket shrouding me. In that state of comfort and relaxation, something jolted me awake.

An image.

Amira's bracelet.

It had been a string of emeralds.

I hadn't thought anything of it as she'd absently fingered it. But now all the pieces of the puzzle fell into place. Gerardo owned an emerald mine in Boyacá and had invited Martin to invest in it. In his letter to me, Martin had mentioned a plan, his "last chance" to make this business work out.

I turned to my side, my mind racing.

Martin had been a guest at the New Year's Eve party that Amira had also attended, but not Farid, which had been a major frustration for her. Had Martin known or figured out then that Amira was Farid's wife and that she was having an extramarital affair with Gerardo?

Martin had mentioned a plan. Did his plan involve blackmailing Gerardo about his relationship with Amira? No, that was not his style. He didn't follow the rules and he was an irrepressible womanizer, I had to admit to my own dismay, but he didn't seem dishonest in his business dealings. At least, that hadn't been my experience with him.

I remembered the two letters Lucas had showed me. They accused Martin of being in possession of an emerald necklace. Was this necklace part of a set, together with a bracelet and maybe a pair of earrings? A set with the bracelet Amira wore? In that case, the necklace must have belonged to Amira and this could have been the precious gift Gerardo had given her for her birthday. After all, he'd had unlimited access to this stone.

If Martin had stolen the jewel that would've certainly given Gerardo a motive to kill him, assuming that he'd been the one to send those two threatening letters instructing Martin to return the necklace in that abandoned chapel.

I recalled the conversation between Amira and Farid a few

nights ago. She'd asked her husband where *he* was and I assumed she'd meant Martin. Could she be talking about Gerardo instead?

I would have to ask Lucas about him.

Yes, that was my next course of action. I had to find out where Gerardo was and he might lead me to Martin.

HAPTER 31

Camila

Medellín, 1924
One year before the gala

I'd never thought I would be the kind of person who would adapt to, much less enjoy, religious life. I'd never been exceptionally spiritual, perhaps because Mama had died when I was so young and Baba was too busy with work to care about mass or our sacraments. Still, we attended mass regularly with Tía Lidia and Tío Ibrahim on Sundays when Baba opened the store, but I'd never been devout or had an inkling of a vocation. Religious life had simply happened to me and the truth was that I'd found the peace and the sense of purpose I'd always longed for.

As a young woman, I'd thought dressmaking would be the solution for my restlessness at home, but I'd known little about that world, though I'd tried through several letters to convince my father to let me give it a try. I asked him to give me a small space in the store to make dresses and try to sell them. I mentioned how good I'd gotten and how I'd been sewing all my maternity gowns, but he didn't even bother answering my letters.

I was left with no other option than to obey Farid's instructions about what would be done with the baby after I delivered: to give the child away. Baba didn't want me back and I couldn't stay in the home for unwed mothers forever.

At least some good came from my time in Palmira.

I'd met Sor Consuelo the day after I arrived at the home. She was the first smiling face I encountered and I would always be grateful for that—most of the women there were so austere.

As the only nurse in the home, she was admired and respected by all. And yet, she never took advantage of her position or power. She'd been a Sierva de Jesús who volunteered to come into the home and take care of our bodies and souls without judgment but with kindness and prudence. She never asked about or prodded into our sad circumstances. Her philosophy was based on the concept that you didn't have to pay for your mistakes every day of your life, an idea that was highly contrarian to what I was experiencing with my close family members. Perhaps because she was so young—somewhere in her mid-twenties—she had a fresh perspective on life.

With her, I learned how to take care of others. Most of the girls didn't know how it was that they'd ended up in their current conditions or how our babies would ever depart their fleshy homes. Sor Consuelo taught us the gory details—that is, when the school director, Doña Inés, wasn't around. She always started with something like, "I shouldn't be telling you this, but you might as well know . . ."

The majority of *the sinners*, as Doña Inés not so secretly referred to us, were horrified with the realities of life, but I was fascinated.

Sor Consuelo saw my uncanny curiosity and started tasking me with small chores to help her during the care of the mothers-to-be and, ultimately, their deliveries. I feared the day I would be in that same miserable position, but I knew it was bound to happen. This baby had to get out at some point.

* * *

After it was all done, my baby gone and my hands empty, Sor Consuelo was the only one to console me—as her name so brilliantly stated. I didn't want to leave her, but my time at the home was over and I would have to face Baba again, though at this point he wanted little to do with me.

The idea of becoming a nun probably would've never occurred to me had it not been for one heartbreaking incident.

It had been a morning like any other. In two days, I would leave Palmira and go back to Cali. I didn't know what to expect upon my return. Baba had not answered my letters and my little siblings had also become unresponsive. I suspected Baba was keeping my letters for Nazira for fear that my words would badly influence her. That was the only explanation for her prolonged silence.

I spotted Sor Consuelo when she was going to the market. She was fond of vegetables and herbs for taking care of our healing bodies after delivery. She said I should rest, but I didn't want to sleep anymore. I'd been doing enough of that for a few weeks and I was ready for my *cuarentena* to be over. I offered to go with her and help her with the basket.

She agreed, which went against all the rules since we girls were not allowed to leave the house. I think she'd grown fond of me as well and wanted to spend time with me before I left.

At the market, while choosing ripe avocados, a strange look came upon her face. I turned around to see what it was she was looking at with that pain-stricken expression. I imagined someone was coming to us to rob us or she'd seen some act of uncalled-for cruelty—such was her level of sensitivity. But there was nothing out of the ordinary, only food vendors and buyers behind me. When I turned in her direction again, she had collapsed to the ground, her hand pressed against her chest.

I started screaming to all who would hear.

Several bystanders—men, women, some ignorant, some knowledgeable—came to Sor Consuelo's rescue, but in the end, there was nothing anyone could do to save her life.

Eventually, I learned that she'd had a heart attack, which was surprising given her youth, but some years later, Farid explained to me that she must've had a heart condition she had been unaware of.

I, however, was convinced she was too good for this world and the pain of seeing so much suffering and injustice had broken her heart.

At her funeral, I decided I would continue with her legacy and join her congregation, if they would have me. My dream was to come back one day to the home of unwed mothers and take her place. Baba agreed to pay my dowry, which was significantly less than I would've required for a good marriage, and he took me to the convent in Medellín without much fanfare. Of course, the secret of my shameful and carnal past was deeply hidden from these pious women—they wouldn't have accepted me as one of their own if they'd known my unforgivable sins.

It pained me that Baba not once tried to persuade me to come back to the house and had so easily agreed to give me away to the Siervas, but my pride wouldn't allow me to change my mind, even when I saw him board the carriage and leave for good.

I often thought of Sor Consuelo, wondering if she would approve of the woman—the nun and nurse—I'd become. I have asked my Reverend Mother countless times to send me to Palmira to take Sor Consuelo's place, but one thing I didn't know, and that took me years and hours of contemplation to accept, was that my wishes ceased to exist when I joined the congregation.

They would send me where they needed me. And so far, nobody needed me in the home of unwed mothers as they'd promptly found a replacement for Sor Consuelo.

But I had plenty to do in Medellín. People never stopped getting sick.

When Sor Marianela, one of the young nuns whom I'd taken under my wing, cautiously approached me in my cell, I immediately knew something was wrong. She always got the hiccups when she was nervous, which didn't require much provocation.

"Sor Camila? There's a gentleman here to see you."

A gentleman? Had something happened to Baba, or one of my siblings? Even though I rarely accepted their visits, I still worried about them.

"What gentleman?"

Another hiccup. "He said his name is Lucas."

Lucas? I hadn't seen him in years! Since that infamous trip to his *madrina*'s hacienda. Something must've happened to Farid because if it had been Baba, one of my brothers would've come.

I fixed my veil, an involuntary sign of vanity that I regretted doing as I was supposed to set a good example for this new nun.

With tempered steps and my hands inside my pockets, I walked into the receiving vestibule and spotted a tall man facing away from me. He held his hat in one of his hands as he admired the life-size mosaic of Santa María Josefa del Corazón de Jesús, our patron saint and founder.

I didn't remember Lucas being this tall.

As he turned around, I recognized his profile and my knees nearly faltered.

Martin.

What was he doing *here*?

I must look ancient. But I had no way of knowing as I hadn't seen my reflection in years.

"Hello, Camila," he said. "Or should I say Sor Camila?"

There was no apparent mockery in his tone. It seemed like he truly wanted to know.

"Sor Camila is fine."

He had filled out since I last saw him and his face clearly showed the signs of time. His skin had layer upon layer of sunburns, a few wrinkles flanking the corners of his eyes, a beard that could use some trimming.

There was not much left of the scrawny youngster he once had been, but he was still an attractive man. I would have to confess this last thought to Padre Hernán.

"Why did you say you were Lucas?"

"I didn't think you'd come down if you knew who I was."

He was right about that.

There was a stack of books in one of the shelves for visitors to look at. I started arranging them by size—I needed something to do with my hands, something that would keep his eyes off my face. If he looked into my eyes, he would *know* the way his presence was affecting me.

"Why are you here? What do you want?" I said.

"Is it all right if I sit down?" He pointed at one of the mustard sofas in the parlor. "I just got into town and I'm a little tired."

I must have nodded because he sat down, but I had no awareness of doing this. Something was boiling inside me.

My shame, my downfall, the pain of having lost my baby were all his fault.

"Lucas told me what happened to you," he said.

I faced him, regaining control of my inner turbulence. "What *happened* to me? Or what *you did* to me?"

Where had all those years of contrition, of learning humility, forgiveness, and obedience, of making a conscious effort to forget every detail of my past life gone? For years, I had honestly tried to forget all the wrongs done to me and the ones I'd done to others. I'd given my best effort to start a new life of devotion and perfection as if I were opening a blank notebook. The disheartening part was that I thought I'd achieved it.

Until now.

Until Martin.

Once again Martin.

"I'm so sorry, Camila. I had no idea that—"

"*¡Cállese!*" I brought a finger to my lips. My anger had momentarily blinded me from the fact that if anyone heard anything about my past life, they would expel me. I'd had nothing but an exemplary conduct since I joined the Siervas. "I don't understand why you're here."

I should leave. I wasn't supposed to think, much less talk about the past.

But the curiosity to know why he'd come to see me and the restrained rage from all these years wouldn't let me "curb my passions," as the mistress of postulants drilled into me during my first year in the convent.

"I wanted to say I'm sorry," he said, running his fingers along the rim of the hat in his lap. "I was so young, so stupid then. Ever since Lucas told me, I've been disheartened just thinking how much you had to endure, to suffer, on your own. I wanted to let you know that I wrote you but you never answered my letters."

He wrote me?

"I never received anything."

"I thought you didn't want anything to do with me. That's why I left you alone." His voice softened. "Camila, I want to know about the baby. I don't have any descendants or any family at all. I would like to reach out to him. Or her."

I wrung a pamphlet in my hands, nearly ripping the cover.

This couldn't be. The past that I had so carefully erased from my mind, that I'd been trying to detach from, couldn't be coming back to me with this obtrusive force. I refused to accept it.

"You must leave, Martin, and never come back."

"But please, I need to know." He stood up and took a step toward me. "I promise never to tell anyone you're the mother. I just need to know how to find the child and if it was a boy or a girl."

I held on to the back of a chair, fighting a violent desire to retch.

"If you don't leave now, I'll start screaming."

"Camila . . ."

"Stop it. You have to go."

He donned his hat, whose sides had been relentlessly squeezed.

"Will you forgive me?" he said.

Was this a test? Yes, of course it was. I should be magnanimous. One of the principles of religious life was to practice humility. Even Jesus had forgiven his tormentors. Then, who was I to deny Martin forgiveness? An inability to forgive was a true sign of pride. And pride was the deadliest of sins, the exaltation of love of Self above all others, including God.

And yet, I couldn't help it. I couldn't forgive him. I'd been despising him for too long. A voice that didn't sound like my own, but the demon that I always tried to tame inside me, spoke in my place.

"Never."

CHAPTER 32

Puri

The dried leaves crunched under my feet as I strolled along the fields of Martin's estate—or what had at one point been his property. In about thirty minutes, I would have to report for my shift but I wanted to be alone for a while, to think about what I should do next. I needed the familiar scent of moist vegetation and banana leaves around me, the trills and whistles of birds, the damp air. Could it be true that Martin had died somewhere in here?

If it was true, at least he'd died in a place he loved.

I took in a deep breath. I wanted to return to Ecuador, my new home. I missed my son, my siblings. But I also wanted to know what exactly had happened to Martin. I couldn't leave until I saw his grave and understood why he had died. I owed it to my son.

There were voices nearby.

Through the foliage, I discerned two figures: one was a man and the other, a woman.

She was yelling at him, but I couldn't quite make out what she was telling him. I skulked closer to them. The man, in a white coat, raised his arm and slapped her hard. She nearly lost her balance and held on to a fence pole.

Their features sharpened.

Farid and Amira.

He raised his arm again. A blast of energy ran through my legs and I rushed toward them.

"Stop!" I stood between the couple.

Farid looked at me as if I had worms gliding down my face.

"This is none of your business, Sor Purificación. This is a problem between husband and wife."

I extended my arms, guarding Amira. "She's a woman!"

He ran his fingers through his scarce hair. "You don't understand. She provoked me."

Behind me, Amira was sobbing.

Farid rubbed his eyes. "I'm sorry. I don't know what came over me. I . . . I'm just so exhausted."

"Then go to bed, Dr. Mansur," I said, firmly. "Things will make sense once you've rested."

Farid nodded. Then he gave Amira one last glance before retracing his steps back to the hacienda.

I didn't know what had come over me. I barely knew these people. Strategically, it had been stupid as my immediate future was in Farid's hands and if anything, he could provide me with the information I needed. But I didn't care. I couldn't stand back in the face of such an injustice, even if I'd ruined any opportunity to speak to him.

Amira's cheek was bright red, her eyeliner smeared from all the crying.

"Thank you, *hermana*. You're an angel," she said.

"I'm not sure about that," I said. I hated when people said how good I was when, in fact, I was being deceitful to everyone.

"You want to tell me what happened?" I asked.

"Not here." She turned away from the hacienda. It was so incongruous to see a woman dressed in Canton silk in the country. Any second her heels would get stuck in the mud.

I followed her. I would be late for my shift, but it might be worth it.

We arrived at an old warehouse with a scarlet pitched roof. My guess was that this was the place where Martin had fermented and dried the cacao beans he'd sent me every month. Today, there were no workers here. What a waste of land and resources.

There was an improvised bench made out of a tree trunk outside.

"I told Farid I didn't love him anymore. I told him I was in love with someone else." She took a seat. "He couldn't take it. Farid is a traditionalist. So is our family. He can't accept that I don't want to live with him anymore. He hit me before I even proposed we get an annulment."

And Farid wanted to convince her to stay by *beating* her?

I sat next to her. "Under what grounds?"

"That I don't know. I was hoping he wouldn't make things so difficult, although my family would disown me if I even mention the word *separation*."

"Do you want to leave with this man you love, this Gerardo? Is that it?"

"I would love to, but it's impossible." Her expression hardened. "He's gone."

"What do you mean *gone*? Where?"

"I suppose he went back to Boyacá. He has another home and a business there."

The emerald mine.

"He hasn't contacted me in months. Since the gala. But I don't want to be here anymore. I want to go back to Bogotá, where the rest of my family lives."

"And your children?" I said.

She hesitated. "They would come with me, of course."

Her answer had been appropriate, but something about her reaction made me doubt she really longed to be with her children. Why, I never saw her with Basim. He seemed to spend all his time with his grandfather or playing the guitar.

"This man, Gerardo, what happened to him? Why hasn't he contacted you?"

"Either he's angry at me or Farid found a way to make him disappear."

A taste of copper filled my mouth. Today I glimpsed a side of Farid I hadn't seen before—though I had considered the possibility that he might have hurt Martin to keep the property. I decided to tackle one option at a time.

"Why would Gerardo be angry at you?" I said.

"Because I lost the gift he gave me, a valuable emerald necklace."

Of course.

"Tell me about this necklace."

She ran her hand by her collar, setting her fingers on the oversized silk chrysanthemums on the shoulder of her dress. "It was so lovely. It had a grand emerald in the center, about this size." She made a big *O* with her fingers. "And four medium-sized stones on each side." Her gaze got lost somewhere in the vegetation across from us. "Obviously I couldn't wear it in front of Farid, but my opportunity came at a New Year's Eve party Gerardo hosted. I think I mentioned it to you before?"

"Yes."

"Well, since Farid wasn't attending the party, I put it on. I wanted Gerardo to see me with it." She crossed her legs. "I had this gorgeous evening gown on, made of imported black satin and chiffon, and a turban headwrap." She placed her hands over her head. "The necklace really stood out. I'd made some *baklawa*, my specialty, for Gerardo to try and I took it to the party. That's how I met Martin. He was standing by the food table, where there were all kinds of desserts and delicacies, and he absolutely loved my *baklawa*. He said the only thing missing was Puri's chocolate."

I plucked a white carnation. "And then?"

"Gerardo was engaged with his guests the entire evening, so he barely paid me any attention. Most of the night, I was left in the corner of the room with a glass of wine in my hand. I was furious. Martin came to my rescue a few times and even invited me to dance."

"Did you know he was your husband's friend?"

"Not at the time. Farid was too busy with work to introduce me to any of his friends. Like I mentioned the other day, he was consumed with his patients and never, ever, wanted to go out with me." She shook her head. "I'd had way too much to drink and got dizzy. Martin offered to take me home, but I was frantic. I wanted Gerardo to take me. He told me to wait until the clock hit midnight. He had to be there with his guests for that big moment. I continued to drink, stewing over being there by myself, over the entire situation with my husband and Gerardo. When I couldn't stand on my feet anymore, Martin took me to the study and helped me lie down on a couch. I don't remember well what happened. I have a vague recollection of talking to him about Gerardo, about how much I loved him and how I hated my life, but I don't remember much more." She scratched the bench's surface with her nail. "I think I fell asleep for some time because when I woke up, I was alone in the study. There was a lot of noise coming from the parlor. I believe the clock had struck midnight and the chimes had woken me up. When I felt strong enough to stand and walk, I returned to the parlor. But there was so much chaos there: confetti, music, dancing. I couldn't find Martin. When Gerardo saw me, he came and asked where the necklace was. That's when I noticed it was missing. I suspected that Martin took it, but I couldn't be sure because I didn't know if anybody else had been in the study. Gerardo told me the necklace was worth a fortune, but by now a lot of the guests had left. People were so drunk and distracted it was impossible to find out who'd taken it. And I felt so sick. Gerardo took me home, but he was never the same after that."

She sniffed.

"The next time I saw him was here, at the fundraiser gala, two months later. That's when we both figured out that Martin and Farid were also friends."

Martin, Martin, what did you do?

"You said Farid may have found a way to make Gerardo disappear. Do you really believe he's capable of that?"

"Farid has seen death since he was a little boy. He's been surrounded by it every day for years. It doesn't faze him anymore. So, to answer your question, Sister, yes, I think he's capable of getting rid of anybody. Of that and a lot more."

CHAPTER 33

Puri

"Don Martin loved my *sancocho de gallina,*" Doña Tulia said, adding cobs of corn into the soup.

I nodded. I'd heard all about her *sancocho.* At the moment I was more preoccupied with preventing her from adding sugar to the broth. The food in the hacienda was getting increasingly bad and the nurses complained that Doña Lula, the "good cook," was never around.

"It was all he wanted after the accident," she said.

I set my raw carrot on the counter—it was one of the few safe eating choices. "What accident, Doña Tuli?"

She covered her mouth. "I wasn't supposed to say anything about that. Now, he's going to be angry with me."

I leaned over the counter, lowering my voice so the other nurses wouldn't hear me. "I could talk to him about it, explain that you didn't mean to tell me his secret." I was half joking, but something about her expression made me think that, for once, she knew what she was talking about.

"That would be wonderful."

I took a bite of the carrot. "So, what accident was it?"

"You know, when they shot him." She lowered her voice. "Fortunately, the bullet barely hit his shoulder, so I cured it."

"After the gala?"

"The gala?" She shook her head. "Oh, no, before that. A week or two after New Year's. I remember because I had just gotten back from visiting my sister that day. I told Don Martin he shouldn't take those walks at night, but he was incorrigible."

I was so confused.

"Wait. Didn't he go horseback riding?"

"No. That was later, in March. This was another time. He asked me not to tell anyone, but you're a nun so that's all right."

At times like these, I doubted Doña Tuli was truly sick in the head. Today, she sounded completely sane.

"Do you know who I am?" I said.

"Sor Puri," she said, matter-of-factly, as she wiped down the counter with a moist rag.

I should take advantage of this moment of lucidity to get all the information I needed. She was, after all, one of the few people who had worked with Martin.

"Tuli, what happened to him the night of the gala?"

She sighed. "Poor Don Martin. He went on a horse ride and never came back."

"Do you know why?"

"They say he fell off the mare, his Giralda."

"And you haven't seen him since?"

"Nobody has." She looked into my eyes. "He died."

Tuli was making perfect sense. Did that mean, then, that someone had tried to kill Martin *before* the gala? It would be consistent with the threatening letter demanding the emerald necklace. Maybe that was why he wrote me, why he feared for his life.

Lula rushed into the kitchen hugging a wicker basket full of eggs.

"I'm sorry I'm late," she said to all who would hear.

The nurses spoke all at once.

"This is too much, Lulita," Bertha said. "How could you leave Tuli in charge of all our meals?"

"Where have you been?"

"You're killing us!"

I stared at Tuli as she continued cleaning the counters. She had a vacant smile, which shortly after gave way to her usual careless humming. It was apparent that she had retreated back to the confines of her nebulous mind.

The soil was still moist and soft, even after three and a half months. I touched the dirt to make sure it was real and read the inscription on the tombstone for the fourth time.

JUAN MARTIN SABATER GARZA
GUAYAQUIL, FEBRUARY 18, 1892 – EL PARAÍSO, MARCH 10, 1925
Q.E.P.D.

Thirty-three years old—Jesus Christ's age; barely six months older than me. I looked around the still cemetery. Sunbeams hit the top of headstones, casting dark, elongated shadows in diagonal patterns. A soft breeze stirred the violet petals in front of Martin's name. A row of ants trailed irreverently along the edge of his grave. How could life go on—with its predictable cycles and mundane pursuits—in the face of our impending mortality? Shaking my head, I scanned the graves surrounding us.

"Are you ready?" Lucas offered his hand to help me up.

I took it and stood up straight. What would I do about this painful lump in my throat?

"Let's go," I said, doing my best to control my voice.

He was staring at me. I probably gave myself away, but I couldn't help it. When Lucas told me he'd found Martin's grave in El Paraíso, I urged him to bring me and couldn't hide my emotion when I saw his tombstone. Not for long, anyway.

At least Lucas didn't ask any questions.

Corroborating that Martin was, in fact, dead was something I wasn't prepared for. I'd been telling myself that it was probably a mistake—or a lie. I'd gone as far as believing that it might have been a man with the same name, but the birthplace and birth date left no doubt that it was the same person.

As painful as this was, it was probably best that I came. I needed to see with my own eyes that Martin was truly dead. It might be the only way to forget him, to end this fixation.

Death was so final.

The strange thing was that beneath the pain, there was relief. I finally had an answer.

"You seem to have had a lot of affection for him," Lucas said as we dodged tombstones on our way back to the cabriolet.

We took our spots on the carriage's buckboard. Neither one said a word as he pulled the harness's lines.

"*Hermana*, did you . . . were you—"

"Please don't ask anything, Lucas."

He was obviously intrigued by my past with Martin, but I wasn't ready to have that conversation with him. Not so soon after seeing my former lover's grave.

This was it; my search was over. There was no point in being here anymore.

I glanced at Lucas's profile, then turned back to the front as if avoiding direct sunlight. I should tell him the truth right now and ask him to help me get back to Ecuador as soon as possible— without a fuss, without saying goodbye to anyone. I could just disappear and save myself the shame of being discovered. But I didn't know how to tell him.

"Lucas?"

"Yes?"

How to even start?

"Sor Camila says you're almost fully recovered."

"That's what Farid said."

"Will you go back to Cali?"

"Probably."

"To your mother's house?"

He shrugged. "It may be time for me to spread my wings."

I was going to miss him. I enjoyed his company.

"I agree," I said. "But could you try to be a little nicer to her? She's your closest family member."

He glanced at me, tightened his grip on the reins as he led the horse toward a sharp turn.

"You know, for years, I felt an obligation to look after her. I still want the best for her. I'm grateful that she raised me. That takes a special kind of person. But I'm hurt by her long deceit. I've been remembering things, you know? As a little boy, I once heard an argument between my parents where my mother— I mean Matilde—complained that my father was taking me to the hacienda too much and she wanted it to stop. I assume my father had been bringing me to see my mother and my sister, but Matilde told him it had to end. That was why I had memories of this place—of the fountain—but I couldn't have been older than five or six when that happened. I remember playing ball with a little girl. I don't know, I think Matilde crossed a line by putting an end to my relationship with my biological mom and my twin."

"She must have felt threatened."

"She was being selfish."

How could I bring up the subject of my own deceit after this? He obviously felt contempt toward those who lied—regardless of their reasons.

"Well, if you decide to leave," I said, "you should give some thought to what I told you about traveling the world with your camera."

"I'm afraid I'm not as enthralled by photography as you are. It's just a job."

"Oh, but it's so much more than that. It's changed the world, certainly it's changed art."

"How so?"

"Well, look at what you can do. You can take a portrait in an instant. Do you know how long it takes an artist to paint one? And how expensive it is to hire someone to do it? Only the elite can afford it. Artists all over Europe are currently creating movements as a reaction to photography. They don't want to create realistic paintings anymore—why bother when a camera can do it in seconds? Photography offers fascinating possibilities. The idea of capturing a moment forever, the opportunity to see foreign lands, other people you would've never seen otherwise, how they live, how the world looks. It's so exciting."

"How come you know so much about art?"

"I met many artists in Sevilla. Years ago."

I failed to tell him that they had been my husband's friends and that the gatherings took place in my own chocolate store.

"I met novelists, poets, painters, even one sculptor. They all mentioned photography as an emerging art form."

I really missed those intellectual conversations. I supposed I got some of that stimulation from my brother Alberto in Vinces, who was a theologist and an architecture enthusiast, but it wasn't the same as those late-night conversations with my circle of friends back home.

"You might be right, Sister Puri, but who's going to infuse that excitement in me every day when you're gone?"

As we drove away, I glanced back at the cemetery, where Martin rested among hundreds of strangers. And that was when reality hit me. I would never see Martin again. My son would never meet his father. Martin would forever rest in this foreign land, far from us. Many found consolation in the afterlife, but I never had. Who knew what really came after we died?

"Life is too short, Lucas. You just have to do it," I said with urgency. "I know that once you find a new place—a new adventure—you'll find that passion on your own. You're more of an artist than you think."

He was pensive for a moment. I tried to entice him by mentioning one of my favorite sites in Andalucía, the Alhambra.

"You have to see it. It's a place like no other."

"What is it?"

"A fortress. A palace. An amazing display of architecture and art. Oh, and the gardens, Lucas, you would get lost in there."

He kept asking questions about Granada and I also told him about Toledo and El Escorial, near Madrid. I could see the burgeoning excitement in Lucas's eyes and his imagination wandering.

When he reached the hacienda and drove past the chicken coop, the mute worker—Nestor?—tipped his hat at us. I still thought there was something unsettling about him, about the way he looked at me, but it was none of my concern anymore. I'd made up my mind. I would leave in the morning, with or without Lucas's help.

CHAPTER 34

Puri

The morning of my departure was crisp and sunny, which I took as a good omen. I still had to ask Lucas to take me to El Paraíso so I could find a carriage to go to Cali, get Angélica, and then board the train to Buenaventura and from there, a ship back to Ecuador. Hopefully, my return home would be less eventful than my arrival.

Would Lucas connect my departure with the confirmation of Martin's demise?

As the sun was just rising, I decided to take a short walk rather than go to sleep, like I usually did at the end of my shift—it would be my way of saying goodbye to this beautiful country after eighteen long days and nights.

And to Martin.

Even though I'd already made up my mind about leaving, there was one thought, one idea that disturbed me. If I left now and never looked back, would it be fair to my son?

He was, after all, Martin's only descendant.

Was it fair that his inheritance would end up in Farid Mansur's hands? Especially if the doctor had something to do with Martin's death. Because I still believed it was too convenient that he'd been the one to find Martin while he was agonizing and had him sign his will in those last few moments of his life—*if* he had truly signed it. I couldn't shake off the feeling that it had been forged.

And yet, Farid was doing good things with Martin's property. He was saving lives. His cause was noble, far removed from any desire to profit, because as I had learned, the hospital was partly subsidized by the Catholic Church, which was one of the reasons they were sending nuns—and apparently there were more to come. Still, there was potential for profit for Mansur after the epidemic ended.

But what about little Cristóbal? I'd also lost my father's hacienda. All my son would have left would be my chocolate business, and who knew how much longer it would last? I could always hire Tomás Aquilino, my father's attorney, to contest Martin's will. I could do it from Guayaquil, but my action would put into evidence that Cristóbal was Martin's son—not my former husband's. What would that knowledge do to him? What kind of scandal would that cause in Vinces? What would my siblings think of me? I knew for a fact that Angélica would never forgive me.

But what was more important: my reputation, my relationship with my family, or Martin's legacy and, thus, Cristóbal's rightful inheritance?

The clop of hooves drew my attention. Riding Martin's mare, Farid galloped toward the stables. This wasn't the first time I'd seen him riding at dawn. The sand created waves underneath the horse's hooves. How unfair that someone else would benefit from Martin's hard work and make his dreams their own. It was infuriating, but I had to admit—despite my annoyance—that Farid looked sublime on top of Giralda. He seemed to belong on the mare's back just as much as he belonged in a hospital, curing a patient or heading a meeting.

That didn't mean he ought to keep my son's birthright.

As he took the mare to the stable, a wagon arrived. The driver was Nestor, the mute worker. I wouldn't have looked twice had I not recognized the man lying in the back of the wagon.

Don Iván Contreras—the former owner of this hacienda.

I remembered his shiny bald head from the gala photograph Lucas had shown me.

Nestor was gesturing for me to come. He jumped to the back of the wagon, hoisted Iván up, and pointed at the man's feet with his chin. I did my part and lifted the man's heavy legs. Once on the ground, Nestor carried him by himself into the building.

I followed them in, curious as I was. Lucas said Martin had figured out something about the previous owner, something he was going to share with him after the gala.

I had to warn Lucas that his stepfather was here.

I would leave right after that. Just as soon as Lucas could take me to El Paraíso.

That was what I was planning, but my urgency to leave died upon making an odd discovery. As the men crossed the courtyard and rushed into one of the cholera rooms, Nestor, the mute who might have been one of the last few people to see Martin alive, spoke.

CHAPTER 35

Lucas

My first impulse when I heard that Iván Contreras was at the hacienda was to choke him until he confessed what he'd done with my mother. But Sor Puri, with her calm demeanor and firm grip, prevented me from taking another step. She'd come looking for me in Don Yusuf's bedroom, where I'd been watching the old man and his grandson embarked on a ruthless game of chess. I'd stepped into the hallway with her.

"You have to be patient," she said in a low voice.

"Yes, yes. I know," I said, fighting my annoyance.

Had I not been patient when I'd seen that man the night of the gala? But so many things had changed after that evening that it was hard to remain collected when our nerves were being tested daily.

"I know he did something to my mother."

Just now I realized my fists were locked.

"That's not all," Puri said. "Nestor spoke."

"*El mudo?* What did he say?"

She bit her lower lip, drawing my eyes to it. "He told Contreras not to worry. He said he would take care of everything."

"And his voice was . . . what?"

"Normal. A little low."

"I can't say that I'm completely surprised. Martin didn't seem to trust either one. He said Nestor was always secretive and somewhat hostile. He didn't seem happy at all when Contreras sold the property and left all his employees here."

"Some people don't like change, I suppose," she said ominously. Something was off with her.

"Can you watch Contreras?" I said. "It's easier for you to get in and out of the cholera room. You know Sor Camila forbade me from going in there."

She avoided my gaze, seemed to think about my request for too long before slowly nodding.

"Great. I'll keep an eye on Nestor," I said.

"Do you think they might have had something to do with"— she crafted her next words carefully—"Martin's demise?"

I gestured for her to follow me down the hall, careful not get my crutches stuck in the grout of the brick floor. I didn't want Farid's family to hear us.

We stopped by a wooden bench, where, only a few days ago, patients waited for a bed.

We sat across the balustrade. Standing on the edge of a flowerpot, a hummingbird explored the pistil of a burgundy carnation.

"I've considered the possibility," I said. "Martin mentioned some findings he wanted to share with me. I always assumed it had to do with Contreras."

Beside me, she let out a deep sigh, as if losing a battle within herself.

"Lucas, what exactly happened during the fundraiser gala?"

I leaned forward, resting my elbows on my thighs.

"If I knew, Sor Puri, I would've told you a long time ago."

CHAPTER 36

Camila

February 21, 1925
Two weeks before the gala

Time had stood still at Colegio Internado Oro Verde. The last time I'd seen those redbrick walls and gray pitched roofs had been at Farid's high school graduation—the day Martin had given me my first kiss outside this very same gymnasium. That had been the beginning of the end. How long ago that rushed kiss seemed now. It couldn't have happened to me, could it? To think that I would never feel the lips of a man on mine again. Back then, I'd had no idea how dramatically my life would change by the end of the summer.

And now I was here again, in my long habit, a grown woman, a different woman; one I would've never envisioned or recognized as the seventeen-year-old with the rapid heartbeat and dreams of one day becoming Martin Sabater's wife.

But the school looked exactly the same, except for the abundant trees that had grown exponentially in the last decade and a few stains on the walls probably caused by the relentless rains. Other than those details, the school remained the same: a compound of buildings erected to prepare young men in all areas of life—science, religion, languages, trades, and agronomy. I always envied my brother for having the opportunity to come here, whereas I was stuck in the house tending to my father and younger siblings.

Today, I was not alone. Sor Eugenia and Sor Marianela had come with me. My brother Farid had found a way to bring me back to the area I'd been avoiding all my adult life. When my brother got an idea into his thick skull, there was no stopping him. And my Reverend Mother stood no chance next to his scheming ways. He'd written her a long letter requesting my presence at the gala to help with the fundraising efforts of the community. He'd taken advantage of the fact that our congregation had once organized a successful charity to open an orphanage in Medellín and had used that as the perfect excuse. *We need their expertise, their connections*, he'd written, and the Reverend Mother had been happy to acquiesce in order to please the man who'd made generous contributions to our convent. Farid's real motivation for wanting me back in El Valle del Cauca remained to be seen.

I descended the landau. We were to stay here for three weeks to help with the fundraiser organization and then go back to our convent, but the Reverend Mother had no information as to where the party was going to be held or any other details. I was just hoping I didn't have to face Martin after our unpleasant encounter in Medellín last year, but for all I knew, he may have gone back to Ecuador. At least I hoped so.

My brother and Lucas greeted us.

I was pleased and relieved to see Lucas. I'd always liked him. I often wondered why I didn't pick him over Martin. Things would've been so different if I'd accepted Lucas's advances when we were young. He'd never been overly direct about his intentions, but I knew—a woman always does—that he was in love with me. Back then, I'd been blinded by Martin's charm. Lucas had seemed too young, too unassuming, too silly to be taken seriously.

"*Hola*, Camila. *Tanto tiempo.*"

Yes, it had been a long time. He offered a hand to help me into the building. Still now, I saw the pain in his eyes at my rejection.

I'd been an idiot; I'd made the wrong choice, but there was no turning back.

My brother was speaking the whole time—it was what he did. He was greeting my sisters, asking how our trip went, talking about the weather, about the fundraiser, and how grateful he was that we'd agreed to help. I would do just that. Help with the effort and leave. Though I suspected that meant I would have to see people I'd been forcing myself to forget all these years.

I knew I could do it.

I'd developed a shield around my heart that protected me and buffered any unpleasant or painful emotion threatening to emerge. I just had to go through the motions, minute by minute, hour by hour, until this mission was over and I could get back to my seat in the landau and head home.

We made progress over the next few days, contacting influential people in the community: business owners, doctors, local politicians. My sisters and I, along with the school principal—Father Carlos Benigno, who'd been nothing but a teacher fifteen years ago—compiled several items for the auction to be held during the gala.

The news that the fundraiser gala would be held at Martin's hacienda hit me like a kick in the liver. First of all, I had no idea he'd purchased a property in the area. Second, why did the gala have to be there, of all places? Farid said it was the perfect venue, large enough, close enough, and apparently spectacular with all the renovations.

I wanted to yell at him, to shake him by the shoulders for bringing me back, but I couldn't say anything. Farid didn't know my past with Martin. If he did, he would've killed him, not held a party at his hacienda. But how could Martin allow this? *He* knew what happened between us.

And yet, he didn't care. He shamelessly remained friends with Farid. As if nothing had happened. As if he'd done nothing wrong.

The night of the gala, I wanted to vanish as soon as I saw Martin standing by one of the pillars of his hacienda's portico. It was a good thing we would be surrounded by people all night and wouldn't have a chance to speak. It shouldn't be too hard to avoid him.

In his tuxedo, he looked stunning. He was one of those men who looked better with age. He'd acquired a calm confidence that in his youth conveyed recklessness and arrogance. His composure made me wonder if he'd known that Farid was bringing me along.

Upon seeing me with Farid, his expression told me my suspicions were correct. He had no idea I was coming.

He greeted me politely, with the same deference he showed my sisters, but he fidgeted with his cufflinks.

"Farid mentioned some nuns were coming to help us with the fundraiser, but I had no idea you were one of them."

"Yes." I glared at Farid. "My brother loves surprises."

And he did, because when I was entering the opulent parlor in Martin's hacienda, Farid leaned over and whispered into my ear, "I have a surprise for you, Mila."

I tensed up. *Did he know about Martin and me?*

"What kind of surprise?" I said, having the distinct feeling he was mocking me. But why? What had I ever done to him?

"Don't worry, *ukhti*. It's a good thing."

The surprise, it turned out, was that my sister Nazira—now a beautiful woman in her twenties, a mother, a wife, and the spitting image of my late mother—had come to the party with her husband. I hadn't seen Nazira since she was ten years old. I'd barely recognized her in that gold beaded chiffon gown exposing the bottom half of her calves. Her dress hit all the latest fashion trends: loose-fitting Grecian drapery, dropped-waist, fringe hemline. Had she not looked so much like our mother, I wouldn't have known who she was. Her eyes, highlighted with dark liner along the top eyelashes, had the same melancholic expression my mother's had had. Her hair, simply adorned with a rhinestone hair comb, was a replica of my mother's dark and abundant mane.

At times like these, I wished I could remove this plain old habit and wear one of those lavish gowns. God only knew what Amira— the fashion queen—would be wearing tonight.

"*Hermanita*," Nazira said, extending her arms. She'd been too young when I left Cali to perfect her Arabic and learn the words Farid and I used toward each other—words such as *ukhti* or *akhi*.

"Nazira, you look lovely," I said, hugging her back.

"I've missed you so much!"

At first, we were tense around each other—we didn't know whether to sit on Martin's expensive furniture or remain standing as the parlor started filling with elegant guests. Nazira sat first and I did the same. We talked about safe subjects, such as her kids, her husband's work, the trip to El Paraíso. In return, she asked about my life in Medellín.

"There's not much to say," I said. "My life mostly consists of prayer and tending to the sick. Nothing you'd be interested in."

She furrowed her brow.

Nazira and I had exchanged letters at the beginning of my life in the convent, but as a nun, I'd been *strongly encouraged* to cut ties with my past and therefore my family, so I'd stopped writing her after my second year of novitiate.

I'd heard some things about her from Farid, who, despite my request to stop coming to the convent, managed to visit a handful of times throughout the years. The Reverend Mother couldn't deny him anything since he was one of our biggest benefactors.

From Farid I heard that Nazira had married an apothecary, the son of one of Tío Ibrahim's friends, and that she'd moved away. I asked her about life in Buenaventura, but she didn't answer. There was something in her eyes that hadn't been there as a child.

"You never came back," she said. "You never even said good-bye."

I knew now what I'd read in her eyes.

Resentment.

And pain.

For the first time since I left, I wondered what she must have felt when she came back from Tía Lidia's house and didn't find me there. I'd been so immersed in my problem, so focused on what I was going to do that I didn't stop to think about my little sister, who'd always seen me as her mother. I'd never wondered what it would've been like for her in that house surrounded by men and an acidic maid.

"I'm sorry," I said. "Please forgive me."

"I was so angry at you. For years." Her eyes filled with tears. "Until I found Ernesto." She glanced at her husband, who was speaking to Farid now. Not far from where they stood was Martin, greeting new arrivals. I looked away. I couldn't stand the sight of him.

Nazira followed my gaze toward Martin. I straightened my back, pretending to be interested in a stunning blond woman who entered the parlor.

"I've done something bad," Nazira said.

I thought I'd heard wrong.

"Excuse me?" I said.

Nazira stood. "Come on. I have something to show you."

Puzzled, I followed her to the patio where dozens of tables had been elegantly set for dinner. The waiters my brother had hired were setting baskets of bread on all the tables.

"What is it?" I said.

Nazira was clutching her mesh golden purse, which perfectly matched her attire.

"These came after you left." She undid the clasp of her purse and removed three envelopes. "For you."

I glanced at the name on the corner: Martin Sabater.

"He wrote you from Popayán." She handed me the letters.

I didn't want to touch them. I didn't want to face the possibility that the resentment—the hatred—I'd nurtured against the man who had wronged me and ruined my life had been unjust.

"Take them," Nazira said. Her tone surprised me. She would've never spoken to me in that tone as a child. Then again, it had been fifteen years since I'd last seen her. I had to accept the fact that I didn't know her. She was a grown woman now. With a husband. With children.

I took them and turned them over. The flap was unglued.

"You read them," I said, more an accusation than a question.

"I couldn't help it. I kept them sealed for a year, but when Baba told me you weren't coming back, that you'd joined the convent, I was so upset I read the letters."

I ran my thumb over Martin's name. Who knew what he said in there? I would certainly not read them in front of her. Or at all. As a nun, I was supposed to renounce my entire past and these letters were an integral part of it. I shoved them in the pockets under my scapular.

"I never wanted to show them to Baba or Farid because I didn't know what they would do to Martin."

She knew about the baby?

"The advantage of being a child is that adults don't think you ever listen or understand their discussions. But I did."

I averted her gaze.

"Tía Lidia talked about nothing else but your disgrace to Tío Ibrahim, and at home all Baba did was drink."

Ave María, what had I done to my father? I had refused to see him for years, but I was certain he would be coming tonight. Farid had warned me. I suspected it was one of the reasons why my brother had insisted so much that I come back—he wanted to foster an encounter between us, a reconciliation. It had nothing to do with the fundraiser.

"He cared for you, *hermana*."

I pretended not to know who she was talking about. "I'm sorry Baba had to go through that."

"I meant Martin," she said. "Read the letters."

"We'd better go back inside," I said. "I have an auction to run."

CHAPTER 37

Puri

The good thing about my disguise was that, for the most part, I remained inconspicuous. Since nuns were expected to be quiet and discreet, people sometimes forgot I was there. So, it was easy for me to observe Iván Contreras without calling attention to myself.

"Start an IV on him," Nurse Bertha instructed me as she tended to another patient who was throwing up.

I nodded.

So far my agreement with Lucas hadn't borne fruit. Nothing out of the ordinary was happening with either Contreras or Nestor, according to Lucas's latest report.

As I was poking one of the veins in Iván's arm, Nestor walked into the cholera room—he must have somehow escaped Lucas's watchful eye. The former mute startled me. Blood squirted all over my apron and the floor uncontrollably. I stared blankly at it, not knowing what to do.

"What the hell are you doing?" Iván said. "Are you going to just stand there while I bleed to death?"

I brought my hand to the bleeding but he kept moving his arm, making both of us panic more. With a gauze pad, I tried to stop the blood flow by dabbing it, but the vein kept bleeding as if it were a hose.

Nurse Bertha came to my rescue.

"*¡Muévase!*" she said.

I moved out of the way, as told, while the nurse brought a gauze pad to the bleeding and applied pressure for about a minute.

"Maybe you should go change before one of the doctors comes," she said, unceremoniously.

Both Nestor and Iván gave me murderous looks as I walked out with a soiled apron and a hurt pride.

As silently as I could, I entered the nurses' room and went to the armoire to change my habit. What on earth? Sor Camila's bed was empty. Only Nurse Celia and Perla were sleeping in the room. I hadn't seen the nun downstairs, either. Where could she be in the middle of the night?

Perla lifted her head from the pillow. "Everything all right?"

"Yes, yes, go back to sleep, *mi alma*."

"What happened?"

I removed my apron. "I'll explain later. Where's Sor Camila?"

Perla returned her head to the pillow. "She never sleeps."

Her eyes were closed again. Had she been talking in her sleep?

At dawn, I went to the kitchen for a cup of coffee. Doña Tulia was pacing the kitchen, talking to herself. I'd never seen her this agitated.

"What's wrong, Tuli?" I asked.

"He's here. He's here."

She was crying. I approached her. "Who?"

"Don Iván. He's mean. Not like Don Martin."

"It's all right, Tuli. He won't come near you. He's sick."

But she kept repeating the same mantra. "He's here. He's here."

"What's wrong with her?"

I turned to face Farid's son, Basim. His voice was surprisingly grave.

"Her nerves," I said. "She's upset that her former boss was

brought here." I lowered my voice. "I guess she didn't like him much."

He nodded and offered a half smile, which seemed so familiar to me, but I didn't know why. Something about his demeanor reminded me of a different time, a different place.

"You're gifted with the guitar," I said.

"Thank you." He looked away shyly, as young men tended to do with adult women.

"Who taught you?"

"My grandfather."

"You're very close to him, aren't you?"

"Yes. He's the only person I can talk to."

I'd seen the two of them go on walks together and yesterday, I'd seen them playing chess when I went to find Lucas. What was it about men and chess? I glanced back at the boy. His eyes were so expressive, so sad.

Just like his father's.

CHAPTER 38

Camila

Hacienda La Reina
March 7, 1925
The night of the gala

I could think of nothing else but Martin's letters pressing against my abdomen, like flames. I'd found the other sisters in the parlor and they took me to another spacious room, where all the items to be auctioned were held: valuable paintings, porcelain sculptures, china sets, jewelry, gowns, and aged cognac. We were tagging them and corroborating they were on our list in the proper order, but I kept making mistakes.

Martin had written me that fall, so many moons ago. If only I had waited a little longer to tell Tía Lidia about my pregnancy, my life could've been so different. I still didn't know what Martin had written. In fact, I didn't know if I wanted to read his letters, but if he'd reached out, it meant he cared about me—at least minimally. If I'd had his address before I'd confided in my aunt, I would've told him about the baby. We could've come up with a plan. Together.

"*Ukhti*, can I talk to you?"

Farid's voice startled me. I turned to him, unable to hide my annoyance.

"Does it have to be now? Don't you see I'm busy?"

"Yes. It has to be now. There's something I've been wanting to talk to you about."

"I'm doing what you wanted me to do, what you brought me here for."

He pointed at the other nuns with his chin. "They can take care of it. Come on, it'll only be a few minutes."

I followed him out of the room, running my hand over the back of a velvet love seat on my way out. He led me up the staircase and into Martin's office.

This could've been my house, my husband.

What in the name of everything holy was wrong with me? *What* was I thinking?

Farid shut the door behind me.

"What is it?" I said, crossing my arms. The last thing I needed was for Martin's letters to fall on the floor—right in front of my brother.

"It's about . . ." He paced the room, unwilling to look at me. "It's about your son."

Every one of my extremities stiffened. Farid hadn't mentioned my son since the day he took him from me, two days after I'd delivered.

"He's almost fifteen now," he said, as if I didn't know his age to the minute. "He's grown so much. He's tall and bony."

Why was he telling me this?

"He's changed a lot in the last year."

"So what?" I said, impatiently.

"Well, he reminds me of someone." He stopped his pacing, stood in front of me, arms crossed. "You never told me who the father was."

I lifted my chin. "It was none of your business."

He scoffed. "None of my business? I *raised* him."

"I didn't ask you to."

"You know who Basim looks like?" He didn't give me a chance to respond. "Martin, when we went to school together."

I didn't even flinch, but my flesh boiled.

"He is the father, isn't he?"

"Is that why you brought me here? To satisfy your morbid curiosity?"

He smacked the cherry desk. "It's not curiosity, *¡maldita sea!*" His chest was heaving. This was the Farid I'd feared as a child. "He betrayed me! He was one of my best friends and what was he doing behind my back? Having *sex* with my sister?"

He made it sound so dirty, so wrong.

"We loved each other," I said.

"You think Martin loved you? You and how many others?"

I had the impulse to remove the letters from my pocket and throw them at his face. *See? I meant something to him! Why would he have written all these letters to me if he didn't care?*

"I'm going to kill him," he hissed.

I grabbed his arm. "No. Wait. What are you going to do?"

He let go of my hand and darted out of the room.

CHAPTER 39

Puri

In the morning, Iván Contreras was doing a little better. He seemed to prefer me over Nurse Bertha, despite my mishap last night. I supposed he didn't care for her ill temper and boorish manners. With my help, Contreras sat on the bed, sipping some *avena*. Lula had prepared the tasty oatmeal drink as she was in charge of breakfast now.

"There's a rumor going around that you used to own this hacienda," I said.

He swallowed before speaking, his face scattered with age spots, like islands on a map.

"Back when I ran this plantation it was one of the most successful in the region. Not the disaster that Sabater turned it into."

"Why did he fail?"

The lines in his forehead accentuated. His ears were so long they nearly reached the edge of his jaw. "Not everybody's born with a business sense. I should've never sold it to him, but I was tired of working. I was ready to retire and move into town."

What about your wife? I wanted to say, but instead, I brought the tin cup back to his mouth. He raised a hand to stop me.

"No more."

He leaned against the headboard. Around us were about a dozen other patients in various stages of decline.

"You sound like you didn't care much for the new owner," I said.

He remained silent, staring at me. Dr. Costa was nearby, tending to a patient. Any second now he might interrupt us, and who knew if I'd ever be able to talk to Iván again?

"You know"—I set the cup of *avena* on the end table—"this might be a good time to say what's on your mind and heart. It often brings people comfort during difficult times."

"What? You want me to confess to *you?*" His tone was so condescending. "Am I that sick that I have to take a nun instead of a priest?"

"No, I didn't mean it that way. I just thought it would relieve your soul to share your feelings with someone else."

"I have nothing to confess, *Sister*, but thanks for your concern. Doctor, you might want to talk to your staff members about not being so fresh with your patients."

Fresh?

Dr. Costa stared at me. I adjusted the mask covering half of my face, hoping to turn invisible.

"I'd like to speak to you when you get a chance, Sor Puri," Dr. Costa said.

I nodded and rushed outside.

Sor Camila and Lula stood by the fountain, talking. Lucas was coming toward me. The bandage on his ankle had been removed and he was wearing shoes, but he used a bamboo cane to help him walk. His eyes told me he had something to tell me. He pointed his chin toward the kitchen area. I removed my mask and followed him to the orchard as discreetly as possible.

The trees were blooming at this time of the year with ripe mangoes and figs. The aroma was enough to get my stomach growling.

It took all my might not to grab one of those fruits and take a bite, skin and all. Buried beneath a luscious branch, I spotted Lucas's distinctive hat.

"Hi," I said.

He lifted the bottom of his pants, showing off his free ankle. "What do you think?"

"Nice. You're almost ready for a race."

His dimples deepened.

"Why are you still up?" he said.

"I was trying to get some information from Don Iván, but it didn't go so well." I leaned on the trunk of a mango tree. It had been an exhausting shift. "Did you make any progress?"

"As a matter of fact, yes. I ran into Farid in the storage room. He was trying to open the safe, but I interrupted him."

"Do you think he has the combination?"

"Maybe. He had something in his hand. Could've been a piece of paper with the code, I suppose."

Under the morning light, his eyes looked greener.

"I think you should try to get it tonight," he said.

"Me? Why me?"

"Because you work nights. I'll keep him busy with a bottle of *aguardiente*. We already agreed to have a drink tonight to relax a little."

"But where would I look?"

"His office, to start."

"To start?"

"If it's not there, we'll look in his bedroom tomorrow when Amira goes for a walk."

"You make it sound so simple," I said.

"It doesn't have to be complicated."

"What if he has the paper in his pocket?"

"If I get him drunk enough, I'll check his pockets," he said.

"Talking about Farid," I said, biting a hangnail on my thumb, "there's something I need to ask you about him."

He clenched the cane's handle. "What?"

"Basim isn't really his son, is he?"

He blinked. "How do you know?"

"I was talking to the boy this morning and I noticed some things."

"What things?"

"He looks like Martin. He has his gestures, his eyes. And he plays chess, just like Martin did."

Lucas nodded. "We used to play chess incessantly in school. It always bothered Farid that he couldn't beat Martin."

"Of course," I said. "His father was a fanatic."

"So I heard. He lost his plantation over—"

"Yes, yes," I said. I didn't even want to remember that. If Lucas only knew how much that game of chess had affected my life. I chose to take the conversation in a different direction. "After talking to Basim for a moment, I just knew."

"Yes, I also figured it out on my own. It's hard not to notice the resemblance."

I licked my bottom lip, trying to gather the courage to ask the next question. "What I don't understand is who the mother is, and why is Farid pretending to be his father?"

"Farid is his uncle," Lucas said, looking around to make sure we were completely alone. "And his mother is Camila." His voice was so low I almost didn't hear him.

At first, I thought the news had shocked me to the point of nearly making me lose my balance. But honestly, I wasn't *that* shocked. I'd been giving this some thought all morning and I had considered the possibility. Why else would Farid raise a child who wasn't his unless he was family? And yet, despite my comprehension and common sense, there was something undeniably wrong happening at the moment. Something that had nothing to do with me. My feet seemed to be standing on quicksand.

Oh, no, not again.

I looked down. The ground was moving, just like the day those men had attacked me. Lucas's eyes widened. He held on to a tree branch.

"*Temblor*," he said.

Madre mía, another earthquake. I tried to hold on to a branch of my own but it was moving. Around us, fruit and branches wavered back and forth in a hypnotic rhythm. I wanted to sprint, but I couldn't move. I was as powerless as an insect under a man's foot. Nowhere to run. Nowhere safe. I had seen the destruction in Cali. I held on to Lucas's arm. He hugged me in return.

"It's all right," he said in a soothing voice. "You'll get through this."

But I wasn't so sure about that. The ground seemed to have different plans as it shuddered under the soles of my shoes. What if the earth cracked open and swallowed us? One of the patients told me that very same thing had happened to her mother not far from here.

I might never see my Cristóbal again.

"Puri, Puri, calm down," he said toward my ear. His breath was warm. I relished being so close to another human being again, to be in someone's arms.

After a few seconds—according to Lucas because it felt like an hour to me—the shaking stopped.

"It's just an aftershock," he said. "We had several immediately after the earthquake."

"I know," I said. "But that was over two weeks ago."

This wasn't an aftershock. *This was an entirely new earthquake!*

Only now did I realize how close our bodies were. He was slightly taller than me, so our faces were just a few centimeters apart; close enough that I could smell his citric cologne. We hadn't been this close since I'd shaved him. Before I could take a step back, he ran the tips of his fingers by my cheek.

"You're so pretty," he said.

I didn't know how to respond. I wasn't good with compliments. Something tickled inside my stomach.

"One day, I'd love to take a photo of you," he said, lifting my chin, studying me with an artistic eye he always denied. Then he let out a sigh. "It's just my luck."

I knew this had the potential to be a major mistake in my attempts to keep up with my disguise, but I couldn't help myself. I had to ask him. "What is?"

"Nothing."

Something inside me was telling me—yelling at me—to say the truth right there and then. *I'm not a nun, you silly man, I'm perfectly able to kiss you right now if you so wish.* In fact, I didn't even move. I simply stared at his lips.

"Doña Tuli, Doña Tuli!"

It was Lula's voice echoing from the other side of the orchard.

I took a step back, my legs trembling under the habit.

"Tuli!" Lula kept screaming.

Lucas picked up his cane from the ground. I didn't even realize he'd dropped it.

"Oh, Sor Puri. Don Lucas. Good thing I found you. Did you feel that?"

I had no voice, but apparently Lucas did.

"Yes." He was staring at me, I could feel it, and his gaze made my face burn.

"*Ay, Virgencita de Chiquinquirá*, that was strong!" Lula said. "I thought the pans were going to fall on top of my head."

I finally found my voice. "Is everything all right in there?"

"Yes. Except that Doña Tulia took off running as if the devil was chasing after her! Haven't you seen her?"

"I haven't," I said. *I've been too busy nearly kissing Martin's best friend.* What on earth was wrong with me?

"Me neither," Lucas said.

"Well, I'm glad to see you, *hermana*. Dr. Costa is looking for you."

Por caridad. Not now.

CHAPTER 40

Lucas

There was a good explanation as to why I was stuck inside the armoire in Martin's study and it had nothing to do with snooping—it had everything to do with desperation. The roll inside my Brownie had gotten jammed in the film chamber after I'd dropped the camera, which was not only nerve-racking in the middle of a major event such as this one, but also frustrating. Crammed between Martin's coats, I attempted to dislodge the film from the take-up spool in complete darkness—to prevent further damage to the photos I'd already taken.

"Are you *sure* he took it?" a man said nearby.

I stiffened—not that I was doing anything wrong—but it *felt* wrong to listen in on someone else's conversation.

"Not entirely," a woman said, "but he was with me when I fell asleep in the study and after he left, the necklace was missing."

I was almost certain this unknown couple had entered the room, but curiosity prevented me from making my presence known.

Moreover, I didn't want to open the closet door and ruin the film, or risk that they might open the armoire upon hearing me.

"So you say." The man's voice was close now—most likely inside the room. "But he never showed up at the abandoned chapel."

"And? That doesn't mean anything. Only that he wasn't intimidated by your threats."

There was a creaking of drawers and steps getting close to the armoire. I'd better shut the camera before they let the light in. Should I say something? It would be awkward having to explain myself, especially after listening to their peculiar conversation.

"Do you really think he would've left something so valuable inside the desk?" she said. "He probably sold it."

"I've thought of that already. But I was hoping he would have a safe in this room."

The voices sounded familiar, the woman's in particular. But I'd talked to so many people at the party already.

"Would you stop for a minute?" she said.

"Stop what?"

"Looking for the damn necklace. I haven't seen you in two months. This might be our only opportunity to be alone."

"Amira, not here."

Amira? But the man's voice wasn't Farid's, I was certain of that.

"You haven't missed me?" she said, her voice softer.

The shuffling of papers stopped. I held my breath.

"Of course I have."

I froze, trying to listen and figure out who this man was. But there had been so many men downstairs.

"You look so beautiful," he said. "I've been wanting to kiss you all night."

They were quiet for a moment and I assumed they were kissing—or something. *Juemadre!* Couldn't they have found another room in this enormous hacienda to go to? The last thing I wanted was to listen to my best friend's wife kiss her lover, whoever that might be.

"What was that?" Amira said.

"What?"

"That noise."

"What noise?"

"Someone's coming."

I couldn't tell if she was talking about me or someone else. I was expecting that any second they would open the armoire door so I made sure the camera was completely shut.

But they never did. In fact, their voices dimmed as if they were walking away. I couldn't make out what they were saying anymore. I waited without moving a muscle until I was reasonably certain they'd left the room.

Slowly, I pushed the door open and stepped out of the closet—a relief, as my back ached from having bent over in such a tight space for so long.

As I headed back to the staircase, I spotted Don Yusuf Mansur entering one of the bedrooms with Farid. The old man was saying something in Arabic and, by his tone, I could tell he was agitated. Farid answered in Spanish.

"I don't understand when you speak that fast. Will you calm down?" Farid told his father.

They shut the door behind them. I stood by the carved oak panel and listened.

"I'm telling you," Yusuf switched to Spanish, "that damn woman is making a fool out of you. I just saw her with that man, that friend of Martin's."

"Who? What friend?"

"The redhead! The mine owner!"

Farid was silent for a moment.

"Are you going to let them laugh at you behind your back?" Yusuf said.

"Are you sure?"

"I know what I saw."

Farid's voice was hoarser than usual. "What *exactly* did you see?"

"They were kissing. In the study. The two idiots left the door ajar."

There was a thump inside the room. For a moment, I feared one of them had fallen down, but knowing Farid's temper, it was more likely that he'd hit a wall or a piece of furniture.

As their steps intensified, I darted away from the door and turned around the corner. Farid strode by without seeing me. His father followed him at a distance.

I couldn't say I was completely surprised about Amira's affair. She was young, beautiful, and so alone. I'd heard rumors about her since they moved to Cali, but I'd never truly lent ears to foolish chatter even though my mother and her friends had perfected the art of gossip. And now Farid had found out, in the worst way, at the worst possible moment. I'd better do something about it before a tragedy ensued. Farid could be so impulsive, so violent.

I'd better catch him before he did something he might regret for the rest of his life.

CHAPTER 41

Puri

A strange apathy took over me as I walked back to the hacienda. I knew I had to confront my feelings about Martin having a child with Camila, but at this point, nothing surprised me about him. I'd been one more in the long line of women who'd loved him, but I'd always clung to the thought that I'd been the only one who'd given him a child.

That notion had woefully changed.

Martin had a son with Camila.

And it must have been so painful, so traumatic that she'd become a nun and given her son to her brother.

But oddly, I couldn't feel anything—no anger, no pain, *nothing*.

The second thing I needed to come to terms with was what exactly was happening with Lucas, and could whatever that was have anything to do with my detachment from Martin—with his death, with him fathering another child, with the fact that I'd made a colossal mistake by loving him. Was it because of Lucas? Was it that time had run its course? After all, I hadn't seen Martin in over four years.

The sight of Tuli scurrying into the heart of the forest stopped me. I wasn't in a desperate hurry to be exposed by Dr. Costa, so I decided to follow the cook instead of returning to the hacienda.

Lucas had remained in the orchard calming Lula's nerves, which were quite altered after the small aftershock we'd experienced. Apparently, the earth was still adjusting to its new setup. So, it would be up to me to find out where Tuli was going.

I made my way through a curtain of thick branches and fallen trunks, brown leaves crackling under my feet, the air musky and heavy. A fragrance reminiscent of yeast, wet moss, and earth permeated. It didn't take long for Sor Alba Luz's habit to get stuck to my sweaty back, as if I'd just taken a bath.

In the distance, I spotted a dwelling of some kind, a wooden structure that appeared to be missing part of a wall. Tuli's turquoise skirt flashed for a minute before vanishing inside. I followed her in, careful not to spook her. I waited outside, debating whether to go in or not. In the end, curiosity reigned.

I couldn't believe my eyes.

Like a jigsaw puzzle, she was piecing together a set of bones, making out the shape of a person on the dirt floor. She was talking to the bones, explaining how the earth was angry again, how it had started shaking this morning.

"But don't worry," she was saying, "I'll look after you. I won't let that mean old man hurt you again."

I wasn't sure how to proceed. I didn't want to startle the woman, but I needed to understand whose bones those were. The first thought that came to mind was that they might be Martin's, but then whose body was in the grave I'd seen?

Holy Mother, what was happening? This was surreal. I approached the old lady.

"*Hola, cariño,*" I said in the calmest tone I could muster. "Are you all right?"

She turned to me, but I didn't know if she recognized me.

"Lula is a little worried about you," I said, making an effort not to look at the bones scattered across the floor, as if they were the most common thing in the world. "Because of the earth-quake."

There was something witchlike about Tuli, with her concoctions and the fact that she seemed to know things that others didn't. And this—what should I call it—*ceremony* of sorts?

"I don't like earthquakes," she said.

"Of course not, but it was just a *temblor*. Everything is fine."

I squatted next to her.

There was no skull, just the long limbs that formed arms and legs, in addition to the sternum and other smaller pieces scattered throughout.

She started collecting the bones and returned them to a wooden box.

"I have to go back," she said.

I knelt next to her. I intended to help her grab one of the bones and insert it in the box, but I couldn't bring myself to touch any of them. A question kept lingering in my mind: Who did these bones belong to?

CHAPTER 42

Camila

Hacienda La Reina
March 7, 1925
The night of the gala

It was hard to believe that only a couple of hours ago civility and class reigned in this hacienda. Sor Eugenia was certain that the current chaos had to do with the empty bottles of wine, rum, whiskey, and *aguardiente* filling the dining tables.

"Alcohol brings out the worst in people," she admonished.

I thought it was something else. I believed it had to do with Martin's desire to impress others. He'd always had a deep-rooted insecurity, an inferiority complex if you will, which I believed had to do with the fact that he wasn't the richest man in the region or that he didn't have an affluent family behind him. But he masked this flaw of character well with his charm, with his conquests, and with his confident laughter. I could see it so clearly now, as an adult, but I'd been blinded to his insecurities in my youth.

This desire to impress, I reckoned, had pushed him to show off his Andalusian mare to all who cared to see. And of course, that dreadful blond woman, that special friend of his, had insisted that they all go for a horse ride—in the middle of the night, with no concern or thought about the fact that everybody had been drinking.

As I ambled throughout the hacienda, I was confronted with a sight I'd never seen before. Frantic guests scattered throughout the property, shoes and stoles missing, women stumbling in the patio with tangled hair and empty wineglasses, men passed out on couches, and the worst part, Martin gone. His mare had returned twenty minutes ago without him.

A search party, led by my brother, was forming. I was trying my best to pretend I didn't care.

"Sor Camila, can I see you for a moment?"

I turned to find one of the kitchen maids—Lula?—standing in front of me. She looked agitated, her lips trembling slightly, her skin as pale as if she'd seen a ghost.

I followed her toward the back of the hacienda, where she led me to a donkey-drawn wagon.

"I know where Don Martin is."

"You do? Wonderful. Let's go tell my brother."

She held my sleeve. "No. Please. Just come with me."

I climbed onto the rustic buckboard and sat next to Lula, who grabbed the traces and guided the donkey into the plantation.

The full moon guided us through rows of cacao and banana trees and a long dirt road straight ahead. Toward the end of the road, the vegetation grew denser, darker. Lula took a turn into the thick forest. The donkey refused to take another step.

"It's here," Lula said, getting out of the wagon. "This way, *madre.*"

I followed her into the woods, stepping on broken branches and fallen leaves. Lula held my hand to help me. She'd grown up here and knew these woods like the back of her hand, she said.

At the heels of a monumental eucalyptus was Martin.

I couldn't get enough air. I didn't want to see what was wrong with him. My hands turned clammy; my mouth dry. I discerned his unnatural position, the tree trunk under his neck, his blurry facial features in shades of blue. I couldn't tell if his eyes were open or closed.

My heart overruled the pride that had reigned over me for the last fifteen years and I knelt beside him.

"Martin? Can you hear me? It's Camila."

He opened his eyes.

"Camila," he said with an effort.

At least his mind was working.

I held his hand.

How could I have thought for a second that I'd forgotten him? That I'd ever stopped loving him? I'd convinced myself that I despised him. I'd wished horrible things on him. But now, seeing him so defenseless, so defeated, I couldn't ignore my feelings—our bond—any longer. I'd caused this tragedy with my resentment, with my unwillingness to forgive.

"Don't let them find me," he said.

"Them?" I said. "Who are you talking about?"

"Don't take me back to the hacienda. Please. They're going to try again."

"Try what?"

Lula spoke before him. "To kill him. Didn't you hear the shots? That's why I came over."

"You're shot?" I made a quick inventory of his body, but didn't see blood anywhere, not that this was the best lighting for an examination. His body appeared to be made out of rubber, though.

"I don't know," he said.

"Can you move?"

He grimaced.

"I can't feel my legs. I can't move them."

We stared into each other's eyes. Mine teared up.

"We need to get him out of here," Lula said with urgency. "That's why I went to get you. I can't carry him alone."

"But where are we going to take him?"

"I know a place. Now let's hurry before they find him."

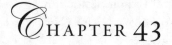

CHAPTER 43

Puri

I hid under the covers and pretended to be asleep as soon as I reached the nurses' bedroom. The last thing I wanted after all the excitement of the morning was to talk to Dr. Costa. I had a bad feeling about his reasons for calling me. He must have remembered me. Maybe it was a sign that it was time for me to leave—even if I didn't have all the answers I needed. It wasn't as if I stood a chance of solving this puzzle, anyway. The longer I stayed, the more questions arose.

The door creaked open. I shut my eyes more tightly.

"She's exhausted." The voice sounded like Sor Camila's.

"All right. I'll talk to her later," the man said.

I had no doubt it was Dr. Costa.

How long would I be able to avoid him? At least one more night? Lucas had asked me to help him find the safe's combination. I *had* to do it. Who cared if they forced me out tomorrow? Who cared if I didn't fully understand what had happened to Martin? He was dead, that was it. I would just have to live without all the answers. I'd been here too long already and had to get back to my son before I contracted cholera myself.

I would just have to forget about Lucas and whatever sensations he had awoken.

I tossed and turned thinking about him, about the way his eyes brightened when he saw me, about the way he teased me, about the feel of his embrace during the *temblor*. Eventually, I fell asleep and woke up after what felt like minutes, but in reality, had been hours. The nurses were getting ready for their shift, which began with dinner.

I would skip dinner altogether to avoid Dr. Costa. Hopefully he would go to bed early, but these doctors were unpredictable. Sometimes they spent all their time in the cholera wing. Other times they couldn't be found.

"You're finally up, *hermana*," Bertha told me while buttoning her uniform blouse over her large bosom. "You must've had fantastic dreams."

She giggled. And so did the other night nurse, a square, quiet woman named Rocío.

Had I spoken in my sleep? I didn't remember my dream except that Lucas had been in it. Oh, no, had I said something about him?

Yet another reason not to go to dinner.

I was lucky not to run into Dr. Costa during the first three hours of my shift. When it was dark and still and most everybody had gone to bed, I crossed the courtyard toward the staircase. Lucas and Farid were on the patio, having drinks. They'd been at it for hours, ever since I started my shift. Lucas nodded at me as I walked past them.

I ignored the surge of energy inside me. I suddenly forgot where I was going.

I had to get a hold of myself. I wasn't a lovesick adolescent. I was a thirty-three-year-old woman—a business owner and a mother.

The hall upstairs was empty.

From the gallery, I could see the door to Dr. Mansur's office. It would only take about twenty steps to get there. And yet, I had a bad feeling about this. I was getting tired of snooping, of hiding my real identity. What would Lucas think of me when he learned I'd been deceiving everybody here, putting patients' lives in danger with my inexperience and, even worse, that I'd also had a child with his best friend? I doubted he would have the same warm feelings for me then. Helping him now was the least I could do before he despised me and cut me out of his life forever, just like he'd done with his adoptive mother.

Lucas had no tolerance for deception.

I snuck into Mansur's office and turned on the gas lamp. I started with the top of the desk, where there was an array of papers. But nothing in there resembled a combination number. I proceeded to the drawers. Nothing. I briefly scanned the inside of books, prescription pads, folders.

A sense of futility took over me. More than satisfying my own curiosity, I wanted Lucas to be impressed by me. After all, I'd solved the puzzle about the man who'd murdered my husband a few years ago. But this seemed monumental in comparison.

Deflated, I headed out of the office.

"What are you doing here, *hermana*?"

I started. Then slowly turned around.

Amira stood in front of me, like a specter in her dark robe. A lengthy cigarette holder dangled between her fingers. The lantern in the hall underlined her features heavily, giving her a grave expression.

She must have seen me come in when she was smoking in the hall, hidden somewhere in the shadows. I should've known better. Amira never slept.

I cleared my throat, looked around the hall.

"Can you keep a secret?" I said, wrapping my arm around hers as if we were the best of friends. "Sometimes, I come here to nap so nobody sees me."

"To nap?" she repeated.

"Yes, it's the only room that's empty and the sofa in there is so comfortable. These night shifts can get very long." I led her back to her room, as if she were a small child. "Promise me you won't tell your husband. I'll be in so much trouble if the doctors or Sor Camila find out."

Amira didn't answer. She simply stared at me in silence.

We stopped in front of her door.

"Well, I'd better go back to work," I said. "Good night, Amira."

"Good night, Puri," she said, her voice a whisper.

Something about the way she'd said my name—without the *Sor*—gave me an ominous feeling.

The rowdy laughter on the patio echoed all the way to the stairs. It seemed Lucas had done a good job at getting Farid drunk, or getting inebriated himself. Now they were singing, cheering to Martin's memory. I walked past them and it didn't escape my notice the way Lucas looked at me with a sort of smile in his eyes. He looked adorable with his short-sleeve ivory shirt and suspenders. I stopped in front of them.

"Maybe you should take it down a notch?" I said. "People are trying to sleep."

"Oh, *hermana*," Dr. Mansur said, "I never imagined they recruited them so pretty. What a waste! Don't you agree, Lucas?"

Mansur was clearly drunk. He'd never been so fresh with me. In fact, he'd been nothing but professional all this time.

"Yes," Lucas said, fixing his gaze on me.

He didn't sound drunk at all.

"Maybe we should help him to his room?" I said. "You have a long day tomorrow, Doctor."

"That's a good idea," Lucas said. "Farid, you must get some rest."

Mansur tried to refuse, the way drunkards do when they want to keep the party going, but Lucas was already up, helping his friend.

"Help me, Sister," he said.

I grabbed the doctor's other arm and the two of us managed to lift him. Farid was quite tall and as I helped straighten him, I felt the solid muscles of his back.

"Maybe we should take him to your room, Señor Ferreira, since Doña Amira is still awake."

Mansur repeated his wife's name and said something in Arabic that didn't sound pleasant, though I had no idea what it meant.

"Sounds like a solid plan," Lucas said.

I could tell Lucas was having trouble balancing his own body without the cane, but somehow, we managed to cross the courtyard. The shirt was tight enough on Lucas that the definition of his shoulders and arms was apparent. I tried not to stare and instead focused on the task of helping Mansur up the staircase. The doctor continued his ranting in Arabic and Lucas and I took turns telling him to keep it down.

They had finally reopened Hospital San Juan de Dios, in Cali—after repairing the damages from the earthquake—so we'd been getting fewer patients and we weren't so crowded anymore. Thus, Lucas had his old room back.

Lucas and I helped Mansur into the room and set him on the bed. I undid his shoelaces and removed his boots.

"We should take his trousers off," Lucas said.

Mansur clung to Lucas's neck. "*Este es mi hermano*," he told me. "You know how long we've known each other?"

Lucas removed Farid's arms from his shoulders. "I love you, too, Turco."

I was already unbuttoning the doctor's light cotton shirt. There was a slim chance that he carried the combination number with him, but it was worth a try. God knew I didn't want to have to look inside Farid and Amira's bedroom.

Under the doctor's shirt was the medal I'd seen when I first met him.

"And this medal?" I said, lifting it.

"Saint Pantaleon, patron saint of physicians. He was a healer," Lucas said, attempting to undo Farid's trousers. "You really should learn your saints, *hermana*."

I swallowed. "Of course I know who he is. I was testing *you*."

He gave me a funny look.

Farid started to sing. I'd never been more grateful to hear the out-of-tune hollers of a drunken man.

"Shhh," Lucas said. "You don't want to wake up your sister, do you?"

"My sister. Good idea. There are a few things I need to talk to her about. Mila! Mila!"

"Shhh," Lucas said. "Your father's room is next door. Come on, Farid, he's an old man. He needs his sleep. You can talk to her tomorrow."

Before every Mansur in the hospital showed up, I checked the shirt's front pocket. Nothing. With Farid sitting on the edge of the bed, I pulled his trousers down, avoiding the sight of his white union suit. I ransacked through every single pocket in his pants but again, I found nothing.

I looked at Lucas in defeat.

All this work for nothing.

"That's fine," he said. "We'll figure it out."

"What? What is there to figure out?" Farid said.

"How to get you to bed without waking up the entire hospital," I said, untucking the sheets.

Farid had entered a new stage of drunkenness: complete exhaustion. He'd closed his eyes already and had gotten into a fetal position on top of the covers.

"Wait, wait," I said. "Get under the covers."

I grasped Farid's hands in an attempt to get him up, but he pulled me down and I landed on top of him so that our faces were only centimeters apart. The smell of alcohol emanated from his pores.

"Well, hello, pretty sister," Farid said. "Nice to have you this close."

"That's enough!" Lucas said, holding me by the waist and pulling me away from Farid's grasp. "Have some respect, Farid. She's a nun!" He turned to me, his beret crooked. "Let's go, Puri."

I'd never seen Lucas like this.

Was he *jealous*?

Lucas turned the light off and shut the door, holding my hand the entire time, as though he feared I might run away.

When we reached the first floor—him limping, me staring at him in shock—he dropped my hand. "I'm sorry about that."

I was more disappointed about him letting go of my hand than not finding the paper with the combination.

"Don't worry about it," I said.

"I don't want you to get in trouble with . . . I don't know, the Lord, because of Farid's stupidity."

"I'm fine, Lucas." I bit my lower lip to not smile.

"He's such an idiot. He's used to having any woman he wants. Just like Martin."

His last words killed my amusement. I'd been just another woman to fall for Martin. What would Lucas think if he knew the extent of my involvement with his friend?

"I take it you didn't have any luck in his office?" he said.

"I beg your pardon?"

He lowered his voice even more. "Looking for the combination?"

"Oh, no," I said. "In fact, Amira saw me there."

"*Mierda*." He brought his hand to his forehead, adjusted his beret. "What a waste of time. I'm telling you, getting Farid drunk was a nightmare. He has so much tolerance. After a while, I was pouring my drinks in his glass whenever he was distracted."

That explained why Lucas was still sober.

"Wait a minute," I said.

"What?"

I headed toward the patio and went directly to the wrought iron bistro table where the two men had been drinking. Sure enough, Farid's white smock was still sitting on the chair's backrest. I dug my hand in one of the pockets and searched for the paper.

Again, nothing.

I searched inside the other one. The feel of the cold metal tube and the flexible rubber gave me an idea.

When Lucas finally reached me, I flashed the medical stethoscope at him.

I was certain that my break was over but I didn't care. I doubted the other nurses would come find me and this might be our last chance to open the safe before they threw me out of here. While I held the candle close to the metal safe, Lucas placed the ear tips of Farid's stethoscope in his ears and pressed the chest piece on the safe's door. With the patience of a saint, he tried different dial combinations, listening attentively to the click that would signal that he got the right digits. After the third turn, the safe unlocked.

He turned to me with a wide smile.

I applauded quietly.

He pulled on the metal handle and opened the door.

Inside was a small stack of cash and several documents that Lucas handed to me. There was Martin's Ecuadorian passport, his *cédula*, contracts with cacao bean buyers—including me—and other papers I couldn't examine as Lucas gently removed a midnight blue velvet box.

The necklace.

He opened the lid, but the necklace had been taken apart. From what we could see, only four smaller-sized emeralds remained, but the large one—the one Amira had mentioned—was gone.

"Look inside," I said.

He felt the empty safe with his hand.

I, myself, brought the candle to the inside of the box, but it was completely empty.

"Amira said there were four medium-sized stones on either side of the big one for a total of eight, plus the center piece."

And yet, there were only four pieces left.

"He must have sold them," Lucas said. "That's how he gave himself away."

"Probably."

"What did you find in there?"

"Oh, just contracts. Nothing important." I didn't want Lucas to see my name on the contract papers. Or Farid, for that matter.

"Let's just put everything away. I don't want Farid to notice someone opened the safe."

He closed the jewelry box and returned it to the safe. Then he extended his hand so I would hand him the papers. My contract was the top one.

I handed him Martin's passport and *cédula* but held on to the other documents.

"Wait, let me make sure there's nothing important here." I scanned through the documents and placed mine on the bottom. But how could I prevent Farid from looking at it at some point? My name was not common. Would he make the connection?

"Hurry, I don't want someone to find us here," he said.

"Just a minute." I pretended to read one of the papers. Maybe I should just confess.

"Come on, *hermana*."

About that . . .

It would be so easy, such a relief to tell him the truth.

But then I remembered the harsh expression he reserved for his mother for lying to him all of his life. He wouldn't take it well. He was a man of high morals. He'd been outraged when Farid had made a pass at me.

I handed him the papers. If Farid found out who I was, so be it.

I couldn't tell Lucas.

I couldn't live with his contempt.

CHAPTER 44

Lucas

There was something wrong with Don Yusuf. He'd always been an outgoing, jolly man, but since the earthquake, he'd become muted and spent hours locked in his room, apparently reading. Or so Basim said. I understood losing your house to a natural disaster could be life altering. Aging could also be a contributing factor for his premature silence, but I sensed there was something else there; something he was keeping to himself.

I intended to know what.

The most effective, and quickest, way to get a man speaking was alcohol. But I wasn't looking forward to this method, not after getting Farid drunk last night. I still had a headache even though I'd drunk a fraction of what Farid had. It had always been that way. He had the tolerance of a bull and his father was the same, which is why I was dreading the drinking binge with Don Yusuf.

From his bedroom door, I flashed a bottle of *aguardiente* at him.

"Ah, Lucas, you read my mind. Tonight feels like a . . . what do they call it—*una noche de copas?*"

Yes, a night of drinks, all right.

Don Yusuf had always had a special affection for me after all the holidays and summers I spent with them. In his own words, I was his "*caleño* son."

We settled on two lawn chairs in the back of the hacienda, overlooking the weathering trees of what had once been Martin's imposing plantation. It was a pity that nobody had taken over the cacao business after his passing. I knew Farid meant well with the hospital, but did he have to take over a place like this and let it go to waste?

The sun was already setting, so we lowered our straw hats to shield our eyes. Basim brought over his guitar and sat on a broken tree trunk by my side. I could see the burgeoning man inside his adolescent body. Basim had an intuition and wisdom seldom seen in young men.

I borrowed his guitar to play my favorite *bambuco*. I'd left mine at Matilde's house—I never intended to stay here for so long. Not that I had any desire to go back to Cali. Not when I was so close to finding out what had happened to my biological mother. It would be a while before I went back home as I also intended to find my twin sister. But who was I fooling? I would've probably already left had it not been for one thing—or should I say, one person.

Ugh, what an idiot I was. She was a *nun*, for God's sake!

I was a sucker for unrequited love.

First Camila, now Puri.

"How do you do that?" Basim said, staring at my fingers as I picked out the tune.

It was amazing how much he was growing to look like Martin. No wonder Farid and his father had figured out the whole thing. It was impossible not to. He must have caused quite an impression on Camila as well.

I slowed down the speed of my arpeggios to show him.

"Like this," I said, indicating what I'd done.

Too bad Martin had never met his son. He'd been so lonely in this enormous hacienda the last months of his life. And Basim was such an agreeable boy.

I handed Basim the guitar and served more *aguardiente* to Don Yusuf.

"*Ya Allah!*" the old Mansur said. "You want to get me drunk or what?"

I smirked, but kept pouring the transparent liquid into his glass.

"Don Yusuf, how often do you and I have a drink? We need to distract our minds from all the horror we're seeing here. Besides, there's always room for one more *aguardientico*."

He took the glass. "You're right about that. I, for one, am ready to go home. I can't stand this place."

He glanced at his grandson, who, oblivious to the true meaning of his grandfather's words, continued to move his fingers along the guitar's neck with growing dexterity.

"How are the house repairs coming along?" I asked.

"From what I hear from Ibrahim, slower than I would like." He rested his hands on the side of the chair and I offered him some *aborrajados* and a slice of *queso campesino* to mitigate the disappointment in his voice.

"What I wouldn't give for an *Arak* with this cheese," he said, longingly.

But *Arak* was not always in high supply around these lands unless an Arab *paisano* happened to visit Don Ibrahim or Don Yusuf or another one of their compatriots.

"That's not the only thing you're longing for tonight, isn't it?" I said.

"Ah, Lucas, you know me well. It's not good for a man to be without a woman. When are you getting married, *ibni*?"

I felt complete acceptance every time he called me *ibni*—*son* in Arabic—and I also knew the *aguardiente* was starting to work.

"Oh, I'm well past the age."

"You're crazy, boy, there's no age limit for men. You can marry at any age. I never understood why you didn't."

Because the woman I loved devoted her life to God.

I shrugged. "I was not lucky enough to find the right person."

"Nonsense," he said. "There's always someone."

"Hopefully things will be different for Basim, right?"

The boy blushed, but continued strumming the guitar. How was I supposed to get relevant information from Don Yusuf with Basim here the entire time? I was going to have to come up with an excuse for the boy to leave. But not yet. Don Yusuf was not done reminiscing about his house, about his late wife, or his homeland.

It took only two hours for Basim to get bored with us and for Don Yusuf to get drunk enough to open up. It was dark now, which was ideal for confessions and secrets, but I could still see him through the dim light coming from the kitchen. This was my chance, my one opportunity to know exactly what had happened the night Martin disappeared.

"It seems like so long ago since the fundraiser gala, doesn't it?" I said, gazing at the star-filled sky.

"A lifetime." He touched the side of his hook nose with his forefinger. "But don't remind me of that dreadful night."

I ignored his plea.

"What exactly happened when you all went horseback riding? What were those gunshots all about?"

"Ugh, Lucas, why you have to talk about this?"

I guess he's not ready yet.

I served him another drink.

This time, however, I didn't have to insist. Don Yusuf was ready for me to fill his glass. He gulped it at once.

"You know you can trust me, Don Yusuf."

"What you want to know, *ibni*?"

I sat forward, squeezing my hat's rim.

"Who shot Martin?"

Don Yusuf brought his hands to his face. "That damn Martin, *ibn sharmuta!* He had it coming. He disgraced my daughter. Her entire life, her future, down the drain because of him."

"So, you and Farid found out that night?"

"We'd suspected it for some time."

"So, this was, what? *Revenge?* Kill him and take the hacienda from him?"

"No. That's not what happened."

"Then?"

He stood up, mumbling in Arabic, and stumbled toward the *cacaotales*. I rushed behind him.

"Why do you make me talk, Lucas? I don't want to remember." He brought his hands to his face.

"What did you do?"

He kept walking. "I didn't mean to hurt him."

It was hard for me to keep up with my stiff leg. Don Yusuf had left in such a rush that I'd forgotten my cane by the chair. A spasm reverberated up my spine with every step I took.

It had gotten dark already but the moonlight illuminated our path. The deeper we got into the cacao fields, the louder the chirping of crickets resounded. I spotted an owl on the branch of a tree, which my mother thought was a bad omen.

Could things get *any* worse?

"Don Yusuf!" I called out.

For the life of me, I couldn't understand why the old Mansur was going into the woods at night. In retrospect, I shouldn't have brought up the subject of the gala, but how could I have imagined it would have such a strange effect on him?

I heard him groan a few steps ahead. I hopped toward the sound.

Don Yusuf was on the ground, rubbing his ankle. Apparently, he'd tripped over a rock or the roots of a tree.

"Are you all right?" I said, crouching toward him.

He was silently cussing in Arabic. "I'm such an idiot."

"What was that all about?"

"Don't ask any more, Lucas, *min fadlak*."

"Here, grab my arm," I said, hoisting him up.

The old man was short, but massive. And yet, he'd never seemed more frail to me. I'd always thought of him as all-powerful, a brave man who had migrated halfway across the world with nothing and had made a small fortune due to hard work. But now, his devastation over whatever it was he did wrong was showing me a different side of him. He wasn't the superhero I'd always thought. He was just a man.

CHAPTER 45

Puri

He found me. There was no more escaping Dr. Costa. He was waiting for me downstairs at the beginning of my shift.

"Can I talk to you, *hermana*?"

My compatriot was a quiet, gentle man who normally had a calming aura. I had seen his effect on patients. I wondered for the first time what had happened to his wife. She'd been so kind to me aboard the *Andes* after my husband died.

"*Hermana*, there's something that's been on my mind since you arrived."

I faced the gray pebbles under my feet, hoping the veil would cover most of my face.

"Have we met before? I mean, I've seen hundreds of people since I arrived in Colombia, but you're so familiar."

Just tell him already. There was nothing keeping me here. Except for this strong desire of doing right by my son, by Martin.

And Lucas, of course.

"I . . . I don't think so." I cleared my throat. "Where would we have met?"

"That's what I'm trying to figure out. Did we meet in Spain, perhaps? I have a cousin who's a nun and I went to her Day of Vesture, so maybe there . . . because I haven't been to Sevilla—"

"Dr. Costa, Dr. Costa!" Perla was running across the patio toward us. "You have to come. *Please*."

"What is it, *tía*? Have you seen a ghost or what?"

She stopped in front of us, panting, and rested a hand on her chest.

"It's Sor Camila."

They'd brought her into a private area of the cholera room, separated by a curtain. Apparently, the nurses didn't want the other patients to panic if they saw their beloved nun sick.

"Have you told Dr. Mansur?" Dr. Costa said, drawing the curtain open.

"I couldn't find him anywhere," Perla said.

I'd never seen Sor Camila without the veil. Her hair was so short. It made her face look different, much younger, and her eyes stood out even more. She looked so much like her brother, but she was so pale, so thin in her white camisole.

"It was just a matter of time before one of us got it," Dr. Costa said. "Wash her habit, Perla."

Nodding, she picked up the habit from a chair sitting by the bed.

The doctor himself administered an IV to Camila to prevent her from dehydrating. I was instructed to stay by her side and report to him any change in her condition. After I got her comfortable, I brought a chair by her bed.

There was so much I wanted to tell her. Especially now that I knew that she'd also had a son with Martin. For reasons I couldn't explain, I felt no jealousy toward her. Not like I had felt toward my sister Angélica. I massaged her legs, which had been cramping, but she dozed off and on the rest of the night.

Her brother didn't come to check on her until dawn. He seemed to have no recollection of the things he'd told me the previous night. In fact, he was so flustered with his sister's illness that he didn't seem to notice me at all.

I was exhausted, physically and emotionally. Seeing someone as unbreakable as Sor Camila stricken by this disease was devastating.

It could happen to any one of us.

I'd been telling this to myself daily. And yet, until today it seemed like an abstract concept. Sor Camila had mentioned they'd lost a couple of nuns but I hadn't seen it firsthand. I couldn't ignore it anymore.

Leaving would be the rational thing to do, but I couldn't do it. Not with Sor Camila sick. After all I'd seen her do, I couldn't just abandon her. It would break her heart if someone whom she believed to be a fellow sister would leave in her hour of need.

This was my time to live up to my disguise. It wasn't just an attire, it was a commitment, a way of life. I recalled Sor Alba Luz's words when I'd slipped into her habit. She'd said it suited me. She said maybe it was meant to be mine.

I was far from a vocational awakening, but maybe there was something to this, a reason that went beyond feeling safe or a compulsion to know what had happened to Martin.

Perhaps I was meant to be here. Perhaps there was a purpose greater than myself.

As I headed out of the cholera room—stretching my back as it had been aching for the last couple of hours—I saw Perla tending to Don Iván. The old man was in the process of retching into a bucket Perla was holding. When he looked up, his gaze narrowed.

There was something rotten about him. Lucas had been right to suspect him. But I had no mind for this man right now.

The nurse's room was in a state of chaos. Someone had opened our armoire and had rummaged through our things. My indignant roommates were complaining out loud, picking up their clothes from the beds and hanging them. Alba Luz's bag had also been turned inside out and the little belongings I had—including my son's stuffed bear—littered the mosaic tile floors. I picked up the bear and hugged it. Seeing my most prized possession on the ground felt like a personal attack.

Had it been?

CHAPTER 46

Puri

I only slept a couple of hours and from the moment I woke up, I dedicated all my attention to Sor Camila. I tried feeding her some of Tuli's miraculous broth, but the nun hardly ate. With all the liquids she was losing—at rapid speed—her cheeks seemed to be shrinking.

"I need you to do something for me," she said.

"Anything you need," I said, removing the cloth napkin from her chest as she was most definitely done after four spoonfuls of broth.

"Ask Lucas to take you to El Paraíso and bring Padre José María."

I was dumbfounded. Her request seemed so final.

"Surely you're going to make it, *hermana*."

"Just do it, Puri, the sooner the better."

I wanted to somehow infuse her with hope, but this woman had been here since the beginning of this epidemic. She knew exactly what to expect.

"Before you leave," she said as I stood, "please tell Lula to come."

Lula? The cook?

I nodded, but something hit me on my way to the kitchen. Why had she called me "Puri" and where had she left the *Sor*? Did she know something?

I'd become so irrational about that.

Lucas was in the kitchen, having *pandebono* for breakfast. Lula warmed *avena* in the stove with one hand while cooling herself with a straw fan with the other. I had a sudden urge to cry as my eyes met Lucas's.

"What's wrong?" he said.

I swallowed painfully. "Lula, Sor Camila asked to speak to you. She's in the cholera room. Sick."

"*Sick?*" both repeated, horrified.

Lula dropped her fan and abandoned her *avena* over the flame without another word.

I removed the pot from the stove. Lucas stood behind me.

"She asked to speak to Padre José María." I could feel the tears gathering in my eyes. "Could you take me to El Paraíso to get him?"

"Of course."

I took in deep breaths as we headed for the stables to get the horse and the carriage. What would happen to Basim if Camila died? Would he ever find out that his aunt was, in fact, his biological mother? I couldn't believe Sor Camila wouldn't be here anymore—she was such an integral part of this hospital.

"Puri?" Lucas said, reaching out for my hand.

I feared that if I spoke, I would start sobbing uncontrollably.

The words finally came out. "Sor Camila can't die."

He wiped a tear from my cheek. "She'll make it, you'll see."

I started. His touch was so unexpected. His fingers lingered down my cheek. I extended my arms and hugged him. The warmth of his chest against mine offered some relief. He brought his hands to my back and held me for a few minutes. My body fit perfectly into his. It was one of the best hugs I'd ever received.

Slowly, I loosened my grip and set my hands on his shoulders.

At that moment, I didn't care if it was proper or not for a nun to hug a man. I needed this. I expected him to push me away, but he didn't. He brought his hands to my face and gently cupped it.

Wait, was he going to . . . ?

His lips touched mine before I could do anything about it—not that I would have. I'd been fooling myself into thinking that Lucas was just a helpful, nice man—a ray of sunshine in the middle of a storm—but I couldn't fool myself any longer. I *wanted* this kiss just as much as he apparently did. It occurred to me that someone might see us. I should take a step back. After all, I was wearing a habit; I must be breaking some sort of sacred law. But I couldn't pull away. Lucas's kiss was doing things to my body, to my soul. It was filling me with an unexpected relief. Soothing me. But as I started giving in to the delicious sensations he was awakening, the kiss came to an abrupt end.

"I'm sorry," he said, the voice of reason. He lowered the rim of his bowler hat. "Please forgive me. I don't know what came over me."

I was too shocked to speak.

What *could* I say?

I could start by telling him I wasn't a nun. That would certainly relieve his guilt.

He turned toward the horse, which had been patiently waiting for us, and adjusted the holster's straps.

I wanted to tell him, I really did. But this was not the right time. We needed to get Padre José María, not get in a big discussion of what I'd done and why.

During our drive to town, Lucas kept his gaze on the road and I was conscious of his proximity, of his leg touching mine, of his manly scent, all along trying to come up with the right words to end this unbearable silence.

"You really think Sor Camila will survive?" I said.

"It could happen. A handful of people have gotten better. And I know Dr. Costa has been working on some kind of medicine. I bet he'll try it on her."

"I hope so. I don't know what's to become of this hospital without her."

He nodded. I wished, only for a moment, that he would throw in one of his jokes, something to lighten the mood.

"But like Dr. Costa said," I continued, "it was just a matter of time before someone else got sick, like those two nuns."

He turned to me for the first time.

"What two nuns?"

"I don't know their names, but Sor Camila mentioned that they had died." At least that had been my impression. She hadn't really specified what happened to them.

"There haven't been any other nuns here. I mean, a couple of sisters came with her to the gala, months ago, but they left right after. Sor Camila has been the only nun here since Farid turned this place into a hospital. Well, other than you."

I dodged his gaze. "Are you sure?"

"Yes. I came to the opening to take photographs, remember? I've memorized almost every face."

A branch of an overgrown tree was blocking the trail. Lucas skewed the carriage.

"But why would she lie about that?" I said.

Sor Camila had also been saying for some time that other nuns from her congregation were supposed to arrive, but none of them ever did.

"I've wondered myself why she'd sent for a Sierva de María instead of someone from her own congregation," he said.

Yes. *Why?*

"She said they were too busy and couldn't send anyone," I said.

Our eyes met, but only for a second, because both of us turned in opposite directions. I rehearsed my confession in my mind.

Since we're talking about nuns, I guess I should tell you something.

I parted my lips. I was going to tell him.

I'm not a nun. I'm barely a Catholic.

Before I gathered enough courage, he stopped the carriage by a small, run-down chapel and stepped down. I'd lost my chance. For now.

When we got back to the hacienda with Padre José María, Sor Camila was hooked to an IV again. I stood at a distance while she confessed, my mind ruminating, reliving my conversation with Lucas about Sor Camila. Why had she lied about the other nuns being here? I also remembered Perla saying something about Camila being here when she arrived. But didn't Perla come at the very beginning, when they first turned the hacienda into a hospital? So why had Camila been here already? It must've had something to do with her connection to Farid.

I stepped outside for some fresh air and sat on the edge of the fountain, lulled by the serene sounds the water made as it fell inside its stone basin.

Now that I thought about it, Camila had had other strange behaviors, like the time I'd run into her in the hallway in the middle of the night, or just the other night when she wasn't in her bed. What had Perla said, that Camila never slept?

"Purificación!" Lucas's voice startled me.

He was walking toward me, his cane in one hand and a piece of paper in the other.

"What's wrong?" I said.

He was frowning.

Lucas *never* frowned.

And he'd never called me Purificación, either.

He extended the paper toward me. It wasn't paper, it was an image.

I took it. A group photograph. My eyes gravitated toward me wearing a black cocktail dress with peacock appliques scattered throughout, my mane in a bun, and a headband with a long feather around it. I remembered this gown—the appliques were gold and turquoise, as was the feather. My late husband, Cristóbal, was by my side, wearing one of his finest tuxedos. There were about eight people sitting around a table, and at the end was Dr. Costa with his wife, Montserrat.

This photo had been taken aboard the *Andes* five years ago, soon after we'd left Cuba. I'd had no recollection of Dr. Costa at this dinner, only the night of my husband's demise.

"Dr. Costa showed it to me," Lucas said, his frown deeper. "He says he met you a few years ago *with your husband.*"

I swallowed.

"Let me explain—"

"You're married? You're not a nun?"

"Yes and no."

He seized the photograph from my hands, politeness aside, and fixed his eyes on Cristóbal.

"How could you—"

"I'm a widow," I explained. "Cristóbal perished during that trip. Didn't Dr. Costa tell you that?"

"He didn't have time, I suppose. As soon as he told me who you were, I came looking for you." He dropped the picture on the ground. "Why are you pretending to be a nun?"

If he was this upset about my husband, I didn't even want to think about what he would say when I told him about Martin's son.

I stared at Cristóbal's image. It had been so long since I'd seen his placid face.

Please help me.

"It's a long story," I started.

He'd set his cane against the fountain and had crossed his arms in front of his chest. I'd never seen him this upset, not even at his mother's house.

"I have all day," he said.

"Well, the truth is"—I chewed on my bottom lip. *Where should I even start?*—"I went to Ecuador five years ago to take possession of my father's cacao plantation after he passed away. Martin was the plantation administrator there. He and I . . . well, we had a short relationship and when he came here, he sold me cacao beans for my chocolate store. Since I hadn't heard from him in months, I decided to come and find him."

"That doesn't explain your *long* deceit."

I told him about the assault, about my fears.

"There's one more thing," I said, picking up the photograph from the ground and staring at my old smiling self, clueless of all the hardships I would have to endure in the near future. "Martin and I have a son together."

He gaped. I reached out for his arm, tight against his chest, but he took a step back.

"And here you were, laughing at me all along," he said.

"No, not at all. I felt terrible about not telling you the truth. I tried so many times."

He was shaking his head, glaring at me as if I were trash.

"Lucas, please, don't look at me that way. What else could I do? I had to know what happened to Martin."

"Of course you did. He's the love of your life, just like everybody else's."

"I never said that. I—"

"I don't want to hear any more, Puri!" He brought his fists to his sides. "But don't you worry, I won't tell anyone what I know, so you're free to continue investigating all you want."

"I doubt it," I said, in a desperate attempt to keep him here. "Someone is on to me."

He lifted an eyebrow, minimally interested.

"Last night, I found my things in disarray, as though someone had been looking through my bag."

His features softened. The old Lucas was back, I dared to hope.

"Yes, well, sorry to hear it." He grabbed his cane. "I wish you luck."

"Wait. You're *leaving*?"

"First thing in the morning. There's nothing else for me here."

"What about María Belén? Don Iván?"

"That old man is going to die and take his secret with him. I'm done wasting my time here."

"What about Sor Camila?"

His eyes glimmered.

"I'm afraid I can't do anything for her. My presence won't make a difference."

And with that, Lucas turned around and left.

CHAPTER 47

Lucas

Farid was beside himself. I'd never seen him so pale, so unkempt. He'd always been a man who prided himself on keeping a pristine image. In spite of the many bad nights he experienced in his line of work and his demanding schedule, he'd always found the time to shave and wash his face.

Today was the exception, which told me how sick Camila really was.

She'd always been Farid's adoration in spite of her illegitimate child and the many years they'd lived apart. He'd told me once that Camila and Don Yusuf were the only people in the world he loved—not his daughters, not his younger siblings, and certainly not his wife. He said that after his mother had died, something got shut inside his heart, and he didn't let anyone else inside.

Sure, he had appreciation for me and had, at one point, cared for Martin. But it wasn't like the love he had for his father and his sister.

"What do you mean, you're leaving?" he told me, hands pressed against the desk's surface.

"Exactly that. I'm done here. I'm fully recovered, as you know well, and I've been here entirely too long."

He glanced at my leg.

"But now, Lucas? Now that Camila is so ill? I need you here, *hermano*, if only for moral support."

I didn't even want to think about Camila. It wasn't like I loved her still. I'd had many years to get over my infatuation, though I still admired and considered her a beautiful woman, but the possibility that she might die in a day or two was something I didn't want to face. I wasn't ready to take her dead body away in that damn wagon, like I'd done with all the others. Not after the blow I just received with Puri's confession.

I shook my head. "I'm truly sorry, Farid. I already made up my mind. I'm leaving tomorrow. So would you please have Nestor take me to Cali first thing in the morning?"

"All right, if you feel you must." He rubbed his forehead. "But before you leave, there's something I'd like to talk to you about."

"What?"

"That nun, Sor Purificación."

Por amor de Dios, did we have to talk about her right now?

"You've gotten very close to her, it seems."

"Not really. Why do you ask?"

"Amira has her suspicions about her."

"About what?" I massaged my lower leg, which had gotten numb. It happened from time to time since the accident. It had gotten so pale and skinny.

"Martin once talked to Amira about a woman named Purificación that he knew well."

I shifted in my seat.

"That's not such a common name," he said.

"So?"

"Don't you think it's a big coincidence that she would show up here after he . . . after he died? Besides, the Puri that Martin mentioned was also a Spaniard and Amira says she's been digging about Martin, about her, asking all kinds of questions. She even found her snooping in my office." He leaned forward, fingers crossed. "Amira made a deal with me. She said she would share a secret that had the potential of solving all my economic problems in exchange for her freedom."

"What economic problems?"

"This hospital has been nothing but expenses, Lucas. The Church is barely giving me any money to support all these people. I don't think I can keep this place going for much longer."

"Maybe you should turn it back into a cacao plantation." I couldn't hide the hostility in my voice. Puri had managed to make me doubt my best friend and what he had done to acquire this place.

Farid made a face.

"Tell me about this deal you made with Amira. What secret did she share?"

"She said Martin was in possession of an expensive emerald necklace and she strongly believes Puri might have it. Part of it is in Martin's safe but the biggest stone—the most valuable—is missing."

"Why does she think Puri has it?" The words came out before I had a chance to think about what he was saying. Puri had just confessed to me that Martin and her had been lovers. She'd even had a child with him. Amira might not be so far off, but Puri didn't have said necklace. Half of it was in Martin's safe and she had no idea where the rest was. Had Farid been the one to look through her things yesterday?

"Amira thinks they might have had a relationship. Something about the way he spoke of her. He could've given her a stone and maybe she came here for the rest?"

"I think your wife has a vivid imagination," I said, noncommittally. I hadn't decided yet where my loyalty should be. With my childhood friend—a known bully? Or with the woman I'd fallen in love with—a confirmed liar?

"I don't know. Amira might be right about her," El Turco said. "She's tried to approach me, too. Look at this." He opened a folder on top of his desk and handed me a document.

It was a contract between Puri and Martin. She was a client of his, just like she'd told me.

"See? I think this is her."

I didn't like what I saw in his eyes. Puri had no idea how determined and heartless Farid could be when he wanted something.

"Now that we're talking about Martin," I said, changing the subject, "would you care to explain what exactly happened the night of the gala?"

He shut the folder. "Oh, Lucas, do we have to talk about that again? I already explained what happened. A jaguar cut in front of me and I shot it. The gunshot spooked the horses and apparently Martin fell down and broke his neck. End of story."

"You shot twice?"

"What?"

"There were two shots."

He shook his head. "Where did you get that?"

"Many witnesses heard two shots."

"Oh, come on!" He stood up. "Why are you bringing this up now? So, maybe I shot twice. How am I supposed to remember that? Who the hell cares anyway?"

"Well, I was speaking to your father a few days ago and he was perturbed by whatever happened there."

He seemed taken aback by my comment. "Of course he was. It was a terrible tragedy." He strode toward the door. "Now, let's go see Nestor and tell him about your trip tomorrow."

CHAPTER 48

Puri

Lucas was leaving today. And he hated me.

He didn't care about his missing mother or Don Iván, either.

I should leave, too.

There was nothing left for me here.

Except for one thing.

Sor Camila was not doing well. She'd been sleeping for hours and when she woke up, it was to expel whatever liquids we'd put into her body.

After she dies, I'll leave.

I wasn't close to her, but I admired her strength, her stamina, and she believed me to be a nun so she would go in peace if I stayed by her side. It was the least I could do.

When she opened her eyes, I approached her.

"Is there anything you need, *hermana*?" I said.

She parted her lips, about to say something, but couldn't.

Or *wouldn't*.

I decided to take a gamble. She might be too proud to do it herself, or too worried about *el que dirán*—what will they say? How many bad decisions were made in life in consideration of what society might say?

I made sure the cream gauze curtain separating Sor Camila from the other patients was well shut and cleared my throat.

"Is there anybody you would like to see, *hermana*? I know that your . . . that Basim has been asking about you. He'll probably be delighted to see you."

"Basim?" Her voice broke. Her lips were so chapped. She'd acquired a bluish-gray tone all over her face.

I held her hand. It was cold and leathery.

"I think you should talk to him," I said.

She squinted a little bit, studying my every expression. I nodded, grasping her hand. She squeezed mine back. A single tear trailed from the corner of her eye.

"Yes, call him." She didn't let go of my hand. "And Puri, come back later. I need to ask you something else."

I'd spent all night thinking about what Sor Camila was hiding—the ifs and whys of her prolonged presence here, her furtive meetings with Lula, and the cook's constant absences. I might have an idea of what Camila wanted to ask me.

After finding Basim and taking him to Camila, I left mother and son alone and went to the kitchen area.

"Doña Tuli," I said. "Where is Lula?"

The old woman scratched her head. "She was just here, serving *sancocho.*"

I thanked her and stepped out of the kitchen through the back door. I crossed the orchard and the chicken coop. The servants' quarters were just a few meters away. I spotted Lula's curly head approaching one of the doors, a bowl of soup in her hands.

I followed her at a distance and watched as she opened the door with one hand while holding the bowl with the other. She glanced back for a second. I hid behind a thicket.

Once she was inside, I carefully crossed the dirt path that connected the chicken coop to the building that housed the servants in the hacienda. I held the doorknob, taking a deep breath, and slowly twisted it.

The door creaked a bit as I pushed it in. I made my way into a dim room. It was dark but even through the gloom, I could see the body lying on the bed.

My suspicions were correct.

CHAPTER 49

Camila

This was not at all the scenario I'd envisioned for telling my son who I really was. Not that I'd actually considered the possibility. I'd always shut down the idea. I'd been tempted to do it so many times since he'd arrived at the hacienda, but there was simply too much at stake.

So I resigned myself to watch him from a distance as he ate or talked to Baba or played his guitar. I had managed to surprise him a few times with the desserts I'd saved for him. If he was anything like the men in our family, the portions they were giving him wouldn't be enough. Basim would thank me and grant me one of his sweet smiles, which reminded me so much of Martin.

Wearing a mask over his nose and mouth, Basim approached me and sat on the chair that Sor Puri had left by my bed. Despite my dehydration, my eyes filled with tears.

"*Hola, tía,*" he said. He was a boy of few words. So different from his father and from my brother. In some ways he reminded me of Lucas when he was young.

I managed a smile through my achy throat. I must look awful.

What a pity to be in such a deplorable state when making such an important confession.

"Sor Puri said you wanted to talk to me."

"Yes, Basim." I reached out for his hand. It was somewhat damp, larger than mine. How had that happened when at one point he'd been so small he'd lived inside of me? He seemed taken aback by my touch, but didn't move away.

"Basim, I have something to tell you, but please, understand that what I did was against my wishes."

He shifted in his seat, his eyes on me.

"Basim, I know you've always known me as your aunt, the nun. But the truth is I wasn't born with a religious vocation. This path was something I had to take because of my circumstances."

"What circumstances?"

"I fell in love when I was seventeen years old. And that love . . . well, it had consequences."

He leaned forward, his eyes narrowed. "What consequences?"

I rubbed his hand to soften the blow I was about to deliver. "You."

His eyes widened, but he didn't pull away.

"I'm so sorry, Basim. I was too young, unwed. I didn't know what else to do. Farid offered the best solution: he and Amira would raise you as their own. You would have a father and a mother, a good home, a decent last name."

Basim brought his hands to his eyes.

"I'm sorry, *mi amor*. I've always thought of you and longed to see you, but I had the consolation that you were better off with them."

After a moment, he uncovered his eyes—as expressive as Martin's.

"Before I go, I need to know that you forgive me," I said.

He shook his head. "There's nothing to forgive. You were just a girl."

For so many years, I'd feared that Basim would hate me once

he found out the truth. It was one of the reasons I'd adamantly rejected the idea of telling him. But this boy was so noble, so generous. I had to hand it to Farid and Amira—they'd raised a wonderful human being.

"I just want to know one thing," he said.

"Anything."

"My father," he said, his eyelashes moist. "Who is he?"

CHAPTER 50

Puri

Martin Sabater looked at me as though seeing a ghost. But he was the only ghost here. I approached the bed. Lula had set the bowl of soup on the end table and was placing a napkin on Martin's chest. When she saw me, she covered her mouth.

"I'm sorry, Don Martin," she said, turning toward her *patrón*, an anguished expression on her face. "I didn't know *la monjita* was following me."

"It's all right, Lula. She's a friend of mine. You may leave us alone."

Lula nodded and, drying her hands on her apron, she promptly left the room.

Martin wouldn't take his eyes off me. And I could do nothing else but stare at the face I'd been doing my best not to forget in the last four years.

"I won't even ask why you're dressed like that," he said.

I couldn't help but smile.

"I should've known you would find me. There's no stopping Doña Puri when she sets her mind onto something."

"No," I said, tears welling in my eyes. "I always suspected you were alive."

Sure, he was alive, but in what state? He must have lost at least twenty pounds since I'd last seen him. His face was ashen, and so much older, but Sor Camila had kept him well shaved and his clothes were spotless. He'd been well cared for in the—what?— three, four months he'd been hiding here.

"I assume you received my letter, then?" he said.

"Yes."

"And the bear?"

I nodded. He was about to say something else, but I spoke first. "What's wrong with your legs?"

"I'm paralyzed, Puri."

"The fall."

He nodded.

"Does Farid know you're here?" I said.

"Of course not. He would kill me if he knew."

"Is he the one—the one who tried to kill you that night?"

Martin shook his head.

"Don Yusuf?" I said.

His eyes widened; he must be surprised that I knew all his enemies. "No, Puri, Don Yusuf shot Amira's lover, a man named Gerardo. He figured out Farid's wife was having an illicit relationship with him and he wanted to save his son's honor."

That had been the first shot.

"So, who shot the second time?"

"How do you know there were two shots?"

I didn't want to bring up the subject of Angélica just now. "It's a long story."

"The former owner of this place, Iván Contreras, shot me," he said, without a moment's hesitation. "But I was lucky to dodge the bullet. Not lucky enough to prevent the fall that would tie me to this bed for the rest of my life."

"What did you find out about his wife?" I said.

He lifted an eyebrow. "You've been talking to Lucas, too?"

"He's been trying to find his mother and help me find you."

His expression turned grim. "That poor woman."

And then I knew. The bones in Tuli's possession had to be hers.

"When we were building the chicken coop," he said, bringing a hand to his back and rubbing it, "I found a set of bones. They had the finest fabrics attached to them, so I had no doubt they belonged to a woman. It couldn't be anybody else but Lucas's mother. The worker that was helping me, Nestor, must have told Contreras that we found her. He was always bitter that his *patrón* had left and I'd purchased the property. He was his most loyal dog."

"You were a threat to Contreras."

"Certainly."

"But why would he kill his wife?" I said.

He shrugged. "One can only speculate, but according to Lucas's twin sister, Olivia, her mother disappeared right after Lucas's father died. Lucas said his mother had been to his father's funeral. Who knows if Contreras got vexed that she had gone there? Or maybe it was an accident. Your guess is as good as mine."

"Contreras is here, you know."

"So I hear."

I sat by his side. My heart was about to break through my ribs. "Is that why you've been hiding here all this time?"

"I have many enemies, Puri. A lot of people would benefit from my death."

"Some are already benefitting."

He shrugged, yet again.

"I'm extremely vulnerable right now. I don't have the strength to confront them. Nor do I care about this place anymore."

I swallowed. "But you should. You have a son."

He didn't blink. "I know."

Maybe he was thinking about Basim when he said he knew about his son. I had to tell him about my Cristóbal. I should've done it a long time ago.

"Martin—"

A ruckus came from the door, making us both turn to see what the source of the commotion was.

A shiver ran down my spine as the door flew open.

Farid.

CHAPTER 51

Camila

March 14, 1925
One week after the gala

It had been seven days since I found Martin in the woods. Seven days since the search party, headed by my brother, had been looking for him.

I was torn. I wanted to tell Farid I'd found him, but Martin made Lula and me promise that we wouldn't tell anyone where he was. I still couldn't believe someone from our circle of friends and acquaintances would be willing to kill Martin. Murder was, in my opinion, the worst of all sins, even if some believed that in the eyes of the Lord all sins were equal.

When I asked Martin who did this to him, he wouldn't elaborate. He simply said he had enemies, which made me wonder if he knew himself. Of course the list included my brother, who now knew—unequivocally—that Martin was Basim's father. But I didn't want to believe my brother would be capable of killing a man who'd been a close friend of his.

Martin was lucky to be still alive. He could've broken his neck and then he would've died for sure. But he'd definitely broken something important, a vital vertebra, maybe. I was no doctor, but my experience told me he might never walk again. Fortunately, he had mobility of his upper body.

"We should have a doctor check you," I said, for the twentieth time. "Even if it's not my brother."

Martin didn't want to hear a word about it. I'd never seen him like this before. He was constantly on guard, turning toward the door at every single sound. Restless. Fearful. This was not the Martin I'd known.

We'd brought him to Lula's room the night of the accident and had kept him hidden from everybody at the hacienda. With all the fuss and chaos of the party, nobody had noticed us, but honestly, I didn't know how much longer we could pull this off.

Sor Eugenia and Sor Marianela reminded me we had to leave in the morning, but how would I leave Martin here, in the sole care of Lula, who was an excellent cook but knew nothing about caregiving?

"What's wrong?" Martin asked me.

"I'm scheduled to leave tomorrow."

"Back to Medellín?" he said.

"Yes."

He managed a smile. "Go. I'll be fine. Don't you worry about me."

No, he wasn't going to be fine, but I couldn't disobey the Reverend Mother. Not for the man who'd been the cause of my disgrace. She was a stern woman and would certainly not approve of my staying, even if I told her the truth. *Especially* if I told her the truth.

"I'll arrange for someone to look after you, Martin."

"Thank you, Camila." He had a faint smile on to disguise the pain I was certain he was feeling. He'd not only fractured his back, but he also had a wound on his head, which kept bleeding.

The hacienda was finally quiet after the commotion of the last few days. Baba and Martin's guests had left and Farid had taken Martin's friend away—the crazy woman who did nothing but scream Martin's name day and night. I'd been halfway tempted to tell her where Martin was so she would calm down for once and let the rest of the people sleep, but Martin had been adamant: nobody but Lula and I should know where he was. If one more person knew, especially someone as loud as Angélica—who would no doubt insist that we take him to a hospital—he would be exposed to his enemies again.

I'd spared Martin the knowledge of where Farid had taken Angélica. I'd only mentioned that she'd left and he said it was probably for the best that she returned to her family and to her country. I'd said goodbye to him already. As a nun, I was not the owner of my own destiny and I had to follow my superior's orders. It was probably best to be away, anyway. Martin moved too many things inside me—good and bad—and I couldn't enjoy the serenity I had finally found in the convent.

When I arrived in Cali, I would hire a nurse or, better yet, a doctor, to come check on Martin. I would talk to the Reverend Mother about him and she might help me.

As I stepped into the carriage that would take my sisters and me away, I gave Martin's hacienda one last look.

I clutched the wooden crucifix on my chest. What would become of him? I shouldn't care anymore, just like he hadn't cared about me all those years ago.

I sat in the back of the rented landau Padre José María had sent for us. It was close to dawn and my sisters were still exhausted after tending to Martin's guests and leading endless prayers for his prompt return.

The two of them fell asleep as soon as the carriage started to move.

I stared at them, at their pristine habits, pure as their souls.

Unlike mine.

I was still holding on to resentments. After all these years, I couldn't let go of "what Martin had done to me" but the truth was he hadn't forced me. I had been happy to give myself to him. I'd loved him so.

How long was I going to blame him for my misfortune? Nobody could've forced me to give Basim away if I didn't want to. Nobody had made me enter the convent and bury myself there. I'd been the one to make that decision, out of bitterness, out of pride.

And Martin, really, had attempted to contact me.

From one of my pockets, I carefully removed the letters Nazira had given me the night of the gala. I hadn't read them yet. I was afraid to know what he had written.

I removed the first letter. It was dated just a few days before Baba found out about my pregnancy.

> *September 20, 1910*
>
> *Camila, my love,*
>
> *How can I begin to express everything I feel for you? Those days at Hacienda La Magna were the happiest of my life. I know you think I'm some kind of lover boy, but I promise you that I'm not. I had only one relationship before you and it was a child's game in comparison. I never felt for her the things I feel for you. She was a close friend and I cared for her, but you're the woman for me, the one I truly love—my first one.*
>
> *I'll never forget that.*
>
> *I'm sorry I didn't write you sooner, mi reina, but I've been working all these months to help pay for my school and expenses. I don't want to depend completely on Don Armand, even after what he did to my father, which you may remember from our conversation that last night by La Reina. The move to Popayán also took more time and effort than I thought, but here I am, all yours once again. I want to come back to see you just as soon as I finish my first semester here in Popayán, but I can hardly wait. I'm sending you my address so you can write me, too. Your letters will most likely make my stay here less painful as I miss you every day of my life—no pressure there.*

I'm going to sleep now and I'll be thinking about you until I do.

I hope to dream of you, too.

Yours forever,

Martin

November 1, 1910

My beloved queen,

It's been over a month since I wrote you. I know the postal service takes some time, but I can't wait to hear from you. I'm going crazy here without you. I go to the post office every day, waiting for a letter from you. I haven't heard from Farid, either, but I've been really bad about writing. You're the only person I've written to, but that's because I can't stop thinking about you. I assume your brother already moved to Bogotá. Did he? Please send him my greetings and also to Don Yusuf and your siblings.

I really miss you, Farid, and Lucas, of course. You all are like family to me.

Please write me whenever you get this letter. I'm very lonely here. I also want you to know that I've been really good and faithful. I haven't gone to a single party or met any other woman. Every time my classmates invite me out, I say no, and they tell me: "Yes, of course, you're waiting for a letter from Camila."

So please, end my suffering, don't make me wait any longer.

Yours,

Martin

January 10, 1911

Dear Camila,

I hope you had a good holiday season. Honestly, Christmas and New Year's Eve without you were awful. I stayed with one of my classmate's family here in Popayán. They're nice but I missed you terribly. Those years I spent with your family in Cali were some of the best of my life.

Camila, I know it took me a while to write you after I moved away, but please stop punishing me. I can't stand your silence. I've been tempted to go to Cali to see you, but I don't want to impose my presence in your life if you've already moved on. I don't want to be the kind of man who won't let go and forces himself upon a woman who doesn't want him.

I've done a lot of thinking during this break about us, about what I want in life. I always thought I wanted to marry Angélica, probably because I wanted to get my father's hacienda back, but the truth is that land means nothing to me compared to you, which brings me to my next point.

I want to marry you, Camila. I want to be with you for the rest of my life, but I understand if you don't want the same thing. Thus, here's what I propose. I don't want to wait any longer. I'm not going to wait for the perfect moment to tell you this, or the next time I see you in person, I'm going to ask you right now if you want to marry me, and if you do, I'll leave everything behind and move to Cali, or wherever you want to live. I'll forget all my dreams of getting my father's plantation back and we can concentrate on a life together. I know you dream of owning a dress shop. I'd be willing to do that if that means having you in my life—even if I think dresses are the most boring thing in the world!

What do you think? Will you have me?

If you don't answer, I'll understand that's not what you want and I promise I will respect your wishes and never bother you again. But please say yes.

Faithfully yours,
Martin

I'd been crying, without even realizing it. Martin had loved me. He hadn't used me, like I thought all these years. And now he needed me. I was the only person he had, the only one who could protect him. What was I doing *here*?

I wiped my tears, put the letters back in my pocket, and turned toward the carriage driver.

"Please, I forgot something truly important. Will you turn around?"

"But, *hermana*, if we go back now, you're going to miss the train to Cartago."

I glanced at my sisters, dozing off peacefully, oblivious to the turmoil inside my heart.

"Then just stop. I'll walk back."

"Are you sure?"

"Yes."

As soon as he pulled on the reins, my sisters opened their eyes.

"What's happening?" Sor Marianela said.

"What was that?" Sor Eugenia said, frowning.

"*Hermanas*," I said, "I've decided to stay here."

"What do you mean, stay?" Sor Eugenia was one of the strictest nuns I knew. Things with her were always black or white.

"Why are you crying, *hermana*?" Sor Marianela said.

"I'm not going back to the convent," I said, feeling a weight falling off my shoulders.

"What?" Whatever sleepiness Sor Eugenia had had dissipated in lieu of my announcement.

"I tried to fool myself for years into thinking that I could be the perfect nun, that I could be humble and obedient, that I could forget my past and forgive those who harmed me, but I'm not that kind of woman. I've never been."

"Surely you're confused, Sor Camila, it's probably all the excitement of the festivities and the missing man."

"No, Sor Eugenia, I've never been more certain of anything in my life."

"But you can't renounce, *hermana*, what would I do without

you?" Sor Marianela said. She'd started hiccupping already. The two of us had become close the last couple of years.

"I will miss you, too, *hermana*," I said, "but I can't continue to lie to the Siervas and to myself any longer."

"What are we supposed to tell the Reverend Mother?" she said.

"I will write her a formal letter informing her of my decision, but in the meantime, please convey my message to her. Tell her I love her and all my sisters, but I can't live a farce any longer."

"*Hermana*," Sor Eugenia said, "I really wish you would reconsider."

"I'm sorry," I said, opening the carriage door.

"Wait, what are you doing?" Sor Eugenia said.

"As I said, I'm staying here. Please, don't let this stop you. Continue with your trip. Blessings, *hermanas*."

I hopped out. The last thing I saw before heading back to the hacienda was Sor Marianela's smile beneath her tears.

CHAPTER 52

Puri

Farid stepped into the room, shock and incredulity flashing through his face.

"Martin," he said. "Baba said you were dead. He saw you fall from the horse and said you were unresponsive." He ran his fingers through his hair. "He came looking for me, but we couldn't find you anywhere. We looked for you for days. Hell, I still look for you from time to time. We assumed a jaguar or another animal got to you. I believed only death would've stopped you from returning to your hacienda."

"So, you buried Gerardo and put my name on his grave?" Martin said, filled with bitterness.

Farid scratched his head. "I can't believe you've been here all along. And you." He turned to me. "You knew? You came to find him? You're that friend Amira mentioned to me, right?"

He stared at both of us.

"I knew you were up to something. That's why I followed you here," he told me, shaking his head. "But no, someone else was helping Martin, right?" He turned to him. "This so-called nun only got here a few weeks ago."

I watched him in silence.

"Camila," he voiced his thoughts. "That's why she was already here when I came back to open the hospital."

"You mean, to steal my property," Martin said.

"She told me she'd heard I was opening a hospital and came to help, but I never understood how she knew." He narrowed his eyes. "She's been taking care of you all this time, *¿cierto?* You're using her all over again, taking advantage of her kindness, of her innocence, just like you did fifteen years ago, but this time, she won't be able to go back to the convent. Not after this, *hijo de puta.*"

He pounced toward Martin, without any notice, and started choking him with his bare hands.

"Stop!" I said, hitting Farid's back, attempting to remove his hands from Martin's throat. But he was too strong and my efforts didn't stop him.

Martin's looked at me in terror, trying unsuccessfully to set his throat free.

I turned around, looking for something to hit Farid with. The only thing within my reach was the bowl Lula had brought. I emptied the scalding liquid on top of Farid's head, burning him with the broth.

He let out a groan and pulled back immediately. Then he brought his hands to his face, which was already turning red. Some of the broth and a drumstick landed on Martin's legs, but he didn't even flinch.

When Farid turned to me, a deep crease between his thick eyebrows, I took a step back.

I'd seen him slap Amira. I'd now seen him try to choke Martin. What would he do to me? Someone he had no feelings for whatsoever?

Farid removed a revolver from the pocket of his doctor's gown.

"I don't know what you want, but I know you're not a nun and you're up to no good." He raised his arm, pointing the muzzle at me. He fluctuated between Martin and me. "And you, I've been wanting to do this ever since I found out what you did to my sister.

You were supposed to be my best friend, my brother, and what did you do? You impregnated my sister. You made her fall in love with you. You ruined her. But that's what you do, isn't it? You ruin everyone and everything you touch. I'm not going to let you ruin this place, too."

"Of course you would see things that way," Martin said. "You don't know anything about love."

"*Love?* Ha!"

"You can dismiss me all you want. Any excuse to kill me so you can keep my property. Well, go ahead and do it. This is no way to live, anyway, but let Puri go. She's done nothing wrong. She just wanted to find me, that's all."

"She *has* done wrong," Farid said. "She came here under false pretenses and got involved in our lives, who knows with what intentions. She's probably after the hacienda, after this land. I saw her contract. She's in the cacao business."

He pointed the gun at my chest.

"Both of you hinder me and I won't stand for it anymore."

He thumbed the revolver's hammer back and leveled the pistol at me. Martin lurched his body sideways, right in front of me. As we both fell to the ground, the explosion of the gunshot overwhelmed my senses, heat building inside me. Martin fell heavily, his back on top of me. I covered my ears and screamed at the top of my lungs.

I didn't stop yelling until I heard Lucas's voice inside the room.

"What's going on here?" he said, taking in the entire scene in front of him.

The sound of Lucas's voice pulled me back into reality. I slid out from under Martin's dead weight and rolled him onto his back. He was still breathing. I glanced up and saw Farid stare at us openmouthed, holding the revolver with a loose grip, his eyes glazed over in horror.

"Turco, what have you done?" Lucas said, removing the gun from Farid's hand. "Have you lost your mind?" He darted toward us. "Martin?"

Thank God Lucas hadn't left yet. He knelt in front of us and grabbed Martin by the shoulders.

Martin was spitting blood. My face was covered with tears, my habit stained with Martin's blood.

"Please, help him," I told Lucas. "Call Dr. Costa."

"And you? Did that *maldito* hurt you?" He was beside himself.

"I'm fine, Lucas, but please help Martin."

Farid, flushed after the burns I'd inflicted on his face, had collapsed on one of the chairs in the corner of the room, his hair soaked, his glassy gaze somewhere on the floorboards.

Lucas rushed past him while I held Martin's clammy hand, whispering that he would be fine, that Dr. Costa would save him, but I had my doubts. Martin was bleeding so profusely he must've been shot in a vital organ.

"Please, Martin, don't die. You can't do this to me. I *just* found you."

"I'm sorry," he said. "I didn't do it on purpose."

How can he joke at a time like this?

Farid got up, scraping the chair's legs against the floor, and left the room. Instead of his habitual brisk and confident walk, he dragged his feet toward the sunlight. He looked like a man defeated by resentment and hatred.

"Puri," Martin said.

"What?"

"Take care of my son."

"Your son," I repeated at the same time as Lucas, Dr. Costa, and Perla dashed into the room. The three of them lifted Martin and carried him outside.

I stayed back with a big lump in my throat. They'd taken Martin before I could ask him if he was talking about my son or Camila's.

Somehow, I found the strength to get up, my scapular splashed with erratic bloodstains as though I were a butcher. I picked up Lucas's cane from the floor and straightened my back. Lula came back into her room.

"Are you all right, *madre*?"

"Yes, yes, I'm fine, Lula. But I'm worried about Martin. There's no time to waste."

The two of us darted into the main building. As I rushed inside, I saw Martin being carried through the courtyard.

Basim stopped next to him, his eyes filled with tears. Had Camila told him everything? Had she died?

"Wait, please," Martin told Lucas. "Come here, *hijo*."

Hesitantly, Basim approached his wounded father. Martin extended his hand toward the boy. Basim took it. With his other hand, Martin cupped Basim's face.

"I'm sorry," he said. "I'm so sorry." There were tears in Martin's eyes. "Please look after your mother."

Basim nodded. Their resemblance was more apparent now that they were side by side. Martin must have seen it, too.

"We have to go," Dr. Costa said. "He's losing too much blood."

CHAPTER 53

Puri

Lucas sat across from me on the opposite bench. I had been waiting in the hall for Dr. Costa to operate on Martin, my hands tucked under my hamstrings, my feet lightly touching the brick floor. Basim had just left to check on Camila, so this was the first time Lucas and I were alone after he'd confronted me with Dr. Costa's photograph.

"I can't believe Martin was here all along," he said, rubbing his eyes. "To think that I even climbed on that building to take a photograph." He scoffed. "He must have heard the ruckus when I fell."

"He was very vulnerable," I said.

"Did he explain what happened the night of the gala?"

I nodded. I knew I had to tell Lucas about his mother, but I was dreading the moment I would give him yet another blow. Hard as it would be, I couldn't hide anything from Lucas anymore. I'd learned my lesson.

"He told me Iván Contreras shot him, but in an attempt to dodge the bullet, he fell off the horse."

"What did Martin discover?" he said.

"Martin and Nestor had found"—I paused, trying to find the

right words, the kindest words to deliver the news—"your mother's remains. I think Nestor told Iván and he must have felt threated by what Martin knew."

Lucas sprung up. "*¡Ese hijueputa!*"

"Wait, what are you going to do?"

I followed Lucas as he hurtled toward the cholera room. Lucas crossed the room, in the direction of Iván's bed.

It was empty.

Lucas turned to Nurse Bertha. "Where is that *malparido*?" he barked.

"Who?" she said, tending to another patient.

Lucas pointed at Contreras's bed.

"Oh, Mr. Contreras. He died an hour ago. Nestor already took his body."

Martin passed away the next day. The bullet had hit one of his lungs and he'd lost entirely too much blood. Dr. Costa wasn't a surgeon, but he'd tried his best to remove the bullet and save Martin's life. It had been a useless effort, though, as it only bought Martin a couple of hours.

I figured it was best not to tell Camila yet. She didn't need devastating news while she was fighting for her own life.

I'd been sitting by her side for the last couple of hours, guarding her sleep. When she woke up, she seemed confused.

"Where's your habit, *hermana*?"

I'd borrowed one of Perla's outfits—this time with her consent—not the orange one, but a more subdued navy, tube-shaped tunic with a dangling necktie, and my bob was finally freed from the bandeau, coif, and veil.

"I don't need it," I said. "I'm not really a nun."

I didn't offer any further explanation and she didn't ask, but she looked at me as if she'd been expecting me to say this at any moment. I must have given myself away at some point.

She surprised me with a faint smile and said, "Neither am I."

Lucas entered the room with some concoction in a bowl.

"Dr. Costa told me to give this to Camila."

"What is it?"

"Some solution he's been working on."

Both of us helped Camila sit up. The mushy solution had a slight banana scent.

"Does it have banana?"

"Yes, for taste and for potassium," Lucas said, bringing a spoonful to Camila's mouth. "He said it has boiled water, salt, and sugar."

Camila ate the entire thing.

"She has to have this every couple of hours. Dr. Costa said he'd check on her in a little bit, but needed to rest for a while."

Of course, he'd been up all night with Martin. Dr. Costa and I had exchanged an awkward look in the hall and I'd apologized for lying to him and asked after his wife, whom he said had returned to Spain before he came here.

I didn't ask any more questions and was grateful for his discretion as he didn't pry into my reasons for posing as a nun, either.

In the next few hours, Camila seemed to gain some of her strength back. Don Yusuf and Basim spent the entire afternoon with her, Basim softly playing the guitar while Camila watched him without blinking. Camila and her father also seemed to make their peace as he held her hand for a long time and she didn't remove it.

When I looked at Camila's father, I couldn't help but think about the fact that he'd shot Gerardo the night of the gala. Would his crime ever be uncovered? I certainly wouldn't say anything. He seemed to be paying for his actions with daily remorse, according to a passing comment Lucas made to me. Honestly, I was more concerned about Farid's whereabouts and what would happen if I ran into him again. Would he attempt to finish the job and end my life?

I left Camila with her family and headed for the nurses' room. I hadn't slept all night either, and the exhaustion was finally catching up with me.

Amira was on the patio, sitting on the bench where we'd spoken the first time we met, a trunk and a suitcase by her feet. She seemed surprised—but not entirely—upon seeing me in street clothes.

"You're leaving?" I said.

"Yes. Finally. I'm going back to Cali to get my girls and then to Bogotá." She cleared her throat. "I'm just waiting for Nestor to come back and take me."

I nodded.

"Puri," she said, "I'm sorry I told Farid about your connection to Martin, but I had to. It was the only way I could think of to be freed of him."

Knowing what I did about him now, I didn't blame her.

"That's all right."

It was the polite thing to say. The truth was, if she hadn't told him, he wouldn't have followed me to Lula's room and Martin might still be alive today.

"Goodbye, Amira," I said. "I wish you luck."

As I walked up the stairs, I thought about Martin and Camila and their son. What was to become of this property that he'd loved so much? What was to become of Basim?

CHAPTER 54

Camila

March 19, 1925
Twelve days after the gala

I never regretted my decision to leave the Siervas. I was grateful for my time with them because they had taught me all I knew about nursing and caring for others. They'd also taught me about myself and the importance of thinking and working for others and how gratifying that could be. I'd done this, to some extent, with my family after my mother died, but I'd felt obligated then and had resented them. Something changed when I joined the convent. I entered a mold that demanded no less than excellence and the disposal of petty feelings. I strived to better myself, to fit into this structure, this model of moral perfection. The nuns had offered me the comfort and strength I needed, *when* I needed it, and I believed that I had become a better person because of them, in spite of the flaws I still had.

I confessed my entire story to Padre José María and he agreed to help Martin and me.

In spite of his age and his line of work, the priest was a romantic at heart.

For the occasion, I wore a narrow beige sheath with three-quarter sleeves that I'd sewn myself. I hadn't been able to find satin in this corner of the world, so I settled for cotton.

Martin looked so handsome in one of the suits I'd brought from his room. It was unfortunate that despite having this beautiful hacienda at our disposal, with its gorgeous vegetation and exquisite architecture, we would have this ceremony in the cook's room, but nobody but Lula and I, and now Padre José María, could know that Martin was here and that he was still alive.

Especially Nestor, who seemed so sneaky.

Fortunately, everybody had left the hacienda already, except for a couple of servants, and I didn't think Farid would be coming any time soon after taking Angélica with him to Cali.

After leaving my sisters in the carriage and walking back to the hacienda, I'd dashed into Lula's room, holding Martin's last letter in my hand, and had uttered a "Yes, I will marry you, if you'll still have me."

I was fully conscious that I might be making a fool of myself after all these years. Who knew if he still loved me or if he'd found someone else—or worse yet, if he'd already married? But I was willing to take the chance. I was so excited after reading his letters that I was unable to hold back. I'd been doing a lot of that in the last fifteen years.

The sadness in his eyes transformed immediately, which told me Martin's feelings for me hadn't changed.

And now I was sitting by his side, a bouquet of wild flowers in my lap. We'd managed to move Martin to a chair and I brought one next to him for me. Lula was our only witness as Padre José María read the Gospel.

And then came the words I'd been longing to hear when I was a seventeen-year-old girl:

"I, Martin Sabater, take you, Camila Mansur, to be my lawfully wedded wife, to have and to hold, from this day forward, for better, for worse, for richer, for poorer, in sickness and in health, until death do us part."

I said my vows after him. This time, the ones I truly meant.

Martin squeezed my hand as I spoke.

"You have declared your consent before the Church," Padre José María said. "May the Lord in his goodness strengthen your consent and fill you both with his blessings. What God has joined, men must not divide. Amen."

Martin and I turned to each other and kissed.

I'd never been happier in my entire life.

CHAPTER 55

Puri

Camila was one of our few patients to make it. Thanks to Dr. Costa's solution and care, others followed. Now that she was stronger and could sit and eat on her own, I knew it was the time to tell her about Martin.

I dragged the chair by her side.

"You look serious," she said.

"I have something to tell you."

She paled.

"We found Martin at the servants' quarters."

Her hand reached for her crucifix.

I avoided her gaze lest I would lose the courage to speak. "He and Farid had a confrontation and . . ."

How could I frame my words without breaking her heart? Was it even possible?

"Camila, your brother shot him."

She brought a hand to her mouth.

"He didn't make it, *mi alma*. I'm so sorry."

For the first time since I'd met her, Camila lost her composure. Her scream was heartrending. I didn't know what else to do other than to hold her. Against my shoulder, she sobbed like a child for what seemed like hours.

When she was calmer, I gave her a warm *valeriana*. She confessed that she and Martin had gotten married in March, which hurt my pride more than anything else. Deep down, though, I was glad that at least during those months of lockdown—not only in Lula's room but also inside his body—he'd been happy with Camila.

As the widow of Martin Sabater and the mother of his firstborn, she was entitled to keep the hacienda. She didn't say what she would do with it, but I suspected she was more cut out for nursing and healing than producing cacao.

Lucas stayed for a few more days to help with Camila's recovery and with Martin's funeral, but I suspected his time here, like mine, was coming to an end.

Since Nestor never came back after taking Amira, Dr. Costa—who was now running the hospital—had hired two more workers to drive the carriage and help with the orchard and chickens. One of them was taking me to Cali so I could get Angélica and bring her back to Ecuador with me.

Camila was taking slow steps now and, like me, she no longer wore her habit. Her first outing had been, sadly, to Martin's funeral. Lucas had managed to change the tombstone on Gerardo's grave and brought Padre José María to conduct the service at the cemetery.

Dressed entirely in black, Camila sat by my side on the front steps of the hacienda, where I waited for the carriage to take me away. Lucas hadn't even bothered coming down to say goodbye to me.

"We heard from Farid," she said.

I turned to her. "Where is he?"

"In Cali. He turned himself in to the authorities. He couldn't live with the guilt of what he had done. He sent me a letter, apologizing for everything."

It was, no doubt, a relief to know he was far away from here.

"Camila, there is something I haven't told you." I'd already explained to her that I'd come here to find Martin because I was worried about my chocolate business, but I'd kept the real reason to myself. "I'm convinced now that nothing good comes from keeping secrets, from hiding the truth. I know that it may be hard to hear, but I must tell you." *Even if you hate me afterward.*

She eyed me with apprehension.

"I have a four-year-old son." I fumbled with the gloves in my lap. "And Martin was the father."

The shock in her eyes was unmistakable. They filled up with tears almost immediately. But instead of a hysteric attack, she spoke with a calm voice.

"I'm not a fool, Puri, I expected him to have a life during those years I was in the convent."

The Siervas had taught her well. She was in full control of her emotions, as devastating as my news might have been.

But her eyes betrayed one of those emotions, something akin to empathy.

Camila and I had gone through the same thing. We'd both loved the same man without being married to him. She placed her hand on mine.

"I'm glad to have met you, Puri. You're an extraordinary woman."

"Likewise." I held her hand, which was finally filling out again. "Martin couldn't have chosen a better partner."

She gave me a long hug.

"I hope to see you again," she said. "You've been a great support during my hardest hours."

I nodded, too touched to answer.

Perla came running, pulling Doña Tuli by the hand. The two of them hugged and kissed me as the carriage stopped in front of me.

I gave one last glance to the imposing entrance of what had once been Martin's beloved hacienda and climbed into the carriage.

I sat down and attempted to shut the door, but something stopped it.

A bamboo cane.

Lucas climbed up with his old suitcase under his arm and a camera in his hand.

"What are you doing?" I said.

"I'm coming with you. You can't be trusted traveling alone. You need someone to keep you out of trouble as you make your way back to Ecuador. And besides, I've always wanted to visit another country. And who knows? Maybe I can get some good shots out of it."

"You do realize that your life may be in jeopardy if you come with me?"

He sat in front of me, setting his suitcase by our feet, right next to his cane.

"I'll take my chances."

I didn't say anything else. I simply swung my arms around his neck and gave him a loud kiss.

PILOGUE

Inside the train car taking us to Buenaventura, I watched Angélica doze off in front of me while Lucas rested his head on my shoulder, eyes shut. I'd spoken to the chief doctor at the mental institution and claimed her as my younger sister. What she needed, I said, was to go back to her family in Ecuador. It had helped, too, that on our way to the asylum, I'd bought Angélica a cockatoo that looked almost exactly like her beloved Ramona and had the same pompous attitude. Lucas thought it would be a hassle to take such a loud bird on a trip with us, but I knew that a heartwarming pet was exactly what Angélica needed to start healing.

She remembered me and, dare I say, looked happy to see me, especially with the white bird perched on my shoulder. She seemed certainly glad to leave her ivory prison.

She'd asked me about Martin, but I would wait to reach Catalina's home in Vinces to tell her the news about him.

Lately, I'd been thinking a lot about my last moments with Martin, about his request regarding his son. Well, he should be satisfied to know that things had been made right by Camila and Basim, and that they had a place to live and a promising future ahead.

But that wasn't it.

There was something else in his tone, in the despair I saw in his eyes.

I had Cristóbal's stuffed bear in my hands, as usual. Why had Martin asked if I'd received it? What did it matter? And why had he sent my son a toy in the first place? In his letter, he'd said he hoped Cristóbal would guard it as it was "one of a kind."

Was it because my son's *father* had given it to him? Had he known? Did he mean my Cristóbal when he asked me to look after his son?

I examined the stuffed bear, running my fingers over its belly. The rough texture of a seam across his belly stopped me. I'd had this bear for months and I was just now realizing the vertical, coarse brown thread dividing his belly in two. Apparently, it had been well covered with the plush.

I grabbed a pair of scissors from Sor Alba Luz's medical kit and gently cut through the seams. The bear's belly opened up, revealing a shiny emerald as big as my fist.

Underneath was a handwritten note.

> *My dearest Puri,*
>   *I have the strong suspicion that you've been hiding*
> *some vital information from me, so in case something*
> *were to happen to me, you have this. Sell it, do with it as*
> *you please, but always know that you and your son have*
> *a very special place in my heart.*
>   *Martin*

Acknowledgments

We wouldn't be holding this book in our hands if it weren't for the following people:

My exceptional editor, Norma Pérez-Hernández, who was the first to suggest that *The Spanish Daughter* should have a sequel. Your enthusiasm and encouragement have been paramount for the completion of this project.

My agent, Rachel Brooks, who insisted that Norma was on to something and made it possible for these characters to come to life. I'm truly grateful for your support and your dedication.

The Kensington team, especially Vida Engstrand and Michelle Addo, who've gone above and beyond to support me and find opportunities for my work.

The writers who always help me with their special talents:

María Elena Venant, whose gift for finding obscure historical details changed the course of this novel several times—I don't know what I would do without your help and brilliance.

Shea Berkley, who helped me untangle a very complicated plot until it made sense.

Susie Salom, aka S. Z. Salom, who always helps me bring out the heart in all my stories.

Jill Orr, for helping me figure out the perfect ending for this novel.

Robyn Arrington, brilliant writer and encouraging first reader.

The people who assisted me with their knowledge and experiences:

Ximena Reyes, for planting the emerald seed in my mind and for talking to me about her beloved Colombia.

Vitalia Brasmer, for sitting with me for four hours to answer all my questions about her native Cali and El Valle del Cauca.

Travis Gutierrez, who for years led a successful school fundraising gala and was kind enough to share all the details with me.

Dr. Elma Gutierrez, for teaching me about deliveries in the early twentieth century and everything that could possibly go wrong.

Diana and Jason Harlan, for providing me with the rest of the medical information I needed.

Dr. Emile Nakhleh and Maggie Asfahani, for coming to my aid when I needed to sprinkle Arabic words throughout the novel.

Laurie and Lindsey Gilbert, for explaining what life is like in a boarding school.

And as always, my family:

Danny, for continuing to choreograph all my action scenes.

Natalie, for being a supportive editor to her ESL mom.

Andy, for the IV demonstration (in spite of the blood!).

My mom, for continuing to answer random questions about her childhood and teenage years.

My dad, for the earthquake memories and the stories about his immigrant parents and their journey to Ecuador.

Mónica and Alfredo, for being avid readers and supporters of my work, and Giancarlo for letting my characters borrow some of his boarding school experiences.

And finally, Ruth and Cheri, who hosted a lovely event, and all the book clubs who have reached out to me, especially Stephanie and her Los Alamos group, Las Lores, La Lectora Latina, Literary Escape, and my Xtraordinary Women in Los Angeles.

The Queen of the Valley

Lorena Hughes

The suggested questions are included to enhance your group's
reading of Lorena Hughes's *The Queen of the Valley*

DISCUSSION QUESTIONS

1. *The Queen of the Valley* features three protagonists: a Palestinian-Colombian nun named Camila; Lucas, a photographer; and Puri, a French-Spanish chocolatier disguised as a nun. Each is connected to Martin Sabater, the missing hacienda owner, in a different way. In which ways do you think Martin most affected the lives of Camila, Lucas, and Puri? Where do you think they would be if he hadn't gone back to Colombia?

2. One of the story's main characters is Puri, a young chocolatier and mother who goes undercover as a nun in search of her son's missing father. Throughout this journey, Puri learns to exploit expectations of virtue to carefully navigate a patriarchal society's rules around women. What do you think Puri discovers about herself after the experience of posing as a nun?

3. The 1920s saw the mainstreaming of photography both as an artform and in journalism, a detail explored through the character of Lucas. Armed with his Kodak Folding Autographic Brownie, Lucas hides behind the camera's lens as he works to uncover secrets about his past. What is your take on Lucas's relationship with his father, who himself owned a photography studio? How does photography play a part in their estrangement? Do you think Lucas was a true artist?

4. Palestinian-Colombian nun Camila wanted to be a dressmaker when she was a young woman. But, later in life, she found a vocation for helping and healing others. What do you make of this change of heart? Did you have a dream or vocation as a child or young adult that changed as you grew up? What was it and why didn't you follow through with it?

5. Camila was Martin's first love and vice versa. Do you believe theirs was true love or mainly the experience of falling in love for the first time? Do you believe that everyone remembers their first love? Can you share a little bit about yours?

6. The story touches on Dr. Farid "El Turco" Mansur's arranged marriage to Amira as well as his parents' before they immigrated to Colombia from Palestine. Do you have any ancestors who had arranged marriages? Do you think those marriages worked any better than those who marry for love? Do you know of any cultures that continue this tradition?

7. Do you believe Martin knew Puri's son was his? How might he have figured this out?

8. Do you think Lucas's resentment toward Doña Matilde was justified? Why or why not? Do you know of anyone who found out the truth about their origins as an adult? Is it a forgivable deceit?

9. Puri's sister Angélica was committed to a mental institution for "going into hysterics." Lucas mentions to her a variety of reasons as to why women could be committed in the past. Have you heard of cases like these in real life?

10. In your estimation, who or what was the Queen of the Valley? Please explain your answer.

Visit our website at
KensingtonBooks.com
to sign up for our newsletters, read
more from your favorite authors, see
books by series, view reading group
guides, and more!

BOOK | CLUB
BETWEEN THE CHAPTERS

Become a Part of Our
Between the Chapters Book Club
Community and Join the Conversation

Betweenthechapters.net